Praise for *Horse Stalker*

"From Robert Digitale's imagination and heart springs an odyssey that beckons the reader with alliances both dark and enlightened, landscapes enchanting and perilous, first love and treachery. The fantastic journey plummets and ascends along the full trajectory of human potential, from the sinister to the holy. Saddle up!"
  —Chris Smith, newspaper columnist,
  Santa Rosa, Calif.

"Veteran reporter Robert Digitale uses his journalistic skills to tell a compelling fantasy of ancient feuds and warriors who must rethink their old ways. He introduces a new kind of hero and women who use their wit and magic to offer a different world."
  —Susan Swartz, journalist and author of *The Juicy Tomatoes Guide to Ripe Living after 50.*

"*Horse Stalker* is a world to lose yourself in, with plenty of adventure and mystery. I took it up and hardly put it down until I had read the last page. Quite engrossing! And highly recommended."
  —Tim Stafford, journalist and author
  of the forthcoming book, *Miracles,*
  and the civil rights-era novel, *Birmingham.*

HORSE STALKER

The Root of Glory: Book One

By Robert Digitale

Franklin Park Press
2011

Franklin Park Press
Santa Rosa, California
Email: robert@horsestalker.com

Horse Stalker
The Root of Glory, Book One
By Robert Digitale

Library of Congress Control Number: 2011932257

ISBN: 978-0-9832435-0-2

Fiction/Fantasy

Printed in the United States of America

To:
My wife, Carol;
Our daughters, Elizabeth, Jean and Deanna;
And my mother, Mary Wise Digitale

PART ONE:

AMONG THE CLAN
OF THE HORSE

Roj

Chapter One

Wonder on the Mountain

In the blackish cave, Roj's mind beheld a vision. He saw a pale horse with a red mane. The animal advanced with eyes afire. Roj knew it was an omen, but of what? To steady himself, he put a hand on the gritty nubs of the rock wall. At once the vision faded. Once more Roj noticed the sound of rain falling outside, and he remembered his own stallion tethered nearby. The recollection caused him to turn back toward the glare of the cave's mouth. To his surprise, he saw the silhouette of a man with a drawn sword standing at the entrance. Roj raised a hand to shield his eyes, even as the stranger called out, "Be you MuKierin?"

"Yes, sir," said Roj. "Are you?"

"I ask the questions, boy. Now step out to your horse."

The young MuKierin passed the stranger and exited the cave, halting beneath a rock overhang that sheltered them both from a drenching rain. There, Roj took his first good look at the man. He was old and small in stature, with sunken cheeks, a thin gray beard and close-set eyes. His tattered, brown robe was tied with a horsehair belt. Around his neck rested a leather thong with a jagged, black volcanic rock hanging upon it—the sacred stone of Roj's people. The man's right hand tightly gripped a small sword. Overall, the stranger seemed a fierce-enough opponent, despite his age and ragged appearance. Roj felt his heart pounding.

"What brings you up the mountain?" the old man demanded. The stranger's eyes glanced left to Roj's sorrel stallion standing forlornly in the downpour. Next he scanned to his right for any signs of movement.

"I'm a horse hunter," said Roj. "I've come up here chasing a great horse."

"What horse?"

"A Spotted Stallion. I've tracked him for over two days. He passed up that main trail not long ago. I might have caught him, but the lightning flashed nearby and I thought I'd better find shelter from the rain. Look at me. I'm soaked. Anyway, I got underneath this overhang and thought I smelled Bitter Root cooking inside this cave. So I went inside to have a look."

The old man took a step back and looked askance. "Rare be the man who can track a prince of horses up this mountain. And never did I hear of such a deed by a boy. Never."

"I'm not a boy," said Roj. "I've lived twenty years, long enough to see both my parents die of the camp fever. For the last four years I've hunted horses in the low country. And I did track that Spotted Stallion up into these mountains."

The old man gave Roj a stern look. "Indeed, you be a strange one, boy. But still you bring trouble. Big trouble."

"What sort of trouble?"

"I ask the questions." The old man brought his glaring face so close that Roj could smell his foul breath—the Bitter Root, all right, just as he had smelled in the cave. "Where be your kinsmen?" the stranger demanded.

"Maybe I don't have any. How can you ask about my kinsmen when it looks like you mean to slit their throats? If you are MuKierin, please let me go. Let me take my horse and ride away."

The old man's eyes narrowed and his weathered face seemed to drain of life. "I be MuKierin," he whispered slowly. In silence, he looked over the young horse hunter. He beheld a young man of medium height, with a thick brown beard and hair that reached the shoulders of his dark cloak. Beneath his outer garment, he wore a simple cotton shirt and trousers with a horsehair belt tied around his waist. Around his neck rested a leather thong with a sacred black stone upon it.

The hermit put away his sword, folded his arms and stepped closer to his intruder. "Hear me, boy," he said,

2

lowering his voice and sounding almost fatherly. "You bring trouble. Plenty bad for me. Plenty bad for you. If you be Barsk, you be dead already and then I slap your horse to run back to the Red River. But you be MuKierin, so under my wing you go. You cannot leave me and live. Now we go, unless there be friends. MuKierin friends. Barsk friends do not count."

Roj nodded and looked away. The sudden encounter with the old man had flustered him. But now he realized that the stranger's fractured dialect came from the old line of horse hunters, most likely those from the hill country between Kierinswell and Orres. Roj decided to take a chance on this ragged MuKierin. "I have a kinsman, my sister's man," he said. "He's following behind me with our packhorse and a spare mount. He'll show up soon enough."

The old man winced at the news, but checked himself and turned away. Stepping out into the rain, he scanned the jagged peaks above the cave. He seemed to be calculating something in his mind. At length he muttered out loud, "The day be long now and the horse be spent...The boy cannot get away...The sky fire be good, but what if there be not enough light left to climb the mountain?"

Roj leaned back against a rock and gently rubbed his beard. He tried his best to look calm. "Please, kinsman," he called to the stranger. "You and I both belong to the Clan of the Horse. The Stone Woman is your mother as well as mine. Please tell me what sort of trouble is lurking in these hills?"

The old man stepped back to the overhang and pursed his thin lips. "There be evil ones nearby," he whispered. "Fierce evil ones. They find you, boy, they eat you."

"What evil ones? Are you telling me a campfire tale for scaring little boys?"

"The old tales hold truth, though the storytellers only guess at the danger. Long, long ago the Stone Woman warn her people to stay off the high places. She say not to pass beyond the foothills above Kierinswell. But the MuKierin trespass here and live, and so the people pay the Stone Woman no heed. In truth, the evil ones play the foxes. At

3

first, they let some come to the high places and live, and so they lure many more here to die. For generations, the horse hunters come up the mountain, but they never go back down. Their bones be trophies here. The people never learn their fate. The dead tell no tales."

"But who are these evil ones? To which clan do they belong?"

"They be not of the Seven Clans, but of their own kind. They be old as stone and fierce as wolves, great warriors who strike from the caves."

Roj stared at the stranger, struggling to grasp his words. "But how do you know so much about them? Why haven't these evil ones eaten you?"

"I be a seeker, boy," the old man replied, a proud lilt to his voice. "One seeker be good. One seeker and one boy be plenty trouble."

"What's a seeker?"

"You ask the Grand Elder in Kierinswell about seekers, boy. There be no answers on the mountain."

Roj frowned. "Very well, then how will you keep me from getting eaten?"

"You go under my wing. A seeker knows the mountain. We go to someone as fierce as the evil ones. But we go soon, while there be light, or we both be dead."

They began their wait for Roj's brother-in-law. Roj used the time to scan the ridges above the cave. The mountains before him rose above a land of high desert, a country of sagebrush valleys and foothills strewn with impenetrable thickets of brush. Water was scarce and found mostly in wells. For good reason the inhabitants called this country the Dry Lands. At least his people, the MuKierin, had the great peaks of the Powder Mountains that rose on the eastern flank of their homeland. The high places had few stands of timber but many cairns and outcroppings of scarred rock. Snow dusted the mountains in autumn and capped them white in winter. For most of the year, the high reaches belonged to the panther and the eagle, or so it seemed.

The old man sat down on a squat slab of rock. From

his pouch he removed a patch of bearskin and placed it fur side down upon his knee. In his left hand he grabbed a long, slender piece of the sacred black stone. In his right hand he took the pointed end of a deer antler and used it to peel off dark, glassy flakes. After using the antler to shape an edge of stone, he grabbed a flat piece of gray sandstone and dulled the black edges. Then he repeated the process. After a few minutes he looked up at his young guest. "Where did you find the stallion?" he asked.

"We came upon him two days ago on the edge of the foothills," Roj said. "It was just the two of us, me and Noli, my brother-in-law. When we saw him, our hunting party was back a ways getting ready to close in on a herd of wild horses. There were about a dozen of us, not a big camp like you see in the South Lands near Orres. Anyway, Noli and I had figured our group would catch a few colts and fillies and sell them in Kierinswell. But then the two of us came over a ridge and saw that stallion loping through the brush. I've never seen anything like him. My heart felt like it would burst from all the excitement of watching him slide past us. He was big and he had a creamy white hide and those black markings across his chest and rump. Well, we went right after him. Noli figured he would soon circle back to the herd. Then we could drive him into the ropes of our kinsmen. But he never circled back. He just kept climbing these cursed hills.

"Noli let me do the tracking, and for two days I never lost his trail. I just seemed to be able to sense his path. I've never felt anything like it before. Even so, this morning I was ready to turn back. I told Noli that my sister would skin the both of us if we got lost in these mountains. But he just called me a boy and said that we'd never get another chance like this. He's steadfast when he makes up his mind, and he's made up his mind to become the first MuKierin to ever catch a Spotted Stallion."

The hermit noticed that a quirt hung from Roj's right wrist, while his left hand was covered with a leather wrap that the horse hunters used to prevent rope burns. He rested his hands on his knees and asked, "Boy, you throw left?"

Roj smiled as he looked down at the stained wrap. "Yes, I always have, ever since I first picked up a rope. I swing a hammer with my right hand and I take hold of my knife with it, too. But I have always thrown a rope with my left hand. I guess it makes me a bit odd."

The old man grunted and once more thrust the antler against the black stone. "I know you be a strange one."

"What do you mean?"

"Long ago they say you come to me some day. They urge me to save you. I say, 'How will I know him?' 'You will know him,' they say. So I know you be a strange one. And so you be, a boy who throws left and tracks a great stallion."

Roj's throat and ears began to tingle. "Wait, kinsman. Who said I would be coming to you?"

"The fierce ones who do not eat the people. One day they see me cry and they give me the promise. 'If he comes, bring him to us,' they say. 'We will take him under our wing.'"

Roj squinted as the old man went back to fashioning the glassy, veined stone. He stood up and asked himself, *Is this old man mad? Has he conjured up this whole story, this tale of fierce ones who will eat you and others who will keep you alive? He seems touched, all right, but what if he is telling the truth? My papa and other men did warn of unknown danger on the high places. Some say a great evil haunts these mountains. All I know is this ground scares me.*

Suddenly he recalled the recent vision, though now only from memory. Even so, it dawned on him that the horse he had envisioned was probably the very Spotted Stallion he had been chasing. He strained to remember whether the dream horse had the same creamy white hide and the distinctive black markings. His mental efforts made him feel strangely weak, and his balance began to give way. He wobbled to a nearby boulder and sank to the earth. When he regained his bearings, he looked up to see that the hermit had stopped his stone work and was staring soberly at him. Roj tried to think of some way to explain what he had just experienced. *No, just keep your mouth shut,* he thought. *This old man won't believe you.*

The two men turned their eyes back to the main trail as Roj's brother-in-law emerged riding a bay stallion and leading a packhorse and a spare mount, a black-faced piebald. As soon as Noli spied Roj near the shadows of the cave, he swung his horse smoothly onto the rocky trace. The rain poured harder and the horses sloshed through puddles until they stopped underneath the rock canopy.

"Greetings, kinsman," Noli said to the hermit. He pulled off the hood of his cloak and shook out his damp beard and stringy hair. "In all my days I've never seen such a rain. I thought I would be sleeping in a puddle all night long."

"Off the horse," the old MuKierin retorted. Noli glanced a moment at Roj, then obediently swung a leg over his sheepskin-lined saddle and slipped down. Immediately the old man grabbed the reins and the halter ropes and led all four horses back toward the main trail. As the host disappeared, Noli stepped forward and grinned at his brother-in-law.

"How did you ever manage to find a kinsman in these lonely mountains?" he asked.

"We stumbled on one another," said Roj.

"Well, at least you found us a dry place to rest from the storm."

"The old man doesn't want us to stay here, Noli. He claims that bad ones are lurking nearby who will kill us if they find us. I don't know if he's telling the truth or if he's mad. But he's dead serious."

"Bad ones? What bad ones?"

"I don't know. He calls them old and evil, and says they belong to none of the Seven Clans. And he says some other people live up here that can protect us from the bad ones. He's offered to take us to them. I know he sounds crazy. Even so, he has me scared. My papa warned me to stay out of these mountains, and now this old man is talking about creatures from some old campfire tale." Roj debated whether or not to tell Noli that the hermit seemed to be expecting someone in need of rescue. For now he kept silent about that. Instead, he stepped into the downpour and looked back

7

toward the main trail. The path up the mountain disappeared in a thicket of prickly brush. The way down vanished among the rocks. Far beyond the ridge a bolt of lightning flashed against the darkened sky. "What should we do, Noli?" he asked. "Part of me wants to turn around and hurry back to Kierinswell. And yet the old man says we can't survive without his help."

"You're forgetting something," said Noli. "We don't want to give up on our stallion. We've got to take the upward trail and find our prize."

"But we can't just ignore the old man's warnings."

"What we can't ignore is the opportunity of a lifetime. Listen, we have a chance to be the first MuKierin to ever catch a Spotted Stallion. Do you hear me? Only a few men have even seen such an amazing horse, and none have ever claimed one for their own. But we have seen that stallion and soon we can take him. Tell me, what greater thing could you do on this earth? And this storm will help us. In this rain that horse will stop and rest. If we find the right spot amid these canyons, we can rope him before dark. So we'll rest here a few minutes and then we'll push ahead."

The two men grew silent as the old MuKierin returned without their animals. At their feet he threw two horsehair ropes. One was Roj's black lariat; the other was speckled with the colors of sorrels, grays and bays. "We go now," he said, pointing to the ropes. "I know these be dear. Take them with you."

Noli bent down and grabbed the speckled rope. "Yes, they're dear," he said. "This was my papa's rope. And that rope belonged to Roj's papa before he died. But if we're leaving, we'll take our horses, too."

"No, they go back down the mountain without you."

"You mean you let them loose?" Noli asked, anger rising in his voice. "Why would you do that? Did the boy here do something to offend you?"

"Those horses be trouble. The bad ones look for you on the trail. We trek over the mountain. No horses."

"No, by the Stone Woman, we're going our own

8

way!" Noli insisted. "And we'll take our horses with us!"

The old man drew his sword. "So be it, boy. Then one of us dies over those horses. You go with me or you fight me. You boys already be plenty trouble. If the evil ones come here, they kill me, too. If you be Barsk, I leave your bones in a pile. If you run, I kill you both so the bad ones leave me be."

Noli stepped back and reached for the knife on his belt. Roj called out, "Wait, Noli. Please let me say something." He turned to the hermit and spread out his arms in a sign of peace. "Those horses are all we possess," he said. "And you want us to just let them wander off?"

"Dead men need no horses. Without me, the evil ones pull you off those horses and split you open. But here you stand in my cave, so now my life be forfeit, too. So I kill you and save my life, or I take you under my wing. No more talk. Choose, Strange One."

"Strange One?" Noli asked, squinting.

"Very well," Roj said, putting a hand on his brother-in-law's shoulder. "Please, Noli, let loose your knife. Let's not spill any blood here."

"We need our horses," Noli replied.

"He has a sword. You have a knife. You can't take him alone. And I can't raise an arm against this old man. Listen to him. He speaks in the tongue of the old horse hunters. And he is offering to help us, even though he should know better than to threaten his kinsmen."

"Two men with knives could take him," Noli sneered. "But I guess I still have a boy for a partner." Reluctantly he took his hand off his blade.

Now the old man let loose, shaking a finger at Roj. "I be MuKierin! I watch over MuKierin! You cost me plenty, more than you know, but under my wing you go. You live or you die under my wing. Now we go!"

Roj frowned, first at the old man, next at his brother-in-law. Slowly he reached down and grabbed the remaining rope, the black one. Warily the younger men stepped back from their host. The hermit shifted a few steps away from the entrance but kept himself between the two horse hunters and the main trail. Roj looked out at the downpour and once more felt the chill of damp clothes clinging to his body. Reluctantly, he left the cave's overhang. Out through the rain the men slogged, moving along a smaller trace and up a rock gully. Roj and Noli led the way under the old man's direction. They were upward bound, passing among the boulders and scrub brush along the slopes. Soon they crested a ridge. There in the afternoon rain, the high country seemed to open up before them. Lightning strikes had set a score of brush fires along the distant hilltops, the smoke drifting up in great, gray plumes. On a slope below them, the ground smoldered black and grayish-white, the sickly sweet odor of scorched earth rising up to their nostrils. The smoke and the clouds came together and shrouded the pale sky in a dreary light that seemed to spread out forever. To Roj, it appeared too vast a country for a man on foot. But the old man smiled at the scene. "The storm be good," he muttered. "The bad ones fear the sky fire. For now, they leave the high ground to us." He kept a defensive stance as he eyed the two younger men. His right hand stayed close to his sword.

Noli drew close to Roj as they hiked ahead up a slope of loose rock. "Get ready to make a break for it," he whispered. "When we get to the top of this ridge, I'll go left. You run right and we'll escape this madman."

"No, Noli, that's too risky," said Roj. "He knows this ground. We don't. We run and before we have caught the horses and found each other, he will have ambushed one of us, maybe both of us, among these rocks. And if he doesn't find us, maybe somebody else will."

"Who? Do you really believe there are bad ones out there? I just think this hermit is crazy. He's been out here alone for too long."

"Maybe he is crazy, but we've got to keep our wits. He's the one with the sword. We've got to be sure we can both get safely away before we try anything."

"We can't wait long," Noli said. "We need those horses. I doubt we can make it out of these mountains alive without them." He turned back to sneak a glance at the old

MuKierin. The swordsman halted and glared back, touching his hand to the hilt of his sheathed blade. Noli whipped his head around and trudged on.

Chapter Two

A Light From Within

They tramped for two hours until they came to the edge of a long canyon that blocked their path. Roj slipped the black loops of the horsehair rope over his shoulder and led the descent down the wall of the cliff. The handholds were wet and the men had to take extra care not to slip. At length, they dropped off a ledge and passed through brush into a dry wash that ran along the bottom of the canyon. The old man drew near and pointed at the sky. A new storm front was advancing on them, its blackened clouds spitting flame and bellowing thunder. Dark sheets of rain painted the sky. Quickly the old man took the lead, springing up a steep bank and into a thicket beneath a cliff of crumbled rock and scrub brush.

Noli grabbed Roj's arm. "Let him climb," he said, nodding to the hermit. "Here's our chance to escape."

Roj turned back toward the canyon wall they had just climbed down. "Where would we go, Noli? It'll soon be dark. We can't find our horses before sundown. And you yourself said we can't escape these mountains without them. That old man knows this. Now that we have traveled far from his cave, he may let us run away. Out here he'll survive, but without him we'll perish. No, we've got to stay under his wing. He's MuKierin, Noli. He speaks the tongue of the old ones. He would never desert two horse hunters, not if we stick close to him."

The three men scaled the second cliff, even as rainwater streamed down its broken face. Roj thought their guide surprisingly agile for his age. Before long the younger men were panting. "We need to rest," Noli complained. "We're horse hunters, not acrobats."

"At the top," the old man replied from above. "There be places to hide from the sky fire. Come quickly, MuKierin! Make for safety!"

The men climbed by bracing their feet against exposed rock while their hands clung to ledges and scrub brush. Roj looked up along the top of the canyon. Far away he spied a dead tree trunk with two great limbs spread like a man reaching for the sky. Suddenly, lightning struck it and snapped off a limb, sending the great branch into a blazing free-fall down the canyon. A blast of thunder tore at their ears as the remainder of the trunk erupted in flames. "Save us, Kierin!" Roj yelled wildly. "Save us, Stone Woman!" In great fear, the younger men strained for the top.

Once there, they found the old man anxiously motioning them to follow. They raced downhill among boulders and brush. Behind them the thunder cracked and roared, pulsing in strange rhythms that made each silence almost as scary as the next eruption. At length, the old MuKierin stopped beside a boulder with a ledge that offered protection. The three crawled beneath it and curled against each other as the storm slammed into the mountain. Roj and Noli covered their ears and cowered. The ground, the air and even the rock seemed to rumble mightily. Lightning flashed around the hilltop and the smell of fire hung near, even through the rain. At last, the storm passed. Only then did Roj notice the old man's hand upon his shoulder, firm and steady.

"The storm be good," he said. "Stay here, Strange One. I be back soon."

Noli and Roj twisted onto their backs and ran wet sleeves across damp faces. "Why does he keep calling you Strange One?" Noli demanded.

"I think his mind is playing tricks on him, making him think I'm somebody else. I told him how I had tracked the stallion and how I throw a rope with my left hand. Then he called me strange and said he knew that I would come to him someday. He said he'd heard it from the people who will give us refuge."

Noli's temper flared. "Now I know he's mad. You should have told me all this back at the cave, before he took our horses. I had my papa's sword on that packhorse. I could have grabbed that blade and fought our way out of this."

Roj frowned. "Noli, you always want to fight your way out of trouble. But I was hoping there might be another way. You can call me a boy and a fool, but I didn't want this old man's blood on our hands."

"Well, the time for a tussle has passed," Noli said with resignation in his voice. "Our horses have run to who knows where and the night is coming soon. We have no choice now but to go with him. But if we ever make it out of here alive, I plan to tell our kinsmen that bandits robbed us. It sounds less humiliating than to tell them that we let some mad hermit turn our horses loose on a mountainside."

Roj shrugged and wiped wet fingers against the grainy earth. "Well, you must admit that he has put us under his wing, sky fire and all. He wants our company no more than we want his. But here he is trudging along with us. He's either going to slay us or become a lifelong friend."

"Yes, he's MuKierin. I'll give him that much. He shakes his sword at us, but he does his duty to the Clan. His mama taught him to look after his own kind."

The rain turned to a light shower. Roj felt cramped beneath the ledge so he crawled out and stretched his legs. He climbed a small knoll in order to get a better look at the ridges around him. At first he saw only shrub-studded slopes and gray boulders. But within a few moments he spotted a strange light glowing in the notch of a distant canyon. The light didn't flicker like a flame. Instead it seemed to grow steadily brighter, a golden beam spreading wider and higher from within the gorge. Roj felt his chest start to tingle, then the feeling reached his fingers and his lips. He scanned for signs of such phenomena on other hilltops, but saw none. He turned back and once more felt a thrill at beholding such brightness. "What are you?" he asked aloud. "Who are you?" The thought came to him that he must make his way to the light and let it wash over him. He began to feel almost weightless, as if with three or four immense strides he could make his way across the great expanse and immerse himself in the golden glow. But gravity returned to his body as the sky convulsed with lightning. Four great bolts struck in rapid succession around the blazing canyon. The golden light remained a few moments longer and then went out.

Roj stood transfixed, waiting to see whether the wondrous sight would reappear. The hermit soon returned and climbed the knoll. Roj called to him, "Kinsman, I saw a great light in the distance, shining brighter than daybreak. And a string of lightning bolts struck all around it. Did you see it?"

The old man sighed. "Once, long ago. Only once."

Roj tingled unexplainably at the words. "Well, let's go that way. Let's make for that light."

"No, the light be beautiful but it signals danger. The fierce ones clash beneath its glow. Even so, for us it be a good sign. The sky fire drives back the evil ones, blocking their path to us. The fierce ones who do not eat the people shall prevail. No, we leave the battle to them but we go on to the ground of the promise. Soon enough you will be safe."

The hermit turned to walk away. Roj remained frozen, longing to better understand what he had just experienced. The old man stopped and turned around, carefully studying his young charge. Noli arose and walked wearily by his brother-in-law. "Come, Strange One," he called mockingly as he caught up to the hermit. For a moment the two men stood together and silently watched Roj. At length the hermit let his right hand slip down to touch the hilt of his sword. Frowning, Roj reluctantly descended the high ground.

Together the three strode down a gentle slope that led them into a small valley. The hermit seemed less concerned now about being spotted. Soon the rain let up. They pushed on, watching the shrouded sun emerge at last beneath the clouds, then sink below a pink and purple horizon. Roj couldn't help but notice the evening's beauty.

The three now walked abreast through a clearing in the brush. Noli asked, "So where has he gone, Roj, that stallion of ours? Do you think you could find him in the morning?"

Roj turned and looked wistfully back along the trail. "No, this rain has washed away all his tracks. He doesn't need to worry about us anymore."

"No one will believe us, but we nearly had him," Noli said. "We nearly caught ourselves a prince of the Dry Lands. Oh, what bad luck we've had today. We let a fortune slip through our fingers."

The old man snorted. "Crazy MuKierin dreams. Crazy. Nobody catches those stallions."

"One day some lucky MuKierin will," answered Noli. "And the boy here was on his track for more than two days. He could have been the one."

The hermit gave them both a sober look. "The boy throws left and tracks stallions. Surely he be a Strange One." They walked on, and the old man seemed to look far off into the fading daylight. "Be the old horse hunters still filling the little ones' minds with the stallions?"

"Indeed, they do," said Noli, "just like when we were boys. Those gray beards still gather the boys around the fire on summer nights and tell their stories. They tell how our forefather Kierin promised that one day a MuKierin will ride a Spotted Stallion out of this desert to a land beside the sea. Then it grows real quiet, and the old ones speak the old words ..."

Here the hermit himself interrupted, "Remember me, horse stalker, when you ride beside the shining waters."

Noli and Roj nodded knowingly. "Remember me, horse stalker," Noli echoed. "Where did you hear the words, in Kierinswell or in the South Lands near Orres, where I come from?"

The old man sighed, his eyes suddenly downcast. "No questions, now. I give no answers on the mountain."

They pushed on in the autumn dusk. Pale light reflected off a few hills but most of the land lay shrouded beneath clouds. The light dimmed and the old MuKierin hastened his pace. At length they reached the base of a steep slope of loose rock. The light was so faded now that Roj's eyes could no longer distinguish one color from another. Their guide halted. "I go no farther," he said. "Up ahead be the ground of the promise. Go and be safe."

The young men looked surprised at the sudden talk of parting. "But, kinsman," said Roj, "why won't you come with us? Don't you also want protection from these evil ones?"

"No, boy, I be a seeker to the end. A seeker goes his way alone." He thrust his hand in his pouch. When he removed it, he held aloft the shiny black stone that he had fashioned earlier that day. To Roj's delight, he saw the old man had shaped it into a small knife. It was not much longer than a man's hand, with a rounded grip and a wicked edge. He handed it to Roj and looked him in the eye. "Go on, Strange One. I choose my own path. So be it."

Roj took the stone blade and hugged his kinsman. Next Noli stepped up and declared, "Old man, I still don't know what to make of you. You're a hermit who lets loose other men's horses. At least, we're still alive. And if you really did help us escape harm in these hills, then we're in your debt and we won't forget it. You are MuKierin. We are MuKierin, too."

From far away came the sound of rocks sliding over rock. "Go," the hermit said. "Go quickly. Trouble may be near."

The two horse hunters stepped forward onto the loosely packed slope, carefully testing the earth as their feet sank into the crushed rock. Roj looked back once and saw the old man disappear into the night. He turned and focused on the climb ahead. He wanted to hurry, but the slope was too steep. Soon his legs were churning and his calves burning. With each step he planted small impressions in the eroding hillside. The two men pushed steadily on, not stopping until they reached the top. Despite the darkness, they could see they had reached a small plateau with a rocky slope above them on their right. On their left, the land seemed to drop off as if it were the edge of a table. Both men sank to one knee and tried to catch their breath. "I hope we're almost there," Roj said. "I didn't like that sound we heard back there."

Off to their left came a muffled tapping noise. A few moments later the horse hunters recognized the rhythm of feet running. They looked at each other and knew at once that those feet didn't belong to the old hermit. Whoever it was, whatever it was, the creature was headed fast their way. "Run for it!" Roj hissed. They sprang up and shot across the top of the hill, their ropes swinging wildly in their hands as they ran. Roj led the way, dodging the brush and the ankle-high rocks scattered before them. The two sprinted up to a small dry wash and jumped across it. The brush was low here but the night obscured their vision. They ran for almost two minutes when they spied a figure far ahead of them, standing on either a rock or a patch of raised ground. Roj slowed to a jog, fighting the urge to hunch over and take in more air. Both men gasped for breath but kept moving—their eyes fixed on the figure before them. Roj's heart beat wildly. No longer could he hear the running feet behind him. Instead, the night had grown still, except for the pained wheezing that rose from each man's throat. They slowed and stepped cautiously forward until they were less than thirty paces away from the looming shape. There they stopped.

Chapter Three

An Emissary of the King

From the figure came a voice so vibrant that it sounded as if it could be heard for miles around. "You may come forward, MuKierin."

Roj's eyes bulged, and he whispered, "That's a woman speaking to us." He shouted back with a voice that in comparison seemed almost a rasping croak, "Was it you that the old man brought us to meet?"

"Yes."

Noli shouted next, "Can you prove it?"

"No. But if I were one of the evil ones, you would now be my captives. Instead, I will let you stay or come as you wish. It is for you to choose."

"Are the bad ones hunting for us?" Noli asked her.

"Yes."

"And is there a bad one just over the hill back there?"

"Yes."

Noli whispered, "Save us, Stone Woman."

"I say we go to the woman," said Roj. "Or do you want to go back and see if she's telling the truth?"

The two men walked forward side by side. Their eyes squinted and their ears strained for any sounds of danger. They drew near and beheld the darkened shape of this stranger, a woman of their height with long curls and a flowing white gown. She didn't appear to have a weapon.

"Very good, MuKierin," she said. "You have chosen wisely. Now, we must go quickly."

She turned to leave, but Noli pleaded, "Wait. Woman, who are you?"

"I am the one who saved you. Please come."

"But what keeps that bad one back there from rushing up and killing us?"

"He is afraid. His fear holds him back from us."

21

"Is he afraid of you or me?"

"Truly he does not fear you, MuKierin. But now we must move quickly. Let us stay quiet until we reach shelter." With that, she set off. The two horsemen hurried behind her down the mountain.

For nearly an hour the woman led them downhill beneath a night sky where the clouds had given way to reveal stars beyond number. Along the skyline, Roj could see little but the occasional silhouette of a small tree atop the ridge above them. The trio came at last to the bottom of a hill. On they hiked along a dry streambed that wound down to a spot where the slopes seemed to press in on either side. Soon they spotted a faint light that shone forth from a cave. On they strode toward the light.

Inside, the cave was illuminated by twin silver candelabra, each with three tapered candles. Between the glowing candles sat a plain, drop-leaf writing desk with a straight-back chair sitting atop a small woven rug of many colors. A white quill pen stood in a holder atop the desk. Roj found the items strange for their setting, but he was quickly drawn away from them by his desire to take his first good look at the woman. She had auburn tresses, large green eyes, a straight nose and sculpted cheeks. His eyes were drawn to hers, which signaled to him kindness and grace. The more Roj saw her, the more he found it hard to look away from her. His brother-in-law noticed this, and it irritated him.

"Let us meet your kinsmen, lady?" Noli demanded. "Please take us to your headman."

"For now I am alone," she replied, looking straight into his eyes.

"Alone, you say? How is it that a woman can be safe alone in these mountains?"

"Watch and see. But I tell you that for now you are safe in my keeping."

"Did you tell that old hermit that this boy here would need a rescuer one day?"

"Why do you ask such a question?"

"I ask because that old man called this boy, my wife's

22

brother, a 'Strange One.' And he said he'd been waiting for him. Did you put such thoughts in his head?"

"Why did the old one call him 'Strange One?'"

"Because the boy throws with his left hand!"

"Also," Roj interrupted, "I told him that I had tracked a Spotted Stallion."

"Indeed," she said, her voice rising. "And is this true?"

"Yes, lady, I tracked the stallion for over two days. And I got close to him this morning, but my horse had no strength for a fight. And then I met the hermit."

"So young you are," the lady said, surprised. "So young and yet you have tracked a prince of the wild ones. Indeed, you have a great gift if you can follow such a creature."

"Well," said Noli, "it was I who knew to set the boy out front as our tracker. But answer me. Did you tell the hermit that the boy would need a rescuer?"

"My people promised the old one that we would care for any MuKierin that he brought to us. You are the first, and he risked his life to save you. That does make you strange, both you and this man."

Roj smiled when she said the word "man." But Noli frowned at her answer. "Lady, this day we lost our horses and all our possessions. We have been ruined, and for what? Tell us about these evil ones. Why don't we know about them or about you?"

"Many MuKierin know of them. They are the Dark Brood, the evil ones who belong to Equis. You have heard of Equis?"

"Yes, Equis is a great city that lies far south along the Red River," Noli said. "They say its rulers do not belong to the Seven Clans. But we have never seen any of their kind. They stay far away from the Clan of the Horse."

"That is because of the kindness of the King. He has forced the evil ones to stay far from your villages, and to come no closer than these mountains."

"What king?"

"Have you not heard of the King?"

"Well, some speak of a king. But others say the King only lives in old stories."

"The Stone Woman knew the King. She told her children to trust the Great King Over the Mountains. Do you know of the Stone Woman?"

"Yes, she is the blessed mother of our clan. But the Stone Woman lived many generations ago. All our people know stories about her, but they're old stories, like campfire tales."

"And what of the White Beard? Have you not heard of Him? The White Beard also speaks of the King, and his stories are not old. He is the King's steward among your people. Among the MuKierin he speaks both to the great and the small."

"Yes, I've heard of this White Beard. They say he's a hermit who lives in the southern hills near Orres where I grew up. But I've never met him, and I don't know much about him."

"Then you shall learn of him, and of the King he serves. And one day I hope you will meet him. But tonight I shall provide you a place to rest, and in the morning I shall help you return to your people."

"Excuse me, lady," Roj interrupted. "I really do want to learn more about you and your king. But my kinsman and I have hardly eaten anything today. Could you spare us some food?"

The lady smiled broadly. "Indeed, you shall sup before you lie down. Let me make the preparations."

"Begging your pardon, lady," said Noli, "my kinsman and I must step outside and care for the things men must care for before they lie down." The woman nodded and Noli roughly nudged his brother-in-law. They left the cave, striding down a gravel slope until they reached a pair of large boulders.

"Let's not go too far," Roj said.

"I may start running and never look back," Noli

replied. "We have escaped the cook's pot and jumped into the coals."

"What do you mean?"

"I mean something's funny here. Did you look at that woman? Of course, you did. You scarcely took your eyes off her. Didn't the old man say he was taking us to someone as fierce as the bad ones? Does she look fierce to you? And why would a woman as downright pretty as that one live here on this mountain, with no man, nobody at all? And why would she rescue foreigners, two dirt-poor horse hunters?"

"Speak for yourself."

"No, you listen to me," Noli growled. "Something here smells funny. Look, she's a foreigner, not a MuKierin. What do we matter to her? Yes, I do think there was a bad one out there tonight, and we heard him running there behind us. But let's think about this. Would a bad one really be scared of this lone woman? How fierce is she? Could it even be that she's in some sort of conspiracy with the old man and that bad one? Maybe all three of them want to trick us into going with her. I know it sounds crazy, but we can't rule it out. I think we're in big trouble with her."

"Wait a minute," Roj protested. "This woman helps us and you start speaking sour words about her. You should be grateful."

"You be grateful. You can get all mushy brained and witless with your eyes fixed on her pretty face. But I'm scared and I'm trying to keep us alive."

"I'm scared, too. Being up in these mountains is enough to scare anybody. But I'm worn out. My body cannot take much more tonight. Let's rest tonight and in the morning we can try to make sense of things."

"Okay, but we need to keep our eyes on her. Tonight we'll have to take turns watching her."

Roj untied and pulled down the front of his trousers. "Not me. I won't be able to keep my eyes open. If you want to stay awake tonight, you go right ahead. And if that woman wants to rip out my heart while I sleep, she's welcome to it."

The men relieved themselves and returned to the cave.

25

There in the amber candlelight, the lady had set two cups of hot tea and a plate of cold biscuits on a low table. The scene made Roj think back to childhood, when his sister Remy made him play with her, two little ones pretending to dine together. Now Roj and Noli knelt at the table, and the woman brought them a plate of deer jerky and raisins. The horse hunters ripped apart the biscuits and stuffed them in their mouths. Roj sipped the tea and nodded his approval to their host. "Lady," he asked, "what can you tell us about the old hermit?"

"What did he tell you?"

"Very little. He called himself a seeker but wouldn't say much more. And he wouldn't come with us to meet you."

"For now I will respect his wishes to keep his ways secret. This seeker desires to live on his own, to be indebted neither to my people nor to the Dark Brood. Even so, he risked his life to bring you to me. Is that not the way of the MuKierin?"

"Yes," said Roj, "he took us under his wing. We're in his debt, and now we're in your debt, too."

Noli shook his head and set down his cup. "What we are is destitute. What a day we've been through. This morning we were drawing close to a Spotted Stallion, a king of horses. In a few more hours we could have put our ropes on him and collected a fortune. Instead, now we're standing on the edge of ruin. We have nothing. It's all because we let that crazy hermit turn loose our horses, along with all our possessions. Now we'll return empty-handed to Kierinswell, if we return at all. If we get out of these mountains, the boy and I could wind up wearing the debtors' chains." Wearily Noli arose and walked toward the back of the cave. There he sat down and wrapped a woven blanket around himself.

The lady stared into Roj's eyes. "Indeed," she said, "I know of the debtors' chains. I have seen how the Seven Clans treat their debtors. They sell them into slavery, even their own kinsmen."

Roj looked down at his half-empty cup of tea. "It's my fault. The old hermit did let loose our horses. Noli wanted to

26

fight him so we could recapture the animals. But I couldn't kill the old man, so we lost them."

"Did you think the seeker meant you good or harm?"

"I knew he didn't mean us any harm. He was strange, but he did bring us to you, just like he said he would."

"Then do not regret your choice. Wisely did you trust the seeker, and he did not fail you. Truly I tell you that you would have perished this day if you had not gone with him. Your enemies were tracking you. The rain and lightning held them back for a time, but you would not have escaped them, even if you had kept your horses."

Roj's mouth gaped. "That reminds me. This afternoon I saw a wondrous light in another canyon. Noli and the hermit didn't see it, just me. But the old man knew about it. He said he had seen it once long ago, and he said the fierce ones were fighting there beneath that light."

"Indeed, the seeker did behold that light many years ago. That day my people tried to save another group of horse hunters. Alas, we found them too late. All had fallen to the Dark Brood. The seeker did not witness their fate, but he saw the light and later he learned of our battle with the enemy."

"But did the light come from you or these bad ones?"

"The Dark Brood has no such light. No, MuKierin, it was my light of power that you saw this day. With that light, I stood before your pursuer and blocked his way. He was forced to retreat and to take another path. Even so, he came close to overtaking you."

Roj's chest once more began to tingle, and he thought back to the great light. "Lady, who are you? How did you come by such a great power?"

"I am one who serves the King. And he has called me to take you under my wing and to help you return to your people. If you are willing, I will go with you and keep you safe."

"And have you saved other MuKierin?"

"No, you and your kinsman are the first to be rescued on this mountain. All those who came before you perished here. Had the seeker not taken you under his wing, you too

27

would have perished."

Roj sighed. "Lady, please tell me your name. I'm Rojiston, the son of Aaln of the Stone Fences, but they call me Roj. And that's Noli, my sister's husband. Lady, please give me your name."

"You may call me Healdin. And now I will ask a question of you, Rojiston, son of Aaln. Your kinsman calls you a boy. How much older is he than you?"

"Four years. Lady, don't judge him by his rough words. He loves my sister and he eagerly took her hand, even though she had only ten silver coins for a dowry. Noli comes from the South Lands near Orres. We met him there last fall while horse hunting with my kinsmen. Noli and Remy soon took each other's hand. He's a good husband. He's even agreed to give up horse hunting in order to learn a trade from my uncle, a candle maker in Kierinswell. Believe me, a horse hunter could hardly make a greater sacrifice."

Healdin nodded and arose. "We have much to learn of one another, Roj. But now I am weary and you yourself have survived a great test, though not the last test, to be sure. Sleep now and we shall speak again on the morrow."

Chapter Four

Suffering and Bitterness

In the night, Roj awakened from an uneasy slumber. Outside the cave, someone was moaning. The young man raised himself and felt his stomach grow queasy at the sound of the groans. Was Noli the ill one? Quietly Roj arose and went forth. There was barely enough light to see the slanted surfaces of the cave wall and the rock path outside. Beyond the entrance, he found Healdin sprawled before him in the starlight.

"Lady!" he exclaimed.

"Water," she whispered. "Please, Roj, fetch me the water skin."

He rushed inside and grabbed the water pouch. He listened for Noli and heard him snoring soundly from the back of the cave, despite his vow to stay awake. Quickly Roj carried the water back to Healdin. She was so weak he had to lift her head to help her take a drink. He gasped to see a slight amount of blood dripping from her mouth.

"Lady, you're bleeding. What's the matter?"

Slowly, Healdin sipped a few mouthfuls of water and lay back down. "The worst is over. The malady often passes in a few hours."

Roj refrained from pressing further about her sickness. "Do you want me to leave you alone?"

"No, Roj, I would have you stay, if you are willing."

"Of course, I'll stay."

"Good. You will be a comfort to me. Please tell me of your family."

"All I have left is my sister," he said as he sat on a rock beside her. "My mama and papa died of the camp fever about five summers ago."

"Tell me of your mother."

Roj felt his throat tighten. "What I recall most about

29

her was her touch. Everyday she hugged my sister and me. My papa said she would spoil us with her hugs. But Mama said she had only hugs to give us, and she would not have us go forth each day without them."

Healdin gave a weak smile. "Indeed, she was a wise woman. I would like to know more of her."

Roj bit his lip. "There's not much more to tell. When the fever came, she lasted longer than Papa. But it laid her low, much as you look now. Near the end, she could not keep down her food. How I hated those days. And she wouldn't let us touch her. She feared the fever would take us, too. All Remy and I could do was watch her go. She gave us no more hugs."

Healdin reached out and took his hand. "Thank you, Roj. This night you have brought me a tender comfort. I perceive that you have not considered your mother's death for many days. I hope some day to help you recall the better times with her, too. Now I beg you, help me return to my bed. I will rest there and fall into a deep sleep. But you must wake me in the morning."

At first light, Noli arose sleepily and stumbled forth on his way to relieve himself. He went to Roj and kicked him lightly. "It's morning, boy," he said. "We've got a long walk in front of us." He turned and saw Healdin sleeping soundly nearby. "Our rescuer looks even less fierce in the day than in the night. Look at her. She looks pale as death."

"She became ill in the night," Roj said. "She was bleeding from her mouth. It scared me, Noli, but she said it would pass. In a moment I'll wake her."

Noli stepped forward slowly, shading his eyes as they adjusted to the early light outside the cave. The sun was rising above the hills, but it had yet to shine in the bottom of the rocky canyon. Noli took a few more steps and then froze at the mouth of the cave. "Roj," he called. "Come here."

Startled, Roj obeyed as Noli raised his right hand and pointed outside. There in the early light stood their four horses, the same ones the old MuKierin had released the day before.

"By the Stone Woman!" Roj exclaimed. "Lady, our horses have showed up. How did that happen?"

"Friends brought them," Healdin said weakly, pushing herself up on her knees. She stood and followed the men from the cave.

"Look at this, Noli!" Roj shouted. "Here is ol' Sandy, your mare-crazed stallion. And the packhorse looks to have all our provisions. We're whole again. We don't need to worry about the debtors' chains or about walking back to Kierinswell."

Noli moved cautiously toward the horses, squinting as if they might be a mirage. Gingerly he stroked Sandy's mane and looked back soberly at Roj. Next he went to the packhorse and removed his sword. He nodded sharply as he attached the blade's scabbard to his horsehair belt. "This sword belonged to my papa," he proclaimed to Healdin, who by this time had reached the cave's mouth. "He served a term as a soldier, and he taught me to swing this blade with all the skill of our forefather Kierin."

The lady turned to Roj, asking, "And do you have a sword?"

Noli snorted. "Ha, the boy doesn't fight. The fighter in his family wears a skirt. That would be his sister, my woman."

"I was given my papa's sword when he died," Roj explained. "But a day came when Remy and I needed food. She held tight to the ten silver coins for her dowry and wouldn't give them up. Instead, she sold my sword. Indeed, right now I wish I had a blade, though the truth is that I don't know how to wield one."

Noli grabbed the reins and turned his horse around. "Roj, let's get ready to go. We're getting out of here. I'll ride in front."

Healdin said, "I would ask that you stay here longer and permit me to rest through the morning."

"No," said Noli. "I want out of these cursed hills. We're going to leave as soon as possible, with or without you."

"I shall ride with you. Let us hope we do not come to regret your haste."

The sky remained clear and the sun was shining in the canyon when they set out from the cave. Noli rode in front, then the lady, with Roj in the rear, atop the sorrel stallion, and their other horses behind him. Healdin rode her own gray mare. They followed the dry streambed for nearly a mile, and then climbed up a path leading over the ridge. At last they came to what appeared to be the main trail. On that wider road Roj took the opportunity to catch up and ride alongside Healdin.

"Did you grow up in these mountains, lady?" he asked.

"No, my people come from far away. We live in a land of green hills and great forests and much water."

"Does such a place exist?"

"Indeed, it does. I hope you will see it some day."

Roj noticed she was wincing. "Lady, are you well?"

"I suffered much last night, Roj, and I remain weak. Perhaps we can rest soon."

Roj glanced toward Noli, who had ridden far ahead to the crest of a hill. Suddenly his brother-in-law halted and raised a hand in warning. On the other side, at the bottom of the slope, the hermit was kneeling atop a small boulder. The old man's arms appeared tied behind his back. Behind him stood some odd creature, but its head and body were covered with a blanket. To Noli, the creature seemed smaller than a human, but he couldn't be sure; it stood completely hidden beneath the blanket. "Horse dogs," the creature screeched in the tongue of the MuKierin. The words seemed weak, more like the sound of a cawing bird than a human. "Show your manhood. Stop hiding behind the woman. I will kill your kinsman unless you step forward. Are you cowards?"

Noli drew his sword and rose up in his saddle. "Let him go, you dog!" he screamed.

"Cowards!" The creature cawed again. "Women! Gutless MuKierin! Will you not stand up for one of your own? Must I kill this old man because you will not challenge me? I shall kill him!"

Noli glared back to his kinsman. "Come on, Roj!" he yelled. "We have the horses. Bring along your fierce woman and let's free that old man." At once he spurred Sandy and yelled defiantly, "For the Stone Woman!"

Slowly Healdin stirred herself, but Roj had already ridden ahead and begun to uncoil his horsehair rope. "Wait, Roj," she cried. "It is a trap." She urged her mare forward after the two men.

With his sword extended, Noli galloped down the trail toward his enemy. Suddenly, a rope was pulled taut and low across the path, catching Sandy's front legs. The stallion buckled headfirst into the dirt. Noli flew overhead and tumbled wildly along the trail. As he did, a strange warrior jumped out from behind the boulders. The fighter looked immense. He was outfitted in worn, black leather armor. On his head, he wore a leather helmet, from beneath which flowed a great mass of shaggy hair. On his face were some sorts of markings. And in his right hand, he held a sword.

"Noli!" Roj cried. He had no sword, but he held out his rope and spurred his horse down the trail. Healdin watched in alarm at his charge.

Onto the trail strode a new warrior, the very one who had tripped Noli's stallion. This warrior, also clad in black armor, raised a sword and made ready to strike Roj down. The young man had little time to react. He swung his horse left, galloping off the trail and down the hillside. Part way down his stallion lost its footing and the animal toppled over. Roj managed to tumble to the uphill side as the animal careened and rolled down the slope.

The two warriors each went after a different victim. The first drew near and stood over Noli. The horse hunter had broken his left arm in the fall and could barely struggle to his knees. Noli closed his eyes as his enemy pulled back his sword. But the deadly blow never came. Instead, the sword thudded to the ground. Noli opened his eyes to see the warrior shudder and collapse, three arrows protruding from his chest.

33

A shriek of victory sounded from the hillside, even as more arrows shot forth. The warrior approaching Roj quickly ducked amid boulders. He scurried behind the great rocks until he reached the safety of a nearby cave. The seeker, meanwhile, was dragged away by the cawing creature, which tossed off its covering and was revealed as yet another warrior, even bigger than the first two and also adorned in black. His height had been hidden because he had been standing in a pit dug behind the rock. This last fighter held the old MuKierin as a shield and backed up to the cave. At the entrance, the captor drove a long knife deep into the hermit and flung him to the ground. Then, the two surviving warriors disappeared into the cave.

The fall had bruised Roj, but he arose from the dirt and ran to the fallen hermit. He tried to attend to the old man's wound, but the seeker stopped him. "The King's power," he sputtered. "Find it for the MuKierin. Do not let the evil ones take it."

"Rest, kinsman," Roj said softly. He scanned the ground for any sign of what the old man might be talking about. A tall, strange woman approached from the hillside and knelt beside the hermit. Roj looked in wonder to see a silver helm upon her head and a breastplate of silver mesh over her white gown. He backed away as she knelt beside the hermit and set down a round shield and a silver-tipped spear. Gently, she put one hand against the old man's wound and a second upon his throat. She looked up at Healdin and shook her head. "He sleeps with his fathers," she said in MuKierin.

Slowly, Roj rose up and turned back toward Noli. His brother-in-law was lying on his back with one knee bent upward. Two more women warriors knelt over him. Roj shuffled over as pangs of grief began to well up inside him. One of the women looked up as he approached. "His arm is broken," she said of Noli. "But he lives."

"Did we save the old man?" Noli asked.

"No," said Roj. "They killed him."

"Blast them! We'll avenge him, Roj. We must.

34

Somehow we must make these dogs pay for what they did to us."

A few paces away, two more women examined the dead warrior. He seemed a giant, with flesh on his face and hands and a mass of unkempt hair flowing from his scalp and beard. Dark brands, not tattoos but actual brands burned on with hot irons, disfigured his cheeks, forehead and arms. The brands on the cheeks depicted lightning bolts and skulls, and a broken star was burned into the center of his forehead. Upon his black armor hung the delicate bleached bones of the humans he had slain, both finger and toe bones. Roj looked on in disgust as the women dragged away the corpse.

Healdin approached, looking weak and shaken. "How I feared for you," she said. "Indeed, I am amazed that you survived."

Roj heard the fright in her voice, but his own heart was pumping too fast for her words to sink into his brain. He turned back toward the dead man and asked her, "Who are these savages?"

"They are evil ones, and they delight in the destruction of your kinsmen," Healdin said. She pointed toward the corpse. "That one was called Yuikki, or 'Sneaker.' The one who chased after you is named Weakling or 'Wuuf' in their tongue. His allies gave him that name to chide him, but do not be fooled, Roj. To your people he has ever been a deadly foe. And the one who killed the old man is Pibbibib, 'Backstabber' in your tongue. He is the leader of these three. It was Pibbibib that pursued you last night. It was he whose path I blocked. For generations, these three have killed horse hunters on this mountain. And now the seeker sleeps with your ancestors, too. We must bury him according to the custom of your people."

"Lady, he spoke of a power, the King's power. He told me to find it, not to let the evil ones take it. What did he mean?"

"We will not speak of such matters now. You remain in danger. Let us bury your kinsman and retreat to safer ground."

35

Six white-gowned women took the old MuKierin's body to a high place off the trail and dug a shallow grave. Roj went with them. He removed the dead man's horsehair belt and black stone necklace. These he placed in a sack, which he took and tied to the back of his own saddle. Healdin stayed behind and attended Noli, whose left arm ached mightily and was starting to swell. The lady built a fire and brewed a special tea. Noli drank it and felt a little better. Afterward, the lady set the broken bone and splinted it with two pieces of white wood. When Roj returned, Noli was sitting atop Sandy, grimacing but anxious to leave this place of death. "We will not go far," Healdin told Roj. "We will stop soon and let your kinsman rest. I must lie down and sleep, too."

They set off with six women warriors in front and as many behind them. Roj felt nauseous. Healdin rode beside him in silence for a few minutes. At length, she said, "Your kinsmen and you were brave but foolish today. My people might have saved the old man if you had not been so rash."

Her words stung. "The old man saved our lives," said Roj. "We were obliged to do the same for him, but we failed him. Now his enemies must become our enemies. We must avenge his death. It is our way."

"It is a bent way," she replied. "But you will not have to go looking for these evil ones. They will come seeking their revenge on you."

"What do you mean?"

"They lost one, too, not that they cared for him. But you stood against them and we killed Yuikki. Now Pibbibib and Weakling must report this disgrace to their masters. They will be branded on their arms and sent out to hunt you down."

"What are you saying? It sounds like we're as good as dead."

"No. You are safe as long as you listen to me."

"None of this makes any sense."

"You must be patient. We will speak tonight by the fire. I have much to tell you."

They rode until early afternoon. By that time two

dozen women had joined the party. Most of them carried great bows and quivers of arrows—rare sights in the Dry Lands where good wood was so scarce. These women wore silver helms and fine mesh breastplates over white gowns. Some held glistening silver shields and wooden lances tipped with silver points. Many rode silver or gray mares. To Roj, these strange females made an unsettling sight. Nonetheless, he accepted their presence, at least for now, and simply hoped there were enough of them to deal with their enemies.

At last, they reached a sand-colored pass above a great canyon. From there, the women could command the high ground and keep watch on the trail below. A camp already had been set up with a dozen beige tents and a picket line that held at least thirty horses. In the center, a thin, wrinkled-face woman stood waiting with folded arms. Healdin dismounted and kissed the old woman. "I must rest," she told Roj, before disappearing into a nearby tent. Meanwhile, two women warriors took Noli off his horse and helped him shuffle to a clean tarp placed on the ground. There he lay down and curled up in pain. Other women took Noli's horse, the packhorse and their own animals to the picket line. No one spoke to Roj, but he dismounted and followed with his own stallion. He noticed that several women already were slinking among the surrounding boulders outside the camp, apparently looking for a place to ambush any intruders. They took with them tan shawls, which they used to camouflage themselves against the rocks.

After caring for the horses, Roj went to help make Noli as comfortable as possible. The trail had been a rough climb, with many a switchback and rock staircase to it, and his kinsman looked worn and pale. The old woman emerged from Healdin's tent and, over a small fire, began to concoct a new brew, this one stronger than the first one that Healdin had made. Noli drank it and soon was sleeping deep and peaceful on the tarp atop the sandy ground. Roj put a blanket on him and turned to Noli's nurse. "Thank you, woman. Thank you for helping my brother-in-law get some rest."

"You are welcome, MuKierin. Call me Mirri."

More women kept showing up and reporting to the old woman. To each, she gave duties. She sent some over to the next hilltop and another group to the rocks just beyond the camp. Meanwhile, she oversaw the cooks as they tended six pots and kettles boiling with soup and stew over a large campfire.

With nothing else to do, Roj walked to the edge of the camp to check on the horses. Healdin's gray mare stood free, not tethered by bridle nor halter rope. Its immense eyes locked on the horse hunter as he approached. Roj slowed his advance and changed course, but the mare followed his every stride. He halted and found himself staring back in wonder. Together they fixed their minds on one another; neither moved for a full minute. Mirri noticed the encounter and walked up to Roj.

"This mare is from the stallion's bloodline," he said. "Somehow I can sense it."

"Yes, they are brother and sister," Mirri said. "The mares do not take on the spots of their sires, but still they belong to a most wondrous breed."

"I can almost hear her in my head."

"Indeed? Then you are a strange one."

Roj frowned. "Too many people have given me that title, and I'm not sure I like it."

"What does the mare say to you?"

"Well, I don't hear any actual words. But I get a strange feeling that she is wondering whether I have enough courage for what lies ahead. It's as if she's asking whether I'm a man or a coward."

"Well, that is no surprise. Every woman in this camp is wondering the same question. But I think the mare may be the first to know the answer." The old woman gave a wry smile and walked away.

Later, the company came together for the evening meal. Roj judged the stew the tastiest of his life. The smell of the venison and herbs soon woke Noli. The cooks, however, first made the injured man drink a bowl of green soup, which they said was made especially to help heal his broken bone.

But the men really went after the stew. They both had three portions. Then they took twist bread—dough wrapped on sticks and placed beside the coals—and wiped up the last bit of gravy off their plates. They washed the meal down with a swig of red wine and lay back on their blankets like the kings of the clan.

After dinner, three women took out stringed instruments and began tuning them. The sun was low now and everything its rays touched glowed golden, from the nearby rock outcrops to the farthest ridges. There, as the last light of day bathed the pass, the women began to make their music. They started soft and gentle—just a fiddle, harp and mandolin—instruments unknown to Roj. Soon, a woman added her voice, and then another as the chorus came round again. The words were strange but soothing. They conveyed a sense that all was right in the world, that night was settling once more over the mountains as it had done countless times before, and the day would come again.

After the song ended, Healdin appeared from her tent. She held a fiddle in her left hand. Other women drew near with rhythm makers, drums, guitars and other stringed instruments. Roj sat up on his blanket. Nearby, Noli drifted between waking and sleep. For a moment, the company stood silent. Presently, a horn sounded far off down the mountain. Closer still a second horn echoed the same five notes of a minor scale: Mi, Rae, Doe, La, Sol. A third horn blew the same flourish just outside the camp. Healdin put her bow to the strings and repeated the strain. Once more her bow sang the notes and then built a lively melody upon them. Other instruments joined in; the rhythm makers kept a syncopated beat. The chorus that followed sounded regal, with a choir of voices singing sweet and strong, and the sound of the lady's fiddle soaring above it all. The song went on so for a few minutes. Then Healdin dropped her bow and one singer took over, and the music changed. The woman sang high and pure, but her voice conveyed sorrow and unfulfilled longings and a hurt over that which was lost. Next came a slow chorus filled with voices singing some bitter refrain. The singer called out plaintively and the stringed instruments echoed her melody. Roj ached to hear a song of such beauty and pain. He longed to know the singer's words, and the cause of her grief. At length her voice began to fade, as if darkness itself was swallowing her up. Indeed, Roj's ears strained to listen as the song gave way to silence.

Then Healdin again raised her bow. Its eerie wail shot across the mountaintop, echoing the singer's sorrow and sending shivers through Roj. The singer joined in while the other instruments played soft and low. Roj's rescuer began a new melody, one that allowed for the singer's song, yet was not bound to it. On and on her fiddle played, higher and higher, and then in the chorus the choir proclaimed: "Fidden Gadaeyo, Ta Elladoena Fidden Gadaeyo!" A horn sounded a flourish and Healdin answered with her strings. Then the choir and the singer joined in. All hint of sorrow was gone now. Boldly they sang the words again: "Fidden Gadaeyo, Ta Elladoena Fidden Gadaeyo!"

Roj didn't mark how much longer the music lasted. All he knew was the song was ending and he wished it would go on and on. He stared at Healdin standing there in the firelight as the music came to a close. Quiet once more descended upon the mountains. The company savored the moment. Roj observed the satisfaction upon each face and the warm glances that the musicians gave one another. He turned to see Noli sleeping peacefully beside him.

Healdin soon retreated to her tent. Roj watched anxiously for her to return to the fire. He feared she might retire for the night. The other musicians left. Three of them entered Healdin's tent. Roj felt an urge to get up and go there, too. What would she think if he asked to speak with her? What would he say? He didn't have a clue. Frustrated, he lay back down on his blanket.

Chapter Five

The Age-Old Story

After a few minutes the musicians exited the lady's tent. Roj kept his eyes fixed on the canvas flap. If Healdin came out, he told himself, he could follow her and tell her how he enjoyed the music. Or he could thank her for the food and care. Or he could say anything, just to be near her. The rest of the camp seemed to be settling down for the night. Roj kept his watch. At last he saw her emerge. Two other women joined her and they walked straight for him. Roj tried not to show how pleased he was to see her moving his way. She drew close and spoke. "It will be cold on the pass tonight," she said. "Your kinsman and you will sleep in my tent. I will sleep with my own in another tent."

"You're most kind," Roj said. "Thank you."

"Help us wake him, and these women will take him there," she said.

Roj obeyed and soon Noli was stumbling sleepily for the tent. Healdin, meanwhile, turned to Roj. "Come sit with me by the fire," she said. He nodded and followed her to a flat stone that could seat two people. She sat down, and he joined her. Neither spoke for a moment. At length she asked, "Did the music please you?"

"Oh, yes, lady. I've never heard anything like it before."

"It was telling the story of your people and mine," she said.

"Was it? What was the woman singing about?"

"She sang of your sorrows and mine, and of your hope and mine. Roj, what do you know of your people and the King?"

The horse hunter tried to remember. "Well, I know that some people say a king will rescue us one day. They think he'll send us a champion. And they say he'll help a man

41

ride a Spotted Stallion out of the Dry Lands to a great sea, a place of shining waters. We've got a name for that man. We call him the Horse Stalker."

Healdin smiled. "Your people remember a little of the old tales. That is good. Listen and I will tell a story. There is much that you must know if you are to understand the old man who died today and the evil ones who killed him."

And Healdin told this story:

My homeland lies far beyond this desert. We call our home the Green Lands because of its forested hills and fertile valleys. There lives the King, the ruler of my people. Long ago he sailed over the sea and brought back to our land a Golden Box, and within it an object of great light and power, the Root of Glory. At first my people understood little of this awesome force, though we learned more once it was stolen. But even in the King's possession we soon grasped that it could touch the hearts of all who should behold it. In some it awakens awe, in others envy, in some fear, in others joy.

In time, some of the King's subjects sought to possess this power. They became obsessed with it, and they could sense such obsession in others. At last these greedy ones came together and, in the darkness, plotted their treachery to take the Root, which they came to call the Great Valuable.

A leader arose among the conspirators: Zoirra, a great captain of the King's guard and a warrior of much cunning. And he devised a plan to steal this power. On an appointed day, Zoirra rode to the castle at River's End. He went unseen up a secret passageway and forced his way into the King's locked chambers. He found the room empty and the Golden Box sitting on a table of white marble. But when he opened the box, a great light flashed in the chambers, damaging his eyes. He cried out and writhed on the ground. He could still see but only by the light of Root of Glory. His confederates heard his cries and found him in the room, helpless and flailing on the floor. No one then was willing to go near the great light streaming from the Golden Box. So they left the box untouched and carried their wounded leader away. Once

Zoirra was taken from the room, he lost all sight. His allies put him on a horse and rode hastily from the castle. Quickly they gathered their followers and fled the Green Lands. Thousands had taken part in the conspiracy. Together they traveled south into this great desert, which then appeared empty.

And in the desert the conspirators made a strange discovery: some of the Root's power had been transferred to Zoirra. Though blind, their leader seemed able to sense the approach of the King's loyal subjects, especially those who had stood long in their ruler's presence. This ability awed Zoirra's underlings, and they named this gift The Powers. Many yearned for such a gift, and those who spent the most time in Zoirra's presence began to sense The Powers coming upon them, too, though their perceiving skills could not compare with those of their master.

So Zoirra grew in power, and yet he remained consumed by his lust for the Root of Glory, especially since only by its light would he ever again see. While he feared to ever touch it, he nonetheless vowed to find a way to control it, regain his sight and destroy the King. So the conspirators defied the king and refused his demand to lay down their arms.

And this is when your people enter the story. In response to the rebellion, the King led his troops to the boundary of the Dry Lands and began to set up a line of defense. As he surveyed these efforts, his scouts brought him strange news: pilgrims were crossing the desert, fleeing a great drought in a faraway country. They were seeking a new home and they already had traveled into the northeastern edge of the Dry Lands. Among the refugees was a young mother named Hannah, whom your people later named the Stone Woman. When the King heard of your ancestors' plight, he feared for them. So he gathered two dozen soldiers and two hundred pack mules and set off to bring them supplies. He told his commanders to prepare more provisions and to follow after him with a larger supply train. Finally, he sent out skirmish parties to defend his own movement from the rebels.

After many days, he found the sojourners, a few thousand men, women and children. They were gaunt from hunger and from the desert's harshness. When they saw the King's immense warriors, they fell down in fear. But the King told them, "I mean you no harm. My soldiers and I have brought you food and water. If you are willing, we will help you cross this desert and reach the green and fertile lands of my kingdom. There, my people will welcome you and provide you the means to build homes and farms for your families." Your kinswomen wept at this news. Your men felt as if a great weight had been taken from their shoulders. That day the leaders of the families met with the King. And the King chose Aesa, the husband of Hannah, to represent your people. The next day they set off slowly across the desert.

The King had warned the people not to go exploring in the desert. But a number nonetheless set out to see the land, including a stocky man named Troppa. Late one afternoon Troppa crossed over to the nearby foothills. There, among the large brown rocks, he heard a voice, the voice of Zoirra. "Beware, man, beware!" the voice called out.

"Who are you?" Troppa asked.

"The voice of experience," Zoirra replied. "I am the voice of one who has paid dearly for placing his trust in another, only to be betrayed. And again I say, beware!"

"Show yourself to me," said Troppa.

"No," said the voice, "For I am only a weak, wounded cripple and I cannot risk myself against one as strong as you. Is it not enough that I am risking so much to give you this warning?"

"Then at least say plainly who it is that I should fear," Troppa said.

Zoirra replied, "That I will do. Fear the one who seems to offer friendship but who means to enslave you. Fear the one who has crippled me and who will take your freedom from you when he deems the time is right. Fear the one who will suck all the life out of your body."

"Do you mean the king?" asked Troppa. "How do I know you speak true?"

"Your heart knows I speak true," said Zoirra. "He pretends to help, because he now has few troops. But when his reinforcements arrive, you will see his true side. You will see he means to put you in chains and make you his slaves."

"Perhaps I believe you. But what can one man do?"

"There is a way to defeat the King," said Zoirra. "There is a power to undo him. I can help you take hold of it. But you must do exactly as I say."

Troppa was both wary and intrigued. "Why not fetch it yourself?" he asked.

Zoirra replied. "I cannot. My people cannot safely touch it, neither can the king's soldiers nor any of his subjects, for we are all of a different race and this power can kill us simply by its touch. But your people are of a race that may safely touch it, I am sure. You could wield this great weapon to free all of us." Zoirra, of course, was not at all sure that Troppa could safely touch the Root, but he certainly wanted him to try.

Troppa asked, "How can I know such a power exists? What proof can you give me?"

"Step forward to the flat boulder," said Zoirra. "You will find a rabbit skin there. Unwrap the skin and behold the necklace within. I have long worn this necklace, but today I give it to you. Put it on and you will sense the power of which I speak. It is but a small sensation of the great force that could belong to you. But it will be enough for you to know that this power exists and that it could be held in your hands."

Troppa went to the rock and took the skin in his hand. For a moment he hesitated, but then he pulled back the skin and picked up the necklace, a red stone on a leather thong. And he put it on and felt his body tingle with a strange sensation. And immediately he desired the source of that power.

That same day Hannah's husband Aesa went to the King and said, "Majesty, may I seek your favor? You found us as poor and desperate wanderers, a people with little left to lose. Still, we know nothing of your land. We know nothing of your friends or your enemies. We know nothing of your past, nor do we know what future awaits us in your land. I know I have no right to ask anything of you. But still I must ask for my family. Please, majesty, promise me that you will not abandon my wife and my children, whatever should happen to me."

The King replied: "Aesa, how will you know whether or not I speak truth?"

Aesa replied, "I may not know for sure, Lord. But, whatever you say, if I hear it from you, I will hold onto the words because I have nothing else to hold onto."

"Then hear me, Aesa," said the King. "I have told myself that I will not leave your people to perish in this wasteland, nor will I stand by while my enemies enslave you. Moreover, I have heard your request. I promise to care for your wife and your children, and for their children. If your offspring will follow me, I will take them to the Green Lands."

Zoirra, meanwhile, took Troppa under his wing and that same night began to prepare him for treachery.

On a morning a few days later, the King's sentries saw a dust cloud in the south. The captain told the King that rebel cavalry appeared to be near. The King decided to keep the people in camp until his supply train could arrive that evening with more troops. He sent two messengers to seek reinforcements, and then he ordered the captain to send out two scouting parties to look for the enemy. Later, the captain took his remaining soldiers to reconnoiter the southern hills near camp, and to wait there for the return of his scouting parties. Troppa saw them all leave, just as Zoirra had predicted. Troppa knew that all was going according to plan.

That afternoon, when the King retired to his tent for his daily rest, Troppa drew near. He brought twelve kinsmen with him. The twelve believed Troppa's story that the King meant them harm, and all were eager to join him in his quest for power. Only the King's chief servant remained in camp, but he was at work in another tent. While his kinsmen waited outside, Troppa quietly slipped into the King's tent. He crept to the King's bed and beheld the Golden Box on the ground beside it. That box, Zoirra had told him, held the power. Troppa touched the box and did not die. He took it in his hands and began to exit. The King awoke and saw Troppa holding the Golden Box.

"Do not open that box," the King declared.

"We know you mean to make us slaves," Troppa said. "We will not stand for it."

"Again I tell you not to open the box. If you could read the golden inscription upon it, you would know your doom. You would read that the power inside that box cannot kill me. I can withstand its pain, and I can overcome anyone who wields it against me. Troppa, it is not too late for you to put down the box. But if you open it, you will find that you can never freely let it go."

Troppa refused to listen. Instead, he fled the King and raced with his kinsmen to their encampment. And when he found Aesa, he declared, "You no longer lead these people. I am now their King!" And he opened the Golden Box and touched the Root, and a great light arose from the box, red and terrible. Troppa removed the root from the box and with it struck down Aesa. The people saw a great flash. And in that moment their hearts were changed, pierced by the light of this power. A longing came upon them, a longing for the Root of Glory. Even so, they ran in fear from Troppa. Some of the women took Aesa's widow, Hannah, in their arms and gathered up her two young children. And together the women fled into the desert.

The King found Aesa's corpse amid the empty camp. He told his servant, "Go at once to the captain. Tell him what has happened. Tell him Troppa has taken the Golden Box and the Root. Tell him Zoirra and the other rebels must be near. Our few soldiers must drive the enemy back tonight, or he will take Troppa and the Root."

The servant asked, "Should I tell the captain to bring back Troppa and the others?"

"No," the King said. "Troppa will not willingly release the Golden Box, and I will not bring these people back by force. I will not enslave them. Tell the captain not to show himself to Troppa. Still, tell him this: I must find a way to remove the Root from these people before they destroy one another. Have him come to me after sunset."

That night, your ancestors hid in little bands among the rocks and gullies, terrified of the King's troops and of Troppa and the stolen Root. Hannah was with her kinsmen. The men there were cursing that they should be so unlucky as to be related to Aesa. And Hannah was crying for herself and Kerissa, her young daughter, and Kierin, her baby son. Late that night, while the others slept, Hannah heard a voice calling her name. No one else heard the voice. In her grief, Hannah thought it was Aesa calling out to her, so she arose sleepily and walked out into the night. There, she found the captain of the King's troops. Immediately she fell down in fear.

"Do not fear, Hannah," the captain said. "The King has sent me to you. He told me to say he has not abandoned you. He made a promise to Aesa to care for you and your children."

Hannah asked, "Then have you come to take us back to the King?"

"No," the captain said. "The King will not force your people to return to him. And he believes none of them now will come willingly."

"He knows us," said Hannah. "All the men fear the King will slaughter them for what has happened today, for that is what they would do in his place."

The captain said, "Then for now, you must lead your people, Hannah. If you will follow me, I will take you to a place of the King's choosing, a place where you can live until the time when your kinsmen will willingly follow the King to the Green Lands."

Hannah began to whimper, "O, Aesa, why have you died? Now I need you, Aesa! Please come back to me. How can I survive this harsh land without you?"

The captain said, "Woman, if you want to save your children, you must hurry. Troppa is near. The danger is very great. Will you lead your people where I am told to take you?"

Hannah brushed away her tears and moaned, "The men will not follow a woman."

The captain replied, "Then they will perish. The coming days will be terrible. Many will kill and be killed because today's treachery. If your kinsmen want to save their women and children, they must leave with you now. Look behind me. I have brought ten mules loaded with food and water. Awaken your people and tell them you are leaving with your children to safety. Then set out southeast toward those darkened hilltops. Let those who wish to save themselves follow you. I will stay hidden so as not to frighten your people. Keep looking to the southeast. In a few hours you will see a candlelight burning in the distance to show you the way."

The captain left, and Hannah awoke her people and gave them some of the food the King had provided. She told them the captain's words and said she was leaving as he had instructed. Immediately the men started to grumble. Several said they would not follow a woman. But Hannah bravely took her children and started walking away with the mules. Some of the men stood up to stop her. But Aesa's brother, a man named Squire, crossed their path and warned them, "Do not block her way. If the King gave Hannah these mules, he surely can slay anyone who harms her. Go wherever you want, but I will follow Hannah and put my life in her hands." That settled the matter. Hannah's kinsmen arose and followed her—nearly one hundred people in all.

That same night a band of Troppa's kinsmen attacked him as he slept. They had seen the power, and each one now desired to have the Golden Box and its contents for his own. There in the darkness they attacked and overpowered him. In the scuffle, one man managed to get his hands on the box and to remove the stolen Root. It became as a sword of fire. Again a red flame filled the sky, and this time many died. Troppa fell there, and so did many others who had reached in vain to grasp the awesome power.

49

The days that followed were filled with great bloodshed among your people. Whole families were annihilated, even the nursing babes. And there was no peace for the men who clutched the Golden Box or held the Root, for they always were gripped with fear that another would attempt to take it from them. In the end, everyone who touched the Root died a violent death. Still, the king's warriors kept the Dark Brood from ever getting close enough to the mortals to capture the Root. In time, both the Golden Box and the Root vanished. The last man to hold them was named Ry. He ran off into the western desert so that his kinsmen could not kill him while he slept. But one night he fell fast asleep beneath a starless sky and awoke to find that the Golden Box had vanished from his side. When he realized he had lost his treasure, he went mad and killed himself.

So the Root disappeared in the Dry Lands, and neither your people nor the King's enemies have ever found it. Thus, it remains hidden to this day. The lost people came to make up the Seven Clans of the desert, of which Hannah's kinsmen, the MuKierin, are but one. But the people never found peace. The power of the stolen Root had touched them and their descendants. Although they no longer can name it, your people still long for its awesome light. Without it, they will never find peace. And so they strive, not knowing for what they seek. They vie with one another for wealth and dominance. They war with one another and enslave one another. And when tempted by the evil ones, they search for the great power, though the quest costs them everything.

As for Zoirra and his evil ones, they became harsh masters over most of the clans. They are known to you as the warriors of Equis, and they collect both tribute and slaves from nearly all the desert clans. But the evil ones have not yet been allowed to rule over the Clan of the Horse, or over the Pappi, the Clan of the Lake, whose lands lie west of your people.

As for Hannah, she became the leader of your people and raised her children and waited for a day when the King would rescue her kinsmen. To the MuKierin she became known as the Stone Woman. And before she died, the King promised her that at the right time he would send a Champion, a man of his own choosing. This Champion would reclaim the Golden Box and the Root and at last lead the desert people to the Green Lands. And this would be a sign: a horseman would arise and change the future. That man would be the Horse Stalker you speak of. But these promises did not come to pass in Hannah's lifetime. She went to sleep with her fathers, as did her son, Kierin, and her daughter, Kerissa. Many generations since have joined her. And your people still yearn to leave the desert. But none ever escaped the Dry Lands.

Healdin ended her story. Roj realized he had hardly taken his eyes off her. He glanced down at the fire, the coals slowly ebbing away. "That's quite a story, especially about the longing that afflicts my people. So we need this power to have peace. But how do we find it?"

"Many have tried from among the desert people. Each clan has its tales of a mysterious power that your ancestors lost long ago. Some people guess it is a sword of fire. Others believe it is a scepter that can force all men to bend their knees in submission. A few even have heard the name of the Golden Box, though its contents remain a mystery.

"But what can this power, this Root, truly do?"

"It can do what the mind of its possessor has the strength to will it to do. In the hand of its owner the King, it can do much good. In the hands of an ordinary mortal, its power remains limited, though still great enough to kill many of your kind. And in the hands of a mortal trained to wield it, it could do great evil."

Roj thought for a moment. "And the evil ones also seek this power. The bad ones we met today belong to Zoirra, don't they? Why do my people know so little of them?"

"A few know," she said. "For the love of Hannah, the King has kept the Dark Brood away from her descendants. He has forced the evil ones into the high mountains, far from your villages. But your people certainly have heard of the

Castle of Equis and its evil servants. And some MuKierin have had dealings with the bad ones."

"The old hermit certainly knew about them," said Roj. "But who was he? How did he come to live in these mountains?"

"Your Elders call him a seeker, a seeker of the Golden Box. His work remains a great secret of your clan. Your Elders have held onto Hannah's words of a coming Champion and for generations they have sent out their seekers in anticipation of that day. Such men spend their lives wandering the desert looking for the box, in order that they may present it to your Grand Elder and that he might give it to his appointed Champion. In truth, it is a futile quest. Even if a seeker could find the box, he would face an unbearable temptation to take the Root for himself. Nonetheless, the Elders think it is for them to anoint the Champion, and so they send out their seekers. This old one was the last of his generation. In his youth he had searched throughout the foothills beneath the Powder Mountains. But before you were born he entered the high mountains. It was then that he first encountered the Dark Brood."

"But why did they let him live? Why did Zoirra's warriors not kill him long ago?"

"The warriors knew at once that he was a seeker. So it pleased them to let him go on searching the mountains for the Golden Box. But in time the old man stopped his wandering. He became content to live in his cave and to remain within this one range of peaks and canyons."

"Wait," said Roj. "You mean the evil ones wanted him to find the Golden Box? I don't understand."

"Remember, the enemy also desires this object of power. But after Zoirra was blinded that day, the bad ones do not dare touch it, though perhaps some day one among the Dark Brood will so dare again. Therefore, the evil warriors hope that a mortal will find the Root of Glory. I even suspect that Zoirra seeks one day to prepare a mortal from among the Seven Clans to wield this great power against the King's Champion. Thus, the bad ones allowed the seeker to live in these mountains. They hoped he would find the box and they would take him captive with it."

"But why didn't the old man see right away how evil these warriors are?"

"You must understand that the bad ones can hide their nature when it suits them, as Zoirra did with Troppa long ago. They can deceive and for a time the old man allowed himself to be deceived. He was a seeker, and a seeker who knows mysteries can become proud. But in time he came to understand their evil. A night came when the Dark Brood ambushed a party of horse hunters in the high mountains. The next day the old man came upon the carnage. He grieved deeply for the lost MuKierin. And my people saw his grief, and they came and comforted him. For so long he had resisted our words. But that day he listened. We told him we would help him if ever he sought to prevent the slaughter of his kinsmen. We said we would take under our wing any MuKierin he brought to us. He accepted our offer. And thus he was quick to take you under his wing. And so you live. I think he knew the evil ones would kill him for this act of mercy. And yet he remained too proud to place himself under our wing, because it could mean ending his quest for stolen Root. The longing for power twisted him, too, and so he perished."

"And now these bad ones want to kill Noli and me."

"Yes. They want their revenge for Yuikki. And they would kill you anyway because you have met me. They hate such encounters with the King's subjects. So they will send Pibbibib, the one known as Backstabber, and Weakling to hunt for you. But you can find safety under my wing. I will care for you."

"And you have your light to protect us," Roj said. "Healdin, it sounds much like the power of the stolen Root."

"Indeed, the two belong to one another. Generations ago the King gave me this power. It is called Mara, the Vine. It is small, merely the size of your own knife, and I wear it sheathed on my leg. Seldom has it been seen, though a terrible day is coming when it will fill the night with fire. But I must

53

draw it with care, lest by its light I blind you and other mortals."

"Generations ago! But lady, you look so young."

"So I am, Roj, among my people. But we are not as you, nor are those of the Dark Brood. Zoirra and Pibbibib and these other rebels all fled the Green Lands long ago. And Mirri and I were among those who pursued them. We have battled one another for generations of the lives of your people. And we shall continue to battle until one side defeats the other."

Roj shook his head in wonder. "Lady, tell me one more thing. Can these evil ones actually touch the Root and live?"

His rescuer's eyes flashed. "You hear this story and immediately you desire to know secrets that have been kept hidden for generations. Again, think what you ask, child of Hannah. Already this day you have gained terrible enemies among the Dark Brood. These warriors would stop at nothing to take such a secret from you. So would those among the desert people who seek the mysterious power. No, for your sake, I will not answer you."

"As you wish," Roj sighed. Glancing away, he let his mind drift back to the events of the day—the music and the stew and the skirmish. The haunting sounds of the chorus and the horror of the dead stirred his insides. He needed to move, to rise and walk off this anxiousness. He looked back at the lady. She seemed everything he was not—so confident and serene. He still questioned whether he could trust her, but he wanted to.

Healdin arose and declared, "Tomorrow we will begin the journey back to Kierinswell. We must find a way to protect you from Pibbibib. Our safest path will be to journey far south to Orres. There, you will meet the White Beard, the King's Steward. He will help us."

The lady departed to a nearby tent. Mirri, the old servant, met her outside and bowed down. "My lady, did you tell the horse hunter the story?" she asked.

"Yes, Mirri. How strange it must sound to his ears.

Even so, he grasps that Pibbibib means to track him down. Thus, for now I believe he will place himself under my wing."

"He has a gift with the royal horses, my lady. He sensed that your mare belonged to the same lineage as the stallion. Indeed, all our company wonders whether he may be the one. Behold, he is the first child of Hannah ever to be rescued in these mountains. And we almost lost him today to the evil ones."

"Indeed, Mirri, this day I worried that he would die before my eyes. In all my years, I have never been gripped by such fear. How unprepared I was for such a feeling. And still he remains in great danger. You must help me, Mirri. I cannot let my fears so rule over me. We have waited so long for this day. I must walk with more care."

"You were ill and weary this day, lady."

"It was more than weariness, Mirri. The terror gripped me as never before. I nearly drew the Vine, even though I might have greatly harmed both him and me. No, you must help me. I must walk the path set out for me. In time we will know whether he is the Horse Stalker, the one who will change the future. If he is, he must persevere in his own way, even as the old story says."

Chapter Six

Forks in the Road

A few nights later Healdin arose beneath the amber light of a half moon. Already she had led Roj and Noli down into the foothills beneath the Powder Mountains. Now the time had come to awaken the men. "The moon has reached the top of its arc," she told them. "We must continue our journey. Late on the morrow we will reach Kierinswell."

Noli wanted more sleep. "Why do you push us so?" he muttered, tenderly rubbing his broken arm. "You say the bad ones have no horses. They cannot catch us before we reach the walls of Kierinswell."

"You will find no safety in that city," she replied. "The enemy has accomplices there, even among your people. Pibbibib is not afraid to climb the city walls at night and go to those who would help him search for you. In time he could find you there. And in that great city, he could devise many schemes to attack you. Staying there would put you and your woman, Roj's sister, in great peril. Instead, I wish to lead you into remote lands where my own people can help me watch over you."

"Can Pibbibib track us even in the countryside?" Roj asked.

"He would lose our trail on the trampled roads around Kierinswell," Healdin said. "But that will not stop him. He may guess that I will take you far from that city. Moreover, he can sense where I have passed, especially the nearer he draws to me. My light of power touched him that day on the mountain when the seeker found you. That day I stood before Pibbibib and blocked his path with the light of the Vine. His mind became awakened to my power, and he began to sense my light. He will not soon lose this awareness. The colder the trail, the greater the difficulty Pibbibib will have in following us."

Noli said, "But these villains have your scent, not ours. Wouldn't Kierinswell be a safer place for the boy and me, only without you? You could lead these bad ones far from us, and we would find peace."

"You will have no peace as long as Pibbibib hunts you. In time he would search all the land of MuKierin, including Kierinswell. A day may come when he will stop chasing you, but he must have a reason to do so. Otherwise, he will keep hunting you until he finds you and destroys you. To him, it will not matter if the hunt takes one year or a hundred."

"I don't want this life," Noli said. "I don't want to get in between you and your enemies."

"Pibbibib is your enemy, too. He hated your people long before you took your first breath. It is time you learned this truth."

By late afternoon of the fifth day after the seeker's death, Roj, Noli and Healdin reached the outskirts of Kierinswell, the chief city of the Clan of the Horse. The two horse hunters parted company with Healdin on a hill a few miles from the capital's south gate. Taking along their packhorse and the extra mount, the men rode along the outer walls and passed within.

Kierinswell was built around three deep wells; each well lay separated from the others by a cluster of flattened hilltops. Walls of adobe brick surrounded the old city, including the main battlement on the north side. But about half of its five thousand people lived outside the walls, many in one-room mud huts. To the west of the city lay vast sagebrush plains. To the east rose the foothills and Fire Mountain, the sacred meeting place of the MuKierin.

Inside the city, Roj and Noli avoided the main thoroughfare that passed by the great market and bazaar. Instead, they trotted their horses along back lanes and up the nearest hilltop. They were bound for the compound of Shone the candle maker. Shone was Roj's uncle, and earlier that year he had taken in Remy, who was both Roj's sister and Noli's wife. Uncle Shone had promised to teach Noli the craft of candle making that autumn.

The two men turned their horses into the candle maker's dirt yard, cluttered with broken-down carts and huge heaps of brush for the fires. The yard at first appeared deserted, but Roj soon spied a half-dozen male servants eating dinner in the shade near the compound's main kitchen.

"Go get your woman," Roj called to Noli. "I will find my uncle."

"Tell him my arm will mend," Noli replied, raising the broken left arm, splinted and cradled in a sling. "Tell him I still value his promise."

"Do you mean you're going to stop riding the wind and settle down?" Roj asked. He gave a sly grin.

"Don't ask me that now," Noli replied. "Your sister wants me here, and I don't wish to anger your uncle. But I truly would miss riding the wind."

The two dismounted and went separate ways. Roj, his quirt dangling off his right hand, strode wearily to the main house. Noli, meanwhile, turned for the large kitchen. He nodded to the male servants hunched nearby over wicker tables, slurping their soup directly from fired clay bowls. Several grizzled faces turned toward the newcomer and beheld his broken arm. "Did a wild one kick you?" one bald servant asked. "Or did you drink too much wine and fall off your horse?"

Noli smiled grimly and passed by them in silence. He lifted the latch and slowly opened a door built of thin sticks. It took a moment for his eyes to adjust to the dim light in the kitchen, but at length he saw Remy. She was sitting alone at a small table, not with the half-dozen other women in the room, and her face seemed filled with sadness. Her eyes stared to the far wall and then dropped to the half-filled bowl before her on the table. Noli swallowed hard and stepped quietly to her side.

"Woman, I have come for you," he said as boldly as he could muster.

She turned, and for an instant she began smiling, happy to hear his voice, glad to have him near her once again.

"At last you have come," she said. Then she saw the broken arm. "Noli, what did you do to your arm?"

"I'll tell you later. Come with me, woman. We've got to leave now."

She shook her head as if the movement might help her to better hear her husband. "What do you mean?"

"Quiet," he whispered, cutting her off. "Come. Roj is waiting for us."

Obediently she followed him out the door. As she closed it, she noticed that all the women servants were staring soberly at her from their wood benches. At once she felt a lump bulging in her throat. Turning, she stepped quickly to pursue her husband as he strode back across the yard toward the female servants quarters. Near the door he stopped and turned toward her. "Hurry and gather your things," he said. "We're going south."

"Noli, please, won't you tell me why we have to leave? I have done well here. Uncle Shone is pleased with my work."

"Bad ones are hunting for us," he replied. "Roj and I will say more once we're on the road. Look, I don't like leaving this place. But your brother wants us to leave the city before the gates close for the night. Now, go! Put on your leggings."

A few minutes, later Remy emerged with all of her possessions rolled into a canvas tarp and tied fast by a rope. Beneath her worn beige skirt she wore gray cloth riding leggings. Roj, meanwhile, had filled two water skins and placed them on either side of a packhorse. He took Remy's gear, plopped it on top of the skins and lashed everything in place. Remy looked as if she would cry. "May I say goodbye to Uncle Shone?" she asked.

Roj frowned and shook his head. "I talked to him for all of us, Remy," he said. "You need say nothing more."

"What did you tell him?"

"I told him that Noli and I are in trouble. I told him he has to take my word about this because the story is too strange to be believed. Indeed, Remy, you won't believe it either. But I gave him my word that I would bring Noli and you back here as soon as I could."

Remy knew that as a woman she had no say in this decision, not even to demand an explanation of why her world was being turned upside down. *We can't lose this chance to build a new life, a better life than chasing horses and sleeping in tents,* she thought to herself. *Please, Noli, don't let our chance slip away.* Her husband led their spare mount, the piebald, to her. He began to help his wife mount, but Roj lightly jabbed his kinsman's broken arm and shoved him aside. Squatting slightly, Roj cupped his hands and waited. Remy began to cry as she raised a foot to his hands and launched herself up and into her saddle. Quickly the two men swung aboard their mounts and spun them for the compound's gate. Away they rode. More tears wetted the woman's cheeks.

They quickly passed out the southern gate and trotted down the main road. Remy could see that the sun soon would set beyond the great plain in the west. But they were heading east into the foothills. They journeyed for a few miles and then left the road for a thicket of prickly brush. In a clearing on the other side, a woman was waiting on a gray mare with a packhorse resting beside her. Remy's mouth dropped when she saw how beautiful the stranger was. She swung her head sharply to look at her husband and brother.

Roj motioned sheepishly at the stranger. "Remy, this is Healdin," he mumbled. "She's going to ride with us."

Remy waited a moment for the men to give an explanation. However, neither Roj nor Noli spoke. Remy swallowed hard and asked her brother, "Are we running from her kinsmen, Roj?"

"What?" answered Roj, not grasping the question.

"Is her papa chasing us? Did you run off with her at night the way that Noli's cousins do down in Orres, snatching a woman from her bed rather than paying a proper dowry? Did you trust to the speed of your horses?"

Healdin's eyes lit up at these words. Intently she watched Roj for his answer. "No!" he stammered. "I did nothing. We met in the mountains. We got ourselves in trouble." He felt his face redden. "She helped us."

"What trouble?"

The men clenched their teeth and said nothing. Healdin asked, "May I speak?" Roj shrugged and nodded. Healdin continued, "Remy, in the mountains your men stumbled upon an old story, a tale of the ancient sorrows of your people. And they learned a great secret of a wondrous power that was lost ages ago. In the days of the Stone Woman, the light of this power pierced the hearts of your ancestors and their offspring, and yes, even your own heart, as strange as that may sound to you. And there are evil ones who would kill your men for learning this secret. Even now, they pursue us. I have advised your men that Kierinswell holds too many dangers. We must flee this city."

"For how long must we flee?" Remy asked.

"I can give you no sure answer. Perhaps you must flee until the day the great power is recovered, or until the enemies who recognize your men are killed. Perhaps one day the evil ones will stop seeking one of your men in order to better catch the other."

Remy shuddered at such a thought. She hardened her face. "And you helped my men. And did you tell them of this power?" Healdin nodded but said nothing. Remy turned to Noli. "And do you trust her?"

Her husband frowned. "I'll admit that she scares me," he said. "But we have no choice, Remy. These evil ones are gigantic warriors. We stand no chance against them."

"I trust her," said Roj. "In the mountains she saved us. We got in trouble, and the bad ones killed a defenseless old man who had risked his life to save us. And Healdin and her followers fought the bad ones and saved us. Before he died, the old man told us we could trust Healdin, and he was right. And now she's offering to protect all of us. That's enough for me."

Remy swung her eyes and stared hard at the strange woman. Healdin said nothing as she studied Roj's face. The horse hunter felt himself blush, but he fought hard to return her gaze. At length, Healdin said, "Let us make our way south to Orres. The White Beard, the King's steward of the MuKierin, gathers horse hunters there for a great challenge on the next full moon. I would have you meet him and hear him speak of the King he serves. Even now, my people have located a nearby band of horse hunters who are bound for the South Lands. On the morrow we can overtake them and accompany them on their journey."

Roj nodded his support. Noli simply shrugged. Remy turned away. *Who is this woman?* she thought. *And why has my brother so quickly fallen for her?*

Chapter Seven

To the Southlands

Late the next morning the four travelers spotted a band of horse hunters and their families journeying south toward Orres. Nearly seventy MuKierin were crossing a sagebrush valley, bound that day for a shallow well among the rocks at a place called Sweetwater. The horse hunters and their families soon caught sight of the strangers coming down the hill behind them. A dozen men on horseback fell back to make the first contact.

Remy and Healdin halted their mounts on the hill as their two men rode ahead. Remy looked in the distance at a group of women and girls driving a herd of goats. A fine cloud of dust rose around the females and their animals. "Look at those poor women," Remy said. "I was hoping to never see such a sorry sight again. Why have you brought us here?"

"We have come here to keep your men and you alive," Healdin replied. "Take heart, Remy. I know your stomach troubles you. Tonight I will brew you a calming tea. Have you told Noli that you are with child?"

Remy looked aghast. "How did you guess that?" she asked. "I haven't yet told anyone."

"All the old women in camp will guess soon enough. You cannot hold down your breakfast. But tonight I will help you. Both of us could benefit from a good tea."

Ahead, Roj and Noli halted and waited for the approaching horse hunters. Noli wore his sword at his side, even though he kept his left arm in a sling. Cautiously he dropped his reins and raised his right hand in a sign of peace. "Greetings, MuKierin," he said formally. "I am Noli of Orres. This is my wife's brother, Roj of Kierinswell. We became separated from our hunting party and are bound for the South Lands. We'd like to join your camp and find safety among you."

Three of the men rode forward. "Name your kinsmen" one demanded.

"I was raised by my uncle, Char of Orres," said Noli.

"I know him," the man said. "He's a misfit and a wild bull. Are you?"

"No. I have a woman to think of, and I obey my elders."

"Did the other hunters forsake you?"

"No," said Roj. "The two of us came upon a Spotted Stallion and we went off after him. But we lost him in the mountains."

"A Spotted Stallion!" exclaimed another rider. He was big and beefy and might have been handsome, except his face was too round and his nose too big. Nonetheless, he stood out from the other riders by wearing a bright red vest. "Listen, my friends, you might be interested to know where we're going. We're headed to a challenge at Orres. The White Beard is calling horse hunters there, and he has promised the winner of his challenge a kingly prize: a Spotted Stallion."

Roj said nothing. But in his mind he once more saw a pale horse, and its mane seemed afire. The vision faded as the red-vested rider spoke again. "Indeed, you two won't scoff at this news, not if you've really seen such a stallion. There are plenty of horse hunters who laugh at me when I tell them about the challenge. I don't care. I'm a horse trader and I believe there really are such creatures. The White Beard sent me a messenger three days ago, and he urged me to come to Orres. And here's what else he said. The messenger told me that the King would show me kindness if I would help anyone who asked to come under my wing, especially any woman. And so I see your women back there and I'm inclined to lend you my hand. My name is Arg Wevol, son of Kit. As I said, I'm a horse trader, and my home is near Kierinswell. Who's your father, boy?"

"Aaln of the Stone Fences," Roj replied.

Wevol nodded. "I know his name. How is he?"

"He died of the camp fever five years ago, along with

my mother."

"I'm sorry to hear that, boy," Wevol said. "Here's what I will do. I'm willing to vouch for you on two conditions. First, you both have to take extra turns on watch around our herd at night. And second, you must agree that if you win the Spotted Stallion, you will loan the horse to me for forty days as a stud for my brood mares."

Both Noli and Roj happily shook Wevol's hand in agreement. They signaled the women, and all rode forward to join the main entourage.

The day passed slowly as the group drove their horses and goats across the sagebrush plains. The horse hunters rested a few hours in the heat of the afternoon. But they were determined to reach Sweetwater, and they arrived at the well a few hours before sundown. However, the watering hole already was being used by a host of the downtrodden: sixty chained debtors, plus a dozen guards bound for Kierinswell.

"Behold your brothers and sisters in chains," Healdin told Remy.

"No, you behold all the women and children in this camp," Remy said. "They'll end up in those chains soon enough if they lose the men in their lives. I've seen women lose their husbands to a bad spill on a horse, or to murderous bandits or to camp fever. That's all it takes and then you have no money and they come and put those chains on you. That's why I went to Kierinswell, to escape this life. And now I'm back here, all because of you. Why did you bring us here?"

"I have come here because I wish to free all your people, both the chained and the unchained. All of them live with a longing burned into their souls, a longing that nothing in the Dry Lands will ever satisfy. For generations, my people have waited for such a day of freedom for your people. And your brother may be the one to help usher in that day."

"My brother! I don't understand. What do you mean?"

"Roj has a gift, Remy, one that even he does not yet seem to fully understand. Your men told you that they pursued a Spotted Stallion far into the high mountains. So

67

they did, but they could not have tracked the stallion for so great a distance unless your brother had the gift. The stallion he followed is not a horse of normal birth. He is of a royal lineage, as is my mare. Ages ago, the King brought these creatures from across the sea, from the same land as the Golden Box. These horses can sense things from afar, and they grasp much of the ways of men. And Roj can sense their ways, unlike you and your kinsmen. My people have been waiting for generations for such a man. The old tales say that he can change the future and usher in the day of a Champion, the one who will help recover the King's great power and free all the desert people. Roj could be the man."

"And what if he is not the man?"

"Then he would be undone. He would try and fail to help his people."

Remy looked at her amazed. "And would you let him try and fail?

"I would not bid him to make the attempt if I doubted him. And only Roj can choose whether to take on such a burden. If he does, both you and I will be sorely tempted to reach out and spare him from danger, Remy. But then he cannot fulfill the charge."

Remy shook her head. "Roj trusts you, woman. Perhaps he has good reasons to do so. But I'm his older sister and I've watched over him all his life. He doesn't have anybody but me. I see the way he looks at you. He'd probably follow you to the ends of the earth. But I need to know more about who you really are."

"So you shall, Remy, even this day. Soon I shall send forth my mare. Observe well this day both your brother and my horse. And do not fear. I shall do all I can to keep Roj from harm."

Roj rode up to the two women. "Healdin," he said, "we must stay back from these slavers at the well. Soon their guards will move the prisoners away, but until then they will not abide us to draw near them. Look and you can see the warning markers they have set out around them. Anyone who crosses those markers forfeits his life." Healdin looked toward the well and saw that the guards had set out small banners on thin poles.

The horse hunters gathered on a gentle rise above the well and waited their turn for water. Wevol, the horse trader, had gone off earlier in the day and had yet to reappear. Noli and Roj waited for his return so they would know where the horse trader wished them to set up their tents. Some of the camp's women already were engaged in that task, lashing together thin wicker frames over which they would place the tent's goatskin cover. The tents were low, too low for any but children to stand in. But in winter the horse hunters dug pits and connected together two or more tents, and then the men could stand, and small fires could be built inside to warm the occupants.

As they waited, Healdin noticed a large group of boys join together on flat ground outside the camp. Two teams formed and soon the boys were racing up and down the game field passing two cloth bags. Healdin saw the players striving to pass both bags into the hands of a single teammate.

"What is this?" she asked Roj.

"Haven't you ever seen Two Bag?" he replied. "When I was little, it was my favorite game. Each team tries to advance from one end of the field to the other. You need to use you head to win."

"And you love strategy," Healdin said. "Even Noli says as much. That is why he put you in front when you chased the stallion up the mountain."

The two sat and watched the game until Wevol returned. When she spotted the trader, Healdin arose and walked to her mare. Roj continued to watch the game, but soon became distracted. He turned and began to concentrate on the lady's gray mare. He noticed that Healdin had removed the bridle from the animal's head. Next, she cupped her hand before the mare's mouth and stroked its mane. The creature looked toward Roj and the two locked eyes on each other. A look of worry passed over the young horse hunter's face. He arose and began to advance slowly toward the mare. Remy, who was seated nearby, watched him.

Wevol, meanwhile, rode with two other men down the slope to the edge of the slavers' warning markers. The chief guard trotted out on a sorrel mare to meet the horse trader. The two sides exchanged formal but wary greetings. Wevol soon waved goodbye to the slaver and started to return up the rise. Even as he did, Healdin's mare bolted down the hill toward the slaves. The horse charged at a gallop, looking as if it meant to run down anything in its path. Behind the animal ran Healdin, sprinting downhill like a deer.

"No, Healdin!" cried Roj. "Stay back from the markers!" At once he raced for his own stallion.

The slave guards jumped to their feet and waved their spears at the advancing mare. The prisoners also stood up, but they couldn't move far because they were tied together at their wrist shackles to one long rope. At the last moment, the mare veered right and slid to a halt before a young male slave, who had bravely stepped forward as a shield for a dark-haired woman standing beside him. The mare paused for a few moments, then inched forward and with its nose gently nudged the young man's chest. Everyone watched in wonder at the sudden calm. A moment later, the horse pivoted and charged the fearful guards, scattering them.

Healdin didn't halt until she had crossed the warning markers. The guard chief drew his sword and spurred his mount to confront her. His face turned grim as he prepared to cut down this transgressor. But immediately he heard a whoop and a cry come from the rise above him. In surprise, he turned to see Wevol bearing down upon him. The horse trader had his sword thrust forward and his eyes squinting fiercely at his target. The chief saw his danger and pivoted his horse left, ducking as Wevol swung in vain at him. The two men spun their mounts and charged one another. Their blades clashed. Their horses jostled together and slid apart.

Roj, meanwhile, galloped down the slope toward Healdin. He slowed his stallion and extended an arm. She took it and swung up lightly behind him. Roj quickly turned the stallion and urged it to gallop back toward camp, even as the guards raced on foot after him. Nearby, Wevol and the guard chief slammed their swords together a second time. But the horse trader retreated as three slave guards advanced on foot toward him. The slavers wisely chose not to give further chase. Instead, they returned to the prisoners at the well.

Roj halted on the rise by his kinsmen. Healdin slid down and straightened her gown. "Healdin, are you hurt?" he asked.

She looked up and smiled. "No, Roj, I am well."

Noli ran up breathless, rubbing his broken arm. "Boy, will you stop scaring me? Do you want to get yourself killed?"

"I knew I had time to reach Healdin and get back here safely," Roj said. "I was ready. I could sense beforehand that her mare meant to rush the slaves."

Remy asked, "Roj, how did you know what that horse was going to do?"

"I don't know, Remy. I saw it in her eyes. It was like they were on fire. And I could sense her almost calling me to follow her."

Remy looked puzzled. "But I was watching you and the mare," she said. "I didn't see anything in her eyes."

The foursome turned as Wevol came galloping past a line of cheering horse hunters who had assembled on the rise. Six of his own servants had taken to their horses and swarmed behind him, a mounted squad with swords at their sides. They stopped in front of Roj and Healdin, and Wevol nodded to his chief servant, bidding him to speak on his behalf. "Woman," the servant declared. "My master says you are fearless. But the next time your wild mare runs away, please allow my master to retrieve her for you."

Healdin smiled and nodded. "It shall be as your lord says."

"So be it," Wevol replied, and he gave her a gracious nod. Next, he looked sternly at Noli and Roj. "Catch that mare and keep her away from that well," he said. "We've had enough battles for one day." He raised an arm and his entourage galloped back past the line of camp admirers.

Out of earshot, Noli growled at Wevol's instruction. "Keep that mare away from the well! Does that fool think I can control this mad woman or her horse?"

Roj waited until he was alone with Healdin to speak. "Woman, what were you doing down there? I warned you about those markers. You might have gotten killed."

"No, I was safe, Roj. I simply needed to divert the guards' eyes."

"What do you mean? I don't understand."

"My mare held a piece of broken pottery in her mouth and delivered it to the young male slave there on the flats. I ran down so the guards would be distracted and not see the exchange."

"Why did you do that? Are you trying to free that slave? Those slavers will want to put you in chains if they catch you trying to help one of their prisoners escape."

"Do not fear, Roj. We will be safe. But please be ready tonight. If all goes well, we will have guests. Noli and you will have the watch. Please take your stand near the slave camp."

The guards soon moved the slaves from the well to a campsite a few miles away. The horse hunters went down and began to draw water for their horses and goats. The women completed raising their tents and the children gathered what little tinder they could find. The sun began to set and the people huddled around the camp fires, preparing the evening meals.

After dinner, Healdin began brewing her tea, and the smell of it spread through the camp. "What aromas are these?" the women began asking one another. "What spices do we detect?" They followed their noses and found Healdin's black iron kettle.

"Please, come," Healdin told them, "Please partake of a taste of my home." She served the women, and all who tasted the tea felt refreshed. Many said later that the drink eased the pain of headaches, strained backs and weary bones. Even Remy drank and felt her stomach settle down.

Two middle-aged sisters, one plump, one skinny, watched for the right moment to confide in Remy.

"Child, your brother's woman is a wonder," said the

plump one. "Why, as I said to my sister Melva here, she's got looks and manners and courage."

"My brother has no woman," Remy replied. "That one is a single woman, and we're her guardians. She's merely coming with us to Orres."

"Indeed?" replied Melva, the skinny one. "I'm stunned. As I was saying to my sister, Ornelia, your brother certainly seems fond of her."

"Oh, Melva, all the men seem fond of her," said Ornelia. "Didn't you see how quickly our gallant nephew, Lord Wevol, went out there to rescue her? That was quite a show. Indeed, if one of us had crossed those boundary markers, I daresay our men would have left us to the spears of those bloodthirsty slavers."

"I'm afraid you're right," said Melva. "But tell us, child, who is this woman? It seems unnatural for her to come into our camp without a man of her own."

Remy nodded. "Everything about that woman is unnatural. When I asked my husband about her, all he would say is that she has to be the oldest woman in the camp."

Ornelia eyes widened and she began to cackle. "Oh, he's a wit," she said. "Do you hear that, Melva? There's still hope for us. When I reach that lady's age, I'll be happy to have half her beauty. Do you see how the men look at her? They can't take their eyes off her. She's got them all under her spell."

The two sisters scurried away from Healdin's tent. "Can you believe this good news?" Ornelia asked. "Is it possible that a beautiful woman at last has come near for our shy nephew to wed?"

"And is it possible that at last we're going to get our hands on a share of the family treasure?" Melva asked. "At last, we might be able to collect that marriage bounty that our dead brother had promised us if we could find his son a bride. We're running out of time to collect those five thousand pieces of silver."

"Arg Wevol could have had plenty of women," said Ornelia. "But he won't let us help find him a bride. No, he demands a beautiful woman and he expects her to come to him. Well, one finally has come to him. And he has noticed her. This could be our chance, Melva. But we don't have a lot of time. We've got to bring them together before we get to Orres."

The women of the camp soon departed Healdin's fire. Remy went with the lady to her tent, while Roj and Noli rested in another tent before their turn at the night watch. Inside, Remy nestled into her blanket and turned onto her right side to face Healdin. "You were right," she said. "My brother seems to possess some strange gift with horses. He was able to read the mind of your mare. But what's going to become of him?"

"We must wait for his answer," Healdin said. "Though he does not yet know it, Roj must make a great decision by the time we reach Orres."

"Listen to me. That boy is my only close kin. You've got to swear to me that you're going to protect him."

"I cannot stand in his place when he faces his challenges. But at the right time, I will give him some of my own power to protect him. Oh, Remy, please hear me. I believe Roj could change the future and usher in a new day, a day where you and your child at last sit at the King's table."

"Let your King come sit with me at my table. Until he does, I've got to take care of me and my family."

"Some day the King indeed may sit at your table. And I believe that even the child within you will step forward to help his people."

"Woman," said Remy, "don't scare me with such talk. Here you settle my stomach down and then you stir it all up again."

Chapter Eight

The Eye of the Horse Trader

Even as the camp settled down for the night, Roj and Noli arose from their tent to begin their watch. Roj took hold of Noli's small sword and removed it from its scabbard.

"Could you kill Pibbibib with this?" he asked.

Noli shrugged. "Maybe in his sleep. Do those blasted ones ever sleep?"

"Who knows. But you better teach me how to swing a sword. I need to get one soon."

"You'll need a better swordsman than me to help you take on Pibbibib."

"You'll have to do for now. Perhaps, one day I shall find the King's lost power and use it to kill that monster and the other one, too. Save me, Kierin! How I want to rid myself of them. Those two are already haunting my dreams."

The two men took up their watches on opposite sides of the herd of resting horses. Roj sat on a rise above them, wrapped in a blanket and cloak and leaning against a boulder. The time passed slowly. Soon he was nodding off.

The dawn was still a few hours away when he awoke to a rustling sound behind him. He perked up at once and pressed himself close against the boulder. *Pibbibib!* But then he remembered Healdin's words. *Could it be some of those slaves? If it is, how many of them are out there?* Slowly he took his knife from its sheath. *Do I ever need a sword!* Again he heard a slight creaking. Something or someone was moving his way. *That's not Pibbibib. He wouldn't make that much noise. That has to be slaves coming here.* Roj stood as quietly as he could and crouched beside the boulder. If slaves were near, he wanted to surprise them and keep them quiet. He held his breath and waited a few more moments. Then he sprang around the big rock. In the dark he couldn't make out the opponent before him, but the figure jumped back and froze. "Stop right there,"

Roj ordered as boldly as he could muster. "Don't make a sound. I've got a blade."

A voice called from his right, "Leave her be or I'll strangle you."

"Her?" Roj said, squinting.

"Please, sir," his prisoner begged in a decidedly female voice. "Don't hurt me."

"Leave her be," said the other figure, surely a man, "or I swear I'll rip your heart out."

"Calm yourself, MuKierin," Roj answered. "I'm not going to harm her. I know the lady who helped set you free. Stay quiet and I'll go fetch her."

"I am here, Roj," Healdin called from behind him. She stepped forward and touched Roj's shoulder. "Put away your knife," she told him. "We must quickly remove their chains and help them flee this place."

"How are you going to do that, lady?" asked the man. "We would need a great hammer and chisel to break these chains?"

"I have a way to free you, if you will trust me." Healdin first took the woman by the hand and led her close to the boulder. There, she threw a blanket over her own head and bent down to touch the shackles on the woman's hands. "All of you must turn your eyes from me or you may be blinded," the lady warned. Soon rays of light shone from beneath the edges of the blanket. The young slave woman gasped in shock and dropped to her knees, but she kept her head twisted away. A moment later her shackles fell from her. The light vanished. Healdin pulled off the blanket and beckoned the man, "Come quickly, if you wish to be free." The man ran to her. Once more the light gleamed under the blanket. Roj looked away but still felt his scalp grow prickly with sensation. Not for the last time did he remember that day on the mountain when he first beheld a great light shining in the distance. But soon the darkness returned. Even as the light disappeared, the man's chains fell to the ground.

Noli caught brief glimpses of light from behind the rock and came running. He drew close and saw the two strangers with Roj and Healdin. "Are they slaves?" he demanded. "If they are, we can't help them. We don't want to get chained up, too."

Healdin replied, "Noli, did you think it was my way to save your life but to stand by while others suffer in the debtors' chains?"

"I never asked to get entangled in your war with the evil ones," said Noli, "and I don't intend to give up my life for two slaves."

Healdin whistled softly and her gray mare trotted up the slope. No bridle or saddle rested on the animal. Quickly Healdin tied a great cloth belt around the mare's neck. She turned to the man and the woman. "Would you be free? If so, you must do as I say."

"Yes, lady, we want to escape those slavers," the man replied. "But why have you done this for us? Why do you care what happens to us?"

"Others will tell you my story. My mare will take you to friends who will speak of the King I serve, the Great King Over the Mountains. This maiden is kin to the White Beard, who serves that same King. Now you must quickly leave this place."

The man swung atop the mare. The woman climbed on behind him. "Roj," said Healdin, "bring them the shackles. Now, hear me, friends. You have no bridle. You will not steer my mare. You must simply hang on to this belt and trust her to take you to safety. It is not far. Soon, you will meet two women on gray mares. They will help you and tell you my story. Now, take your shackles and drop them far away in the flats."

Roj handed the man the chains and said, "This lady saved me, too, and my sister's husband. You can trust her. She won't let you down."

"I am MuKierin," the man said to Roj. "I pay my debts. I won't forget what the woman and you did for us tonight. I owe you."

Healdin whispered in the mare's neck and the gray horse sprang off, cantering into the darkness. Noli drew close to Healdin. "And what are we going to do in the morning when the slavers come calling?" he demanded. "You can bet your life they will track those two here."

"Do not fear the slavers," she replied. "I will not let them take you."

Noli shook his head in frustration and walked back toward camp. Roj turned to Healdin. "Woman, there were so many slaves back at the well," he said. "Why did you decide to save those two?"

"The woman is a distant cousin to the White Beard, the very one who assembles the horse hunters in Orres for the great challenge. She has the honor of being the first whose shackles were removed in the name of the King. But she will not be the last. When the Champion comes to your people, he will break the shackles of many held in the debtors' chains. In this way, the MuKierin shall know that the King has sent forth his chosen one.

"Remember this night, Roj. I hope this man and woman will help us."

She started to walk away, but Roj called to her, "Wait, woman. Tell me more about your light of power. I never guessed that you could break chains and shackles."

She drew close to him. "Yes, Roj, my light can cut through iron and bring down lightning on my enemies. The Vine is a fire, small but filled with power. The King gave me this light, and I wield it in his name. I wear it sheathed on my leg, and it is with me always."

Roj fell to a knee before her. "Healdin, who are you? How can anyone stand against you? How can any of these bad ones hope to ever overcome you? And how did Pibbibib survive that day when he met you on the mountain?"

"You ask many questions, Roj. In time you will learn firsthand of me. As for the warriors of the Dark Brood, they fear my power but they will not change. Long ago they saw the light and power of the King, and yet they rebelled against him anyway. Truly, they will not surrender because I possess the Vine. No, they still desire to defeat the King and all his subjects. They still hope to find the stolen Root of Glory and to use it to defeat their enemies. As for Pibbibib, he lives because the King warned me against killing him. The fate of that rebel and the coming Champion are somehow tied together. And so I spared his life that day. But never forget that you remain in great danger from that evil one. Now, return to your watch. The night soon ends."

At dawn, Healdin once more became ill. Remy heard her moaning and found blood flowing from her mouth. The pregnant woman nearly became sick. "Roj!" his sister called. "Come quickly! The foreign woman is spitting blood."

Roj ran and fetched a water skin to Healdin. He noted that she seemed to give up less blood than she had done on the night of their first meeting. But still, she looked worn and pale. Gently he raised her up and helped her drink from the water skin.

"Lady, what's wrong with you?" he asked.

"Do you not know?"

"No, I don't understand what's happening to you."

"It is the power I possess, Roj. I cannot wield the Vine without succumbing to this malady."

"What? Then why do you ever use it? You should just keep it in its sheath."

"There are times that I must take hold of it. I wielded it that day on the mountain in order to save you from Pibbibib, and last night I used it to free your two kinsmen from the debtor's chains."

"But Healdin, this is terrible. Why would your King ever give you such a hurtful power?"

"It was not always as it is now, Roj. The Vine became cursed on the day when Troppa stole the Root of Glory. And it will remain so until the day when that power rests once more in the hands of the King. Until then, I must endure. I am the keeper of this power."

Slowly, Roj reached down and took her hand. "I'm sorry, Healdin. I'm sorry you ever got mixed up with me and my people. You were right when you said our ways are bent. My ancestors never should have stolen the Root. And you never should have come with Noli and me. You need to go back to your own people. I can't bear to see you suffer so."

"I cannot leave you, Roj. Please let me stay now and rest in my tent. The worst is past, but I must sleep. I must stay here this morning. I am too weak to travel."

Gently he helped her lay back down. "I'm not leaving you, Healdin," he said as he exited the tent. Outside, he noted a strange commotion in the camp. He looked to the north and saw a squad of the slavers approaching. The chief guard rode in front on his stallion with half a dozen soldiers following on foot. Only Roj and Noli guessed the reason for this visit. Nonetheless, Wevol already was preparing for another fight. The horse trader untied his own mount and strode forward with his sword at his side. This time, a half-dozen of his servants stood ready behind him. Noli grabbed Remy and escorted her to the rear of the crowd where the women and children stood watching. But Roj ran to Noli's tent and grabbed his kinsman's sword.

"I've lost two slaves," the chief guard announced to the camp. "Bring me that woman with the gray mare."

"What's the woman got to do with your slaves?" Wevol asked.

"Her mare ran to one of the two slaves that escaped. I want to know how she helped them break free and then I'm going to arrest her. She's going to pay for this."

Wevol's eyes grew big. "Is she now?" he growled. "And what proof do you have that she helped your slaves disappear?"

"I told you the proof," the guard leader replied. "Who else could have done it? Nobody else drew near them. And you can see for yourself that somebody helped them. Look at their shackles!" He raised the chains that once had held the man. "Someone took fire and cut through the lock. Don't tell me my slaves did that. Now, bring me the woman!"

All the camp looked in amazement upon the broken shackles. As they did, Roj hustled forward to take a place in Wevol's line of armed supporters. "How stupid do you think I am?" the horse trader asked the chief guard. "Do you call that proof? Go away. I don't care whether or not the woman's mare came near your slaves. Why not accuse the horse? Perhaps it was the mare that cut the chains with fire."

A few horse hunters chuckled. The chief guard, however, raised a hand and pointed at Wevol. "I've been deputized by the Elder of Orres to do my duty. I can arrest anybody who helps a slave escape. And those who get in my way will regret it."

Wevol's eyes flared. He jumped on his horse and shouted to the guard, "Don't threaten me. I've got papers from the Elder of Kierinswell. And they authorize me to do my business without having to bend my knee to the likes of you. That woman has come under my wing, and I'm not going to hand her over without a shred of evidence that she's done anything wrong. Now get out of my sight, or we're going to cross swords again."

The guard leader gave a defiant pose, but his men were badly outnumbered. "I'm leaving, but I'm not finished with this," he declared. Slowly, he turned his horse and rode away with his men on foot behind him. The horse hunters whooped and cheered the retreat.

"Yes, brothers! Yes!" Wevol declared in his loudest voice. "Blast the slavers and all those who get rich off the misery of their own people. And, yes, I mean those slaver Elders, too. Now let's move this camp. The true sons of Kierin are going south to the challenge in Orres."

Slowly, the people returned to their tents. Noli strode up to Roj and asked, "What were you doing with my sword, boy? You're a horse hunter, not a warrior."

"They were coming to take Healdin away. Do you think I was going to stay out of that fight?"

"You're going to get yourself killed, and your sister's going to blame me. Come on now. Let's pack the horses and get out of here."

"Healdin's sick again, Noli. She's too weak to move. I'm going to stay here with her until she's able to ride."

Noli froze at the news. "And what if the slavers return?" he asked.

"Let's hope they keep heading north for Kierinswell.

But I'm not going to leave her here alone. Maybe you should take Remy and stay with the rest of the camp. We'll catch up before nightfall."

Remy exited Healdin's tent as the two men approached. "The foreign woman looks bad," she said. "Does she have the fever? She reminds me of Mama in the days before she died."

"No, she doesn't have the fever," said Roj. "She had this illness once before with us in the mountains. She'll get better once she's rested for a few hours. I'm staying here with her. I'll be fine. Noli and you can leave us and go south with the camp."

"Nonsense," said Remy. "Noli and I are staying with you." Roj began to protest, but his sister raised a hand to silence him. "What do you know about caring for a sick woman? She's a single woman. That puts her under our charge. We're staying."

Within the hour, the horse hunters and their families began to venture forth. Wevol didn't like the news that Healdin was ill and needed to stay behind. But he kept his people moving and made his owns plans to keep an eye on her. Soon, the land lay empty except for a single tent still standing on the flats. Roj and Noli stood beside it and stared north, looking for slavers. "You take the first watch," Noli said. "I want to know if those guards return, not that I'll be ready for them."

"May we can bluff 'em," Roj said. "We'll cover Healdin up and tell them that she's your wife and she's come down with the fever. Indeed, Healdin does look like she's got the fever. Maybe the slavers won't recognize her all covered up. Maybe they'll keep their distance."

The morning passed slowly. A few hours before midday, Healdin's mare trotted back to the tent. Roj took the creature and the rest of the horses to the well for a long drink. Remy prepared a meal of dried meat and hot tea. They ate silently as the men scanned the land toward Kierinswell.

At midday, Healdin emerged from the tent. She walked out slowly to her mare standing near the other horses tied on the picket line. The woman looked worn but somewhat revived. Roj went to her as she gently stroked the mare's withers. "Lady, can you ride?" he asked.

"Yes, Roj, my strength has returned to me. Thank you for staying here."

He smiled at the words. "Remy's made some food for us. We'll eat and get ready to leave this place."

She started back to the tent but stopped when she saw movement, not from the north but to the south. Noli noticed her gaze and turned that direction, too. "Do you see something?" he asked.

"I see three horsemen sitting atop their mounts."

"She's right," said Noli, "There are riders watching us on that hill. Are they bandits?"

"No. Wevol the horse trader rides among them."

"Wevol?" asked Roj. "Why would he be watching us?"

Remy looked at Healdin but said nothing. Noli noticed her gaze and turned to Roj, but the younger man just kept staring at the distant horsemen. "Roj," said Noli, "let's hurry and get ready. We have a long ride ahead of us. Tonight I want to sleep in the safety of the camp."

Chapter Nine

Of Feasts and Shawls

Wevol rejoined the horse hunters at their new camp a few hours before Healdin and Roj. The hunters' families had gone before him and set up their tents in a small valley that looked out to the eastern foothills. Ornelia and Melva took note of their nephew's return. "Where's the beautiful woman?" Melva asked. "Hasn't our nephew been keeping an eye on her?"

"He's too shy to draw near to her," Ornelia said. "And he may even think she belongs to another. The boy needs a matchmaker, Melva. That's our job."

At dusk, the two aunts approached Wevol as he sat alone by the fire. The horse trader's servants were busy preparing his supper. Both women knelt before him. Ornelia said, "Dearest Arg Wevol, may we speak about your future?"

Wevol's eyes flared. "Aunt Ornelia, what mischief are you up to now?"

"Mischief? My dear, I dare say we simply wish to bring you news that may lift up your spirit."

"Is that so? Or do you simply wish to add to your purses, perhaps with a marriage bounty?"

"Oh, your tongue is a whip. Your father on his death bed made me swear that your Aunt Melva and I would watch over his only child. Ever since that day, we have tried to fulfill our duties as sisters. And now we bring you good news of this new woman in our midst. Isn't she a beauty, so full of grace and spirit? We thought she belonged to that boy who rides beside her. Perhaps you also thought this. But she does not have a man. Indeed, we confirmed this directly with the other new woman."

Wevol's chest rose slowly, and he strove to compose his face. "What if she is unmarried? What does that have to do with me?"

"Didn't you see how she smiled at you? Twice you have come to her rescue, and she knows it. She can see you're a leader and a man of money. And we saw her smile at you yesterday. It made my heart flutter to see it. But she won't be with us for long. Once we reach Orres, she may be gone forever. So we wanted you to hear this news in case you have feelings for her. Believe me, nephew, she doesn't have a man of her own."

Wevol turned his head and seemed deep in thought. "And so you think I can be led like a lamb to the butcher?"

"That is most unjust," Ornelia complained. "You have never allowed us to bring you near a woman. But now one appears who has caught your eye. Oh, yes, that much is plain. We see you watch her, and we know you stayed behind today to protect her. And who could blame you? She turns the eyes of all the men in camp. Indeed, you're the one who talks about receiving the kindness of a king. Perhaps she is the sign of that kindness. If she is, let us help you. We can arrange a small feast in order that you can get to know her better. It would give you time to see if she might be the one for you."

"I don't want to be mocked as some lover's fool."

"Yes, we understand. Here's what we can do. We can say that you are giving the feast for the coming challenge in Orres. The woman is a healer who makes a wondrous tea. We have tasted it and felt its power. We can tell the people that she will serve this tea at the feast in order to strengthen the riders who intend to risk death atop the great stallion. You can approach the woman and ask her to prepare the drink for the men. Melva and I will be with you. This woman is kind, and she's in your debt. Surely she'll agree. All you have to do is give this little feast. I think it even will help you gain favor with the riders. That tea really will help them with the challenge. Indeed, you may end up getting the woman and the use of the stallion for your mares. You could wind up the biggest winner of all."

Wevol turned and stared at Ornelia. "I feel exactly like a bird caught in your net. You're right, I do want to get to know her, but I'm afraid that she won't have me. She seems too high and regal to ever marry a horse trader. But I will agree to let you prepare your little feast. Spend what you must. I'll pay for the chance to sit beside her. I am willing to pay to let the horse tamers drink her tea. If I don't do this, I'll always wonder what might have been."

"That's the spirit," Ornelia replied, and she stood up and clapped him on the back. "We'll send for you soon. But don't fear. We're going to have that feast. You're going to sit beside this great beauty and dip your bread in the same bowl with her. And you won't ever forget it."

A few hours later, Healdin entered the camp with Roj, Remy and Noli. The sun had set and the fires of the people were burning around the camp. The foursome began to unpack their horses when Ornelia ran hurriedly to them. "Oh, Healdin our healer, we need you," she gasped. "Melva has taken a bad spill. I helped her to bed but she is breathing poorly. Would you please help her, perhaps with your healing tea?"

At once, Healdin unpacked a small leather bag and followed the old woman. Remy, meanwhile, watched and wondered.

Ornelia called back to Healdin as they passed between the tents, "Oh, I hope this won't be the death of her. Poor Melva, my sister, never complains." They reached Melva's tent door and pushed through it. There, beneath a single candle, the skinny woman lay upon the floor, her bare head unsupported by any pillow.

"Who's there?" Melva croaked weakly, keeping her head still and her eyes focused upward.

"It is I, sister," Ornelia replied. "I have brought Healdin with me. She's going to bring you a healing touch."

"Oh, sister, I told you not to bother the healer woman. I'm breathing now. I'll be fine, really."

"Well, she's here now, so let her help you. Perhaps her soothing tea will ease your pain. Please, let her for my sake, Melva. I'm going to feel so much better once I know you're resting peaceful again."

Just then the tent flap drew back and Melva's bony,

gray-haired husband bent to look in. He entered, followed by Arg Wevol. The horse trader looked completely caught off guard by the scene. Melva turned her head and called, "Lord Wevol, oh goodness! Why has my nephew been brought to see me in this poor condition?"

Her man glared impatiently at her. "He's here because your sister told me to fetch him," he huffed. Immediately he exited.

"I asked for him to come," Ornelia interjected sweetly. "I knew our good nephew, Lord Wevol, would be quick to lend you his help."

Healdin leaned her head toward the trader. "Sir, are you learned in healing?" she gently asked. It took the horse trader a moment to grasp the question. His aunts waited with mouths agape for his reply.

"No, no, woman, I'm not," he said, trying not to appear an idiot. "But I'm here to help, however I can. It's just that I don't exactly know what's the matter with Aunt Melva."

Ornelia broke in, "But, of course. Your Aunt Melva wouldn't have bothered you, but I knew you'd be willing to help if you could. Ah, Healdin, here stands a good man, as you well know, since twice he has come to your rescue. Oh, child, I must tell you that we have boasted to my nephew about your wondrous tea. Perhaps you'll think us silly old women, but we couldn't help ourselves. That tea of yours was such a healing balm for all who tasted it. And when we told our nephew about it, he thought it might help the men who mean to risk their lives riding the great stallion in Orres. So he wants to call a feast so that the men can drink your tea and find strength for the coming challenge. Isn't that so, my lord?"

Wevol swallowed as he looked into Healdin's eyes. "She's right," he said, summoning his strength. "It would be an honor to give such a feast, if you're willing, that is. I really do want to learn more about this miraculous tea."

Healdin smiled at him, and the horse trader's eyes brightened with new life. "I am willing," she said. "Perhaps now, however, I should give attention to your aunt and her injuries." Everyone nodded, but no one moved. Healdin continued, "Lord Wevol, perhaps you would feel more comfortable leaving the tent while I uncover your aunt's injuries." The horse trader blushed and scurried away.

When Healdin returned to her tent, Remy quizzed her, "Did the old woman take a bad spill?"

"I think not. The horse trader soon came to offer his help at her tent. And he asked me to prepare a tea for the men who will seek the stallion of Orres. He plans to gather the camp for a small feast tomorrow evening. And I will make the tea."

For the second time that evening, Remy watched and wondered. That night she slept little, and early the next morning she set off to visit Ornelia's tent. Outside stood a few women, including Melva, and they giggled as Ornelia ran her fingers along the edge of a red shawl. *A courting shawl!* Remy thought. Keeping her composure, she ambled forward and nodded to the women. Ornelia's eyes flickered briefly when she spied her. But she managed to smile and give a greeting. "Good morning, kinswoman. How grateful we are to you for bringing the healer woman to us. Tonight the entire camp will enjoy a feast in her honor."

"I thought the feast was for the men who would seek the stallion, not for a man who seeks a woman," Remy said, her eyes fixed on the red shawl. "However, I am pleased to see that your kinswoman has recovered. I thought she might be leaving us to meet the Stone Woman."

"Ah, child, the healer woman restored me," Melva replied unfazed. "All our fortunes are brighter because of her. Perhaps you'd wish to work with us as we prepare the night's feast. Ornelia, isn't there some work for our good sister here to do? After all, she did help bring us the healer woman. Surely we should find a way to thank her for that."

"No," said Remy. "Many thanks, but I must attend to other duties. Good day."

Ornelia drew close to her sister as Remy walked away. "Melva, I fear that girl wants the healer woman for her little brother. She might try to ruin our hopes."

"We must watch her, sister," Melva said. "She must not spoil this chance of ours."

Remy, meanwhile, went directly to Noli. "That horse trader has feelings for the foreign woman," she whispered.

Her husband stood watering the horses while Roj remained back at the tents packing their gear. Noli grinned at her. "For Healdin?" he snickered. "He's not that stupid, is he?"

"Well, his aunts are working hard to play matchmakers. This feast tonight isn't for the horse tamers involved in the coming challenge. It's about her. They've even got a red courting shawl for her."

"Well, Wevol's going to end up playing the lover's fool," Noli said. "That foreign woman won't have him. Can't he see that?"

"He sees only what he wants to see. That's the way it is with all the men who look upon her. They see only her beauty. But she scares me, Noli. Is Roj falling for her, too?"

"No. The boy cares about horses, not women."

"I'm not so sure. He's almost as old as you were when you took my hand. I worry about him, Noli. And these two aunts give me the chills. They're mean enough to stomp on anybody that gets in their way. I don't want them to hurt Roj."

"What do you want me to do?"

"Keep an eye on him. And keep him out of danger."

Noli led the horses back to the tents. Roj already had wrapped most of the loads in canvas. "Boy," Noli said, "what are you thinking? Do you want to try to win the stallion of Orres?"

Roj looked surprised by the question. "I don't know. You were the one who pushed us hard to chase that stallion up the mountain. You said it would give Remy a better life."

"That was on the mountain. But we've got to consider the dangers at Orres. There are men who want that horse and they might try to harm anyone who stands in their way. And that stallion may be too great for any man to tame in a challenge. Here is what I think. Hold back and watch. Don't step forward tonight at the feast with the other horse tamers. Just wait for the right time."

"That's fine," said Roj. "It doesn't matter to me."

That afternoon, the horse hunters and their families reached their next camp early. Wevol's servants immediately erected a pavilion on a flat stretch of ground that was ringed on one side with boulders the size of ox carts. Nearby, Ornelia and Melva arranged a series of cooking fires. The servants slaughtered two goats and set them on iron spits turning over the fires. They also hung a large kettle there for Healdin's tea. They filled the kettle with water and soon set it to simmering. Next, the servants set up a spacious tent beyond the reach of all the smoke.

Remy watched the women for a time, but soon she went in search of her brother. At once, she set him on a series of chores. She had him fetch water, repair her saddle and later sit still while she trimmed his shoulder-length hair. Healdin, meanwhile, remained in her tent, preparing the ingredients for the tea. An hour before sunset she emerged and went to the kettle of steaming water. Remy noticed that Ornelia and Melva soon were by Healdin's side, motioning toward the spacious tent. *They want to wash and perfume her. They want the horse trader to catch her scent.* Healdin, however, politely declined and stayed at the kettle.

Roj was back repairing Remy's saddle when four drummers began a driving rhythm, the signal for the members of the camp to gather. Roj left the saddle and strode to the area of the boulders. There, many of the single young men had gathered. Healdin, however, took a seat on a pillow beneath the pavilion. A minute later, the drummers stopped and next began a slower beat. The people began to clap to the rhythm. Arg Wevol appeared, wearing his sword and a new scarlet vest. He nodded formally to Healdin and sat beside her. The two then scanned those gathered around them, but Wevol's gaze soon returned toward the lady. His eyes looked at her, first on her lap and then rising slowly toward her face.

Roj saw this and thought, *His eyes are stuck on her. Is he falling for her?* It made no sense. Here was a woman who had lived for hundreds of years. She was older than the Stone Woman and she commanded warriors and was the keeper of a mysterious power. And then Roj realized, *But Wevol doesn't know any of that. All he sees is a beautiful woman. Of course, he wants her. Who here wouldn't want her?* And for the first time, Roj contemplated that he might want her, too. *But Wevol's a greater man than me. You can be sure she would choose him over me, should she be looking for a man, which she isn't.*

The servants began to serve the meal. Healdin and Wevol feasted on wild desert hens that had been caught that day. The rest of the camp ate roasted goat meat and various desert tubers. Wevol's servants opened a skin of red wine, and the men of the camp drank eagerly.

Soon the drummers played a new beat, and two women stood to chant. Roj recognized the fast-paced verse. He had known it since boyhood. The people soon joined in:

> "Kierin told us of a dream,
> (remember me, horse stalker).
> A mighty horse, a crashing sea,
> (remember me, horse stalker).
> A rider on the spotted one,
> (remember me, horse stalker).
> A light upon the favored son,
> (remember me, horse stalker).
> Remember me, remember me,
> remember me, horse stalker.
> Ride beside, ride beside,
> beside the shining water."

The people ended the chant with applause and cheers. In this interlude they turned and chatted about how the feast had proven most acceptable. Roj, however, couldn't take his eyes off Healdin. He thought back to the night on the mountain pass when she had led her company in music, a melody much higher and more regal than the simple chants of his people. That was music, he told himself, the likes of which these horse hunters had never heard.

Healdin spoke briefly to Wevol, who nodded and stood with his arms raised. The people grew quiet as the horse trader said: "Brothers and sisters. We will have a story. Listen to the Lady Healdin."

She arose and smiled. "You sang of Kierin and his vision," she said. "But few recall all that your forefather saw in his dream. Thus, hear my tale. The vision came to Kierin in his manhood, a generation after your people had entered the Dry Lands. In his dream, he saw one of his descendants riding a Spotted Stallion into the Green Lands, the home country of the Great King Over the Mountains. And the rider passed all the way to the King's castle at River's End, on the edge of a great sea. Kierin saw the sun setting over the sea and the waves shimmering and reflecting a great light that sprang forth from the rider. And Kierin looked to the hills above the sea and the slopes were covered with people, with MuKierin and Barsk and Pappi and kinsmen from all the Seven Clans. And he began to cry for the beauty of the vision. In time he shared it with his people. And that is how his kinsmen began the saying, "Remember me, horse stalker, when you ride beside the shining waters." Over the generations, they forgot the vision and remembered only the saying. To them, it described the good fortune that would come to the one who could catch a Spotted Stallion. But the vision was really about the fulfillment of the hopes of the Stone Woman and her son. They looked forward to the day when their children would leave the Dry Lands and find a home with the King."

Healdin ended the tale and motioned to Wevol's servants. They brought forth a great serving bowl. Healdin took a ladle and filled a large clay goblet. Slowly she lifted it above her head and said, "Let the men who would ride the stallion come forward." Six men, all about Roj's age, began to make their way through the crowd. Roj watched them and felt his heart begin to stir. But he recalled Noli's words and stayed in his place. The camp grew silent. "Remember the vision," Healdin told the six. "When you stand before the stallion of Orres, recall Kierin's dream and the hope of the Stone Woman."

93

Each horse tamer drank from the goblet and passed it to the next man. All six drank and returned the cup to Healdin. The lady took it as the men walked back toward the boulders. Wevol sat down on his pillow, expecting her to join him. But Healdin followed the horse tamers, passing through the people until she came to Roj. There she lifted the goblet and asked: "Roj, will you drink this cup?"

Roj glanced briefly at Wevol and saw the horse trader once more standing, but now with his mouth slightly agape. Remy also looked on the scene with alarm, but she remained out of her brother's line of vision. Healdin stared at Roj, and his heart began to race. "Lady," he asked, "do you want me to drink it?"

"Truly I do, Roj. Early in the morning we can ride together, and I will tell you why."

For the briefest of moments, the young man recalled Noli's words of caution. But now, all Roj could see was Healdin standing there before him with her two hands extending the cup to him. The sight nearly took his breath away. "Very well," he said. Carefully he took the cup and downed the tea. It warmed him and washed over him with exhilaration. Perhaps it was simply the touch of Healdin's hand as she took the goblet back from him.

The lady turned and strode back to the pavilion. There she raised the goblet and said, "Lord Wevol has graciously agreed that I may serve the healing tea to any who desire to drink of it. Let all who ache in body or soul come forward. Yes, come and receive your restoration."

Women arose first, but soon a few men also stepped up to a line that was forming in front of the healer woman. Healdin again filled the goblet and began to serve each one who came to her. And all who tasted felt the tea's healing power.

As the line formed, Ornelia and Melva rushed to Wevol. "Isn't she wonderful, nephew, so strong and so beautiful?" Ornelia gushed.

Wevol stood tightlipped and looked forlornly at Healdin. "Yes, but not for me," he said at last.

"Oh, lord," Ornelia protested, "she knows you're a man of strength and means. Any woman would desire you. This beauty may be independent, but she would never turn down your hand. If you simply allow us to arrange a small dinner for you ..."

"No," Wevol interrupted. "You've done enough. She took the cup to him, not to me. I watched her do so. I'll take that as a sign not to pursue her. Good night, aunts." With those words, he left the pavilion, even as the people continued to draw close to Healdin. His aunts half-heartedly started to follow after him, but then they spied Remy watching them.

"What did you do?" Ornelia demanded fiercely as she approached the younger woman. "Did you turn the healer woman against my nephew? Did you push her toward your poor, lovesick brother?"

"No," insisted Remy. "I didn't do anything. My brother is too young to think about women. I didn't do anything to hurt your nephew's chances."

"So you say. But yesterday that woman smiled on our nephew. Now tonight our hopes for his happiness have been dashed. Need I mention that our nephew's father had promised Melva and me a marriage bounty of five thousand pieces of silver on the day that Arg Wevol should wed? That money is gone now, and I suspect you're to blame. That makes me one furious woman. So you'd better watch your step."

At dawn, Healdin went to Roj's tent and awakened him. They saddled their horses and rode together in the coolness of the early morning to a bluff overlooking a great expanse of the high desert. Here the foothills gave way to a plain that extended for miles west toward the canyon lands of the Red River, the home of the Barsk clan. Below the bluff, Roj noticed that another slaver's caravan had camped on the dusty wagon road toward Kierinswell. The guards were rousing their prisoners and forcing them to their feet.

"Behold your brothers and sisters," Healdin said. "Consider the injustice of those who wear the debtors' chains. Tell me, son of Hannah, will you help these children of the

Stone Woman?"

Roj stared soberly at the slaves. "Healdin, I'm not sure how I can help them."

"I wish you also to consider the fate of all the lost people. In the Dry Lands dwell the seven clans: the MuKierin, the Pappi, the Barsk, the Cheyok, the Grotudi, the Jantuun and those who are Nomads and who call themselves the Quolli. Hannah and her son, Kierin, hoped for a day when all these people would journey with the MuKierin to a new home in the Green Lands. Tell me, Roj, will you help bring about that day?"

"Lady, I don't know how to do such a thing."

"Finally, consider the troubles of your sister and her man. Pibbibib, the Backstabber, and Weakling are ever searching for Noli and you. Even now, I fear those evil ones are making their way toward Orres. Tell me, Roj, will you help your kinswoman and her man find a safe place from these evil ones?"

"Yes, of course, I will. For Remy, I'll do whatever I can. But why do you ask me these questions?"

"I ask you because I believe you are the man to help your people and to give safety to your sister. I believe you can become the Horse Stalker, the man who wins the Stallion of Orres. That man can change the future."

"What do you mean?"

"You have a great gift, Roj. It helped you track the Spotted Stallion into the mountains, and it allowed you to sense the mind of my mare at the well at Sweetwater. With such a gift, you can accomplish what no other man at Orres can do. You can ride the Spotted Stallion. You can win that great horse. No one has ever done such a thing among your people. If you win the challenge of Orres, it would signal a new day for the desert people. Certainly our enemies would be alarmed by this great deed."

"But, Healdin, what makes you so sure that I possess this gift? Yes, I did seem to sense the mind of your mare, but not other horses."

"My mare is not as other horses. She is of a royal

lineage, as are all the Spotted Stallions, brought long ago by the King from a land across the sea. You tracked such a stallion into the high country. The old stories of my people say that a man with your gift will herald the coming of the Champion. But hear me, Roj. The gift alone is not enough. Other men also tracked the stallions into the high country. But they all perished there at the hand of the evil ones. You, however, survived both by your wits and because you trusted the seeker and me. Your wits and your trust saved you. You would need such qualities to prevail in the challenges that would await the victor of Orres."

"What challenges would await me?"

"If you win the Stallion, the eyes of many would fall on you. The Dark Brood would fear that you might become the Champion. So would certain men among the Desert clans. These men have long sought the Root of Glory, and they will not rest until they have it. They would suspect that the Horse Stalker might be able to lead them to the lost power. Both the desperate men and the Dark Brood would come after you. Eventually you would need to confront them and overcome them."

"But, Healdin, I'm not the Champion. And I don't know where the Golden Box lies hidden."

"You speak true, Roj. But for the sake of your sister, we would mislead your enemies. For a time we would let them pursue you."

"For the sake of Remy? What do you mean?"

"Your sister is with child. Indeed, ask her and she will tell you. Soon Remy will have a son, and this child will be dear to the King, for one day he too will be called on to help his people. But first the mother and child will need protection. You fled Kierinswell with Remy to escape Pibbibib. But a pregnant woman cannot travel far. Your sister will face increasing danger if she must flee from the evil ones while she carries her son. She needs a refuge, one where she can be safe and where her man can care for her. But that will depend on you."

"Tell me how I can help her."

"As I once said, Pibbibib can be induced to leave one MuKierin alone and go solely after the other. But we must give him a good reason to abandon Noli and chase only you. With the help of the King's servants, all the Dark Brood can be persuaded to fear that you might become the Champion, the one meant to retrieve the stolen Root of Glory. Pibbibib then would follow after you with no more thought for your kinsman and your sister. Then Noli and Remy could find safety again with your uncle in Kierinswell. Thus, we could help provide her the refuge she needs.

"But hear me, Roj. Such a path would put your own life at great risk, and it would take you far from your kinsman. You would choose a hard way. I know this all too well, for I too have journeyed far from my own homeland. Thus, you must give careful thought on whether you will make such a sacrifice for your sister and for the King."

Roj dismounted and dropped his reins to the ground. He walked away and looked beyond the slave caravan to the great sagebrush plain. After a minute he turned back to Healdin. "If I become the Horse Stalker, how would I change the future?"

She shook her head. "One day you will sense the answer in your heart," she said. "On that day I will confirm it."

Roj frowned. "Woman, if I do what you ask, would I go alone or with you?"

"You would remain under my wing. My people and my friends among the MuKierin would help me watch over you. A day would come when you would face your enemies without me. But I would give you some of my own power to protect you and to help you prevail."

Roj sighed with relief. "Poor Wevol," he said.

Healdin looked perplexed. "What do you mean?"

"The horse trader wanted you to go with him. He wants you, Healdin. I saw it in his eyes. For a time I feared you might go with him. No matter. Now I'll go with you and do as you say. I don't understand this talk of a Champion or the fate of the desert people. It's enough for me to trust you

98

and to know that you'll watch over me. And I do want to help keep my sister safe if I can. I have no other family but Remy. I'll pay any price to protect her. But you have to help me. I truly don't know how to win such a mighty stallion."

"Your choice pleases me, Roj," Healdin said. "I will prepare you for what you must do in Orres. And we also will prepare for Pibbibib. Even now I can sense he is drawing near."

Chapter Ten

The Challenge of Orres

On the following night, two immense warriors emerged on a stone outcrop in the foothills north of Orres. In ages past each one had been as fair as any of the King's own. But now they wore their rebellion on their faces. They had branded their cheeks with images of skulls and lightning bolts, and a broken star was burned upon each forehead. They wore leather helms, and their hair hung down over their shoulders like great tangled manes. Little human bones adorned their dark armor. As they drew close to the overlook, the two slipped easily onto the rocky ground. Lying there on their stomachs, they peered through the darkness toward the thickets of prickly brush on the slope beneath them.

"The time has come to turn back," said the smaller one, known to friend and foe as Weakling. "I have let you have your way, but we have failed to find them. Now let us turn back to the safety of our own ground."

"I will not return empty-handed," replied the larger warrior, the one called Pibbibib, or Backstabber. "We would be beaten and mocked by our masters and sent out again. You know that. No, let us look here in the South Lands. She has brought them this way. I can sense it."

"Why would she still be with them?" Weakling asked skeptically. "Why would she care about these little vermin? What do they matter to her?"

"Have you still not heard me? She has them under her wing! For what purpose I cannot say, but I know that those two horse dogs have been in her care ever since they escaped us. On that day when we found the loose horses, I correctly guessed that the old seeker had found horse hunters and was taking them to our enemies. Yuikki and you went to his cave, but I raced cross country to cut them off. The sky fire struck the earth all around me. It seemed as if the Great Enemy himself was shooting deadly bolts of fire at me, but still I went on. And I would have overtaken the horse dogs but for her. She stood before me and blocked my way. From beneath her gown she unsheathed her power, the small light of fire. You have never seen it. Few of our kind ever have gazed upon it. But I beheld it in that very hour. It appeared as small as a dagger, but in her hand it blazed brighter than the morning star, as bright even as the Great Valuable of our cursed Enemy, the very power that Our Highest Master ever desires. It burned far too bright for me to look at for more than a moment. And with its light, she called down the sky fire and forced me back down the mountain. Even so, I did not give up. I tried another trail and almost caught the dogs, but they heard me chasing them and ran behind her skirt. Truly, all I could do that night was catch the seeker and bring him down with me as bait for our trap the next day. And we could have taken the dogs, but you fools failed me. You let them get away and Yuikki ended up with a belly full of arrows."

"I will have my revenge for that day," Weakling growled. "But still I do not understand your tale. Why did she not kill you that very hour when you stood before her on the mountain?"

Pibbibib bellowed his answer. "Do not ask questions that have no answers! She is a She-one and she does what she pleases. She is often kind. It is her weakness, and I will use it against her. But I tell you that she has gone south. Laugh if you doubt me, but I have sensed her ever since that day on the mountain. I have never felt anything like it in all my years. It comes like a faint scent of her in my mind. And I tell you that she has gone this way, and the two dogs remain under her wing."

"As you say, as you say," Weakling relented. "But still you take us a hard way. These southern hills belong to the Cleavers, and we will find no help from them. They may even harass us, curse their dark souls."

"I fear no Cleavers. Hear me, fool. She has plans for these two MuKierin dogs. We both know it. And among our kind, only we know their faces. That makes us warriors of great value. This secret of hers has become our good fortune, and we should make the most of it. It gives us the chance to escape from our mountains and chase after her, and I rejoice in that. To me, those hills have become the blasted edge of nowhere. I want to venture closer to the battle. Indeed, we now can become masters of fortune and have a grand adventure. And when the right time comes, we will slay these horse dogs and have our revenge."

The two warriors left the hilltop and continued south. They tramped along until a few hours before dawn. The sky remained dark when they made for a ridge with enough boulders to provide them refuge for the coming day. But as they drew close to the rocks, four dark figures suddenly emerged. Pibbibib drew his sword and stepped beside Weakling. The two made ready to repulse the ambush. For a moment no one moved, each side seemingly waiting for the other to strike the first blow. Only the hiss of air between teeth disturbed the silence. At length one of the four ambushers growled, "Behold, Pibbibib, the wild beast, has come down from the north. Perhaps we should fall down in fear before him?"

"No," another sneered, "let Backstabber fall down before us now. He has ventured into our domain. Let him tell us why we should not slice him in two and then carve upon the Weakling for good measure." The other warriors cackled their approval.

Pibbibib had seen from the first that these huge creatures didn't belong to the King. They wore the dark armor of the Dark Brood and had the Broken Star branded on their foreheads. To the uninitiated, they looked as he did. But their cheeks bore the brand of knives cleaving hearts in two, not the marks of skulls and lightning bolts that he wore. These evil ones belonged to the other order—Cleavers, his own kind called them. And the Cleavers called his kind "Slinkers." These ambushers were charged with killing the King's Champion on the day when he should appear. Pibbibib, in contrast, belonged to the order seeking the stolen Root of Glory, or the Great Valuable, as the Dark Brood called it. As

103

such, he took a defiant stance, holding up his blade and waving to the one who had just spoken. "Come closer, if you dare, and I will whisper why I have journeyed here."

A huge warrior, one as large as Pibbibib, pushed his way past the four ambushers. He swaggered to his right, glaring at the newcomers and leaving his sword sheathed as a sign of his fearlessness. "Show me!" he demanded.

Pibbibib and Weakling sneered at this order, but reluctantly they complied, pulling back their black capes and revealing the latest brands upon their arms. Cautiously the great warrior lowered his face to examine Pibbibib's forearm, for the new, small burn marks there amounted to the bearer's orders and his authority to carry out the demands of his superiors. "Yuikki's revenge?" The leader snorted. "Now why has Yuikki's revenge brought you here?"

Again Pibbibib bared teeth to show his disrespect. "We search for two horse dogs. They likely will journey south to Orres."

The leader's eyes widened. "And how did you vermin learn of the Challenge at Orres?" he bellowed.

Weakling stepped back in fear. Pibbibib growled at his companion, "Hold firm!" Even as he spoke, he kept his eyes on his interrogator. "We have shown you the markings," he said. "We have made clear our orders. We need not tell how we know of challenges and such." Indeed, Pibbibib was bluffing. He had known nothing of the challenge until this one let slip the news.

The leader took a step back and pondered the matter. "What do the horse dogs have to do with Yuikki?" he demanded.

Pibbibib grinned with disgust at this one's stupidity. "That secret belongs to my master, the Great Suktoos. Ask him, if you dare."

One of the four underlings guffawed at him, "Who whacked Yuikki, or is that a secret, too?" Pibbibib's smile vanished; he refused to acknowledge the question. In response, the four smaller warriors began to slam their fists on their black shields and taunt, "The She-dogs throttled him.

Aaieee! What a disgrace! The cave yokels have allowed the She-dogs to bleed them again."

Their leader snickered, too. "What do you expect of cave dung?" He turned back to Pibbibib. "Very well, cursed ones," he said, "you had best find some courage if you would journey to Orres. The enemy will be waiting there for easy pickings like you—and not just She-ones, mind you. The blasted Tor himself may bring down some real enemy warriors, He-warriors, to slay worms like you. Indeed, a good scrap appears certain, and we shall be ready. But all that involves secrets best asked of my master, the Great Mooschus, if you dare. So stay out of our way, or we will send your bones off in a sack to your cursed Suktoos."

Pibbibib and Weakling began to back away, still wary of these fellow members of the Dark Brood. The two warriors kept their weapons ready, sensing the great temptation they presented, knowing that those who outnumbered them would try to draw blood at the slightest opening. Pibbibib would have done the same in their place. He had cut many such as these over the ages, giving a scar that forever after would testify to his prowess as the "wild beast" of the northern mountains. While the two factions were bound by a common hatred of the King, the members of each order nonetheless viewed one another as potential targets. "Iron sharpens iron," their leaders liked to say. "We shall keep one another on edge, so our enemies never catch us off guard. If you get cut, it shows you were weak." Some wags privately noted that the division also made sure that no rebel ever got too powerful to challenge the great master Zoirra. Instead, power remained divided between the two orders and overseen by Zoirra's top underlings, the commanders Mooschus and Suktoos. Whatever the true reasons for the division, whenever members of the two orders met, no one dared take his eyes off the other side.

Pibbibib suspected that the four ambushers would follow him. Thus, he stayed quiet and strode briskly through the prickly bush. He led Weakling across one hill and then a second. At last, the two warriors stopped and looked back.

"We should run back to the caves!" Weakling pleaded. "We do not wish to get caught between Tor and the Cleavers."

"Do not let that fool back there scare you," Pibbibib replied. "He would be the last to know what the Enemy's commander means to do."

"But what if he speaks true?"

"Then we will have the advantage. Listen, fool, Tor will look for Cleavers. We do not travel like them nor fight their way. We can avoid the enemy. And that stupid one back in the rocks let it slip that the horse dogs will hold a challenge in Orres. That gives us reason enough to go there. Our two vermin may journey to such a gathering. And if they do, we can find them there."

The following night the two warriors reached the outskirts of Orres. By that time the village had filled with horse hunters who had journeyed from throughout the South Lands to attend the White Beard's challenge. Many showed up simply to see the wondrous prize: a Spotted Stallion. That night the taverns overflowed, and three hundred campfires burned brightly in the valley surrounding the village.

In the darkness, Pibbibib and Weakling advanced to an empty crossroads near the north side of the village. Pibbibib knelt beside a large boulder. "We shall dig in here," he said. "Let the Cleavers have the hills to the east. The enemy will expect them there, closer to their sanctuary in the mountains."

"Perhaps the enemy has retreated," Weakling said. "We have seen no sign of Tor or his kind."

"Fool, if Tor and his underlings are near, they will stay hidden but strike like a hammer when the time is ripe. But they will not catch me unaware."

"I just want the days to pass soon, so I can take another horse dog. Here I sit famished, and you refuse to let me kill any more of these vermin."

"You have gorged yourself on these little creatures ever since we left the mountains. But now you must stop and digest them. The time has come to lie low. We will bury ourselves here in the dirt and wait for what may come."

"I do not approve of the path you have chosen," Noli said to Roj. "And your sister will give me a tongue lashing when she finds out what you mean to do."

Dusk was settling in over the great encampment on the outskirts of Orres. Horse hunters and their kin from throughout the South Lands had gathered for the challenge. Noli and his brother-in-law were passing on horseback through the camps, hoping to meet up with Noli's kinsmen. Everywhere, men were gathered around fires, passing wineskins or shaking leather cups of pebble dice.

"Do you have a better way?" Roj asked. "Remy can't stay on the run when she becomes great with child. Let me do this, and you will have the chance to take her back to Kierinswell and find safety there. Then she can rest before the coming of your child."

"But we will not be able to watch over you," Noli said. "And I do not trust the foreign woman."

"But I do trust Healdin. And we have no other way to keep my sister safe. Therefore, I will go with Healdin, and you will go back to my uncle and become a candle maker. When will you tell Remy?"

"Not until you prevail. If you win the stallion, I will point to our new wealth in the hope that it will lessen her anger at me."

They turned onto a main road through the tents. Noli looked up and recognized a rider on horseback. "Jen!" he called. "What good fortune to find you."

The rider waved a greeting. "Uncle Char sent me to watch for you," he said. "Where is your woman?"

"She rides with the camp of Wevol the horse trader of Kierinswell. We came ahead to find your camp."

"Come. Let me take you to Uncle Char."

The three rode around the edge of the encampment until they came to the north end of the village. Orres consisted mostly of low adobe huts and an occasional two-story inn. But it also contained the largest structure in all the South

Lands: a two-story debtors' prison. The adobe fortress had a few barred windows high on the second floor, but none close to the ground. Its front entrance featured a fence and a gate of iron bars. Inside, it held more than one hundred prisoners, paupers sold into slavery for their debts.

The three riders made their way to a great canopy raised on the edge of a large, barren field across from the prison. There, a raucous throng of men were gathered. Five men in red robes stood beneath the canopy, separated from the horde by a circle of ropes. Many of those clamoring outside were waving bags of coins. Roj guessed that the men were placing bets, presumably on the challenge to come. In the midst of the chaos, a gray-bearded man with a round leather cap stepped back from the canopy. He saw Noli and waved a small scrap of paper at him.

"Uncle!" cried Noli. "I see you're still trying to gamble your way into the debtors' chains."

Uncle Char smiled at his nephew and put the paper in a small leather pouch. "Not today, boy. Today, I bet the sure one," he declared, giving Roj a wink and a smile. "Come, boys. You can find shelter under my canopy. Today, I must take you under my wing."

"But how did you know the boy and I would come to you?" Noli asked.

"The old horse hunters told me," Char said softly as he drew close. "They came at night and said in their old tongue, 'Be ready, Char. He comes to you. You be kin to his kin. Thus, please care for him at Orres. The White Beard himself will hold you to account.'"

Char walked ahead as the three younger men dismounted and strolled through the camp. They stopped at a small canopy and a campfire where four other young men sat shaking the leather cups filled with pebble dice. Char kicked dirt on them and chased them off. Roj recognized two of them as Noli's cousins. The uncle waved and bid the newcomers come join him on the goatskin floor. "A little wine," he said. "I will wine and dine you."

"Just one cup," Noli said. "Then we must go back for

my woman. Who else knows we have come to you?"

"Only our kin," Char said. "They will never speak of you outside the family. They know their duty. They know you rest under my wing."

"Good," said Noli. "We must take care, Uncle. Bad ones hunt for us."

"They shall not touch you. We are true MuKierin, not like those who sell their brothers for a few copper coins. Come, sit and rest."

Jen returned with a plate of dried meat and fruit. Char brought out a small wineskin and grabbed four goblets. Roj could see that his cup had been recently used by another for tea, but it would be improper to mention this to his host. Char raised his goblet. "To your health," he declared.

Roj noted Char's round leather cap, the kind worn by the old horse hunters. The hat signified that Noli's uncle no longer rode headlong after the wild horses. Its beaded band was unique, featuring a string of red Xs against a white background. "Do you know the White Beard?" Roj asked.

"My uncle knows him," said Noli. "They call him a hermit who lives in these foothills. Isn't that right, uncle?"

Uncle Char smiled at Roj. "He is a misfit, as I am a misfit. But he calls himself a misfit for the King. Truly I know little of the King, but the White Beard has earned my respect. He despises the slave trade and he fears no one. He tells our Elders many words that they do not wish to hear. He says the King remains displeased with them because they think only of themselves. He says the Elders have been so ever since they first began to rule over our people, in the days after the Stone Woman and her son, Kierin, went to sleep with their fathers."

"Indeed," said Jen, "the Elders judge themselves aristocrats and lords who rule over us. And they rule with iron chains. But they have put no chains on the White Beard."

"They fear him," Char replied. "Many love that old man, even among the rulers. The Elders have their factions. Some are slavers and others hate the slave trade. Some of the anti-slavers love the White Beard, at least for now. But up here in Orres, the Elder Morros is a slaver, and nobody hates the White Beard more. Remember that, boy," he said, nodding to Roj. "Keep away from that one. Do not trust him."

Noli downed his cup. "I must go fetch my woman," he said. "We also travel with another woman, uncle, a foreign woman."

"The White Beard has sent me word of this woman," Char said. "I will welcome her beneath my tents."

The next day, Wevol's servants arrived and set up a great canopy near the dusty field by the prison. A large group of horse hunters sprawled on the ground beneath its shade. They had little to do that day but stare at the eastern hills and wait. To pass the time, they drank and played pebble dice. In the afternoon, Noli went to Wevol and said, "My kinsman has sent me to say that he remembers his vow."

Wevol gave him a proud look. "Your kinsman takes a drink from the woman's cup and dreams that he can ride the great stallion."

"Soon we will know what he can do," Noli said. "But he sent me to tell you that if he should win the stallion, he will fulfill his vow and give you the animal as a sire in your stables for forty days. And you shall fulfill your vow to give him a share of the offspring."

"As I said, he shall have a twentieth of all the colts and fillies born from that stallion," Wevol said. "And after forty days, he shall reclaim the great horse for himself."

"As you say," said Noli.

When the sun began to sink in the western desert, an entourage appeared on a hilltop east of the village. A rider on a black mare led the way, followed by two columns of horsemen. Beside the black mare trotted a magnificent spotted horse, which stayed in step without any rope upon him. Down in the camp, Noli's Uncle Char stood and declared in a great voice, "The White Beard comes to us!" All the horse hunters stirred. They soon could see that the approaching columns contained fifty old men. Each rider wore his hair and beard long. Upon the riders' heads sat leather caps, much like that worn by Uncle Char, though with different bands of beads. Seven of the riders held green banners with a horse's head painted upon cloth. The banners attracted attention, but even more so the stallion beside the White Beard at the front of the columns. His creamy hide bore the dark spots of his kind. Each of his strides showed grace and power.

"Look at him, Roj!" whispered Noli. "He prances like a prince, like a fighter shadow boxing."

Roj nodded. "He looks just like the stallion we chased into the mountains. I'm sure he is the same horse."

"Blast my broken arm!" Noli growled. "That creature rightfully belongs to us. But I can't go out there and claim him."

"No," Roj deadpanned. "You'll have to go to Kierinswell and become a candle maker."

The White Beard rode to the opening on the edge of the horse hunters' tents. A man approaching the age of fifty, he was stout and his head was crowned with a mass of silver-white hair. His white beard reached his chest. His nose was a bit bulbous and his eyes were a keen, deep blue. He stiffened in his saddle and, with stern eyes, surveyed the gathering. At least five hundred men and boys already were crowding before him, while the two columns of riders had formed a semicircle behind him. The old man lifted a carved wooden staff above his head and called in a loud voice:

> Horse Stalker, Horse Stalker,
> Step forward my son,
> The people await you,
> The day has begun.
> "The darkness surrounds us,
> A war must be won;
> Horse Stalker, Horse Stalker,
> Step forward my son."

No one moved. No one seemed to grasp what the old man meant. The White Beard smiled. "I have brought the stallion for the man who can ride him," he called to the crowd. "Let the stallion's rightful owner come and claim him." At these words the horse hunters erupted with whoops and cheers. Poetry might baffle them, but a challenge they understood. Some of the younger men began to line up beside the White Beard, until thirty or so stood before him. The rest formed a great circle, a human corral, with the stallion and his challengers inside the perimeter. By this time nearly every man from Orres had joined the circle. Roj, however, didn't get in the line of contestants. He stood stiffly at a break in the great circle.

"Fifty drum beats!" the men began to chant. "Fifty drum beats!" An old horse hunter stepped forward with a flat leather drum. The White Beard dismounted and attached to the stallion a leather halter with a short lead rope. "Fifty drum beats!" the men cried. "Fifty drum beats!"

The White Beard handed the halter rope to the first horseman and took his seat on a long rock wall that separated the field from the town. For a moment, all the commotion ended. The men grew quiet and the oldest horse hunter at Orres stepped forward into the circle. Raising a crooked arm, he called out the words that every MuKierin knew from boyhood: "Remember me, horse stalker, when you ride beside the shining waters." The younger men whooped their approval. "Ride him, horse stalker!" they shouted. "Ride him." The drummer began his slow steady rhythm. The horseman swung aboard bareback. The men began to count to the beat of the drum: "One, Two, Three." At once the stallion erupted in a sharp frenzy of bucks and twisting jumps. The rider lost his balance and careened to earth. Many flinched and shook their heads. The man hadn't lasted seven beats. "Bad luck," they said to each other.

No better luck came to the next man, who hit the dirt in six beats. The stallion flung the next rider off the right side after eight beats, and the one after that flew over the great horse's head in ten. After the fifth rider lost his bid, the White Beard stepped forward to allow the stallion a chance to rest and take water. Then, five more riders took their turns, none lasting longer than twelve beats. Fifty beats began to seem as long as the time from breakfast to supper. The day waned and the sun's light began to slip away.

Roj's eyes widened as the twentieth rider stepped onto the field. The man seemed a giant, nearly as tall as Pibbibib, with a big pot belly that protruded from beneath a grimy leather vest. His wore his hair shaved except for a slender, dark braid that hung beneath his shoulder, and leather cuffs adorned his wrists. Behind this sunburned hulk stood a thin, bearded man, wearing a gray robe and grasping a leather pouch with its strap slung over this shoulder. Uncle Char drew close to Roj, "Behold, behind the galoot stands the skinny steward of the Elder Morros. He brings some mischief, boy."

The White Beard looked soberly at the pair standing together. "Does this one know the rules?" he asked.

"Indeed, he does," the steward replied, stepping forward. "And you dare not deny a MuKierin his chance at the challenge."

The White Beard said simply, "Let him step forward." He handed the big man the halter rope. The Stallion immediately began to dance and circle the hulk. Slowly the giant began to take in the rope. The stallion reared slightly. Even as its front hooves returned to earth, the giant stepped quickly forward and jumped up, throwing his right arm over the great horse's head. The stallion tried to escape backward, but the big man took its head in both arms and twisted it until both horse and man toppled to earth. Then the giant wriggled beneath the stallion's neck and wrapped his legs around it. The horse lay on its back, its four legs flailing in the air.

"Start the drum," demanded the skinny Steward.

An old horse hunter protested in the old dialect, "But he be not riding the horse."

"His legs are on the horse and he controls it as the rules set forth," the steward replied. "Start the drum or he will win by default."

The drummer looked at the White Beard, who nodded to proceed. "One, two, three," the drummer counted to the sound of the beat.

113

The stallion remained on its back, seeking in vain to find a solid base for traction or leverage. But the giant cradled the horse's head upon his left shoulder and fought to keep the animal upside down. He held the horse's jaw in his left hand and gripped an ear in his right. "Seventeen, eighteen, nineteen," the drummer called. A few men joined in the count, but most simply watched, too stunned to take part. "Twenty-five, twenty-six, twenty-seven." The stallion began to kick its legs and rock its rump from side to side. As its motion increased, the stallion's head began to fight the man's clutches. "Thirty-three, thirty-four, thirty-five." Back and forth the head wriggled, its teeth snapping wildly. The stallion whinnied high and shrill, and with a great lunge it cracked heads with the giant. The heads separated and came together again. This time the horse's teeth found one of the big man's ears and clamped down hard. "Aieee!" the giant squealed. He released his hands in order to fight for his ear. In that instant the stallion twisted left, found its footing and sprang up. The horse's legs clawed for traction and freedom, but in the escape two hooves caught the giant, one in his groin and another in his midsection. The giant flopped and turned, even as the horse wheeled left near the crowd and reared itself high above the men. The circle nearly broke as MuKierin everywhere jumped back in fear and awe. But the White Beard quietly advanced and stood there to protect the crippled hulk. The horse reared again but advanced no further. "Take this wretch from the field," said the host of the challenge. It took ten men to lift the broken giant and take him away into the night.

"Where did the count end?" Morros' steward demanded. "Did he not hold for fifty beats?"

"No," said the drummer. "He released his grip at forty-three. And the stallion strode upon him at forty-eight."

Slowly the White Beard approached the stallion, grabbed the halter rope and led it to water. A few minutes later he returned alone. "Enough foolishness," he said. "Let us rest a minute, MuKierin. Come close and sit before me. I have something to say to all of you." The men stepped near and sat down cross-legged on the churned earth. "I see that some of you have been cut from the same stone as me," the White Beard began. "You think that many horse stalkers may stand among us, and that one of them will succeed by the strength of his hands. I once thought that, too, but now I see things as an old man, and time has shown me my folly. Do you see that prison standing there?" He pointed to the two-story debtors' jail at the edge of the village. "For years I have desired to tear down that wretched place. But still it stands there, a testament of our injustice toward one another. Can you see these old hands of mine? They no longer possess the strength to crush its walls or bend its bars. Now I know that I will not tear it down and free the many slaves languishing there in their misery. Even so, I know that some day that jail will fall, because the Great King over the Mountains wishes it so.

"In the same way, many of you wish to see a kinsman ride this great stallion. But do any of you possess the strength or skill to stay upon its back? It would seem that none of us do. But still, I know this stallion will be ridden because the King wishes it so.

"Do you not know that the King has always provided for us and protected us? He did so in the time of the Stone Woman. Let me tell you of the early days of her rule over us. In the very first harvest season here, the Barsk set a war party to attack our people. They had many warriors and horses, and they seemed fearless. Along the Red River they already had made two other clans bend the knee in submission to them. But our foremother would not bend her knee. Instead, she arose and walked east from Kierinswell to Fire Mountain, the sacred meeting place that was given to her by the King. After she lit the signal fire, an emissary of the King came to her by night. And he assured her that the King's own would help her.

"And when the Barsk encamped on the plains west of Kierinswell, the King's warriors surprised them at night. They sounded trumpets, drove off the horses and sent the Barsk into a panic. None were harmed, but they all fled, leaving their baggage and horses behind. Indeed, they returned in disgrace to their villages by the river.

"And the next morning, our forefathers ventured forth to the empty camp and plundered it. They claimed victory and gave no credit to the King. Oh, how it angered the Stone Woman. She knew the victory was not ours. She knew it belonged to the King."

The White Beard paused a moment and shook his head. "We have changed little since that day. The King watches over the MuKierin, yet we boast that we remain free by the strength of our own hands. We enslave our brothers and think we will never face a day of reckoning. And we refuse to see the signs all around us. Tonight, my brothers, you will behold such a sign. But will you see it? Or will you refuse to open your eyes, even as our Elders do? Those who keep their eyes shut are as good as blind. But those with eyes to see shall not look in vain tonight. They shall see a sign of hope. They shall see that even as the King cared for us long ago, so he still cares for us today. And that hope should give us confidence that one day he will keep his promise to deliver us."

The old man pointed east and asked, "Do you see that little light burning in the darkness?" The men all hastily turned to look. Indeed, a faint beacon was shining near the top of a distant hill. "The King has given this sign that the time has come," The White Beard continued. "The sign shows that the Horse Stalker stands among us, not many horse stalkers but one. And the King calls him to step forward and claim his prize. This man has found the favor of the King. This man, and not the Elders, will change the future. The Horse Stalker knows that our leaders do not control our destiny. He knows that our hope rests with the King."

A murmur rose around the circle. Was the old man talking about the Champion? Were the old tales about to come true?

An old horse hunter brought forth the stallion. The White Beard raised his hand for silence. "No more pretenders," he shouted. "No more foolishness. Horse Stalker, step forward my son. Come and claim the stallion."

Slowly, Roj arose and came forth from among the crowd. Arg Wevol's mouth dropped. The stallion snorted and pawed the earth. Near the tents, Remy looked at her brother and began to cry. Healdin touched Noli's arm and handed him a woman's veil. "It is time for us to mount up. Your uncle and your kinsmen have packed our horses. Take hold of your woman and have her wear this veil. I do not wish her face or mine to be seen by our enemies. Now, bring her. We must not tarry."

Roj strode slowly to the White Beard. "Who sent you to me?" the old man asked, so softly that no one but Roj could hear him.

"The King and his servant Healdin," Roj answered.

"Indeed, then you are the one. Look around you. All of these MuKierin and many more now are tied together with you to the same rope. Therefore, walk with care, my brother. If you stumble, many will fall with you."

Roj nodded, "You may be right, but I fear I will fail all of us."

"By yourself you cannot prevail. But the King has sent Healdin to prepare you. And others will do what they can to help you. Now listen to me. I want to give you one more bit of advice. If you can stay upon this great horse for fifty beats, do not dismount from him until he runs far from this village."

Roj clenched his teeth and turned to behold the stallion, its halter rope still in the hands of the gray-bearded horse hunter. All the other men had backed up to re-form a circle. *Take a breath*, he told himself. *Take another. Get some air.* Quietly, nervously Roj addressed the horse as Healdin had taught him: "Fidden Gadaeyo! A shawna Ta Elladoena Fidden Gadaeyo." The stallion began to dance on the end of the rope, then stopped and seemed to stare down its latest challenger. Roj peered intently back. *Remember me, bold one. Of course, you do. Now what am I supposed to do next?*

Suddenly the horse's mane flamed red. Roj dropped to his knees. The stallion's eyes seemed on fire. Roj turned to see if anyone else had seen what he had seen. No, it was another vision, for him alone. Again he stared at the creature. A

117

thought formed in his mind. Quickly he turned to the old horse hunter with the stallion's rope. "Take off the halter," Roj told him. "Take it off him. I won't need it."

Carefully the old man obeyed, and the stallion sprang forth. It began to lope around the field where the men who had formed a large oval, akin to a race track. The watching MuKierin readily backed up as the horse approached them, but Roj noticed that the stallion swept especially close to those sitting on the long rock wall. At once he shouted, "Off the wall!" He ran for the low stone fence and yelled again, "Off the wall! Off the wall!"

The stallion was circling counterclockwise along the far side of the field as Roj approached the long stone fence. It rose nearly three feet high and was two feet thick. Its surface had been finished with mortar and appeared almost level. People on the wall swung off as Roj jumped atop and began to run along its length. The men looked at him in wonder. The stallion circled left and began to advance beside the wall. Roj increased his pace. Soon, the horse began to draw near him. For a moment the stallion slowed and the two ran side by side. Then with a burst of speed the great creature pulled slightly ahead and veered right where the wall ended. Roj pushed his legs faster and at the wall's edge gave a great leap forward. Through the air he flew and descended cleanly upon the stallion's back and gripped its mane.

The MuKierin roared with astonishment. "The drum!" The White Beard called. "Count the beats. Count for the Horse Stalker!" The stallion slowed into the first turn, then gave a burst of speed as it raced along the side opposite the stone fence. Again it slowed, took the turn and galloped past the wall. The horse made two more laps, then slowed and cut diagonally across the field and took a slow right turn that allowed it to reverse course.

At last, fifty beats drum beats passed, and a roar rose up from the people. "Horse Stalker!" they yelled. "Horse Stalker! Horse Stalker!" The stallion skidded to a stop, reared slightly and came to face the White Beard. The old man stepped up where all could see him. "MuKierin!" he shouted.

"All of you here are witnesses of this challenge and of the winner who has emerged. Has the horseman won fairly?"

"Yes!" the men yelled. "Fairly!"

"So be it!" The old man sang out. "From this time forth, let this stallion be his, and let this man be known as Horse Stalker."

The MuKierin roared their approval. Even as the shouting faded away, a tall man stepped into the center of the circle and raised his hand. He was clad in a gray robe, but he yanked back his hood and revealed a shining helm. Many recognized him as the captain of the elder's guard. From within his robe he revealed a sword. "Horse Stalker," he called out, "My Lord Morros, the Elder of Orres, would speak with you."

Roj felt a wave of fear slap him. But the White Beard's voice boldly called out, "Your pardon, captain, but the King wishes the Horse Stalker now to depart this village."

"Do not stand against me, old man," the captain warned. He raised an arm and a dozen more hooded men stepped into the circle with him. "The Elders legitimately rule over our people. They deserve your obedience. Those who refuse to give it willingly will give it nonetheless."

"I give them their due," the White Beard replied. "Truly I do. But I give the King my heart. And tonight the King bids me say one more word." He pointed to the Stallion and cried, "Ashkani!" At once, the old man pushed over the man directly to his left. "Make way!" he cried. Next he shoved the man on his right and toppled with him to the ground. Even as the White Beard went down, the great horse and its rider bolted directly toward the hole that the King's steward had created in the crowd. The stallion easily jumped the stone fence and raced off through the streets of Orres. "After him!" shouted the captain. He pointed to the White Beard. "My lord will hear of this. The council will know of your treachery."

"Tell the Elders all that you saw tonight," the White Beard replied. "Tell them that the Horse Stalker rides for the King."

Clutching the stallion's mane, Roj peered ahead as the creature galloped through the dark, empty streets of Orres. At the far edge of the village, the horse hunter spied shapes in the road, three riders trailing three extra horses. They began to trot away in advance of him, even as one of the horses in front whinnied. The stallion answered in return and slowed to a trot once he had overtaken the others. There, Roj recognized Healdin, Noli and Remy.

"Follow me," Healdin said. She pushed her horse into a canter. Roj and Remy came next with Noli in the rear leading the two packhorses and Roj's sorrel stallion. They exited the south end of the village. Healdin circled west and then north.

In the moonlight, Pibbibib and Weakling arose from the sand pits into which they had buried themselves. Staying low, they took their places amid a series of low rocks not far from the northern crossroads. Pibbibib looked out to the east and saw the light that the White Beard had brought to the attention of the horse hunters.

"Behold," the warrior said. "The enemy draws near."

"Perhaps the Cleavers have set the light as a trick," said Weakling.

"No, that light is a sign that the Cleavers once again have been routed. And there is a strange feeling in the air."

"I sense nothing. Perhaps your fears are getting the better of you."

A few minutes later they heard the sound of horses from the south. Pibbibib clenched his teeth. "She approaches!" he hissed. "I can sense it." Instinctively the two warriors fell to the ground. A few moments later they saw Healdin and the others race through the sage beyond the road. Healdin wore a veil, but Pibbibib still recognized her. As she passed, her right hand reached down toward her leg. Pibbibib's heart jumped. Would she draw her power? Healdin hesitated and her light remained sheathed. The four riders passed into the darkness.

"Up, fool," Pibbibib ordered. "We must go after them."

"After them?" Weakling snorted. "But they ride for that blasted light in the east. You yourself said the enemy has taken the higher ground."

"Did you not see them? She rides with the two horse dogs. And the very one you should have killed on the mountain sits atop the Spotted Stallion. He must have won the Challenge of Orres. Think, stupid. Our leaders will praise us and reward us for news of this MuKierin dog. The Great Enemy must favor that one. I knew she had some reason to keep them with her."

"But we will have our throats slit if we go after them."

"No, we walk with care. Indeed, we must. It worries me that she rode right past us. Did she guess we were here? I do not know, but we must take special care in case she joins up with Tor's warriors in the eastern hills."

"Indeed," Weakling cried, "she may have too many warriors with her now. Let us not run after her to our destruction."

"We will pursue them in our own way and at our own pace," Pibbibib said. "We need not rush. That dog belongs to you and me. We remain the only ones who know his face. Rejoice, for this is a hunt for the ages! Indeed, let us venture forth and see what became of the Cleavers. No doubt, they have become carrion, but our masters would delight in such news. Soon enough we can turn northeast. Even now I begin to better recognize her scent. I can pick it up whenever we cross her path. In time we will learn where she takes this little dog."

Healdin was crying as she led Roj and the others east from Orres. At length they approached the top of a hill overlooking the village. Suddenly, a group of riders appeared on the ground above them. Roj's heart jumped, and he could only hope that they had met up with friends. Healdin raised her hand to signal she was stopping. The waiting riders pulled back to give her room, and the two groups soon converged.

An old woman drew near. Roj saw it was Mirri, the same one he had met in the mountains. "All stands ready, my lady," she said. "We await your word."

121

Behind Mirri waited many mounted warriors, both male and female, and the males looked immense, every inch the size of Pibbibib. Healdin saw fear on the faces of the three MuKierin. They didn't seem to notice her tears. Quickly she wiped her eyes and said, "Now we have come into the safety of my people. All here have pledged loyalty to the King. You are in safe hands. Dismount for a few moments. We all have long journeys before us."

As Healdin dismounted, Mirri came to her and asked, "How did you fare, my lady?"

"Once more the fear rose within me," Healdin replied. "After we left the village, I could sense Pibbibib as we passed by him, and once more the urge came upon me to draw my light to protect Roj."

"Was the urge greater or lesser this night than the first?"

"It was much greater, Mirri. But this time I recognized the fear and would not give in, though the temptation became ever so strong. I soon found myself crying from the feelings."

"Oh, lady, is this not part of the curse of the Vine?"

"So it seems. It is so new, Mirri, but I sense that these fears will continue to grow stronger within me."

"And what will you do when this young MuKierin next encounters the Dark Brood, lady? How will you resist these growing fears?"

"I must pull back. I cannot stay by Roj's side when next he meets Pibbibib. I must not draw my power, for his sake and the sake of his people. I would harm him. No, I must let him stand alone, as the old tales say. And yet I must do what I can to protect him. When the time is right, I must give him some of my power."

Nearby, Roj went to Remy and took her hand. "Sister," he said, "I need to say good-bye and leave you for a time. Noli and you now can return in safety to Kierinswell. Healdin assures me that the bad ones will follow me now, and not you. They will think I may be able to lead them to the King's lost power."

"What do you mean?" Remy asked with worry in her

122

voice. "Why must we part? We will not leave you, Roj. Who would watch after you? I have cared for you ever since you were a baby. Mama asked me to look after you. Who do you have but me?"

Roj leaned over and kissed her cheek. "You are the only family I have. But now you must look first to the safety of this child. You can't keep running with me. You know that. You must do this for your child. Noli will take you back to Uncle Shone, and you'll be safe there. The evil ones won't look for you any more."

Remy began to cry. "You did this for me and the child inside me. But I still worry about you, Roj. It's not just the evil ones chasing after you. I'm afraid that you're falling in love with this foreign woman. I think it's going to bring you so much sorrow."

Roj bent his head to hers and said softly, "I'd be a fool to give my heart to Healdin? She's not like us, Remy. We both know that. Look, Wevol wanted to marry her, but she wouldn't take his hand. She won't take mine either. She's older than the Stone Woman, and she isn't going to marry some poor horse hunter."

"That's what you say, but your heart isn't listening to your words. I've seen how men look at her. I've seen how you look at her, too. Your heart is wild and you can't control it. You may end up with a broken heart."

Her words stirred Roj, but he quickly resisted them. "Go," he told his sister. "Your husband is ready to leave this place." Remy hugged him and walked away. Noli helped her upon her mount. A small group of warriors surrounded them as they rode off for Kierinswell. Even as they departed, Roj turned and saw a young man approach the Spotted Stallion. It was the same slave that Healdin freed at the well as Sweetwater. "What's he doing here?" Roj asked.

"He has pledged the King his allegiance, as did the woman we also freed, the one who is kin to the White Beard," said Healdin. "She has become this one's wife. His name is Ash. I wish him to become known to the stallion. So I have asked him to take the great horse to Arg Wevol.

Remember, you have given the horse trader the service of the stallion for forty days. My own people will see that he safely reaches his destination." Ash mounted a horse and nodded silently to Roj. The great horse and the former slave would travel together with a company of the King's warriors. As they left, another warrior brought Roj his own sorrel stallion.

"You have done well," Healdin said. "Now my people will take your sister and her man safely to Kierinswell. But we must turn east, and return to the mountains where I first found you. Even now a battle is raging there for control of the high ground. You have brought about a new day, Roj. Now the enemy will strain mightily to find you."

Chapter Eleven
A New Enemy

Pibbibib knew his masters well. As he predicted, his Slinker captains desperately wanted news from the Challenge of Orres. All the Dark Brood had been stirred by rumors of the MuKierin who had won a Spotted Stallion. The two orders, both Slinkers and Cleavers, had sent spies scurrying forth in search of details. Pibbibib and Weakling eventually encountered two scouts of their order in the hills east of the Sweetwater well. Immediately they passed on their secrets of the Horse Stalker, the same man they had been tracking for nearly a month. Pibbibib also presented a sack full of trophies collected from dead "comrades" of the other order. Among the fallen were the same five Cleavers who had challenged Pibbibib and Weakling on their way to Orres. Pibbibib had scalped them all. "These show we came near the battle," he told the scouts. "Now take them, while we search for the trail of the horse dog." He said nothing of his ability to track Healdin's "scent."

The scouts took the sack and the news to their sergeant, who immediately took it to his captain. Soon two mounted couriers set off riding south. The messengers traveled in daylight and darkness, regularly changing horses at special outposts kept by their order. In four long days they had journeyed more than three hundred miles to the Castle of Equis, a stone fortress nestled among the largest city in the Dry Lands. The city of Equis lay far to the south along the Red River, the one great waterway that flowed through the desert. The great battlement was the oldest thing built by hands in the Dry Lands. The castle had been standing even before the rebels fled from the Green Lands. The Dark Brood found it deserted and quickly made it their own.

It was there among the dim shadows of a great room that a single creature sat at his desk, reading the latest dispatches by the light of candles and one long, slit window.

A mammoth figure, his cheeks bore the brands of human hearts with knives thrust through them—the sign of those seeking the enemy's Champion. No one among the desert people could calmly behold that face, especially when it exhibited its fury. The face belonged to Commander Mooschus, chief of the Cleavers.

Suddenly, the great room's door crashed open and an equally impressive figure stood in its entrance. The same Broken Star was on his forehead, but his cheeks displayed lightning bolts and skulls—the sign of those who sought the Root of Glory. There in the doorway stood Commander Suktoos, the chief of Pibbibib's order, the Slinkers. Both warriors wore only black. Suktoos had a long goatee, Mooschus, a thin mustache. Mooschus glared at the intruder. "Leave me, Suktoos," he growled. "I must attend to matters far greater than you can fathom."

Suktoos raised a sack and smiled. "I bring you a gift, my dearest one. These belong to you." He threw the sack at the other's feet. Mooschus ignored him. Suktoos shook his head. "Do not deny the truth, Mooschus," he cooed. "They belong to you, to be sure, all five of them. They say more corpses littered the ground, and I do not doubt it. But these five especially captivated one of my true warriors. It seems your five had been swaggering and bossing my own around. And then—rip and slash—the enemy got the better of them. Now the maggots feast upon them. So my warriors brought back these items to remember them by. It seems your dead ones no longer have any need for their scalps, or their other body parts, for that matter. But I insisted on returning them to you. My own would grow too fond of them. And I know how sensitive you become about your failures. No need to remind you of them time and time again."

"Is that all you have to say?" Mooschus replied. "Very well, you have had your frivolity at my expense. Now depart from me, you evildoer."

"Very well," Suktoos said. He feigned an exit and smiled again. "Oh, I almost forgot the message I was sent to bestow upon you. The Master has taken a special interest in the horse hunter who won the challenge of Orres."

"Do not bluff me. The dog is a simpleton."

"So says your intelligence. But my intelligence says this simpleton already has made contact among the highest-ranking members of the Enemy. My intelligence says he also has made contact with a seeker of the horse dogs, an old one of their clan who searched in the mountains for the Great Valuable that our Master desires. And we both know that the old White Whiskers has declared that this same simpleton is the Horse Stalker who will change the future. That explains why the Enemy pounced so quickly upon your underlings, leading to their unfortunate demise."

Mooschus turned to glare at his co-commander. "Do you deceive me with your tales?"

"The Master thinks I speak true. Indeed, he has sent me to fetch you. You have been summoned, Mooschus. The Master apparently believes you have failed us. So rise and make your way to our Malevolent One."

Mooschus stood slowly, bracing himself for what he was about to endure in Zoirra's presence. It would not be pretty. "This horse dog is not the Champion," he insisted. "I will find him and prove it."

"I think not. The Master already has sent Lord Mackadoo to find the man."

Mooschus sneered at the name. "I do not need any interference from Mackadoo!"

Suktoos shook his head. "Of course, pet. And I always defer to your sound judgment. But our Master already has made his decision. Without your input, he has sent forth his special emissary. He has chosen Mackadoo, this deadly underling who is under neither your thumb nor mine, who reports directly to Our Master, who openly yearns to rise to either your post or mine. Ah, yes, his selection for this assignment did not fill me with delight, either, my pet. Mackadoo poses a threat to both of us. No doubt he hopes someday to hold both our scalps in a sack, if ever we should give him the chance. For my part, I do not intend to let the incompetence of your underlings become my undoing.

However, it remains quite possible that your fools may cost you dearly. Yes, my pet, I worry often that one day those beneath you may cost you everything."

Mooschus started for the door. "Those beneath me will bend to my will. The Master knows my power and retains his confidence in me. You shall see. I will not be undone by one horse hunter."

Pibbibib raised his head and listened for sounds among the rocks. It was a cloudy night, and Weakling was snoring. Pibbibib should have been sleeping, too, except that he had been on edge all night, sensing, it seemed to him, that the lady Healdin remained nearby. He strained his ears until he again caught a noise, gravel sliding ever so slowly down a hillside. He reached over and put his hand across Weakling's mouth. "Visitors," he whispered. Weakling's eyes opened wide, and he nodded in acknowledgement. Pibbibib raised himself to a knee and crawled to a nearby boulder.

They had taken refuge in the stony crag of a ridge top, giving them at least two routes of escape. But flight carried the risk that someone would be waiting in ambush. Pibbibib preferred the role of ambusher, so for now he stayed on the high ground and waited. The noises were ever so light, but he had an ear trained for hearing. He could tell that his adversaries were approaching from both sides of the ridge. What remained a mystery was exactly how many warriors now surrounded him, though he guessed it was at least a half dozen. Such a night sortie was a dangerous exercise, especially since it depended upon the warriors arriving from different sides at the same time. These were not your average Cleavers, Pibbibib told himself. He feared the Enemy might be coming at him.

Weakling crawled up beside him. "We're surrounded," he whispered.

"Back to back," Pibbibib replied. "We shall cut through them and escape."

The hilltop grew eerily silent. Weakling wanted to draw his blade, but Pibbibib stopped him. The sound might give them away. Thus, they crouched and listened. At last the quiet was broken right beside them, as three fist-size rocks landed around them. One clattered on a stony bench and toppled to the ground. Pibbibib saw it as a signal, alerting those surrounding him to attack. Feet started tramping from both sides. A moment later the first dark shape emerged on the right. Pibbibib jumped at him and swung a short blow. A shield blocked it, even as a second attacker swung at him. Pibbibib had just enough time to thwart the blow and pivot left, where he swung low to attack the first one's legs. Another shield again blocked his sword. *This enemy had two shields!* He apparently was meant to take the blows while his allies surrounded and overwhelmed Pibbibib and Weakling. All this Pibbibib considered as he slammed his body into the shield bearer and used him to knock over two other attackers. Next, he stepped back to gain his bearings. Even in the dark he felt certain that his attackers belonged to the Dark Brood and not to the King.

Nearby, Weakling crashed into a warrior and fell beneath him. The two gripped each other and the attacker grabbed Weakling by the throat. Another warrior came at them aiming a sword, but Weakling pushed the adversary over in time to catch the thrust of the blade. The sliced warrior howled. Weakling squirmed free and noticed that the same brands of his order adorned his opponent's cheeks—the symbols of lightning bolts and skulls. "Wait!" Weakling exclaimed as he rose on one knee. "I am with you! I am no Cleaver!" Another warrior, a Cleaver, kicked him in the gut and toppled him down to his belly.

"Enough!"

Pibbibib turned and saw that the order had come from one who had fallen to the ground. *He must be a sergeant.* The other warriors reluctantly complied with his order. Their chests heaved as they pulled back a few steps and warily eyed their two victims.

The sergeant was limping. He apparently had gotten sliced by one of his own comrade's blades when Pibbibib had knocked them to the ground. The sergeant slammed his own sword back in its scabbard, and growled, "Show me!"

He will have his revenge on you, Pibbibib thought. *Do not let him stick you, though.* He held his sword tight in his right hand and let his shield fall to the ground. The sergeant, however, wasn't careless enough to reach for the empty left hand. Instead, he grabbed Pibbibib's right wrist and examined the brands on that arm. Suddenly, and without looking up, he swung and gave Pibbibib an all-out blow to the chin. Pibbibib's head snapped back, his torso bending as spineless as a rag doll. The sergeant then yanked on the right arm and sent Pibbibib sprawling onto his face.

"Defy me, will you?" he yelled, clutching at the wound on his thigh. "Want to try that again?"

Perhaps he will calm himself now, Pibbibib thought as he got up on one knee. *But watch for the knife. He'll try the knife if you give him an opening.*

"These are the ones," the sergeant called to his warriors. "Just as I vowed, these are our cave yokels."

Pibbibib sneered but held his tongue.

"It took so little time to find you worms," the sergeant chided. "Grab a few Slinkers by the throat and they always talk. Then we just needed to keep our eyes out for a trail of corpses with their right earlobes chewed off. No doubt we have little Weakwi here to thank for that handiwork."

Pibbibib glared at his ally. "I told you to stop marking your victims," he growled.

Weakling looked offended. "I make my notch on those ears to show that I can do as I please with the horse dogs," he protested. "It is my way."

"Enough!" the sergeant bellowed. "We will take you with us. Get up."

Pibbibib had noticed the sergeant was a Cleaver. This was no time for weakness. He spit bloody drool to the ground and replied slyly, "Some of your chums tried to boss us around a while back. They had no sense. Tor and the She-dogs got them, every one of them. You should have seen those Cleavers without their scalps."

"I know who scalped them, scumbag. But unless you

want to face my master's wrath, you will obey at once and come with us down this mountain."

Weakling's eyes bulged in fear. "Mooschus is here?" he gasped. Pibbibib growled at him again.

The sergeant guffawed mightily. "Blast, you are stupid hill yokels. Do they teach you nothing up there in Cave Country? No doubt you would fail to know your own master, the cursed Suktoos, even if he hit you upside the head. Look, fool, can't you see that we have different marks on us? We are from both orders, but we all work together. We are elite, not riffraff like you. All you need to know now is that my lord wears the red ruby on his forehead. That means he can chop off your heads and drop them at your master Suktoos' feet, and no one will say he overstepped his bounds. Step out of line if you dare to put it to the test."

The sergeant led the party down the hillside. Pibbibib noticed how the warriors kept alert. Perhaps they also feared that the Enemy remained near. But they met no one on their descent from the ridge. After nearly an hour, they emerged onto a piece of flat ground. The sergeant gave a subtle bird call, and two new warriors emerged from the rocks. The party halted. Pibbibib and Weakling huddled together, fearing at any minute they might face another round of blows. Their guards, however, drew two paces back to form a larger circle. Suddenly, all the warriors drew to attention and dropped to one knee. Pibbibib considered springing free at that moment, until he saw the foolishness of such an attempt. More warriors already had reached the circle, led by one larger than the rest. He was adorned in a black cape and armor, and he wore a jewel upon his forehead. Even in the night it seemed somehow to flicker with a faint, scarlet light. Unlike his underlings, the hair beneath his black helmet was cropped short and his cheeks were free of any brands. On his forehead the mark of the Broken Star lay hidden behind the ruby. In his hand, he held a great sword with a small skull on the end of the hilt.

His eyes met Pibbibib's, and it was more than the prisoner could bear. Pibbibib looked down in submission. The

131

jeweled one spoke softly, so much so that the prisoners strained to hear each syllable. "You each have one chance to prostrate yourselves and tell me why you are here," he said. "I will start with you," he said, pointing his blade at Pibbibib.

Pibbibib cringed. This beast wouldn't even give him the consolation of breaking Weakling first. Flinging himself on the dirt, Pibbibib cried out, "Master, we look for the horse dog who won the Stallion."

"So do I," the lord replied, touching Pibbibib's ear gently with his blade. "And how will you know him?"

"Master, we know his face. We saw him in the mountains before he won the stallion. We saw him with the She-dogs. We saw him with She who holds the little light of fire."

"Is she with the horse dog now?"

"Yes, master. She has gone with him up the mountain."

"I guessed it was she that I sensed above us in those hills. But I need not follow her. I will wait until the MuKierin reaches out for the Stallion." The lord swung around to Weakling. The smaller warrior prostrated himself, hiding his face and moaning softly. The jeweled one raised his sword and thrust it smartly into the dirt near Weakling's scalp. Next, he bent down and called in a mock-soothing voice: "Little worm, do you know what I shall do to your friend if he has lied to me? Do you know what I shall do to you if you fail to tell me the truth? Tell me the truth, little worm. Have you seen the one they call Horse Stalker?"

Weakling raised his head and nodded, squeaking as much as talking, "Yes, master. I swear it. By the Great Master, I swear it."

The lord rose up. "Brand them!" he roared. "They work for me, now. We will take them with us to the Stallion. They shall be our eyes."

Pibbibib perked up his head. The lord noticed and gave a grin that caused the lesser warrior to quickly turn away his gaze. "You amuse me, worm," the jeweled one said. "I know what you think. You have become valuable to me now, and I cannot kill you. Indeed, that is true. I want you to live long enough to show me the Horse Stalker. Among our kind you may be the only ones who actually know his face. But remember this: I only need your eyes. You have many other parts of your body that I can eliminate without the slightest worry. Ponder that long and hard should you have the slightest thought of disobeying me."

The lord strode off. The soldiers set to making a branding fire. It became the sole light on that starless night. "Roll up your sleeves," the sergeant barked at Pibbibib. "I want to smell burning flesh. We still have a score to settle, scumbag."

Indeed, we do, Pibbibib thought, his composure coming back. "Who is he?" he asked, trying to sound brave.

The sergeant set a short branding iron in the fire. "He is the lord with The Powers," he said. "The Powers of the Great Valuable rest on him and protect him from his enemies. Our Great Master has bestowed them upon him. And The Powers also rest upon those who serve him. He is the Lord Mackadoo."

"The Powers?" said Pibbibib. "Well, I approve. Weakling, roll up your sleeve. We shall receive The Powers, too."

Weakling shook his head. "I just want to go back to my cave."

Roj sat alone watching the western sky fade to purple. He had come with Healdin and her warriors into the foothills east of Kierinswell. Soon he would ride to Wevol's horse farm.

After the Challenge of Orres, Healdin had led him north, and they had ascended the same mountains where Roj first met the King's people. But much had changed since that night. The King's warriors had come there as a large army and overwhelmed the forces of the Dark Brood scattered among the high country. The Slinker warriors either fled their caves or died in them. The King's army soon took control of the mountains, and Roj was able to find rest in the high country for a few weeks. The time passed all too soon, and then he went with Healdin down into the foothills. Her scouts led the way, and they passed into the lower hill country without seeing any signs of the enemy.

On this evening, Roj looked away from the fading light of the western sky, and saw Healdin riding up the trail to him. "The time has come," she said. "My scouts tell me that the enemy is watching for you at Wevol's farm. They have taken the horse trader and his people captive. You must help free them."

"Will you go with me?" Roj asked.

She paused to consider her answer. "I will ride with you. But for your sake and the sake of Wevol's servants I must stay back from the horse farm."

"Why?"

"Pibbibib is likely there watching for you. He would sense my presence if I draw too near." She paused a moment and measured her words. "And I do not wish to be tempted to draw my power. I might hurt your or Wevol's people. Thus, my followers will help you this night. Later I will ride forth and let Pibbibib catch the scent of my power. And then I will take the stallion and ride that great horse far away from you. That way the enemy will not be able to track you when you leave the land of your people. Later, I will release the stallion and he will return into the hills above Kierinswell. He will remain in this country until the day when he sets out to find you."

"The stallion is going to come looking for me one day?" Roj asked.

"Yes," she said. "You have seen him before in visions. But you will see him once more with the red mane."

In the darkness, Pibbibib sat with his back against the wall of a stone corral. Roj's Spotted Stallion stood inside, near the center of the large enclosure. No other horse was kept there.

The sound of shuffling feet disturbed the night's silence. The feet halted, and a voice from around the corner of

134

the corral whispered, "It is I, the hungry one." A moment later Weakling emerged. He then flopped down next to the Backstabber. "No food again," he griped. "Those goons on the hill refuse to share their scraps, and I cannot find a goat or a calf within a day's walk of this place, except perhaps Kierinswell. And that remains off limits, as are the horse trader's servants and their little vermin."

"There might be goat meat around if you had not throttled that herder on the other side of the valley," Pibbibib observed. "All the horse dogs ran away after that, and took all their animals with them."

"But I had to eat him!" Weakling protested. "The hunger had overwhelmed me! No one looks out for us. I wish I was back in my nice dark cave in the hills. I could take care of myself there."

"You would be a feast for worms by now. The word is the enemy went up on the mountain and butchered all our old chums. That stupid sergeant says not one of them got away alive. I think he may be telling the truth. You can thank me that you are still alive. It is a good thing we have followed our little horse dog, first for one master and now for another. Otherwise, you would have had your head lopped off."

"Even so, I say we run for the hills as soon as we can."

"And then what would we do? The cursed Tor and his warriors hold the hills. If we went up there, the enemy would pounce on us, too. Listen, fool, you cannot go back, not unless you want your throat slit. That is not for me. I have other plans. Look, we do well here. We report to Mackadoo now. He walks tall, so tall that he answers neither to Suktoos nor Mooschus. I want that kind of tallness, too. And with him, I will gain The Powers. You cannot do that hiding in your cave. You find The Powers down here with Mackadoo battling the enemy."

"You can have The Powers. I am going to find a dark place and curl up for the night."

"No, stupid, you will go back and take your place on the other side of the corral."

"But the Horse Stalker will not come tonight,"

Weakling protested. "Mackadoo's own say as much. They expect him to enter Kierinswell tonight. Even Mackadoo has gone down there. The goons say they have snitches that know his location at this very hour."

"I put no stock in goons and snitches. Not a one of them has a brain half the size of mine. When Tor makes ready, he shall come down here and slay those fools over there at that fire, just as he did to our own warriors in the mountains. But he will not slay me. I shall be ready."

"Indeed?" Weakling replied. "Very well, let me put you to the test. You say The Powers have come upon you. Tell me, oh magnificent one, how close does the Horse Stalker stand to us at this very moment?"

Pibbibib bit his lips. "Blast it all, I cannot say! But I know he stands closer than you imagine. I sense something, even fainter than when I followed the She one who holds the little light of fire. And so we will watch for our prey."

The night grew cold and the two warriors eventually began to doze. So did the other guards who were camped together on the hill above them. Quiet settled over the horse farm. But two hours before dawn Roj crawled down the hillside and slipped through an open window into Wevol's hut. Landing softly inside, he crawled over the dirt floor to the horse trader's bed. He took a breath and placed his left hand over Wevol's mouth. The horse trader's eyes flashed awake.

"Keep quiet, or I will slit your throat. It is I, Roj, who have come to help you," he whispered. "I have come for the stallion. Do not scream." Slowly he removed his hand from Wevol's mouth.

"Boy!" the horse trader hissed. "Why have you come here? We heard you would speak tonight before the Elders in Kierinswell. Do you not know that the bad ones are watching outside for you?"

"The White Beard spread false rumors that I would ride to Kierinswell. The tale allowed me to come here unsuspected. Now tell me, does a watchman stand between the stallion and me?"

"An evil one waits for you at each end of the corral.

Even at night, they watch for you. Oh, what despicable creatures they are. And more evil ones hide on the hill above us. You cannot escape them."

"Listen to me," said Roj. "In a few moments a battle will begin. Stay inside until it ends. Then gather all your servants and leave this place. Take the horses, especially the mares, and leave for Kierinswell. Go to the Elders and tell them what has happened. Even now our leaders may have put the White Beard in chains because I did not appear before them tonight. They will hold him responsible for my absence, though it allowed me to free you. Thus, you must tell the Elders that these evil ones entered our land and waited in ambush here for me. Tell them I came here on this night in order to free you. Urge our leaders to free the White Beard, as you yourself have been freed."

"Yes, of course, Horse Stalker, but please help me understand this madness. It has been an unholy terror here since these evil creatures arrived. Why do they want you?"

"They seek an object of great power that the desert people stole from the King and lost in the days of the Stone Woman. They think I can lead them to this weapon. These evil ones mean to kill and enslave our people. But the Great King Over the Mountains, the one the White Beard serves, has sent warriors to rescue you. So don't forget what he's done for you this night. A day may come when he will ask for your help."

"I won't forget, Horse Stalker. I promise."

Roj climbed back out the window. Wevol's hut stood a short distance from the stone corral. The young MuKierin gathered his breath and dashed for the fence. He easily bounded it and raised his voice for the horse to hear him, "Fidden Gadaeyo! Ash kalay! Fidden Gadaeyo!"

Weakling popped up his sleepy head and gasped to behold an intruder standing beside the great horse. Immediately he raised a horn to his lips and blew out three deep blasts. Roj leapt aboard the stallion and, without bridle or rope, urged the animal to gallop toward the other end of the corral. Pibbibib stood up and smiled. He correctly had sensed his prey was near, and now the MuKierin was riding straight for him. The warrior jumped the fence, drew his sword and raised it with both hands above his shoulders. Roj and the stallion galloped straight toward him. Backstabber didn't fear. At the right time, he planned to swing a savage blow and strike down the great horse.

From the other end of the corral, Weakling once more blew his horn. Immediately an arrow slammed into his right forearm. Weakling howled in agony. More arrows shot past him as he flung himself down. Pibbibib heard his scream and glanced toward the hill behind Wevol's hut. He caught a glimpse of movement and immediately hit the dirt. Three arrows whizzed past his head. A war whoop sounded on the hill. The King's forces were taking the high ground. Roj and the stallion rushed past Pibbibib and jumped the corral fence. The warrior made no attempt to stop the escape. Instead, in great fear he flung himself over the side fence and ran toward Weakling. On the hill above him, he could hear screams and whoops and the crash of steel. His allies were fighting for their lives.

Weakling came running toward him. "They hit me!" he yelled, weaving unsteadily and clutching his right arm. "They hit me bad."

"Shut up," Pibbibib hissed in a voice just above a whisper. "Keep quiet and run."

In the darkness, the two scurried between the servants' huts and slid down a hill into a deep gully. Pibbibib grabbed his companion and flung him down there. "Lie here and shut up," he said.

"If they search for us here, we are done," Weakling moaned.

"And if we venture out any farther, we shall find ourselves on the open ground with no place to hide. We shall stay here and hope that they will leave us be."

"The arrow remains in my arm. Take it out! Oh, how it hurts!"

"Not yet. You would make too much noise."

They waited anxiously as a commotion rose among

the huts. They could hear servants screaming and shouting. Soon they detected the voice of Arg Wevol barking orders. Horses came stamping out of barns and corrals. Within five minutes all the MuKierin had galloped off, leaving behind an eerie silence.

A short time later, Pibbibib felt his hair tingle and his throat tighten. He flipped onto his stomach and peered back up the hill. He saw no movement in the darkness, but still he had to force himself to lay still. "She is drawing near," he whispered.

"She?" Weakling asked.

"Fool, She of the little light of fire! She is coming down from the mountains."

"What? You have doomed us. Let us run!"

"Silence! Lie still or I swear I will slit your throat. We have no choice now but to stay hidden here and hope she will leave us be."

Soon the sensation lessened and Pibbibib's fear subsided. He deemed the woman had come no closer than the hills above Wevol's hut. Dawn came an hour later. Only then did Pibbibib cut off the tip of the arrow and pull the shaft out of his ally's arm. Weakling howled mightily. Pibbibib went back to one of the abandoned huts and found an old cloth to wrap around the wound. In the early light Mackadoo arrived at the horse farm. The sergeant and a handful of warriors accompanied him. At the campfire on the nearby hillside, they found six of their own shot full of arrows or run through by swords. The party advanced downhill and spotted Pibbibib and Weakling in the gully.

"How did you maggots survive?" Mackadoo demanded furiously. He looked ready to kill them both.

"We stayed awake and watched while the others slept," Pibbibib replied. "But the enemy came with too many warriors. We barely escaped with our lives. And that proved a good deed for you, master. We saw the one they call Horse Stalker come and take the stallion. Only we could have known his face."

"It seems you were left alive precisely so that you

could give me this news. It makes me wonder about you worms. You keep showing up at such consequential moments. It seems much too coincidental. I begin to believe that you must be acting in league with the enemy."

"But, master," Weakling protested. "The enemy would not have us."

Mackadoo's sneer almost turned into a grin. "Indeed, you have spoken the only sensible words that could spare your lives. Of course, the enemy would not have two steaming piles of dung like you. If any other among our kind could recognize the Horse Stalker, I would not have you either."

Pibbibib replied, "We remain alive because each day I gain more of The Powers. Through them, I stayed awake and watched, even though your own said the Horse Stalker would ride to Kierinswell this night. They died, but I live."

Mackadoo began to scrutinize Pibbibib's face. "What do you know of The Powers?" he asked in wonder. "To so quickly acquire The Powers, you must stand in the presence of the Great Valuable or beside one who has reached out to take it."

"In the presence!" Pibbibib gasped. Immediately he seemed to check himself. He shrugged and replied, "Perhaps I have found another way. The Great Master has reached out for the Great Valuable and you, my master, have stood in his presence. And I have stood in my master's presence. Perhaps The Powers also can come quickly to some that way."

Now it was Mackadoo's turn to shrug. "Perhaps," he said. "The Powers remains a mystery. And perhaps you have tasted something of them, though I doubt it."

Pibbibib took a step closer. "Someday, I could help you find the Great Valuable."

Mackadoo's eyes grew wide and his mouthed smiled slyly. "Could you, worm? Indeed, someday I may need to look for the Great Valuable, even though the task now falls to Suktoos and the Slinkers. But for whom would you find it— for yourself or for the Great Master?"

"One is meant to hold it. I would find it for him."

"Listen to him, sergeant. He survives a few arrows flying over his head and he begins to see himself crowned in glory. Indeed, I vouch that he desires to take hold of the Great Valuable for himself. Listen, worm, I would gladly let you grasp it and smell you burning up like man flesh that falls on the coals, for indeed, its mere touch would mean your death. But our Master has other plans. He intends to find a dog from among the mortals and to twist him to do our bidding. That mortal will take up the Great Valuable and use it at the proper time. Such a one could overcome the coming Champion of our cursed enemies. But the Great Valuable is not meant for you."

Mackadoo turned his stallion away. His sergeant pointed a gloved hand at Pibbibib. "I am watching you worms," he glared. "Count on it."

As their master rode off, Pibbibib drew his sword and plunged it into the earth. "Now I begin to understand," he told Weakling. "At last I see how The Powers have come upon me."

"You are mad!" Weakling replied.

"No, I am a true master of fortune! Remember what happened that day on the mountain when I chased the Horse Stalker? I followed him, but she blocked my way. And she unsheathed the little light of fire and let it blaze before me."

"I remember your story," Weakling said, "And I remember that she easily could have killed you had she wanted to."

"Ah, curse your memory! Listen to me! On that day I beheld her power and it touched me. She used that power to push me back down the hill."

"What of it?"

"What of it?" Pibbibib growled. "Think, stupid. I came into the presence of her light and The Powers came upon me. Until now I did not know what had happened. But now I begin to understand."

"But Mackadoo said The Powers come from the Great Valuable that our Master desires."

"What does Mackadoo know? He said The Powers

remain a mystery. And he knows nothing of this little light of fire. Why should The Powers not come from her light, too, especially when she released its mighty force upon me? Why, it may exceed the benefit of standing in the presence of our Most Malevolent Master. He has not been near the Great Valuable for hundreds and hundreds of years. But I stood in the presence of her light less than two moons ago."

"And do you now think that you could take hold of the Great Valuable? Mackadoo says its touch would destroy you. And even if you survived, the Great Master does not wish you to hold it."

Pibbibib lowered his voice and drew close to his ally's ear. "What if I could take hold of it?" he asked confidentially. "Who would become the Great Master then?"

Weakling gave a look of horror. "That sort of talk will get us roasted alive!"

"Hush your voice and hear me," Pibbibib continued. "Perhaps the Great Master fears to ever touch the Great Valuable again. But despite his fear, he still may suspect that one of us could indeed take hold of it and become all powerful. Would this prospect not worry him? So, perhaps he scares all of us with tales of how we would surely die if ever we touched it. That way, we remain under his thumb, and he still can use one of the mortals as his puppet."

"But what if the old rumors ring true? Perhaps you would die if you touched the Great Valuable."

"What of it? I am not afraid! If I die, I die in a flame of glory. But if I take it in my hands and live, who could stand against me? I would reign over all. I would be Pibbibib no longer but would take a new name: Ekdonuk, Great One. And you would be my Number Two."

Weakling looked as if walls were closing in upon him. "I do not wish to be your Number Two," he whined. "I say we forget this talk and flee back to the hills. Please, let us run back to the high ground and hide in the caves."

"No. We shall never go back to the hills. We shall find the Horse Stalker. Perhaps he also has been touched by The Powers. We will eat his heart and take more power from him.

And we will not stop there. We will seek for the Great Valuable. If possible, I will clutch that wondrous force in these very hands. I will hold The Powers!"

PART TWO:

AMONG THE LAKE PEOPLE

Healdin

Introduction

The news of the Challenge of Orres reached many ears. Rumors soon spread of a Champion among the MuKierin, or at least one who would prepare the way for such a hero. The gossip stirred fear among the Elders. They grew even more worried when strangers from other clans arrived in Kierinswell and started asking about the Horse Stalker. Among them were members of a secret society that had long coveted the Golden Box and its mysterious contents. The society's members belonged to many clans, and their backers included men of considerable wealth and power.

One evening, two members of this society met west of Kierinswell in a village called the Stone Fences. The first man, bald and middle-aged, took a private room in the back of a squat adobe tavern there. The second man joined him shortly after sunset.

"Come sit by the fire," said the first man, his face set off in shadows as he sat in a stout chair. He spoke in the Common Tongue, which was used for speech between the clans. "We need no candles lit. Now, tell me the news."

The newcomer strode through the darkened room to an empty stool. He appeared about Roj's age but slighter in build and nearly a head shorter. His brown eyes glinted bright and boyish, and a trimmed goatee set off a handsome chin. Before he sat down, he repositioned his sword.

"The Horse Clan talks of nothing but the Challenge of Orres," the small one said, glancing at the fire's red embers. "The White Beard has outdone himself. Fat elders and toothless gray horse hunters and all sorts of malcontents want that old man's ear. But few can find him. And no one seems to know his next move."

"And what can you tell me of this MuKierin who won the Challenge of Orres?"

"Very little, it seems. Those who know him don't talk and those who talk don't really seem to know much about him. One thing is certain. The man has truly scared the Elders of the Horse Clan. They publicly dismiss him, but in secret they have sent out a hundred spies to look for him. We sit next to such agents in the taverns. We slyly question them, and they do the same to us until we realize that we're sniffing for the same scent. But no one seems able to say what became of the man."

"Even so, this news will please our benefactors," said the other man. "It appears that the old tales are true, and the MuKierin really are our best link to finding the Golden Box and the great power that lies within it. But, tell me, what do the old tales say about this Horse Stalker? Will this man know how to find our treasure?"

"Some of the old MuKierin say 'yes.' Some say 'no.' All merely guess. The old tales do speak of such a man riding a Spotted Stallion to a land of shining waters. But no one knows more. Some say this man is the coming Champion. Some say he plays some other role. In any case, we dare not ignore him. The Dark Brood certainly is looking for this horse hunter, too. We cannot let those villains take him first, especially if he could lead us to the Golden Box. But we must first answer this riddle: How will we find the man?"

"Oh, my friend, he must have kinsmen. Go back to Orres, the place where he won the stallion. Start there and make a careful search to learn all you can about this man and his people."

The newcomer rose slowly from his stool. "Very well," he said, "But some say he already has left the Horse Clan. Even his kin may not be able to find him."

"Even that could prove to our advantage," said the other. "We have good contacts among the other clans. And a MuKierin far from home would be a strange bird."

Chapter Twelve

Beyond the MuKierin

"I don't like this land."

Roj looked west across sagebrush plains that stretched out farther than he could see. To the southwest, he could make out distant mountains, but he wasn't headed toward them. "I don't like it," he repeated. "I like the hill country. You can hide in the hills, if you have to. Here, your enemies can see you coming for miles."

His listener, Jerli the horse trader, nodded as he pulled tight the cinch on his roan stallion. Behind him three wranglers were tying up thirty horses for the day's journey. The horses, including a dozen pack animals, were being tied together head to tail in two long strings in order to move more quickly across the flat lands.

"I never minded it," Jerli said. "I've crossed this ground for twenty years and never had a problem. We always stay far enough to the north that the Barsk don't bother us. And the Pappi like to stick close to the lake. The only folks you ever see out here are other horse traders like us. But we'll reach a spot with a hill tonight. You can hide there if you've a mind to."

"How long before we get to the lake?" Roj asked.

Jerli rubbed a short, gray beard. He was thin faced and his gray eyes could stop you in your tracks if he locked them on you. But whenever his blood started to rise, he seemed able to check himself and pull back from saying something he'd later regret. "We've got someplace to go before the lake," he said. "We'll get there tonight, complete a few chores and then push on to the Pappi."

Three nights before, Roj had joined in the raid on Wevol's horse farm. Afterward, Healdin had taken Roj's Spotted Stallion and ridden south. Her aim was to lure away Pibbibib, who could not only track the stallion but also could sense the power from Healdin's great light, Mara the Vine. Once she was sure the Backstabber could no longer follow her, she planned to free the Stallion in the hills above Kierinswell and then rejoin Roj. The Horse Stalker, meanwhile, had turned west from Wevol's farm and traveled with the King's servants to this camp. Jerli and his wranglers had arrived last night. The campsite had no well, and the party was getting low on water. But the horse trader didn't seem concerned.

Even as the wranglers prepared to move that morning, Roj was still trying to make sense of things. "You're not like Wevol," he said to Jerli. "He's also a horse trader, but he's probably never been to the lake."

"Different end of the business," said Jerli. "Wevol trades with the horse hunters out in the back country. He gathers up the wild colts and fillies, and then his people break 'em. Then I buy 'em and take 'em to the Pappi. They like their horses trained. These here will satisfy them just fine."

"So you're the man to help me escape from my own country."

"You won't draw much attention coming with me," said Jerli, "as long as you don't go looking for trouble. My job is to help get you settled over there among the Pappi. I know a trader who lives on the lake. I think I can get him to take you in. Later, the Lady Healdin can join you there."

"What about the Dark Brood? Won't they be there, too?"

"No, we won't find them where we're going. The White Beard says that the King's warriors chased them off the lake a long, long time ago. There was a big fight. The bad ones took a licking, and the King has kept them away ever since."

"Well, I don't see how going there helps me change the future."

"Don't know about that. My job is to get you away from here and to keep you alive until the lady comes. Somebody else can take it from there."

The party headed west with the horses strung out in

line and plodding across the sandy soil. Every hour or so Jerli dismounted and walked stiffly beside his stallion. The sky was clear, but the autumn day stayed cool enough that they didn't have to halt for long in the afternoon.

Eventually they veered northwest off the regular trail. By evening they came to a small valley. Jerli led the party along the eastern slope to a place where a well had been dug beside a rock outcrop. Roj looked west and beheld the sun sinking behind a sharp-faced hill on the other side of the valley. Jerli noticed and said, "I'm going to take you over there before we leave this place. I need to show you something on the top of that hill. But first we've got a job to do here in morning."

"What job?" Roj asked.

"A little digging. I'll show you in the morning. Right now we've got to make camp, water the stock and get supper cooking. Come on, you can help me draw water."

Jerli took a cloth bucket on a rope and led Roj to the outcrop. "The King's own dug this well ten years ago," he said. "The White Beard calls this place Newell. He says this is good ground. Nobody claims it, not the Pappi nor the Barsk nor the MuKierin. We're in the no-man's land on the northern edge of civilization. The White Beard brought me here when this well was first dug. He pointed north and said, 'If you could ride far enough in that direction, you would reach the Green Lands of the King. Imagine what it would be like to look upon that ground.' Of course, you and I would die of thirst if we ever tried to go there alone. We don't know the way. There are only a few wells in that wasteland, and we probably couldn't find any of them. Even so, the King's servants can cross back and forth there. You'll see."

The men ate by a small fire as darkness settled over the desert. They went to bed early and the wranglers took turns in the saddle watching the herd of tired, hungry horses. The night passed quietly, and Jerli didn't rouse his wranglers or Roj until well after sunrise. While the men were eating jerky for breakfast, the horse trader dug into a small depression near the well and found a cache of grain for the horses.

"Is this the digging job you mentioned?" Roj asked.

Jerli smiled. "Nah, you won't get off that easy. No, I waited until morning to uncover this for the horses. We'll feed them and try to keep them from wandering off."

After breakfast, the wranglers gathered round a worn blanket and pulled out cups to play pebble dice. But Jerli came to Roj and handed him a small shovel, a pick and a small metal bar. Together they climbed up the rise from camp. They came to a place where the ground leveled out in a great circle. Jerli stepped into the center and pointed to the earth. "This looks good," he said.

Roj frowned. "This reminds me of working as a boy with my grandfather," he said. "He would never tell me what we were about to do."

"It's pretty simple. You're going to dig with the pick and shovel."

"Yes, that much I've figured out. But what am I digging for, buried treasure?"

"Not exactly. Today we're going to bury a treasure. And you're going to get the honor of helping."

Reluctantly Roj began to cut into the earth. It was slow going at first because he needed to clear away a tough desert bush with roots that didn't easily succumb to the pick or shovel. Finally it gave way and he started digging in earnest. After about a half hour, he turned to Jerli and pointed to a hole that could hold a small trunk or box. The older man shook his head. "Bigger," he said. Roj frowned and returned to his work. After a while, he had carved a hole big enough to set two young boys into the earth side by side. Again he looked up for a sign. "Bigger," the horse trader said. Roj wiped his brow and grabbed the pick in order to carve loose a new section of earth. Jerli came up with a water skin and handed it to him. The younger man took two long drinks and passed it back.

"If it wasn't for this great honor," Roj said, "I could do without all this digging."

Jerli nodded appreciatively. "Of course you could, Horse Stalker. But this honor is all yours and you still have a lot of digging to do."

Roj went back to work, cutting through the hard earth with a pick and then flinging the broken clods away with the shovel. After another hour he had made a hole big enough to fit a bed for a man and his wife. Jerli smiled approvingly. "That's pretty good," he said. "You've made the hole big enough. Now, make it a little deeper."

The sun had passed its high point in the sky when Roj noticed the horse trader hiking to the top of the rise. Wearily, the younger man climbed out of his hole and trudged up after him. When Roj drew near, he spotted a pack train in the distance, winding through the sage. He counted a dozen riders and perhaps twice as many pack animals, mostly mules by the looks of them. Mules were rare in the Dry Lands and few MuKierin used them. Roj distrusted their nature.

Jerli straightened himself and announced, "Our guests will be here soon. I better go check on your excavation. We wouldn't want to disappoint them."

Together the two men walked back down the slope. Roj dropped into his hole. It now was nearly waist deep. The older man nodded silently and turned away. *At least he didn't say, 'Deeper,'* thought Roj. His arms felt like they would ache all night.

Down the hill came the pack train. Three warriors with spears rode in front. But most of the others weren't clad in armor. They wore brown tunics and carried no weapons. One such servant trotted up astride a black mule to Roj. A small beard adorned his thin face, and the long brown hair on his head was pulled into a ponytail. He looked down to inspect Roj's labors. "Good hole," he declared in MuKierin.

Roj forced a smile.

The rider motioned, and other servants led a pack mule to the hole. It was carrying two large sacks, tied up in canvas and lashed to the pack saddle. Four servants, two on each side, carefully lowered the two sacks off the mule and placed them in the hole. Roj helped them untie the bundles and pull away the outer canvas. Inside was a great sack made of thinner canvas, sewn at the top. One of the servants cut loose the great thread that had closed the sack and kicked it down. Out fell loose clumps of rich, dark soil.

Roj turned to Jerli. "Did you have me dig out this hole just so they could fill it back in with more dirt?" he asked.

"You might say that," the horse trader replied. "Just watch. You'll learn something."

In all, the servants unloaded bags of soil from ten mules. All of it went into Roj's hole. After the sacks were emptied, the King's servants took shovels and filled the sacks with the dirt dug from the hole. They laid these newly filled sacks off to the side. The workers leveled off the new soil and then made a new hole in the center of it. Roj watched and wondered as the eleventh mule approached. On its right side a small vine was lashed to the animal. Gently the servants removed it and carried it to the plot of new soil. With care they lowered the vine's roots into the hole. One servant held it straight as others filled in the dirt and pounded two long poles on opposite sides of it. They lashed the vine to the poles and tied to its small trunk four guide ropes, which they spread out and connected to four small stakes.

Roj beheld the vine, which reached almost to his shoulder. Its branches were bare but its gray bark seemed to give off a slight luster.

"They call this vine Ta Ellowyn," Jerli said. The White Beard says the name means 'the Living Fire.' It grows in the Green Lands. The King's people there make a golden elixir from it, which they also call Ta Ellowyn."

"Why are they planting it here?" asked Roj.

"They're preparing this place as a refuge for the future Champion and his followers. The vine can help in time of need. And the new soil makes this ground a part of the Green Lands. Those who live here will be Greenlanders. And you helped prepare the ground, so you can become one, too."

"What's a Greenlander?"

"That's someone whose home is in the far north with the King. The Lady Healdin is a Greenlander. The Stone

Woman and Kierin became Greenlanders, too. They never got out of this desert, but they looked forward to a day when their offspring would make it to the King's land."

"Are you a Greenlander, Jerli?"

The horse trader tilted his head and smirked at the notion. "Yeah, I guess I am. I may not ever get there, but I'd sure like to ride among its great forests and look out on that blue sea. If I don't make it, maybe you'll dip your toes in that cold saltwater for me."

That night the King's servants stayed and prepared freshly killed chicken, plus onions and bread they baked over the fire. The wranglers and the Greenlanders sat close together at the base of the hill. Overhead the stars shone brightly and a sliver of moon hung above the western sky. After dinner one of the King's servants arose and brought a small cup to Roj. "I bring you a taste of Ta Ellowyn, a droplet set in this warm tea," he said. "Will you take it, Greenlander?"

Roj hesitated. "Is it strong?" he asked.

"If you drink it, perhaps you will see visions. Today you prepared a place for the Living Fire. Tonight the Living Fire may provide understanding for your journey."

Roj nodded silently and accepted the cup. The brew steamed and tasted sweet like honey. At his first sip he felt his skin tingle and his mouth slacken. At once he set the cup down. His tongue went numb and his eyes began to go dark. He leaned back and felt his head come to rest upon his blanket. For a moment all seemed black. Then, almost from the corner of his eye, came a vision of horses, wild ones dashing madly over the plains. And a band of young MuKierin galloped after them. Roj couldn't recognize them, but he felt that one of his close relatives was riding among them. Soon the riders passed over the horizon. Darkness returned until a new vision appeared. This time, Roj beheld a train of slaves, shackled and tied together on one long rope. They seemed to be MuKierin, and they stumbled wearily, perhaps on their way to the mines or to other lands. Into view came a young man to block the slave caravan. Guards drew swords and ran forward to oppose the newcomer. The man lifted what appeared to be a staff. First, one guard and then another fell at its mere touch. On its tip sat a shiny object, but not something as sharp as a spear point. Instead, it seemed somewhat rounded. The second vision faded and a third one emerged in Roj's mind. It took place on a mountain at night, and a man was standing trial before black-robed men. And a group of men took the accused and beat him.

Roj found himself weeping. The third vision faded and the fourth and final one appeared. Again it seemed to take place at night; again a hilltop rose in the distance. But this time there was a face that Roj recognized. It was Noli. His hands were chained, and men with swords surrounded him. They stood on a mountain. Roj sensed that they were looking for something. Then a pillar of fire rose up from the hilltop. The light seemed blinding. And Noli began to run away.

Roj wept again until he felt the sorrow give way to weariness and the weariness give way to slumber. If he dreamed the rest of that night, he remembered none of it. The next morning he opened his eyes and gazed around in the early light. He found himself on the ground covered with many blankets and a sleeping cap on his head. Jerli sat nearby, staring into the fire. All the King's servants had vanished. Roj raised himself on one elbow and called, "Where did they go?"

"Back to their home in the Green Lands. They left before dawn. How did you sleep?"

"I'm not sure. I had some strange visions last night. What do you think they mean?"

"You're asking the wrong fellow. It's time for you to get up. You better grab a bite to eat. I've got something to show you."

As the wranglers gathered the horses, Jerli and Roj rode across the flats toward the nearby hilltop. It rose steadily on its right and left flanks, but its front presented a face too steep for men on horseback. Jerli turned left to make the ascent. Broken rock and small bushes adorned the slope before them. The men often stood in the stirrups in order to help their horses climb, but the animals found good footing and chugged steadily to the top. There the horse trader dismounted and began to scan the ground for some landmark. Roj watched him, but he could see nothing out of the ordinary on the hilltop. Nonetheless, he made sure his stallion followed carefully in the older man's track.

"What are you looking for?" Roj asked.

"There are three rocks out here that look like men's heads. I need to find them." A few moments later he called out, "Yes, here they are. Climb down, son. I've got something to show you." Roj obeyed and came up beside the horse trader. Jerli pointed to three rocks grouped together with a bare spot in their midst. "Now pay attention," he said. "Buried in between these rocks is a bag holding clay vials filled with power."

"What kind of power?"

"I'll explain that in a moment. Now come over here." He led Roj over to a second clump of smaller rocks a few paces away. He bent down beside them and began to dig with his fingers in the loose earth. Soon his hands managed to grab hold of what looked like a root. It wasn't. A moment later Jerli lifted up some sort of cover over a hole. Roj helped tilt it up. The cover was made of skin and tied to a small frame of wood. The older man pulled it completely up and said, "Go ahead. Have a look inside." Roj bent down and peered into the rectangular hole. It looked like a grave, except it was considerably deeper and a little wider.

"What is it?"

"It's a fire chamber. The King's servants put it here. We're standing on one of their signal mounts. Here's how it works. If you take one of the clay vials back at those rocks and fling it down into the chamber, the vial will break and a great fire will leap up out of this chamber. Don't ask me how it works, but those vials contain one powerful potion from the King's land. One vial will unleash a blast of fire fifty feet above this chamber. It'll roast your brain if you get too close to it, so be careful with those vials. And you have to shield your eyes from the blast or it can blind you. The base of this chamber is lined with a rock pavement in order to break the vials. Once you send up a pillar of fire into the night sky, the King's servants will see it and come to the rescue. Do you understand?"

"I think so, but why are you showing me this?"

Jerli went to his saddle bag and removed a cylindrical leather case designed for holding scrolls. "The White Beard made this map for you. Take it. It shows the path to this mountain from the Great Lake of the Pappi. Each year you're supposed to come here and water the vine that we planted across the valley. All it needs is one good drink each summer and it will thrive here. You're to come here once each year until the Champion appears in the land of the MuKierin. And every time you come, you should camp up here on this hilltop. If you're ever in danger, you'll grab a vial and send up a pillar of fire as a signal for help. Do you understand?"

"Yes, I do. But now let's get off this mountain. I don't like this place. Last night I had a vision of a mount and a pillar of fire."

"Did you?" asked Jerli, his eyes keen with interest. "We better remember that. And you'd better remember to shield your eyes."

Chapter Thirteen

Longing on the Mountain

Baern the trader had set aside the morning to go fishing. Certainly he didn't need the fish. He could buy all the scaly creatures he ever wanted from those who made their living on the boats. But he was Pappi, a child of the Lake Clan. He had fished since boyhood, and no one ever thought it strange for a Pappi man to go fishing. More than that, he never tired of the hours he spent on the vast blue waters of his homeland. The quiet he found there comforted him. So on an overcast morning, he and a servant shoved off from shore in a long, narrow boat made of reeds.

The Pappi considered the reeds of their land almost as dear as the lake itself. The people fashioned the reeds into boats and baskets. Indeed, their woven baskets had become some of the most valued artistry in the Dry Lands. Leaders from all the Seven Clans prized Pappi baskets, especially those decorated with intricate designs of dark and light patterns. Traders from every clan came to the lake for Pappi baskets and dried fish.

Baern had taken over the family trading business from his father, a thin old man who still lived with his son on the eastern edge of the Great Lake. The wealthiest Pappi traders lived several miles across the water at South Shore, the chief village of the clan. There, the lake's outlet poured forth into the canyon of the Red River, the main waterway of the Dry Lands. It flowed south for nearly two hundred miles before dying in a wasteland known as the Salt Marshes. The South Shore traders dealt mostly with the Barsk and with the southern clans. But Baern's father had chosen the eastern shore and built up his business with the Horse Clan. For years, MuKierin traders had come from the east, bringing fast horses in exchange for woven baskets and other wares. These MuKierin traders looked to the Pappi to serve as the middlemen who gathered goods from the southern clans. In general, the lake people weren't known for their horse sense, but a few traders had become learned about the animals. Indeed, Baern's father still fancied himself a much better judge of horseflesh than his son.

Baern had silver hair tied in a pony tail, and the broad, pale face of his late mother. Like her, he had a smile that often appeared almost beatific, and yet this day he was hardly at peace inside. For weeks he had been expecting someone, and he didn't like to wait. To ease his mind, he went fishing. It reminded him of his boyhood when his father taught him to hoist a sail and to read the winds that rushed over the lake when dark clouds filled the skies. All his life he had found solace on the water.

This morning he made his catch and returned home with his servant. As his boat approached shore, he spotted a large herd of horses coming up the main road from the south. His heart fluttered, and he fought to check his emotions. Leaving behind his catch, he climbed out of the reed vessel and trudged up to the top of the bank. Soon the horses and their keepers arrived. Among them he spotted a familiar face, Jerli the MuKierin.

"Hello, my friend," Jerli said in his fractured Pappi. "I am here. I keep my promise."

Baern tried to give his best gentle smile. "Have you brought guests?" he asked.

"Yes, this one. He is Roj." He turned to Roj and said in MuKierin, "This is my friend, Baern."

The men nodded formally. Jerli climbed off his horse and greeted Baern the Pappi way by putting his two hands together and placing them atop Baern's joined hands. "Let us talk," Jerli said.

The wranglers took the horses to a series of corrals made of bundled sticks with stone columns at the corners. Meanwhile, Roj and Jerli followed Baern to the center of his estate. It lay on a rise above the lake. There stood a two-story, stone structure. It contained a trading house and the master living quarters. Nearby was a paved courtyard surrounded by raised stone flowerbeds. The estate included a dozen adobe servant huts, plus several barns and storage sheds. On a slope above the courtyard grew a large garden and beyond that a vineyard, evidence that this land had plenty of water. Roj took it all in as he followed his host into a courtyard. Beside the path leading to Baern's office sat a small, stone sculpture: a water dragon with great fangs and a long jagged tail. Roj stared with wonder upon it. Then he noticed a servant looking sternly at him. The man was about Roj's age. *That one looks MuKierin,* Roj thought. *He has my features, even if he dresses like a Pappi.*

Inside the trading office, Baern and Jerli stood on opposite sides of a stone counter. Baern served his guests small cups of tea. "I bring you twenty good horses," Jerli said in Pappi.

"What else did you bring me?" Baern asked, looking at Roj.

Jerli smiled. "You and I must ride together. I must show you something."

"When you last visited me, you said that a king was preparing to make his move in the Dry Lands. Is this young man part of those plans?"

"Yes."

"Tell me more."

"Come with me tomorrow and you will learn much. We will help you take the horses as far as the north shore of the lake."

"I will need the headman's blessing to take foreigners north with me."

"As you say."

Baern's father entered the office from his adjoining bedroom. "Who are these foreigners?" he asked gruffly, coughing hoarsely. His eyes flashed when he recognized one of the visitors. "Ah, Jerli. Did you bring me more horses that waddle like ducks?"

"Hello, good friend," he said, and he gave the old, bald man the double-handed greeting of the Pappi. "Come ride my horses. You will fly like a goose skimming over the water."

"No, my friend," the father replied. "My days in a saddle are over, but not in a boat. I will be buried on the waters in my boat." Again he coughed.

"May you live long, father," Jerli said.

Baern spoke. "Father, tomorrow I will take the new horses that Jerli has brought me around the lake to The Sisters. Jerli and his men will come as least part of the way with me. I will be sure to get Circ the Headman's permission."

"See that you do," his father replied. "And have Jerli be careful if he goes to The Sisters. That town does not love foreigners the way I do."

Baern exited his office and signaled to his MuKierin servant. The man came quickly, as if he had expected the call, and he looked sternly at the visitors. Jerli told Roj, "This is Tie, Baern's servant. Go with him, and he'll show you where we'll sleep the night. I'll be along later."

Roj and the servant exited and walked up to the packhorse that held Roj's gear. They led it to a series of huts that housed the estate's servants. "You're MuKierin," Roj said, "even though you don't wear the black stone on your chest. What are you doing among the fishers?"

"I am a slave," said Tie, "My own people sold me into slavery. I don't need such kinsmen, and I don't wear their stones."

Roj's eyes flared. "You never should have been sold to foreigners. That's against our law."

"MuKierin law means nothing here."

"Nonetheless, something ought to be done."

"Not by you. Stay out of this, if you value your own life."

They unpacked the horse and led it back to the corrals, passing again by the stone water dragon. "Do such creatures really live in the lake?" Roj asked.

"No. The ones in the lake are far fiercer than this one. Their claws cut like swords. And they love to eat the children of the Stone Woman."

Roj frowned. *This is one hard MuKierin.*

Early the next morning, Roj got up and went to check on the horses. Later, he walked to the lake and beheld a great mist rising off the water, even as the sun began to rise in the pale eastern sky. A few fishing boats skimmed across the lake's surface about a stone's throw offshore. Along the bank, the trader's servants were loading a larger vessel for the day's trip across the lower end of the lake to the South Shore.

"Do you fear the water?" a voice called. Roj turned and saw Tie, the MuKierin slave.

"Of course," said Roj. "I've never seen anything like it. And I know nothing about boats."

"Why would you? You're MuKierin, and you have lived your life sleeping by wells, not beside such a vast and brooding lake, this giver of life and death. When the wind howls off the mountains, the waters rise and fall in waves that will swamp any boat that these fishers can build. And the lake's bottom is so deep that you would drown long before you ever touched the bottom."

"And it has fierce dragons, doesn't it?"

Tie smiled. "That's what the Pappi will tell you. Dragons guard their homes and ride upon their war banners when they march into battle. The dragons represent the Pappi's fierceness. Perhaps there are dragons, perhaps not. I have never seen one. But they will fight like dragons to hold onto their lake."

"Well, I won't take it from them," Roj said. "I don't want it."

"Then why did you come here, horse boy? Are you running from something?"

"I want to become a horse trader. I need to learn the ways of the Pappi in order to do business with them."

"That's too bad," said Tie. "If you were running from the MuKierin, then I would help you. If I could do something to hurt the MuKierin, I would do it."

"You're a hard man, Tie."

"I was put in chains and taken where I didn't want to

163

go. You try that and see what it does for you."

In mid-morning Baern got on his horse and left his estate with Jerli, Roj and the wranglers. Baern also brought along his slave, Tie. The party took the string of horses along the lake's eastern shore. They rode north on a main road with scarcely a turn in it. Along the way they passed a few large estates, each with clusters of mud huts for the servants. They entered a village, and Roj saw men butchering a hoisted hog. The workers stopped to give grim looks to the strangers. Roj noticed that Baern waved a hand at the men in greeting, but Jerli didn't look up from the road.

Beyond the village they came to a small stone fortress that reached into the lake. On the water a boat seemed to be making for a dock or entrance on the far side of the compound, but it was hidden behind high walls. Jerli and Baern stopped, and the MuKierin motioned for his wranglers to wait outside. "Roj, stay with Tie and the horses," Jerli said. He dismounted and walked with Baern to the main gates of Circ the Headman.

Roj dismounted and made his way toward a half-dozen boats pulled up on a small beach nearby. A few fishermen knelt beside the vessels and cleaned their nets. Roj wanted to take a closer look, but he wasn't sure how the fishers would react.

Tie came up to him. "The Pappi have a saying: Never have more wives than boats. They live by that rule. They love their boats, even when they have a cold heart for their wives."

Together the two men ventured a few steps closer. Roj noticed the boats seemed to look the same in the front and the back. The top of each side had a curved gunwale, which also was made of reeds. "How do they make the boats?" he wondered.

"Never ask a Pappi that question," said Tie. "Never. They hold that secret close to their hearts. They don't want their enemies to ever build vessels. That way they can always rule the water. I have lived with the Pappi for years, and they would never tell me their secrets. A foreigner might be deemed worthy to buy a boat, but never to make one.

"Even so, horse boy, you can learn something by what you see here. For these boats the builders formed long bundles of reeds about the thickness of a man's upper leg. They tied these bundles together into two groups, one for each side, and then used other bundles to link the two groups. Then they beat the sides into the desired shape, and they interwove the two groups at the bow and stern."

"What a wonder," said Roj.

"Yes, but it's a short-lived wonder. After a few years the bottom rots out and then you need another boat."

"Even so, I'd like to ride in one some day."

Baern and Jerli emerged from the fortress with a Pappi man. He was lean with a dour face and a pointy chin, and he wore a black robe. He stopped when he saw Roj and stared sternly at him. Roj remembered Jerli's reaction with the hog butchers, so he kept his eyes down. A moment later the black robe turned and disappeared.

"Who was that?" Roj asked.

"The headman's steward," said Tie. "Don't get him mad at you. You're Baern's guest, but you don't want to get on his bad side."

Jerli smiled at Roj. "We've got the blessing to ride north," he said. "But first we're going up into those eastern hills. Let's go." The horsemen left the fortress and rode off into the barren, dun-colored hills that stretched out along the lake. Behind the hills rose several mountains, including Mount Jerol, a cone-shaped peak that jutted high above all lake country. Roj imagined it in winter with a crown of snow.

In the midst of the hills they halted in a little valley. There, Jerli had his wranglers make camp. "Baern and I are going up on this mountain for the night," the horse trader told Roj. "I want Tie and you to camp up on top of that hilltop over there. We'll be back in the morning."

"I don't want to stay with Tie. Why can't I ride on with you?"

"Baern wants somebody to stick with his servant. Tie's not ready for what Baern's going to see tonight. But Baern wants him nearby. So that's the compromise."

165

Roj felt annoyed. "Why do I have to do things your way? When do I get a say in things?"

Jerli nodded. "Fair enough. When I come down from the mountain, I will have done all that I can for you. Then we'll do things your way."

"I'll hold you to that," vowed Roj.

The wranglers camped with the herd below, while the foursome took their horses and ascended a slope covered with scrub brush. When at last they reached a flat stretch of ground, Baern and Jerli left behind the younger men. Roj and Tie set up camp while the two traders rode further up the mountain.

"I see that you're my keeper," Tie said as he gathered sticks for a fire. "Will you make sure that I don't run away?"

"I'd love nothing better than for you to run off," said Roj. "Do you want me to point the way home?"

"I wouldn't go home. I'd escape around the lake to The Sisters."

"The Sisters? I thought that was where Baern was taking you."

"That's where Baern is taking the horses," said Tie. "I'll go there if the horse trader and you go there, too. Otherwise, I'll go back with you to Baern's estate. Then Baern would take as many horses as he can handle and go there by himself. The rest of the horses would go back with us. Baern would take the other horses with him another day."

"How will he get home?"

"He's going to sail back home. He already has made plans to send one of his large vessels to The Sisters to pick him up. And it's big enough to hold all of us."

"But you wouldn't need to sail back," said Roj. "You'd run off and escape when we turned our backs on you. And I wouldn't blame you."

"No. You don't run off empty-handed in this country. That's a good way to get caught and have the Pappi whack off a few of your fingers or toes. No, I'll make a better plan than that if I ever do escape. Even so, I'd like to go there and see the sights and go back on the boat."

166

"I'd like to take the boat trip, too," Roj said as he sat down on a small boulder. "But what's so special about The Sisters?"

"I've never been there. But they say it's a wild, unruly place. It's a city that trades with the Quolli, the nomads out in the west lands. They're a wild people. If you're going to become an expert trader, you ought to see it for yourself."

"Maybe I will. I might be stuck in this land for a while. I sure don't want to stay cooped up at Baern's place the whole time. And I do want a ride in a boat."

"Of course, Jerli may not want to go to The Sisters. He may say you have to go back to Baern's."

"Maybe he'll do what I say," said Roj.

Up the mountain, the sun was drawing low when Baern and Jerli reached a long, treeless ridge that looked down upon the lake. Below them the deep blue water spread out for miles. The two men dismounted among sparse shrubs and low boulders. "You have a good land," said Jerli, casting his arm about. "It is a land of much water. Many want your land and your water. They will try to take it from you."

"The Barsk have tried before," said Baern. "But we still rule the blessed waters."

"Yes, but you pay tribute to them. You bribe them each year with fish and slaves."

"We compensate them for past war injuries. It is complicated, but it is a way to keep the peace."

"You pay tribute to the Barsk. The Barsk pay tribute to the Dark Brood. But Equis still seeks your land. Only the Good King and his people stand in their way."

"So you say," said Baern.

The two men sat in silence as the dusk settled in around them. Already dark shadows were spreading below them along the edges of the lake. Baern looked east and was unprepared for what he saw. A great company of riders was coming toward them along the top of the ridge. A few moments later he heard a piper begin to play a sweet dirge. The pipe soon died down and a woman's voice pierced the air. As she sang, the hair stood up on the back of Baern's neck. Here came words that the trader had never heard, but a melody that he seemed to recall from childhood. The song was simple, and yet it rose and fell in ways that pricked his heart. Then several instruments joined in, horns that sounded like tamed bulls, a flute that sang like the loveliest bird's call, and then strings that seemed too ethereal for this world. A small gong crashed and suddenly came a great chorus. The company's horses seemed to step livelier. Baern could see that every rider was either singing or playing an instrument. They had released their reins and were focused solely on their music.

Who are they? Baern wondered. *What do they want of me?* On they came. The trader could see now that the women seemed his height or a little taller, but the men appeared much bigger—at least a head and shoulder above him. A few of the men wore armor of tanned leather and some women wore breastplates of silver mesh over white gowns. These warriors carried long spears or bows with quivers of arrows. But most of the company appeared to be minstrels. The riders dismounted and approached the two men. A woman with golden hair and a velvet green gown came and touched Baern's hand and placed within it a small flower, a red blossom with a fragile green leaf. Baern couldn't hold back a smile, but to himself he wondered, *Are they lake fairies? Have they come for me?*

Though he often tried, Baern could not conjure again the wonder that fell on him that night. The singers sang almost until dawn, wrapping their Pappi guest in a great fur robe when the dark grew cold. As Baern grew weary, the musicians returned to the first melody, only this time he understood some of the words:

> Oh, my heart feels a longing
> For a home I can't see;
> 'Tis a yearning that beckons
> To a lost destiny.

From the heights of the mountains,
From the depths of the sea;
Comes a voice that is calling,
Yes, it's calling to me.

And my heart burns with fire
And my soul feels the flame;
For it sings in the silence,
And it calls me by name.

Baern fell asleep to the music. He awoke the next morning to find the company gone. Only Jerli remained beside him.

"Who were they?" Baern asked, still wrapped in the robe.

"They belong to the King," Jerli answered. "I brought you to meet them so you could see their power and their beauty. They are good, Baern. And they have sworn to protect Roj. Will you help them?

"Why do they need to protect him?"

"The Dark Brood wishes to kill him. The old tales say he can change the future. I do not know how he can do this. But the bad ones hate him and search for him. Even so, the King's favor rests upon him. There is a great woman who will come soon to your home. Her power can withstand the Dark Brood. She can watch over the young man and you and all who live with you. I trust her, Baern. I trust her with my life."

"Will you stay with the boy until she comes?" Baern asked.

"Yes, for you I will stay."

"If you will stay, I will meet the woman and speak with her. I hate the Dark Brood. But I do not want to be crushed by them. I must know more before I promise to risk too much for this young man."

"Baern, you are my friend, as is your father," said Jerli. "Thank you. The woman will come. You can test her. She will not fail you. But I beg you to watch over the young one, no matter what happens to me. The fate of Pappi and

MuKierin and all the desert clans may rest with him."

In the early morning light the two men rode down the slope and joined Roj and Tie. The wranglers already were making ready for the day. Jerli went to Roj and said, "Baern's going now to take some horses on to The Sisters. What do you say we ride back to his place and wait for his return?"

"I'd rather go to The Sisters with him," Roj replied.

Jerli frowned. "Well, that's a tough place. They don't like foreigners there, especially MuKierin."

"Have you ever been there?"

"Yes, once when I was young and stupid."

"Well, you said we would do things my way when you came down the mountain. I figure I ought to see a little of this country and learn about its people. And I say we go with Baern. I want to ride on that boat back home."

Jerli nodded soberly. "We'll do it your way," he said. "But I'm sending my boys back to wait for us at Baern's place. I've got to watch out for them, too."

So it was decided: Baern, Tie, Roj and Jerli would continue on to The Sisters while the wranglers would return to Baern's estate. Jerli and Roj sent their own stallions back with the other horsemen, and rode forth on two horses from the herd. All those animals would be sold at the town, and the four men would return by boat to Baern's estate.

The land on the lake's north edge was bare and desolate, and Baern's group made good time passing over it. The four men reached The Sisters by late afternoon. The town was built on a bluff above a long cove, with two prominent hills behind it. The region's headman had a fortress standing on a nearby point. The fortress at The Sisters extended into the lake. From the distance Roj could see boats entering and leaving by water through a gate built into the fortress wall. Guardsmen stood atop the wall near both the land and the water gates.

Baern went directly to the headman and quickly sold him all the horses. The Pappi leaders were seeking more mounts for their cavalry. The MuKierin steeds were greatly prized and would serve soldiers well. Baern next turned to the town's trading houses. He wanted rope and pots, spices and woven baskets. Baern took his slave and his two MuKierin companions from the fortress to the town. There was plenty of time to look around. Roj stood beneath a canopy outside one trader's shop and gazed in wonder at the Pappi baskets. Afterward, he spotted Jerli off to one side with Tie. The horse trader was speaking forcefully to the slave, not angrily, but in a way that Roj could see was heartfelt. *What's he saying?* Roj wondered.

In late afternoon they returned to the fortress with a score of shop servants toting all sorts of goods. Baern was invited to dine that night with the headman. Roj was happy to hear it. "That leaves us free to look around," he told Jerli.

"Tie and I will go with you," the horse trader replied. "Let's just try to stick together."

The three men ventured forth that night to find scores of tents and booths set up near the beach below the town. Quolli traders had arrived from the south, and had brought along drummers to draw a crowd. Not wanting to miss out, many of the Pappi merchants had joined the bazaar. A large campfire burned on the edge of the gathering. Roj led the way among the booths. He found one with shells and beads and stones. *Remy would like these,* he thought as he looked at a red necklace. *What about Healdin? Would these interest her? I guess not. She may be a woman, but her country probably has far greater gems and stones.*

The Quolli drummers grew silent for a few moments and then pounded their drums to roar like thunder. Three female dancers appeared near the fire. Roj and his companions gathered there among the crowd. The drummers began a slower syncopated beat, keeping their volume slightly lower than they had for most of the evening. The dancers fluttered bare arms as sparks and burning embers rose in the night air. Roj circled around to get a better view. The people were converging, and he had to dodge and weave through the crowd. He stepped around a clump of bearded fishermen and almost ran into a young woman in a dark head scarf. Her eyes locked on his.

"MuKierin!" she exclaimed. "Help my friend!" She pointed uphill among the tents to a woman in the grip of a large man. "She MuKierin like you! Save her!"

Roj could see the man pulling the woman toward the tents. He immediately thought of slavers and kidnappers. "Hurry!" pleaded the woman near him. "Save her!"

Roj looked around and saw Jerli and Tie advancing from the other side of the fire ring. "Go to those two MuKierin," he told the woman. "Have them follow me."

The woman nodded and hurried off as directed. Roj turned to see the other woman being dragged around the corner of a row of tents. He rushed her way, but then slowed his pace. This was a bad town, he reminded himself, and he quickly might find himself facing more trouble than he could handle. He decided to advance just past the first tent. There he could keep sight of the kidnapper and still wait for Jerli and Tie to help him figure out the next move.

He came round the tent and immediately spotted the kidnapper and the woman. Out of the corner of his eye, he caught movement coming his way. The next thing he knew two strange men were upon him. One flashed a knife in front of his face. They grabbed him and pushed him forward after the man and the woman. Roj thought of resisting, but the hand with the knife was now resting against his ribs. He knew his abductors could kill him if he tried to struggle.

Hurriedly the men trotted up the rise and forced Roj into a tall tent lit by a single candle. Inside, he saw the same man and woman. The woman quickly stepped to the back of the tent. The man stepped forward and punched Roj in the gut. The young MuKierin doubled over. His attacker knocked him down and rolled him onto his stomach. Roj moaned as loud as he could. One of the other men came with a small leather-covered club and struck Roj on the back of the skull. "No talk!" the man barked. The other man quickly bound Roj's hands behind his back.

The woman exited the tent, but almost immediately she was propelled back inside, knocking down the two captors who stood over Roj. Jerli stormed in behind her with his knife drawn. The third kidnapper in the tent drew a blade and came at him. He sliced Jerli's arm, but the horse trader countered with a knife thrust into the man's leg. The kidnapper fell over wounded. Into this melee another woman was thrown in the tent—the same one who had first duped Roj. She landed on one of the male kidnappers, knocking him over for a second time. Behind her, came Tie. The slave quickly spotted Roj at his feet. He scooped up the young MuKierin and rushed back outside.

"Untie me!" Roj moaned. His hands were still bound behind him.

"No!" yelled Tie, who clutched him by the arm. "They'll catch us. Just run. Run!"

Jerli fought his way out of the tent and ran after his comrades. Two kidnappers gave chase and began to gain on him. Suddenly the horse trader swung round and lashed at his opponents with his knife. The movement caught the two men unprepared. One kidnapper tripped and fell. The other had to swing wide and retreat. Jerli stopped before them and backed slowly toward the beach. Then, he turned and ran for all he was worth.

At the water's edge sat several small reed boats. Tie came to the first one and quickly dropped Roj into the bow. He shoved the vessel into the lake, climbed in and began to paddle with a ferocity that would have matched any native-born Pappi. Out into the cove the boat raced.

"Where's Jerli?" Roj demanded. "We've got to go back and help him! Turn around!"

"No," said Tie. "We go back there and we're all dead men. Jerli told me to get you out of there."

"No!" screamed Roj. "Curse you, Tie! Turn around!"

Jerli reached the other boats and turned back to survey the beach. A gang was coming at him, followed by a crowd curious to see a fight. Jerli waded out into the water up to his shins and took up a spot between two of the beached boats. To his eyes, the gang members appeared to be Quolli. Some of them caught sight of Tie and Roj in the departing boat and sounded an alarm. Two men ran for the boats near the horse trader. When the first approached one and tried to step into its bow, Jerli came at him with his knife. The man pulled back and fell down in the water. The second man grabbed a paddle and swung it at Jerli. The horse trader ducked and grabbed the boat's other paddle. He flung it in the lake. Then he splashed over to the next boat and grabbed its two paddles. One he tossed into the water. The other he kept as a weapon.

The gang gathered nearby to strike, even as the onlookers began to inch back and watch from a safer distance. Through the crowd a Quolli man came limping, the same kidnapper Jerli had stabbed. He appeared to be the gang's leader, and he directed the others to spread out and encircle their enemy. As they did, the limping one drew a sword and came down the beach at Jerli. Alone in the water, the MuKierin backed up and waited between the boats until his opponent put both feet in the lake. Then Jerli charged with the paddle aimed directly in front of him. The leader cocked his sword and swung, knocking away the paddle. But Jerli lunged forward and plunged his knife into the man's chest. The leader toppled, mortally wounded. The other gang members stumbled over the boats and joined the fray. Jerli managed to fight his way back out into the water. Still the men came after him. Retreat seemed his only option. Suddenly the lake bottom dropped off and Jerli sank in. The gang members pulled up short. They couldn't swim. But neither could this foreigner. Jerli splashed helpless before them. The attackers began to laugh and cheer. The drowning man thrashed on the surface, sank and reappeared to take a great gasp of air. No one helped him. He continued to struggle until, at last, he sank and the water covered him.

On the boat, Tie navigated the vessel toward the back of the headman's compound. Roj kept yelling at Tie to turn back. "Listen to me," the slave said. "If you value our lives, you must quiet down. We soon will come to the fortress. The guards on the wall will be on edge from all that noise back there. Don't give them a reason to beat us or put us in chains. We need Baern to protect us, but first he must be brought to us. Hear me. We are not yet out of danger."

Tie drew the vessel close to the water gate. A guardsman on the wall barked out a warning. Tie stopped the boat and spoke in Pappi. After a brief exchange, the guard called out to others within the compound. More soldiers appeared on the wall, and Tie was peppered with more questions. He kept his answers as short and calm as possible. The two MuKierin stayed outside the walls until Baern appeared. The trader spoke to the guards and, at last, the iron water gate was raised. Tie paddled the small reed boat inside to a stone pier. There, Tie and the guards hauled up Roj, who was both bound and red-faced. Someone cut the cords off his hands. Baern and the head guardsman drew near.

Tie was ordered to translate. "My master wants to know what has happened," he said.

"Tell him we've got to go back for Jerli!" Roj angrily answered. "I've got to go back now!"

Tie gave the answer, then a longer explanation of all that had taken place. Baern and the head guardsman exchanged a few words, and the soldier left to make some preparations. Baern next spoke to Tie.

The slave told Roj, "My master says the soldiers will go look for Jerli. You and I must stay here. You are now among the Pappi. As a foreigner, you must do nothing to bring condemnation on us. My master will handle this matter."

Baern left the darkened pier. Roj cried to Tie, "What happened back there? Who were those men?"

"Most likely they were Quolli kidnappers. They make their money taking men and women and selling them into slavery. Around the lake they rarely try to kidnap a Pappi man or woman. That might get them arrested and put in chains. But they are quick to grab a foreigner like you or me. They knew that the Pappi wouldn't lift a finger to help you. They just didn't count on Jerli and me crashing in on them."

"What about that woman they kidnapped?"

"What woman?"

"There were two women. One said the other woman was a MuKierin who needed saving. I later saw that same

175

woman in the tent. I sent the first woman back to find you."

"They were both part of the gang. They were bait to lure you up away from the fire. The woman you sent to us tried to trick us and keep us from following you. But Jerli put a knife to her throat and made her come with us. And when we got close to the tent, he gave her to me and I threatened to kill her if she made a sound."

Roj winced at the realization that he had been conned. "So, have they kidnapped Jerli? Could he still be alive?"

"I don't think the horse trader would let them put chains on him. And he was fighting to keep the kidnappers from catching you and me. The more he cut them, the more they would want to kill him."

Roj dropped to his knees and cried. "We shouldn't have left him, Tie!" he moaned. "It wasn't right."

"It was what he wanted."

Roj looked up, amazed. "How do you know that?" he demanded.

Tie hesitated. "This afternoon he asked me to help him keep you alive. He said you're a special man. He told me that if you should die, so would my chances for freedom. And he promised me that one day I would be set free if I helped him save your life."

Roj's eyes flared with anger. "So you sacrificed his life for your freedom."

"No," said Tie. "The truth is he gave his life for you."

In the morning, the headman's steward gave Baern a report of what his soldiers and agents had learned. The kidnappers were Quolli, and they had slipped away soon after the fight. Jerli had fought and killed one of the gang before he drowned. The horse trader's body had yet to be found, but enough Pappi witnesses had confirmed the events that the steward felt sure that the MuKierin had not been kidnapped but had perished in the lake.

There was little for Roj to do that day but stand on the fortress wall and stare across the water. Baern's vessel had yet to arrive, and the trader had determined that they wouldn't leave The Sisters until Jerli's body was found. Baern forbade both Roj and Tie to leave the compound.

Jerli's corpse washed ashore the next morning. Baern and Tie went with the steward to retrieve the body. The trader paid to have it taken and buried in a graveyard on the edge of town. Roj again was ordered to remain at the fortress. Tie told him, "My master does not wish anyone to see your face." So Roj climbed the wall and watched as the Pappi master and slave set off to pay their last respects to the horse trader.

Baern's ship arrived late that afternoon. It was a reed vessel, more than thirty feet in length and fitted with a stout mast. The ship pulled up near the fortress to a stone pier that reached out into the lake. Soon its crew and a group of servants from the compound began to load it with the wares that Baern had purchased. Roj wanted to help, and the trader allowed him to take part, though not to go beyond the pier. Soon all the goods were stowed aboard and the crew cast off and anchored for the night in the waters near the fortress.

Late the next morning a breeze was stirring, and Baern was ready to leave The Sisters. The trader led Roj and Tie to the pier, where the vessel's crew awaited them. The crew members shoved off and hoisted its main sail. Two of them took long poles on either side of the vessel and pushed the boat out through the shallows. The wind caught the sail and propelled the boat into deeper water. Roj sat in the bow and watched the lake glide past. He soon turned and saw the town grow distant. The vessel plowed slowly along, laden with wares and passengers.

In the stern, Baern called to Tie. "When we return," he said, "you must help me speak to Jerli's wranglers. We must settle with them for the herd they brought to me."

Tie nodded and asked, "Master, what's so important about this stranger? Why would Jerli die for him?"

"I don't know. But you must help me try to learn more. I know that Jerli believed the young man was special, and he had asked me to help watch over him. But now Jerli's dead, and I'm left without answers. What does the stranger say about himself?

"He doesn't want to talk. I think he blames himself for

the horse trader's death."

"Well, let him be for now," said Baern. "A woman is coming soon to stay with us and to join the young man. Jerli said she would give me answers. Let's hope so. In the meantime, keep on the lookout for trouble."

Chapter Fourteen

Searching for Clues

In the hill country south of the great lake, Weakling trudged up a crumbling, steep hillside. The afternoon was passing quickly, and the warrior had yet to find a good lookout for the road below him as it curved amid the barren landscape. In this land beyond the South Shore, the hills seemed to press in close together. Here stood a country fashioned over many centuries by wind and water. It made for deep canyons, of which the deepest lay a mile away with the Red River snaking through its bottom. The hills between the Barsk and the Pappi long had remained deserted. Each clan considered the land too rugged and hardscrabble to draw much sustenance from.

Weakling felt his usual pangs of hunger, but he took comfort in the wide road below him. It meant a trading caravan might pass by in the days ahead. The thought of feasting once more on humans helped propel him a good distance up the slope. He stopped once to brush back his mass of shaggy hair and to wipe the sweat from his brow. On he pushed, passing a mass of boulders, when suddenly a fierce shout rose behind him. Cringing, he jumped and drew his sword. A solitary warrior emerged from a hole in the rocks. Weakling stepped back as he beheld the stout hulk, a warrior in black armor with a great yellow beard and tangled locks flowing from beneath his helm. To his relief, Weakling recognized the face and took comfort in the brands of lightning bolts and skulls on the other's cheeks—the symbols of his old order.

"Zhaggee!" he cried.

"Weakwi!" the other roared, pointing his sword at him. "Why, I thought they skewered all you cave diggers over in horse country. How did the cursed Tor miss you?"

"Ah, I left before the enemy swooped into the hills. Say, can you spare any morsels for an old comrade to gnaw on?"

"Perhaps I can share a dried strip of flesh. Come over and let us chew together. What brings you here?"

Weakling sat down and waited impatiently for his treat. "Ah, I watch for a horse dog. Our betters hope that someday he might pass this way. And what of you, what games do you play here?"

"Big fish. We have some little dogs sniffing for the Great Valuable. Mum is the word, but they seem to think that one of your horse dogs might know where it is. We want these little spies to snag him, and then we'll snag both him and them. We know our sniffers well and we throw them clues whenever we can. Anyway, some suspect that this special one might have gone over to the lake vermin."

"Do you truly think that a horse dog could lead you to the Great Valuable?" Weakling guffawed. "Not a one of them could find the Golden Box if you hit them over the head with it. But they do taste good."

"Ah, yes, as you should know," said Zhaggee, passing him a strip of flesh. "You always were a master of fortune. I remember how you always bit off an earlobe of your victims. Now that seemed a nice touch, but I always wondered, Why the right one? What of it?"

"Well, cursed one, there's no mystery. My reason is simple. I need to make my mark on this world. Some masters of fortune want it all. Not me. I just want a good meal and a sign to show everyone that I enjoyed myself. You come upon a corpse with that right earlobe missing and you know who swallowed it."

"And swallowed a bit more, too, more is the pity for the poor buzzards that come afterward. And speaking of buzzards, did you ever get free of that old gasbag Pibbibib?"

Weakling shrugged. "Well, no, he and I departed the hills together. We passed through a nasty scrap or two back in the summer, and he watched my back. But now he begins to puff himself up, dreams of grandeur and such. I just want to

180

find a good place to live off the land. What about here, what foraging orders do you have here?"

"We can strike only at night and only if we can take the whole party. Escapees are not allowed. So that explains why I am almost out of dried flesh from watching this blasted road. The Pappi and Barsk dogs rarely take a chance here at night anymore."

"Well, I can take the vermin day or night, as long as I think they can tell me something of interest before I break their necks."

Zhaggee nodded to show he was impressed. "Well, you are big fish," he said. "When the next one passes by, you go down and interrogate him. And then we will haul him back up here and gnaw on his bones."

Weakling smiled appreciatively. "Spoken like a true master of fortune. What a life we could have if our betters would just leave us be to enjoy ourselves. But, no, they always have their schemes, and usually that means us putting our necks on the line."

Zhaggee smiled but said nothing in reply. Something had caught his attention on the ridge above. A moment later he spied a figure darting downhill into the cover of a small gully. Zhaggee rose and took a step away from Weakling. "What more do you want to tell me?" he asked, even as he made sure his knife was at the ready.

Oblivious, Weakling replied, "Such as?"

"Such as what has become of your gasbag?"

"Oh, he strides about nearby. No doubt he shall appear soon."

"Methinks he already has."

"Indeed? Where?"

"On the hill above us. Now why does he slink about so?"

"Truly, Zhaggee, I don't know." Weakling stood up to take a look. "I told you he has not been himself of late. Give me a moment and I will assure him that only you and I sit here." Weakling cupped his hands and hollered, "Hear me, you big ogre! It is I! Old Zhaggee from the Red Brigade rests

181

here with me. Come on down and greet him!"

"I want him to stay back twenty paces," Zhaggee said.

"Why?"

"Because sometimes the Backstabber plays rough. They say he scalped some of our own over in horse country."

"Now, Zhaggee, they already were corpses when he scalped them. And they were Cleavers. And besides, a few days before they had tried to poke us."

"Even so, he stays back, for your sake as well as mine."

Weakling stiffened at that comment. His eyes froze as at last he noticed that the other warrior had a hand on his knife. Meekly he acquiesced, "Indeed, Zhaggee, we will do as you say."

A few moments later Pibbibib came over the slope and strode toward them. "You can rest right there," Zhaggee told him.

"Says who?" demanded Pibbibib.

"Says the both of us, right Weakwi?"

"All is well," Weakling called out as pleasantly as he could muster. "Old Zhaggee and I were just passing the time, and talking about how a little man flesh would sit well in the belly. What say we find us a little vermin to gnaw on?"

"No," answered Pibbibib. "We need to move on."

Zhaggee called out, "Weakwi here says you are looking for a horse dog. Describe him to me, so I can watch for him, too."

Pibbibib grinned with derision. "Come up here and I will describe him to you."

Weakling winced at the indirect threat. "Zhaggee," he said, "we have become elite since we last saw you. We stand bound in the service of the Lord Mackadoo, who makes us keep secrets."

"Elite, you say?" asked Zhaggee. "Well, you masters of fortune have become too fine for riffraff like me. But let me tell you how our sweet reunion now will end. Backstabber, you will climb back up that hill alone. When I feel safe enough, I will let your chum join you. Otherwise, who can say what may happen to little Weakwi?"

Pibbibib sneered at the words, but he turned and hiked up the slope. Once on top, he sat on a rock and waited for his ally. Zhaggee then let Weakling start up the hill. As he departed, the warrior from the Red Brigade scampered in the other direction. He was taking no chances. Weakling, meanwhile, didn't stop climbing until he reached the top. He wore a frown on his face when he looked upon Pibbibib. "Why must you always set our chums on edge?" he scolded. "Must you threaten everyone, even from our old order? You might have gotten me throttled."

"What would you have me do?" asked Pibbibib. "Sit down beside someone who will try to stab you the first time the fear grips him in the throat? Do you truly want to spend time with that miscreant? You can have him. Tell me, what game does he play now?"

"There is some horse dog the Red Brigade wants, and they have some other little dogs spying for him among the Pappi. They intend to take him once the spies find him."

"You fool! That is our horse dog!"

"How can you be sure? Zhaggee says this one knows where the Great Valuable is. Do you think our dog knows any such thing?"

"Perhaps not, but he might know one who does. And who else would they search for? Listen, brainless one, we may not know where our dog is, but even Mackadoo thinks he may be hiding among the Pappi. That is why he sent us here. It all makes sense. All our troops still tremble at the thought of going back to the lake and suffering another slaughter there by our enemies. So the goons of the Red Brigade entice these little human vermin to go among the Pappi to search for our horse dog."

"Mackadoo has no fears about sending us among the Pappi," Weakling complained. "He seems ever so happy to risk our necks."

"I can keep you out of trouble, just like before. I gain strength every day."

"Ah, do not sing me that song again. Tell me, oh

mighty one, how will your blasted Powers help us if we do not know who the little spies are? They will grab our horse dog and then Zhaggee's boys will take him from the spies. And we will end this chase with empty hands and emptier bellies."

"Not if I have my way," vowed Pibbibib. "I will muck up their game, and The Powers will help me, just wait and see. For now we will keep to the borders of the Pappi and watch for these spies. We will do our best to find them and get them to lead us to our horse dog before Zhaggee's chums get him. I still mean to take our prey. And so much the better if he knows how to find the Great Valuable."

In the land of the MuKierin, three riders paused on a ridge above a camp of horse hunters. Among them was the boyish member of the secret society—the small one of slight build, the goatee and eyes that glinted brightly. He had come with two accomplices to a sprawling collection of tents south of Orres.

"There lies the tent of the fat, old woman," said one of the riders. "She lives with two men and another hag, a thin one. The fat woman has promised to sell us news of the Horse Stalker's kin."

The small one nodded and asked, "And where do the troublemakers dwell, the ones the fat woman fears and who refused to speak to you?"

"Their tents lie on the other side of the camp. The fat woman says that they're the kinsman of the Horse Stalker's brother-in-law. Those men certainly showed me nothing but scorn the first time I came here. They quickly spread a warning through the camp that anyone who spoke to me would have his tongue cut out. Even so, the woman came to me in secret, but she would not allow me in her tent. 'Send another,' she told me, 'a man not known to my enemies. And see that he brings a large bag of gold.'"

The small one smiled. "You did well. Now let's hope this greedy woman knows what she's talking about. In Orres the people with a hunger for gold knew nothing, while those who knew the real secrets would not come near us. No doubt they thought those blasted Elders had sent us to spy out the Horse Stalker." The small one tightened his reins and waved to his companions. "Hide here and watch for me. I will return after dark."

He rode down with a pack horse in tow. Dusk was settling over the camp. On the edge of the tents, a dozen thin goats wearily sniffed the ground in search of any morsel of foliage. From the tent emerged Ornelia, the woman who had arranged the feast between Healdin and Arg Wevol in summer. She wore a beige blanket wrapped about her head and shoulders. The small one dismounted and walked to her. He stared deeply into her eyes and spoke the secret passwords, "Good evening, Desert Rose. I have brought wine."

She replied with a smile, "Greetings, lord. I welcome you. Please come in. Our men will unpack your animal."

The small one pulled two large sacks from his saddle. He slung them upon his shoulder and followed the woman into her tent. Standing inside were Melva and their two men. The husbands immediately noticed the newcomer's sword hanging beneath his black cloak. Bowing, they stepped briskly outside to attend to their guest's horses. Ornelia directed the small one to sit down on goatskins by a fire. Melva and she took a seat on either side of him.

"My associate said that you could help me find the family of the Horse Stalker," the small one began. "Is that so?"

"Yes, lord," Ornelia said, "we can help you."

"Most people have refused to speak to my associates. Why would you help me?"

"Can't you guess?" she replied. "For gold, we will speak. Moreover, we are hoping to learn a little more about this mysterious man. Isn't that so, Melva?"

"Yes, that would add honey on top of the sweetbread," Melva replied. "Perhaps, lord, you'll help us grasp why everyone cares so much about this horse hunter. Why is he worth all the gold that you have brought to us?"

"Ah, Melva," interrupted Ornelia. "Remember our bargain. First, I get to take my guess. You see, lord, I believe I know at least part of that answer."

"Do you?" replied the small one.

"Perhaps I do. I think you're seeking the man because of the woman. Am I right?"

The small one was taken aback by her words, but he tried not to show it. "Perhaps you are," he said. "Go ahead and lay out your theory."

"Well, you must know how beautiful she is. All the men in our camp couldn't take their eyes off her. My guess is that the horse hunter helped her run away from some aristocrat, perhaps from an Elder or the son of an Elder. That broken-hearted lover now is ready to spend whatever it takes to find her and to have her brought back to him. Am I close to the mark, lord?"

Not within a hundred leagues, he thought. But he smiled slyly and replied, "I don't dare confirm how close you are to solving the riddle. I can say no more, for I am bound by propriety, woman. But now, will you help me find her?"

"What would I earn if I helped you?" Ornelia sweetly inquired.

The small one tossed the two sacks at her feet. They thudded with the heavy clank of gold coins. Just then the two husbands stepped inside with a skin of wine, a sack of dried fruits and other foods taken off their visitor's pack animal. Their eyes froze on the sacks, as did the eyes of their women. "You have my answer," their guest said. "Now tell me how to find the Horse Stalker and his woman?"

Ornelia tipped her head and smiled. "First, go to Kierinswell and find an old candle maker, a man called Shone. In his home you will find the troublesome sister of the Horse Stalker and the sister's man. The man has gone there to learn the candle trade and end his days hunting the wild horses. They go by the names of Remy and Noli. Surely they can help you find this man and his woman."

The small one nodded. "I have heard the man's name. That is good. How do you know them?"

186

"They joined our camp before the Challenge of Orres. They left a bad taste in our mouths. But within the camp we heard the gossip of their move to Kierinswell."

"I understand they have family in this very camp. Tell me about their kin."

"The head of the family is an old horse hunter named Char, the uncle of the sister's man. He won't tell you anything. And he would have his young kinsmen murder us if he knew we had spoken to you. You must promise that you won't tell anyone of our meeting."

The small one raised his hands to signal understanding. "I also want to keep this meeting a secret," he said. "In a moment we will pour the wine and toast our mutual good fortune. But first, please tell me one more thing. I have yet to gaze upon this beautiful woman. How can I be sure when I have found her?"

"Oh, sister, allow me to answer," said Melva. "Generous lord, you will know her because she is a healer woman."

The small one smiled slyly at Melva. A few moments later all five men and women raised their goblets and drank the wine. Their guest soon took his leave. In the dark he rode through the forlorn goats and beyond the camp to the ridge where his accomplices awaited him. "Good news," he called to them. "They told me all that I needed to hear. Let them quaff their wine and count their gold. Soon they will fall into a deep, drunken sleep."

"Nonetheless," said the man who had first met Ornelia, "I want to draw close now and wait."

"Do it your way," the small one replied. "But I have one more task for you. There's another man in this camp, a leader named Char. He is a troublemaker and a relative of the one I want to kidnap. Get me Char's sacred stone. It will prove useful in my plans. Buy it or steal it, but bring it to me at our usual meeting place in Kierinswell."

That night Ornelia, Melva and their men divided the gold into piles. Next, they feasted on the bounty of dried fruits and wine. They built up the fire in the middle of their tent and toasted their great wealth, which would enable them to live in comfort for the rest of their lives. It wasn't until late in the night that they curled up around the fire and fell asleep. A short time later, a shadow entered their tent, but the silence of the camp remained undisturbed. In the late morning, however, a neighbor woman noticed a goat poking its head inside Ornelia's tent. Curious, the woman pulled back the flap covering the tent's entrance. Inside she found the four occupants in their blankets, all with their throats slit.

There wasn't a gold coin to be found in the tent.

Chapter Fifteen

Then Came Healdin

Healdin came to Baern's estate at night, riding down from the hills with her servant Mirri. Both women were adorned with veils. Baern's gardener came out of his hut to greet them. At once he scurried off to tell both his master and Roj of this long-awaited visitor. Baern lit candles and waited for Healdin at his office. But Roj ran from his hut and found her waiting in the courtyard on her gray mare.

"Healdin," he called. "How I wish you had been here. Jerli's dead."

"What happened?" she asked.

"It's my fault," answered Roj. He felt himself choking up. "We went with Baern to a town called The Sisters. Jerli didn't want to go, but I insisted. I got myself into trouble and Jerli had to rescue me. He got me to safety, but some bad men came after him at the edge of the lake. He fought in the water until he slipped and drowned in the lake."

Tears flowed into Healdin's veil. "We will talk when the time is right," she said. "But now I must speak to your host."

Roj led the two women to Baern's office. The trader was waiting at the door. He bowed to greet them.

Healdin spoke to him in perfect Pappi, "Gracious Baern, thank you for watching over Roj. May I speak with you?"

Baern smiled at her in amazement. "Greetings, good woman. I am astounded that you speak my tongue. Yes, please come in. I also wish to speak with you."

Healdin sat down in a chair by a table with a glowing candle. Roj took a seat in a darkened corner. He didn't understand the words being spoken, but he wanted to hear Healdin's voice and stay near her. "Baern," she began, "this is my most trusted servant, Mirri. We came to you at night so

189

that we wouldn't attract attention. I know you went with Jerli up into the hill country above the lake. I believe that he began to tell you the story of my people."

Baern stood and rested an elbow on his stone counter. "There is much he didn't tell me, woman," the trader replied. "How is it that you speak my language?"

"I have walked among the Pappi for scores of years."

"Come now, you seem much too young to have done that."

"Oh, no, I am not too young. I even set my eyes upon you once long ago."

"Really? When was that."

"You were a boy in a red cap," she said. "You had just returned in triumph from a fishing trip with your father. Together you had been out most of the night in his boat, and you had caught nothing. Your father wanted to return home, but you insisted that you try one more time. You put down your net, and it filled with fish. You brought your catch to the nearby town that morning and told the fishermen and all the people your story. And your mother was there, and she came and hugged you. She called you her brave, little fisherman. I was there, too. I heard your tale and smiled to see your joy."

Baern looked dumbfounded. He immediately recalled this story, even though he hadn't thought of it in years. Once more he gazed at Healdin. She didn't appear to be much more than thirty years old. His mind raced to grasp how the woman might have learned this episode from his childhood. *Who could have told her? And why does she wear that veil? What is she hiding?* At last, he said, "Woman, don't play with my mind. It scares me. If anything, it makes me want to send you and this man away."

"As you wish," Healdin said. "What shall we speak of?"

Baern pointed at Roj. The young man looked pained by the attention and lowered his head. "Tell me about him," the trader said. "Jerli made it sound like this young one holds the fate of my people. Is that true?"

Healdin started to answer, but she was stopped by the

sound of Baern's father coughing from a side room. The old man entered the office and demanded gruffly, "What is all this? Who troubles us at this late hour?"

"Father," said Baern, "this is the woman that Jerli told us about. Believe it or not, she speaks our tongue."

The father's eyes widened and he coughed again. "Does she? Lady, I want you to know that Jerli was my friend, even though I often chided him for knowing so little about horses. Please believe that I am truly sorry for his death. We have lost a good man."

Healdin smiled. "I am pleased to meet a friend of Jerli. But gentle father, your cough wears greatly upon you. Please allow my servant to prepare you a healing tea." She turned to Baern and asked, "May we have a little boiling water?"

Baern led Mirri outside to the estate's main kitchen. They soon returned with a large cup and its sweet, steamy scent filled the room. The father took a sip from the cup and his sneer softened to a look of wonder. "Now here is tea fit for drinking," he said. "What do you call it, lady?"

"It is a taste of home," Healdin said. "If you drink it and lay down to rest, you will rise refreshed."

"Very well, this old man will leave you now for a well-deserved slumber. But we will speak again, lady. There is something about you that gets under the skin." With that he retired to his room beside the office.

Baern left the counter and drew close to Healdin. "Woman," he asked, "are you a sorceress?"

"I am a leader of my people," she said. "My King knows the suffering of your people. And I have seen the chains that bind them. For many years I have battled the evil ones who kill the Pappi and those from all the desert clans. And I tell you that this young man signals the start of a new day. Many will be set free, and many will fall. Will you help us, Baern?"

Baern looked again at Roj and said, "Jerli was one of those who fell, wasn't he?"

"Jerli found something worth dying for. His life was not spent in vain."

"And what of this young man? Are you sure he's the one? He doesn't seem up for whatever task he must face."

"I believe in Roj. And I will give him some of my power for the battle he faces. When the time comes, I believe he will give his all. Will you help us?"

The trader retreated to his stone counter. "What do you want me to do?"

"Permit us to stay here until Roj goes forth on his challenge. Mirri and I will guard you and all those here on your estate. We will stand between you and anyone who might try to harm you."

Baern took a moment before he answered. "Woman, you still scare me. Do I have a choice in this matter? If I do, then I say that you may stay here until I tell you to leave. Tonight you may stay. I will see that you are taken to one of my empty servants' huts, not far from where this MuKierin resides."

Healdin arose. "When you say the word, we will go. I am glad we had this talk. It is not a bad thing that you fear me, Baern. Indeed, my enemies fear me much more than you do. But remember this. I am not from the Dark Brood. I am not the one who wants to rip your heart out and eat it." With those words she made her exit. Mirri followed, nodding slyly at the trader. Baern and Roj were left alone, staring at each other in awkward silence.

In the morning, Mirri found Roj washing his face beside his hut. "Come with me," she said. "Our lady will give a feast for Baern and his household. You can help me with the preparations."

They rode to the nearby village to buy a slab of beef and four live chickens. Mirri wore her veil. In town, she spoke the Pappi tongue as well as her lady. The butcher agreed to immediately send a servant with the meat and chickens to Baern's estate. Mirri next went to the spice venders and made a few purchases. The townsmen treated her with respect, but they eyed Roj suspiciously.

The chickens arrived soon after Roj and Mirri returned to the estate. Mirri immediately killed and plucked the birds.

Healdin soon appeared outside with the veil still covering her face. She began making chicken broth in a large kettle hanging over a fire outside the kitchen building. After the broth began to simmer, Healdin sorted through a score of food sacks she had brought to the estate.

Roj stood near her in silence. For days he had been thinking about what he wanted to say to her. But now that she was near, he couldn't seem to start a conversation. At last he asked her, "Why are you doing this dinner?"

"I wish to offer a gesture of appreciation to Baern and his people," she said. "We will make a meal and make a way to bridge the chasm between us. And you will help us."

That day Roj learned about brown-tipped mushrooms and the tasty cooking oil from a tree in the Green Lands, plus other foods that were foreign to his people. When the chicken broth had simmered long enough, the women put another large kettle directly onto the coals and poured in a small layer of oil and cubed steer meat. They browned the meat and removed it. They threw in sliced onions and cooked them until they lost their whiteness and then sautéed the mushrooms. Soon all those ingredients were thrown back in the kettle, along with a portion of the chicken broth and a few strange seasonings. Roj hung the great black pot over the fire to simmer. Baern's servants began to take notice of the cooking. They whispered to one another in groups of two or three.

After three hours, the concoction had simmered into thin brown gravy with red tints throughout. Healdin brought out a spice and poured a few dashes of it into the kettle. Roj bent over her shoulder to take in the aroma. The new ingredient smelled sweet and aromatic. Later, he tasted the gravy and found it had a slight kick.

Mirri came and placed another kettle on the coals. Once more she cooked onions in oil. Roj looked puzzled at her work. He asked Healdin, "Are you going to make another batch of gravy?"

"No," she said, "but now we need your strength, child of Hannah. Come watch Mirri and help her stir."

Healdin lifted a sack and poured into the kettle a heap of rice, a food unknown in the Dry Lands. Mirri poured in more oil and then handed Roj a great wooden spoon. "Stir," she ordered, pointing to the strange white grains.

Two female cooks came from the kitchen, where they had been roasting the chickens that Mirri had prepared. They drew close to observe Roj and Mirri browning the rice in a light coating of oil. Mirri answered several of their questions and invited them to smell the simmering gravy and chicken broth. Roj nodded kindly as the women exchanged words in Pappi. He wondered if the trader's servants thought this meal as strange as he did. When the cooks left, Roj asked Mirri, "What did you tell them?"

"I told them that their tongue has no words to describe our foods. But they politely agreed to take a taste when we have finished."

After a few more minutes, Mirri took a ladle and poured enough chicken broth into the kettle to cover the barely browned rice. The kettle fizzled and the rice bounced off the bottom as the broth bubbled wildly. "Keep stirring," she told Roj. "We still have much to do."

Baern stepped out from his office to watch Roj stir the bubbling rice. The look on his face showed that he understood something strange was unveiling before him. Roj couldn't tell if this pleased the trader or filled him with apprehension. Baern's lips remain tightly closed and he looked deep into Mirri's eyes. After the trader left them, Roj told Mirri, "He knows you are different. Perhaps tall women worry him."

Mirri kept adding an occasional ladle of broth while Roj stirred and stirred. It seemed to him that they would keep mixing this concoction until his arms fell off. But eventually the rice soaked up the broth and began to stick together. Mirri soon began adding the gravy they had made earlier in the day. The aroma of the two merged and filled Roj's nostrils with wonder. His mouth began to water. "What do you call this?" he asked Mirri.

"Paradise," she said with a smile.

Healdin emerged from her hut. She inspected the rice

and began the final preparations. Baern's cooks rang the dinner bell and the entire household converged on the stone pavement of the courtyard. Long tables and benches had been set up there. Even Baern's father came forth, leaning on his staff and taking his seat of honor in an arm chair at the head of one table. "Girl, I want some more of that tea," he called to Healdin. "No more coughing for me." Healdin bowed and went off to brew the tea while Mirri brought the old man a plate of rice and roasted chicken. "What is this?" he demanded sharply.

"Gentle father, here you will find a taste of the great feast that all men long for," she replied. "Please enjoy it." Baern stared dumbstruck at such words, but his father simply shrugged and spooned up a mouthful of rice. He paused, smiled and chewed heartily. "Now this tastes good enough for the Chief of the Seven Dragons!" he exclaimed. The servants seated at table nodded approvingly and tasted, too. They swallowed and smiled and declared to each other how delightful it was to discover such a delicious new dish.

Roj shook his head and thought, *How she does it! Behold, the true fisher.*

The three guests soon joined the other diners around the tables. After the meal, Mirri brought out a lute and Healdin her fiddle. Together they played the same slow dirge that Baern had heard that night on the mountain with Jerli the trader. Once more he recalled the lyrics: "Oh, my heart feels a longing, for a home I can't see..." The household gave heartfelt applause when the song ended. But Baern stood up and walked alone over to the lakeshore. There he stood long beneath the starry sky, gazing upon the water.

Nearly all the servants tarried in the courtyard that night and helped with the cleanup. The men brought new fuel and built up the cooking fire to ward off the cool night air. Even after the pots and dishes were put away, many stayed to talk with Healdin and Mirri. The cooks spoke of Pappi cuisine and their own secret recipes. Others shared of the aches and ailments that troubled them. Mirri made more of the healing tea and passed it around.

Tie came to Roj. "She's a healer woman, isn't she?" he said. "All the servants are talking about how she cured the old man's cough. It has plagued him for years."

"She's a wonder," Roj said. "And she's a good woman."

"Is she your woman?"

"No. You can tell people I'm her guardian, if you like."

"That's too bad. The Pappi men will want her if she has no man. She's beautiful and she will turn their heads. And they will soon hear about her. The servants can't wait to spread the news about her healing power. Circ the Headman has a boy who's been ill for months. He'll pay dearly for news of such a woman. And it would go badly for you if she refused to help the child."

"If I know her, she won't refuse a sick child."

As they talked, Healdin approached them. Tie dared to ask her, "Lady, who are you?"

"I am a friend of the Stone Woman and her children," she said. "Tell me, Tie, do you know how the mother of your clan came by that name?"

"No, lady, I don't."

"Her given name was Hannah, and she once caught some of your kinsmen stealing mules that belonged to the clan. She ordered an executioner's stone be set up for the thieves. She even made them sleep beside that stone the night before they were to die. The next morning she took a sword in her hand and raised it over the prisoners. But she did not strike. She told the people that she still grieved the loss of her own man by a violent death, and she was slow to inflict such pain on the families of the thieves. She said she was willing to give the men one more chance. But they must agree to wear a necklace with a small black stone upon it. They must wear it for the rest of their lives. It would remind them that their lives had been spared once but would not be spared a second time if they were caught stealing again. Then one thief told another, 'We are marked men now.' Hannah heard his words and removed from beneath her own collar a necklace with the same black stone upon it. 'Yes,' she told the man. 'You are marked. So am I. Thanks be to the King, I am marked, but still I live.' That was the day that Hannah became known as the Stone Woman, for both her fierceness and her kindness. And in time all your people began to wear the black stone in tribute to her."

Healdin walked away, even as the two men stared after her. Roj turned to Tie. "I told you," he said. "She's a wonder."

Chapter Sixteen

An Unwelcome Proposal

Within one day, word of the healer woman reached Circ the Headman. Circ ruled the eastern shore. He had many soldiers and servants, as well as four wives and 11 children. Among them was a boy who had been unable to eat solid foods for months, turning him thin and listless. Once Circ heard about Healdin, he immediately sent his chief steward to Baern's estate to fetch her. The black-robed envoy arrived there trailed by a half-dozen guardsmen. Healdin readily agreed to help the boy, and Baern personally escorted Mirri and her to the headman's stone fortress. The two women continued to wear their veils.

At the lakeside fortress, the steward personally led the guests into the great hall and up a nearby stairway to the boy's chambers. Neither Circ nor the boy's mother appeared there. But a servant woman stood by with a black kettle of steaming water. From it, Healdin quickly brewed her healing tea. As the sweetness of its aroma filled the room, the boy raised his head off a red pillow. When all was ready, Healdin held a cup to the boy's lips and helped him drink the tea in small doses. Immediately his stomach felt better and he took a long nap. When he awoke, he asked for roasted chicken and ate it heartily.

Late that afternoon, as Healdin prepared to leave, the steward went to his master and told him of his son's healing. The headman replied, "Show me the woman!" He was brought to her as she stood with Baern and Mirri in the main yard of his fortress. Despite her veil, Circ could tell she was beautiful. He nodded stiffly to her but did not address her. Stepping away, he quietly told his steward, "Give her a rich gift, along with my thanks. She seems a worthy wife and would make a fine addition to my household. Have your spies learn more about her. And declare a holiday in her honor—

with a suitable celebration. I want to show her how much I think of her."

Healdin received a luminous red gem, and the next day the villagers enjoyed a feast of roasted pig and goat. As a result, news of the healer woman spread throughout the east side of the lake. Roj didn't like the attention she was getting. He worried it would bring trouble. But he found it hard to say anything to her, just as he was still unable to speak much about what had happened that night with Jerli at The Sisters. Instead, he often paced about until he couldn't stand it any longer, and then he saddled his stallion and set out for some solace in the eastern hills.

One day while he was out riding, two trading vessels approached the estate from the north. Servants alerted Baern, and he went at once to the shore to greet the visitors. Each boat held six men. From the vessels emerged three men dressed in fine wool with fur trimming. Two men were about Roj's age, and the third was much older. Immediately Baern recognized the oldest guest. "Master Rupe, welcome," Baern said. "To what, do I owe this great honor? What brings you from your trading business on the South Shore?"

Rupe, a stocky balding man, stepped forward and gave Baern an enthusiastic embrace. "Good Baern," he said, "I have been chained too long to my counting table. Should we not all spend more time upon the blessed waters? Thus, I have flown from my nest. We set our course first to Circ's fortress and paid him our respects. And now we have come to visit a fellow merchant. I have never seen your beautiful estate, so I determined in my heart to do so. I hope you do not mind the intrusion."

"You have my heartfelt welcome," Baern said, though he wondered greatly at his guest's motives. "Please come with me and let me offer you tea and refreshments for your journey."

They entered the trader's office where servants quickly spread out trays of light breads and cups of tea. Rupe introduced the two strangers. "This is my son Tooky and our associate Arta," he said. "It gladdens me that they should see the trading life on the quiet side of the lake. It gives evidence that one does not need to pay outrageous tariffs to the Barsk in order to enjoy success."

"You speak with kindness," Baern replied after he directed his servants to leave. "And you have always shown me true hospitality when I have visited the South Shore. Even so, Master Rupe, do you journey simply so that you may take to the waters?"

"Ah, Baern, I suppose that would seem strange, would it not? Perhaps I can never stop looking for opportunities. Such is my way."

"Do you look for opportunities with Circ or with the traders here?"

"Opportunities with Circ? Hah! No, indeed, my friend. Oh, but your headman marks his territory like a dog. Thus, I dared not show myself here without first offering obeisance to him. I assure you that we brought him the appropriate gifts."

Baern smiled politely. "Our headman remains ever protective of his realm."

"Protective. I dare say he does, as well as informed about those who live inside his boundaries. He talked at length about a veiled woman who healed his son. He said she is a guest on your estate. Your headman seems quite taken with her. I believe he even became concerned that we would take an interest in her, too. He made it quite clear that he would deal ever so severely with us if we tried to abduct her and run back across the lake. I was astonished that he would speak so bold a warning to three gentlemen."

Baern answered meekly, "No doubt he merely meant to speak as a protector of the woman."

Arta, a slight man with large eyes, slim lips and a slight goatee, cleared his throat and spoke. As he talked, his eyelids blinked sharply every few seconds. Baern had to be careful not to stare at him. "Your headman said the woman has a MuKierin for a guardian," Arta declared. "Is that so?"

"Yes, one of the Horse Clan watches over her," Baern replied. "Why do you ask?"

The young man's eyelids began to blink again. "Mere curiosity," he replied. "The MuKierin rarely come among our people."

An awkward silence followed. Baern, as host, felt obliged to carry on a conversation. "Perhaps you would wish to meet the woman," he said.

The three men looked with furrowed brows at one another and quickly shook their heads. Rupe smiled and declared, "No, good Baern, you would bring trouble upon us all. I want to be able to swear to your headman that I did not even lay eyes on the woman. No, but I would like a brief tour of your estate, just the two of us. It will give us the chance to talk. I wish your thoughts on the upcoming tariff negotiations with the Barsk."

The party soon exited the office. Baern and Rupe went up toward the vineyard while the younger ones returned to their vessels. Baern gave Rupe a leisurely tour of his land, though they spoke little of trading or tariffs. At length, they returned to the shore and bid farewell to one another. The boats shoved off. Inside the lead vessel, Rupe turned to Arta and said, "The MuKierin rides in the hills. He probably will return in a few hours. Do you wish to try to take him today?

"No, my friend, I will not act this day. Do not fear. You will receive rich payment for making it possible for me to visit this trader and learn more about the man and the woman. You have done enough."

"Well, have it your way," replied Rupe. "But I'm warning you. Circ the Headman now will have his eyes on this place. Indeed, that man has his blasted spies everywhere. And I believe he wants that woman. He will not sit back and let you take her from this place. That much has become clear from our visit with him today."

"I suppose you're right," said Arta. "That does present a problem. But my associates want to make sure that this is the man we are seeking. If he is the one, we'll find a way to deal with the headman."

"Even so, mark my words. If I know that old lecher, he will worry about our visit here today. I would wager that he now will act quickly to prevent losing this woman. He will do what he can to make her his fifth wife."

"Would he kill the MuKierin? That would not do."

"No, the MuKierin remains Baern's guest and under his protection. And he need not kill him. I believe he will seek to barter for the woman."

In the late afternoon, Roj returned on horseback to the estate. Tie was waiting by the corral. "Circ the Headman, the ruler of this region, has sent his steward to see you. He has been waiting an hour here. He wishes us to meet him over the hill."

"What does he want with me?"

"He didn't say."

"Should I stay away from him?"

"It would go ill for both my master and me if you refuse to see the steward."

Roj frowned. "Very well, take me to him."

They found the steward seated in his black robe on a stone wall in front of Baern's greening vineyard. He was lean with a dour face and a pointy chin. As the two MuKierin approached, he rose and quickly signaled to his servants to fetch ten horses tied nearby on a picket line. Roj noticed the man commanded the servants with only the nod of his head and the flick of a finger. He stepped forward a few paces to set himself off from his underlings. In his right hand he held a riding crop.

"Greetings, child of the horse woman," the steward said in the Pappi tongue. His eyes were dark and intent.

Roj recognized these words; he had heard them before. He bowed his head and replied in the Lake tongue, "Greetings, child of the waters."

The steward launched into a brief speech. Tie interpreted, saying "The steward wants me to translate for you. His master has commanded him to come and speak with you. His master bids you to examine these ten horses and say whether they are worthy for a headman."

"Why is he asking me?" Roj inquired.

Tie spoke to the steward, and then replied, "His

master says the MuKierin know horses. Thus, if you deem them worthy, then his master will be pleased. The steward says the servants will parade the beasts around you, two horses to each man, and you shall give your verdict as to which one reigns among them."

The steward clapped his hands and backed away from Roj while the five servants began to lead the horses in a circle on a nearby piece of flat ground. Warily Roj entered the circle. Each servant held the halter ropes to two horses, grays and bays and blacks with especially shiny coats. First the men walked the animals, next they trotted them, and then the steward clapped his hands and they reversed course so that Roj could better see each animal. The MuKierin knelt down in order to observe the high-stepping legs that glided past him. The steward clapped and the servants stopped and turned to face the stranger.

"What do you say?" Tie asked him. "Are they worthy for a headman?"

Roj took a few minutes to approach all the animals, grasping the halter ropes and stroking each animal's neck. He turned to the steward and said, "They appear sound and of good stock. They comport themselves well. I believe the headman can be pleased with these horses."

"And which do you consider the best among them?"

"Tell him I wouldn't know that until I put on a saddle and rode each one. But the black one here appears to be the king of the herd. And his eyes take in all things."

"The steward says you have chosen well. And would you accept the black stallion as a gift?"

"I don't understand. Why does he ask me this?"

Tie queried the steward. The slave's face grew sober as he conveyed the answer. "His master wishes an exchange. He wishes to give you the stallion and these other worthy horses in exchange for the woman."

"Is he joking?"

"No, he's not joking," Tie replied soberly. The steward demanded an interpretation of their exchange and Tie gave it to him. The Pappi spoke and then Tie declared, "He asks whether you consider it an unfair exchange. Normally a Pappi man would offer only one or two horses for a woman, and they would not be of the quality of these horses."

Roj felt his anger rising. "Tell him she's not like any other woman."

"Then the steward asks how many horses you desire in exchange for her?"

"Tell him he couldn't find enough horses in all the Dry Lands."

A longer exchange passed between the steward and slave. Tie said, "He wants to know whether you are trying to keep the woman for yourself. Do you intend to wed the healer woman?"

Roj didn't like the question. It reminded him of the talk with his sister. He hadn't wanted to tell Remy his feelings about Healdin and he certainly didn't want to bare his soul to this stranger. But he felt he must say something. "I do not believe the woman could love me," Roj said. "I do not believe that she would choose to marry me."

"He says his master doesn't care about love. He will give you twenty horses and throw in a woman, a virgin from among the headman's slaves."

Roj wanted to strike the man. *Calm your heart,* he told himself. *Don't do something stupid again.* Aloud, he said slowly, "Tell him I remain only her guardian, not her kinsman. I have not the power to arrange a marriage. Tell him he can ask Healdin directly if she will marry the headman. But I think I know her mind on this matter. I think she will refuse him."

Tie soon related the steward's answer: "He says he doesn't care what the woman wants. In this land, she has no say. You control her fate. You must speak for her. Will you give up the woman?"

Roj turned his back on the two men. *What fools men are. I want her. Wevol wants her. Now this headman wants her, too. Can't we see she is too wonderful for our hands to touch? We all might as well try to catch the summer wind.* He turned back to face the steward. "Tell him I'm sorry. I cannot give her up to any man, not even the headman, not for all the wealth of the Pappi."

The steward's eyes glared as Tie translated the words. He raised his riding crop and began beating the slave until he knocked him to the ground. Roj rushed between them and received a lash to his own head, a blow meant for Tie. The steward raised his arm but refrained from again striking Baern's guest. Roj held his ground. "Go," he said, pointing north. "Go now."

The steward cursed at Tie, even as he backed away and turned to his saddle horse. He climbed aboard and galloped north, trailed by the servants and the ten prize horses. As they departed, Roj turned and extended a hand to Tie, but the slave refused it. Roj asked, "Why did he beat you?"

"He beat me because he knew he couldn't beat you. You are Baern's guest and you stand under his protection. You remain safe for now. But any Pappi may beat a slave to death. Afterward, he need simply send the slave's owner a few goats or fifty chickens."

Two servants had observed Tie's beating and quickly summoned their master. Baern rushed out of the trading office, his stout frame waddling fast as Roj and Tie walked sullenly back over the hill. "Has my servant caused an offense?" Baern asked in Pappi. Tie had to translate the question.

"Tell him the offense was not from his servant," said Roj. "Tell him what happened."

Tie explained the exchange with the steward. Baern's face grew more worried as the story went on. He spoke, and Tie translated: "My master asks your forgiveness for such behavior. He said it's no excuse, but he wants you to understand the effect that the woman seems to have on Pappi men. Perhaps it comes from her healing powers. Even though she remains veiled, she holds a powerful attraction to the men."

"Tell him I know all about the effect she has on men," Roj said. "Perhaps we should leave this place tonight. I'm sorry. Tell Baern I've already caused him too much grief. I don't want him to get on the bad side of the headman."

The trader paused to consider his next move. He didn't look at Roj as he gave his answer. Tie translated, "No, my master says he wishes you to stay. He says he is doing this not for you, but for Jerli. You will be safe if you stay under his protection. Even Circ the Headman would not dare raise his hand against you here. But if you leave, evil might befall you."

"What a mess I've made in coming here," Roj said. "Tell your master I still want to leave this place, but I suspect Healdin will want us to stay. Even so, I'm not staying if it's going to get you killed, Tie. I have to know that you won't be harmed." The slave hesitated to pass on these words, but Roj demanded, saying, "Tell him or Healdin will do so for me. You also have to be protected from that steward. Tell him."

Tie translated Roj's words, and gave this answer from Baern: "My master says that I'm a slave and a slave's life hangs by a thread. But for your sake, he says he'll keep me close to home until the danger passes."

Roj felt his insides stir. "Tie, you tell him that Healdin doesn't like men chaining up other men. Tell him! Baern doesn't have to worry about me, but that woman is a force to be reckoned with. Jerli would have said the same thing. Why, I've seen her break iron chains and free slaves. So don't think things are going to stay the way they've always been. One day she's going to have her way. The Dark Brood can't stop her and neither can all the slaveholders in the Dry Lands."

Roj strode off to cool down. Tie translated for his master. Baern turned to Tie and demanded, "What do you know about all this talk of freeing slaves?"

"I know nothing, master. Some MuKierin do believe that one day a Champion will emerge from among our people. I don't know whether this man thinks he is such a hero. But I've never heard anyone talk about such a woman freeing slaves."

"We must keep an eye on her. In the meantime, you will not leave the compound without my permission. Obey me in this. Oh, what a dark day has befallen us! Behold the effect that this healer woman has on men. Circ has barely laid eyes on her and already he covets her. And, by the dragon, she wore a veil. What if she had been bare faced? Hear me, Tie. Danger surrounds us and we must walk with care."

At dusk, Roj went to Healdin as she sat by the shore. "Healdin," he said, "will you let me go?"

She looked puzzled. "What do you mean?"

He sat down beside her. "I've made a mess of things ever since I came here. Maybe I'm not the one you thought I was. Maybe you should just let me go."

"Go where?"

He looked out across the lake, its colors fading into gray. "I don't know. Someplace far away. Someplace where I won't get anybody else killed."

"Ah," she said, "far away." She lowered her head and paused a moment before saying, "Jerli was dear to me, Roj. Did you care for him?"

Roj ached at the words. "Yes, I did, Healdin. It may not look like it, but I did. I know now that I should have cared for him more than I did."

"What did you love about him, Roj?"

Roj couldn't look her in the eye. "He was an honest man, Healdin. And he didn't think about himself. He didn't need to step in to save me, but he did. He looked out for his wranglers, too. He was a good man."

"Yes, he was. How can you and I honor him?"

"I'm not sure I can do anything to honor him now, Healdin."

"Roj, you now have only two choices. You can run or you can fight. There is a time for both. You have been running ever since I met you. You needed to run at first in order to save your sister and Noli. But if you run now, you're doomed. Your enemies won't stop chasing you. They simply will track you down and destroy you. That is not what Jerli would have wanted for you. Is that what you want?"

"I'm so confused, Healdin. I don't know what I want. Do you still think I can overcome my enemies?"

"I believe in you, Roj. But we will only know what you can do if you are willing to stand and fight them. Will you do that?"

"Will you help me fight them?"

"I will do what I can, but I cannot fight beside you. In battle, I would be too tempted to use the Vine. I might not be able to control it. I might harm you as well as your enemies."

Roj shook his head. "Why wouldn't you be able to control your power? You've always done so before, haven't you?"

Her lips grew taut. "I cannot tell you now. Trust me in this. In time you will understand. But for your sake, you must face your enemies without me."

"But I need your help, Healdin. I'm not sure that I believe in myself anymore. If you still want me to stay, then I'm willing to do whatever you say. But I don't see how I can succeed without your help."

She stood up and extended her hand to him. "Come with me," she said. "Now is the time to prepare you. Come."

He took her hand, arose and together they walked to her hut. Mirri came at her call. The three entered and inside the servant lit a few candles. Roj asked Healdin, "How will you prepare me?"

"First, I will reveal the meaning of the words you spoke to the stallion in Orres. Do you remember them? In Orres, you said the words 'Fidden Gadaeyo.' In my tongue, 'fidden' means to illuminate, to shine brightly. And 'gadaeyo' is the darkness."

"Light the darkness," Roj whispered.

"Yes, light the darkness. Shine in the darkness. It is the greeting of my people and the words we speak aloud when our enemies surround us. And we call the Root of Glory, 'Fidden Gadaeyo.' It is the Darkness Shiner. And its rightful owner is the King. We call him 'Ta Elladoena Fidden Gadaeyo,' the Great One Who Shines in the Darkness. And now you will share in his power." She reached out and touched Roj's hand. It trembled and he looked down to see that she had placed within his palm a small scabbard. From it he drew forth a black stone blade, the very one the old seeker had fashioned and given to him that first night on the mountain. Healdin reached and took the blade. "For you I will make this a fierce weapon against the evil ones," she said. "I will give you some of the power from Mara, the Vine."

She went to her table, took a small vial and poured a golden liquid over the blade. "This elixir comes from the vine of my homeland, Ta Ellowyn, the Living Fire," she said. "You helped plant such a vine with Jerli, and you drank a tea with a drop of Ta Ellowyn mixed in it. And tonight the Living Fire will help me to protect you. But first, you must turn and close your eyes. Do not open them even for a moment. I do not wish you to be blinded by my light." Roj slowly twisted his head toward the hut's wall. Healdin waited and then reached for the scabbard on her leg. She removed her light. The hut filled with a burst of brightness. Roj's eyes remained closed, but his knees buckled and he collapsed to the ground. He bent down and put both hands over his eyes, even as he felt his frame shudder. Healdin brought the two objects together, the white light and the black blade. The liquid on the stone knife sizzled into vapor, leaving behind only a fragrance like sweet incense. The lady then sheathed her light. The room once more went dim, a place of candlelight and shadows. Slowly Roj's eyes adjusted. He looked at Mirri, who seemed unfazed by it all. Healdin handed Roj the sheathed stone blade. "You will wear this on your leg, just as I wear the Vine on mine," she said. "Your enemies will not suspect it there."

"But you have uncovered your light," Roj said. "Will it not make you ill again?"

"You are my charge," she said. "For you, I will do what I must do. Now hear me. You will use your blade only in the greatest need. But you must always wear it. Always."

Nearby, Tie had watched the three guests enter the hut. From outside he witnessed a great white light stream forth from the cracks in the shutters. It made all the hairs on his head tingle. Immediately he ran and told Baern what he had seen.

A week later Arta, the young Pappi who had visited Baern's estate, rode along the eastern shore. Beside him rode a dark-haired foreigner, a stout man with a thick beard and rosy cheeks. It was early morning and the men turned the horses down to the shore to let their mounts drink, each animal extending a front leg far forward and dipping their heads low to reach the waters.

"This headman seems a nuisance," the foreigner said in the Common Tongue used for speech between the clans. "He wants this woman, and he will keep us from having her. I would rather take both the MuKierin and the woman. Then if the man refuses to talk, we could torture the woman in front of him."

"Perhaps your way seems good," said Arta. "But it would bring us many problems. The headman has spies everywhere, and he will fight hard to keep us from kidnapping the woman. We Pappi know that a boat can fight the wind or it can run with it and so benefit from the breeze. If we let him have his way, this leader will helps us. Give him the woman and he will help us take the MuKierin. What good is a woman anyway? What would a woman know of the Golden Box? Does not the man hold the key to finding our prize?"

"I suppose we can succeed without her. But we still must make sure we have the right man and that he will lead us to the treasure."

"Well, you said you know a MuKierin who can identify this one they call Horse Stalker. Let us bring that man here and use him to make sure we have the right man. If he is the one, we will make the Horse Stalker talk. We can torture his kinsman in front of him. And we can make him believe we hold the woman, too. He need not know that the headman has her."

The foreigner nodded. "Very well, but we also must be prepared for the possibility that the Horse Stalker knows nothing about where the Golden Box can be found. Perhaps the White Beard holds that secret."

"Even so, my plan can still bring us success. We will have the Horse Stalker as a hostage. And we can threaten to kill him. Thus, we can force the White Beard to give us our prize."

The two conspirators rode to a nearby village with a tavern built of thick stone slabs. In a private back room, the headman's steward sat at a table with his back to the wall. The two men entered the tavern and walked up to him. Arta spoke in Pappi, "Greetings, fair steward. Good wishes we extend to you and your lord."

The steward answered in the Common Tongue. "We will speak words for your companion's ears, too."

"Ah," Arta said to the foreigner, "I told you this steward was a learned man of the world." The visitors took their seats. The three men soon poured themselves wine and leaned their heads in close over the table. The young Pappi continued softly, "I trust my letter of introduction proved helpful to you."

"It did. It said you had news of a troublesome MuKierin in our midst. Tell me more."

Arta's eyelids began to blink sharply. "We wish to take hold of this troublemaker, this guest of Baern the trader. Then you and your master would be rid of the man."

"And why would you take him?"

"We are tracking a man who committed murder back in his homeland. An Elder demands revenge. We believe he is the man. Do you know his name?"

"No, my master cares nothing for the man. Do you know the name of the healer woman under his protection?"

"No, we care nothing for the woman."

"Is that so?" replied the steward, carefully watching Arta's eyes. "Then you would leave her here?"

"Yes, if that is what your master wants."

"Yes, that is what he wants," replied the steward. "If you took this man away, my master would step forward as her redeemer."

The dark-haired foreigner cocked his head in puzzlement. "What does this mean, 'redeemer?'" he asked.

Arta explained, "Among the Lake People, we offer protection for a woman without a man. Any man from our clan may step forward to seek her hand and become her redeemer. If more than one steps forward, they will bid for her."

The steward nodded. "If you take the man, my master would become the woman's redeemer. But how will you know whether you have found the man?"

"We know another MuKierin who can identify him," said Arta. "We will bring him here. Will you help us, good steward, to take the accused alive? He remains a dangerous and desperate one, so we must take care. We know your eyes roam far and wide over this land. We wish an opportune time to take him. You can help us take him alive and unawares. For this service, you would share richly in the reward."

The steward turned away, calculating the matter in his mind. "My master would smile to see a murderer taken off in chains," he said. "Nonetheless, he will demand certain protections. He stands as the law here, not any MuKierin, not even an aristocrat. They may not take away even a murderer except with the headman's permission. Thus, first, you must bring me formal charges against him, endorsed with the signet ring of a MuKierin Elder. Once you provide such a paper, my master will grant you written permission to arrest him. And after I help you take him, you will sign an affidavit signifying that the wanted man has been delivered to you alive so that he may stand trial in his homeland for his crime. You will sign it in my presence, at a place of my choosing, and then deliver unto me my share of the bounty. And some of my men will accompany you at this man's arrest to make sure that you comply with these requirements. Do you agree?"

Arta looked at his comrade and received a nod of confirmation. "It shall be as you say," Arta said. "You are a wise man. This way your master can show that he did not instigate this arrest. He simply did his duty to carry out justice. I trust that this will help him with the healer woman. She will see that your master acts justly."

"That is my hope," the steward replied. "Now let me add one final condition, gentlemen. You will stay far away from the woman and the trader's estate. I have my spies there.

Your presence near the estate would void our agreement. My master guards jealously what he longs to hold. He will crush anyone who gets in the way of what he wants. And right now, he wants this woman."

Chapter Seventeen

The Walls Close In

It was Noli who first noticed the stranger entering the courtyard of Uncle Shone's candle-making compound in Kierinswell. The autumn afternoon was winding down, but the women servants had yet to begin their preparations for the evening meal. For his part, Noli was ready for the day's work to end. Even so, he reached within and plucked up a merchant's smile in order to properly greet the stranger. The man stood with stooped shoulders and held a floppy hat in both hands. He had a pudgy face and hardly any beard. Noli wondered if he might be a delivery man. He stepped forward and asked the stranger, "Kinsman, may I help you?"

The man curtly replied, "I have something for you." From behind his hat he brought forth a black stone, which he placed in Noli's hand. "Do you recognize this?"

Noli blanched. "Yes, this belongs to Uncle Char. Why did you bring it to me?"

"Your uncle has been sold for his debts, which are many. He has appealed to you to prevent his downfall by settling with the ones he owes. I have been hired to bring you his stone. Will you intercede for him?"

"Yes, of course, I must. What do I need to do?"

"You know the tavern, the Cat and the Kitten. You must be there in ten minutes or your uncle will be sold to the Barsk."

"Ten minutes! That isn't enough time to gather all the treasure needed to pay off a man's debts."

"You don't need to bring the coins now," the stranger said. "You simply will hear the terms of payment to free your uncle and then you will pledge in writing to meet those demands. But you must go quickly and you must leave unseen. Sneak out a window from your kitchen to the side street. We'll be watching you every step along the way. If anyone goes with you or follows you, the men who hold your uncle will vanish without a trace. And your uncle will never escape the debtors' chains."

"Very well, look for me at the tavern."

Noli watched the stranger exit the yard. Immediately he turned and ran for one of the sheds. Inside, he hurried to a tarp and threw it back. There lay his worn leather saddle and his old speckled horsehair rope. Beneath those he reached and grabbed his father's sheath and sword. He wrapped these in a cloth and scampered back to the shed's entrance. To his relief, the surrounding yard sat vacant. He crossed to the kitchen and entered by a side door.

His movement, however, did not go unnoticed. Ash, the slave that Healdin had freed at the well at Sweetwater, had come with his new bride to live at the candle maker's compound. Each day he had watched all who entered the yard. He had seen the pudgy-faced man walk up to Noli, and then he had beheld Noli hasten to the shed and the kitchen. Quickly Ash trotted over to the shed. At once he saw the tarp pulled back from the saddle.

Inside the dim light of the kitchen, Noli could see little except the cleaned chopping tables with tiny beams of sunshine streaming onto them from the slits of the latched windows. The rooms seemed empty. Noli went to the first set of shutters and threw them back, causing the hinges to creak eerily. He brought over a stool and used it to climb atop the counter beneath the window. With much effort, he wriggled his way out the window and dropped down to the alley below. He landed hard and rolled over. When he regained his footing, his right knee ached sharply and forced him to limp. He hobbled off as quickly as he could. Along the way, he fastened the belt around him and positioned the sword on his left side. The street was busy with merchants and passers-by. Several waved to him. He nodded back at them but dared not open his mouth for fear it would slow him down. He reached a street corner and turned left, dodging a pair of parked donkey carts with their drivers sprawled sleepily beside them. Now he could see the two-story tavern and its veranda. A pair of men sat outside playing pebble dice at a table.

As Noli drew near, the pudgy stranger stepped out from the alley on the far side of the Cat and the Kitten. With one finger, he beckoned him over. The candle maker slowed his pace and began to look around him. A few men stood across from the tavern, but they seemed absorbed in conversation. Noli stopped on the street in front of the stranger.

"You have come just in time," the man told him. "Let us go back to the stable and talk with your uncle's creditors."

Noli hesitated. "Have them come inside the tavern, and we'll talk there. I like it inside, and they'll still get their coins."

The stranger said nothing but cast a glance to Noli's right. Noli turned to see a man moving toward him. He spun left and saw two more men advancing from the other side. Noli looked ahead at the tavern, but saw he already would be cut off from reaching it. With no other good option, he bolted straight at the pudgy man, knocking him aside and running down the alley. He feared that the stable would hold danger, so he turned right onto an alley immediately behind the tavern. Before him a single man blocked his path. He appeared about Noli's age but slighter in build and almost a head shorter. His eyes glinted bright and boyish, and a goatee set off a handsome chin. Indeed, he was the small one who a few months earlier had visited Ornelia and Melva on the night their throats were slit.

This small one drew a long, elegant sword and beckoned to Noli, "Come here, big man. We have business, you and I."

"What do you want with me?" Noli demanded.

"I have spent weeks looking for you. I want to kill you."

"Why? What did I ever do to you?"

The small one raised his sword and slashed the air back and forth with it. "I simply enjoy killing. Come to me, big man. Let us see what you can do with that pig sticker of yours."

Noli didn't reach for his sword. Instead, he turned and ran. But even as he retreated, his four pursuers turned into the alley. Noli sprang at them but could not break through. The assailants flung him down and held him there until they tied his hands behind his back. Then they pulled him up and rushed him inside the stable.

"What do you want with me?" Noli cried.

"You'll learn soon enough," the small one replied.

"This isn't about my uncle, is it? You want my woman's brother. Well, I don't know where he is, and I wouldn't tell you if I did."

"Soon enough you will tell me anything I want to know," the small one replied. "What a ripe idiot you are." He turned to his accomplices and barked, "Gag this fool and get him onto that cart. We have a long ride in front of us."

The men stuffed Noli's mouth with rags and tied them in place. They hoisted him into a cart pulled by two stout, gray horses. They covered him with a tarp and had the pudgy-faced one and another kidnapper sit on him. The small one opened the stable doors and the cart jostled out into the alley and down the lane, bound for the city's west gates. Three horsemen followed, trailing packhorses and spare mounts. The cart set out at a brisk trot, but it was evening and the streets were clogged with pedestrians making their way home.

Back at the compound, Ash had gone directly to the kitchen. There he found the shutters thrown back and the stool at the counter. Quickly he spun round and made for the front gate. When he exited the compound, he swung left and right but could see no sign of Noli on the lane. Clenching his teeth, he began trotting toward the main thoroughfare. He looked down each alley he passed but didn't leave the street. Suddenly three horsemen came around a corner a few blocks ahead of him. A cart followed. People scurried to get out of the way. Ash stepped aside and studied each face as the riders passed him. He noticed the pudgy-faced man sitting in the back of the cart. *There's the fellow,* Ash thought. *What's he sitting on? Is he holding Noli down?* The cart soon passed from sight. Ash turned and sprinted back to the candle maker's compound.

Noli's kidnappers passed out the city gates and onto the main road toward the Stone Fences, a town on the western edge of MuKierin civilization. The cart bumped along on that road for only a few minutes when the driver pulled the team to a halt.

The small one rode up to the cart. "Get him off there!" he ordered. Two men threw back the tarp and dragged Noli off the back end. They pulled off his gag but kept his hands tied in front. Noli needed but a moment to get his bearings. His eyes confirmed his worst suspicions. He recognized the road and at once he feared he was bound for the west, likely for the great lake of the Pappi. Worst of all, he suspected he was somehow going to become bait to catch Roj. A kidnapper brought a bay mare over to Noli and helped lift him aboard. The small one grabbed the mare's lead rope and set out west with Noli in tow, followed by three of the other kidnappers. Meanwhile, the cart driver and the pudgy-faced man returned to Kierinswell.

The kidnappers struck off at a trot and stayed on the main highway for a few hours. But when the sun disappeared from the horizon, they left the main road and ventured cross country in order to pass south of the Stone Fences. Even at dusk, they kept watching anxiously behind them. They pushed their horses at brisk walks and trots for four hours, stopping occasionally for brief rests. They passed the Stone Fences, making sure to stay out of sight of the village. The night settled in with clear skies and a half moon rising in the east. The men halted, dismounted and set off on foot to give the horses some relief. The kidnappers tied a rope around Noli's neck and led him stumbling over the plain.

So they proceeded, at times walking or riding, until the night was nearly half over. Noli had begun to doze in his saddle, but he awoke when the party made another stop. Immediately he heard new voices. He rubbed the sleep from his eyes and found he was surrounded by more horses and at least two new strange men. "Get down," the small one ordered him. "We will put you on a new mount. We have many miles left to travel before we rest." Noli obeyed and received a new horse, a pinto that reared slightly as soon as he climbed aboard. Noli leaned against the horse's neck, the better to keep from being thrown. He also decided to try to sleep all he could. *Let these cutthroats stay awake all night. I'll rest and try to look for escape when they stop to sleep.*

The kidnappers halted shortly before sunrise on a rocky plateau with a good view of the trail behind them. They chained Noli to a pack saddle, set a guard and then three of them proceeded to catch a few hours sleep. Noli tried to sleep but the chain kept irritating him. It chafed his wrist, reminding him of his dire predicament. How, he wondered, could he possibly break the chain and overcome four opponents.

Back in Kierinswell, Ash had gone back to the candle maker's compound and then to a nearby stable. He took a saddle horse and rode straight for Fire Mountain. The sun was sinking behind him as he climbed through the eastern foothills. When at last he spotted the sacred hilltop, he urged his horse into a canter and scrambled up the steep old road that circled around the base. It was dusk when he reached the top. The valley beneath him sat empty. Ash raised a horn to his lips and gave three great blasts. He took a few deep breaths and repeated his alarm. Then he climbed down from his horse and waited. Darkness was spreading slowly across the sage valley below him. Soon he could make out the approaching shapes of two riders. They crossed the valley and ascended the hilltop. Each was a great male warrior with a lance in one hand and a shield in another. When they drew close, they nodded to Ash and stared silently at him.

"Bad men have kidnapped Noli, the brother-in-law to the Horse Stalker," Ash said. "I don't know where they've taken him. I think they put him on a cart and left Kierinswell."

"Then the day has come," replied one of the warriors. "We must send the Spotted Stallion to seek out its master."

"But the bad ones have quite a head start. Can the

stallion find him in time?"

"He will outrun any horse of the Dry Lands. The stallion will find the Horse Stalker and also alert our people by the great lake. We will send him away tonight. As for you, go back to the Horse Stalker's sister and comfort her."

Late the next morning, Noli's kidnappers arose and ate a few strips of jerky. They gave their captive nothing but a cup of water. Hunger already was beginning to gnaw at Noli's insides, but he told himself he must show these men a stern face. One of the kidnappers soon began to pack while the other three drew their swords. The small one cast a harsh look at Noli and declared, "We cannot do without our exercise. Perhaps you would care to join us someday." The small one took his fighting stance, a sword in his right hand and a long dagger in his left. Two collaborators circled him and quickly attacked with their blades. The small one deflected both assaults and responded with sword thrusts. The three parried across the camp. The small one showed himself an accomplished swordsman. Seizing an opportunity, he caught one opponent off balance. With a blow from his shoulder, he knocked the man to the ground. Next, he fiercely attacked the other, thrusting aside his opponent's sword and setting the point of his own dagger against the other's chest. The kidnapper conceded.

The small one turned with both blades still drawn and gave Noli a look of disdain. The captive decided this was no time to back down. "The evil ones from Equis will give you a better fight," he said."

The small one growled, "We can deal with their kind, I assure you."

"Perhaps, but watch your back. The Dark Brood always seems to use a turncoat. Perhaps one of these rogues might serve as the traitor?"

The small one raised his dagger and glared at Noli. "One more word," he said, "and you will speak no more. Believe me when I say that I would happily deliver you to our destination without a tongue."

The small one fastened chains on Noli's wrists before

the kidnappers set out that morning. They moved slower than the previous day, but they rarely stopped to rest as they crossed a great sagebrush plain between the Powder Mountains and the Red River. The land did not lie flat but its gentle slopes seemed to stretch on for miles. That night they camped in a little gully. Noli had received only a little water at morning and evening. He had eaten nothing since noon the day before. Even so, he still wouldn't let himself beg from such men. He slept fitfully that night from the cold, as well as from the thirst and the hunger. Thankfully, the next morning one of the men gave him two cups of water. He sipped it carefully and wet his lips, even as a sense of despair washed over him.

That day the plains again stretched out before them. Noli looked out to the southwest and beheld a chocolate-colored mountain with three bands of lighter rock running in layers along its face. Soon he could make out a string of tooth-like hilltops, the gaps between them accentuated by extended shadows. A few hours later they began to pass a series of hills. From above, one looked like great lumps of rounded dough; another appeared as the claw of a great bird and a third brought to mind a hand with seven fingers. Noli had never ventured this far west, but he guessed that the kidnappers were staying well north of the canyons of the Red River. Even so, it appeared they would have to pass over a small mountain range to reach the great lake. Those hills now seemed less than ten miles away.

By the time they reached the base of the first slopes, the sun was sinking beneath the hilltops. The kidnappers dismounted and began grumbling with one another. Noli didn't know the language. He guessed it was the Common Tongue used between clans. And he soon suspected that they were debating whether or not to call a halt for the night. The small one was wagging a finger. His voice rang sharp with authority. The others acted lethargic. The talk soon ended, and the small one strode briskly back to Noli. "Get down," he told his captive. "The horses need a rest. You will walk up the slope."

The party began to climb. The soil on the hillside gave way just enough to make each step an ordeal. Noli struggled just to lift up his feet after they sank into the earth. It wasn't long before he quit looking up toward the top of the hill because it seemed impossible to think about ever reaching it alive. Then, as one of the kidnappers passed by with a string of horses, an idea came to him. Noli increased his stride and with his chained hands caught hold of a stirrup on the last animal. The kidnapper was leading the animals at a good clip, but Noli held on anyway, pulled ever upward. He noticed that the small one was by this time far in front. The others seemed too worn out to care that their captive was hanging on for all he was worth.

Halfway up the hill, the three lagging kidnappers called a halt. Noli fell to his knees. The man leading the horses took out a water skin and took a drink. The two others came and quickly demanded that he hand over the skin. Noli watched until he could stand it no longer. "Brothers," he whispered, "please, have mercy." The last one to take a drink brought the skin over. It contained less than a cup but Noli downed it all. A few moments later, the small one yelled down at them. Noli rose and set out, once more clutching the stirrup.

The dusk was growing deep by the time they reached the top. Even so, they could look out and see in the distance that several more ranges of hilltops blocked their way. Another argument ensued, but this time the small one gave in. They camped there that night. The captors even fed Noli a stick of jerky and gave him a few more swigs of water. He sat down and quickly shut his eyes. But that night, at the higher elevation, he shivered much and slept little.

The sun woke them early on the fourth day of Noli's captivity. The morning's journey included many unending treks up and down canyons on crumbling, light-colored gravel. The party rode most of the time, and Noli slept whenever he could, though often the trail ran along the edges of canyons with drops too steep to risk a nap. The kidnappers ran out of water and the small one cursed his collaborators for wasting drinks on their captive. Eventually Noli noticed more brush and even a few small trees on the slopes they were to cross. In the afternoon they climbed to the top of a ridge and Noli's eyes widened. There in the distance, he saw it: the great lake, blue and immense, with a small range of mountains rising behind its northeastern shore. *What a sight,* he thought, *and what a wretched way to come see it.*

Out from the nearby rocks, two men emerged and hailed them. The startled kidnappers nearly jumped out of their saddles, but soon they laughed and called back with relief. The two on foot drew close and began talking in the Common Tongue. Only a few words were exchanged and then the riders followed the two men as they trudged down the ridge to the place where they had hidden their horses. There, they passed around a water skin to all of their parched comrades, but not to Noli. Soon they set off downhill to a camp at the base of a slope by a small well. Noli at last received a drink and then collapsed beside a saddle to which he was quickly chained. The men spent the rest of the afternoon in camp. Later, a dark-haired man with a thick beard arrived, the same foreigner who had traveled with Arta to meet the steward of Circ the Headman. The kidnappers quickly gathered around him and listened as the newcomer spoke softly for several minutes. Noli lay too far away to even hear what tongue they were using. The men soon began stewing a chicken in a kettle over the fire. For Noli, who had eaten only a few sticks of jerky in four days, the smell of that simmering bird was too much to bear. It took a few hours of boiling but eventually the cook judged the chicken done and even Noli received some broth and a couple of bones with a few moist bites upon them. His kidnappers also gave him two pieces of a flatbread and a bit of boiled root. It was hardly a satisfactory meal, but after so much deprivation, he ate it with relish. Moreover, he was allowed to consume all the water he wanted.

Quickly he fell into a deep sleep, but his captors kicked him awake a mere four hours after sunset. In the dark, the party set out, riding single file down a slope and through a canyon. They crossed two more hills and emerged onto the eastern plain of the Pappi. Far off to their left, they could see the lights of a small village by the lake, but they veered away from it and continued riding north along the eastern shore. Noli wrapped a blanket around his shoulders and shivered himself to sleep. On they rode in the darkness. At last, the dawn appeared behind them. The sun soon swung up above the barren hills at their backs. It was then that Noli awoke, feeling a great weariness. Ahead, he saw they were coming to another village on the lake.

The men entered and stopped in a small square near an immense shed, made of both adobe and stone. The building appeared to touch the lake waters. The small one dismounted and barked at Noli, "Get down." Wearily, the captive complied. He was directed to sit on a stone wall in the middle of the village square. "You will stay here until I move you," the small one said. "If you try to escape, I will slit your throat and take great pleasure watching you bleed to death." He tied a rope tightly to Noli's left leg and fastened the other end to a ring in the wall.

Noli began to survey the square and its inhabitants. At one end, a few workmen were repairing a donkey cart. Nearby, servants walked past hauling great woven baskets on their heads. None of the villagers seemed to pay him any attention. To them, he seemed simply another MuKierin slave brought west, likely to be sold to one of the larger landowners. *But I haven't endured all this so they could sell me into slavery. So why am I here? And when will this nightmare end?*

That same morning, Roj and Tie walked south from the estate to the next village. A boat builder was preparing a new vessel for Baern, and he had sought the trader's approval for the design. Tie was delivering Baern's letter, and Roj was sent along to keep Tie safe. The two MuKierin hiked along on a crisp, autumn morning. On their way, they looked out on fishing boats skimming over the deep blue waters. Tie soon noticed that Roj wore a frown. "What's wrong with you, horse boy?"

"I had a dream last night that I was riding over a cliff," Roj said. "I was chasing some wild ones, and they leapt into a canyon and I could not stop my stallion from jumping in after them. And when I awoke, I sensed that something had changed. Do you ever get a funny feeling inside you, Tie?"

"No."

"Well, I do. I can sense the thoughts of some horses. And all morning I have sensed that something's out of kilter."

"Well, say nothing about it to the boat builder. They're superstitious. He'll blame you if anything goes wrong with his boats.

Roj looked up to a hill above the village and felt his heart jump. There, on the barren slope stood a Spotted Stallion. At once Roj knew it was his stallion. The great horse reared straight up on its hind legs. When its front feet returned to earth, it stared down at the two men.

"Is that what I think it is?" asked Tie.

"Yeah," said Roj. "It's a Spotted Stallion. It's my Spotted Stallion."

Once more the unexplainable happened. For Roj, the stallion's mane turned red, the same fiery glow that he had first envisioned in the seeker's cave and again at the Challenge of Orres. This time the horse appeared much farther away, and the eerie glow made the animal seem almost ghostly.

"Can you see that, Tie?" Roj asked. "Does the stallion's mane look red to you?"

"No," said Tie. "I see the horse, but its mane looks as white as snow.

"It's a sign, Tie. He's come for me."

The stallion bounded up to the top of the hill. It reared again and disappeared from sight. Roj watched all this with his mouth agape. "He's running east," he said. "I've got to follow him."

"But we've come to the boat builder," Tie said. "Behold, there stands his shed."

Reluctantly Roj turned to look back at the village. He

still wanted to follow the stallion, but his eye quickly fixed on a solitary figure sitting on a wall facing them. "That man's from our people," he said.

Tie nodded. "He's got the look of a MuKierin sold into the debtor's chains."

Roj strained his eyes for a better look. "Maybe not," he said. "I may know him." Quickly he took off for the square. The seated MuKierin noticed his approach and stood up. It was Noli. He recognized his brother-in-law and began to wave. "Run, Roj!" he shouted. "Please run!"

Roj turned and saw that three men already were coming up from behind him to block his retreat. Each man wore a sword. "Tie!" Roj shouted. "Go back and tell Healdin that my enemies have found me. Please go!"

"I'd better stay with you," said Tie.

"No, Healdin needs to know what's happened. She'll send help. Please go now while you can."

Tie bounded to the side and veered across the square. The three men ignored him and drew close to Roj. One pointed for him to move toward the boathouse. Roj obeyed. As he approached, a small man and a dark-haired foreigner stepped beside Noli. The small one called out in MuKierin, "Welcome, Horse Stalker. We have brought you a present. Let's go into the boat barn and have a talk." The foreigner and the small one led the way, with Noli shuffling weakly behind them. Roj felt great anger rising inside as he looked upon his chained, mistreated brother-in-law. But fear also touched him, the fear of confronting so many strange and desperate men.

Inside, despite his desperate situation, Roj couldn't help looking around at a place that foreigners were forbidden to enter. He noticed that the back end of the boathouse stood open to the lake and offered a picturesque view across the water to the western shores. On the ground and to one side of that opening, amid the tools and hoists and pulleys, lay a small two-man vessel. But toward the front of the boat house, built on blocks, sat the beginning of a larger trade ship, the one Baern had ordered. In the few moments Roj had to

227

observe, he saw that the vessel was being constructed of long, fat bundles of reeds, placed one on top of the other and running the length of the vessel. However, his eyes soon were drawn again to the back end of the boathouse. There he noticed a worn trench had been dug there, extending out to the lake and allowing the waters to enter inside the structure, a space protected beneath the boat house roof. Inside the building there seemed to be nearly a dozen men, including some Pappi and some MuKierin.

As he made sense of his surroundings, Roj watched two kidnappers grab Noli by his arms and drag him down into the flooded trench. The kidnappers waded up to their knees, roiling the muddy water. They shoved Noli face down beneath the surface. The chained man kicked and twisted, struggling in vain to break free. Roj cried, "Stop! Leave him alone!" Even as he spoke, his mind reeled once more with the image of the stallion running east."

The small one barked an order and the two men lifted their captive's head above the water. He told Roj, "I will leave him alone when you tell me where to find the Golden Box. If you don't know where it is, we'll drown your kinsman and send the corpse to the White Beard, along with one of your fingers. We will tell that proud old man that you'll be next if we don't get what we want." He nodded and the two men once more forced Noli's head under the water.

Roj watched his kinsman's legs and torso slosh helplessly in the trench. Noli seemed to fight a little less with every passing moment. Roj knew he must do something fast, anything to save Noli. Again he saw the image of the stallion running east. "Wait! Stop! I'll tell you whatever you want to know."

The small one gave a call, and the two kidnappers once more lifted up their soaked captive. This time they flung him onto one of the trench's earthen banks. Noli rolled over, his chest heaving as his lungs took in air. The small one demanded, "Horse Stalker, don't lie to me. Do you know where to find the Golden Box and the great power that lies within it?"

"Yes," Roj lied. "Yes, I'll tell you whatever you want to know." He looked anxiously at Noli.

The small one smirked and spoke in the Common Tongue to the dark-haired foreigner. His speech, though foreign to Roj, conveyed an edge of triumph. But the foreigner seemed less intent on listening to the kidnapper and more concerned with staring at the Horse Stalker. Roj sensed immediately that the man was trying to perceive whether or not he was lying. He glanced back briefly to Noli, his tangled hair still drenched with water. Roj saw their fates now rested with him. He hardened his face and turned to stare down his captors.

The small one again spoke in MuKierin: "Horse Stalker, what proof can you give us that you know the Golden Box's hiding place?"

"What proof will you accept?"

"A map. I will accept a map."

Roj's mind seemed to drift for a moment, and once more he envisioned the stallion running east. Immediately he sensed he might find a way of escape. "I have a map," he told the small one. He carefully watched the expression of his captor. "But if you want the Golden Box, you must agree to spare both me and my kinsman here."

The small one moved closer to him. "Where can we find this map?"

"It's in my hut back at the Pappi trader's estate. The woman I watch over could give it to you, as could her servant. But you have to say the right words."

"What words?"

"You must tell them you want the map that the White Beard made for me. It shows the way to a special hilltop. If you mention the old man's name, they'll know that I want them to give you the map."

"The White Beard made it for you, did he? And where is this hilltop?"

Roj decided there was now no turning back in this gamble. "It lies to the northeast in the no-mans land between the MuKierin and the Pappi. I've been there. You can get to it from the East Point Trail. I can lead you there, with or without the map."

Quickly the small one and foreigner walked to the front of the boathouse. Waiting there for them was another conspirator, Arta, the Pappi who had visited Baern's compound in search of Roj. And nearby stood three of Circ the Headman's guards, there to make sure the kidnappers stayed away from Healdin. The dark-haired foreigner looked back at Roj and asked his collaborators, "The Horse Stalker says he can take us to the Golden Box. Can we believe him?"

The small one said, "He says he has a map and that the way to the treasure lies beyond the East Point. He says he knows the way well enough. Let's send our Pappi friend here to get the map. I will tell you what you must say to his woman and her servant. If he doesn't have a map, we can always kidnap the woman."

"We cannot kidnap the woman," Arta replied. "As I have said many times, we have not enough men to take her. Circ the Headman is scared that we really want the woman and not the man. That's why his steward has made clear that he wants us to stay well clear of her. And that's why he sent these three guards to watch over us. He insisted that I, alone, go to meet the steward at the trader's home. I'll go there and get the map, if it exists."

"That sounds good," said the foreigner. "And I'm glad the Horse Stalker says he has a map. He must know that we'll learn soon enough if he's lying. If he is, I'm going to kill his kinsman right in front of him."

"Don't worry," said the small one. "He has a map. I can see it in his eyes."

The foreigner said to Arta, "Go get the map and come after us. We'll leave a man behind for you at the East Point. That's a good place to meet you. How long will it take you to get there?"

"I can reach the pass in three hours," said Arta. "These guardsmen will escort me back to the trader's home. I'll sign some legal papers for the release of the Horse Stalker. After that, I'll pay the steward his bribe, get the map and make for the East Point."

"Our man is going to wait for you at the pass for four hours," the foreigner said. "Up there, he'll be able to see you coming. Don't fail us, Arta. If you don't make it to the East Point, we'll take the Horse Stalker and go after the treasure without you."

Chapter Eighteen

Into the Wild Lands

The kidnappers chained Roj's hands and set out for the East Point. Arta, however, turned north with the headman's three guards for Baern's home. The four riders trotted briskly along the main road along the lake's shore. Soon they began to overtake Tie, who was running back to the trader's estate to warn Healdin. The slave quickly slid down an embankment and out of sight. Ignoring him, the riders passed by without slowing down.

At Baern's estate, Arta found more than a dozen of the headman's soldiers waiting for him. He was surprised by such a large gathering, but he tried not to show it. The headman's steward stepped from Baern's office and waved him over. Arta dismounted and followed him inside. Immediately the steward announced, "I shall now begin my inquiry to make sure that justice has been done this day." Arta immediately noticed that these words weren't meant for him but for the trader, Baern, who was standing by his main counter. The steward continued, "I consider it proper that our good kinsman Baern should witness these proceedings, since he welcomed the accused into his home."

"I do not believe the young MuKierin committed murder," said Baern. He pointed to Arta. "This young gentleman has visited my home before. I suspect him of some treachery in this matter."

The steward tightened his jaw. "I did not come here to judge the innocence of the MuKierin. Neither is it my job to question the character of this Pappi gentleman. I came here to make sure that all men abide by our laws. Now, let us hear the report."

"Today we apprehended the guilty man," said Arta. "His own kinsman identified him. A MuKierin elder has signed the warrant. Now the prisoner will go to Kierinswell

233

and stand trial for his crimes. I have prepared the affidavit of his arrest and I now will sign it in the presence of all." He unrolled a scroll and sat at a table with quill and ink. Quickly his hand scribbled his name to the parchment. He left it there and stood. "Before I depart," he said, "I wish to retrieve one piece of evidence. The murderer confessed to stealing a map and taking it with him. It lies inside his hut. It will help to prove his guilt. The healer woman knows its location."

"The healer woman is away helping a needy child," the steward replied with a sly smile at Arta. He waited until the younger man grasped that her absence was no coincidence. The headman was taking no chances of losing the woman. The steward continued, "However, if you briefly hand over your sword to my guard, you may go and question the woman's servant."

Arta could hardly help from sneering at the charade being played out for the benefit of the Pappi trader. "Gracious steward," he gushed, "I will do as you bid with heartfelt thanks. I know you would think it improper of me to give you any token of my thanks in response to the discharging of your duties. But ask your men later and they will vouch that I consider myself indebted to you for all that you have done." With that he turned and walked out the door, followed by the three guardsmen. He unbuckled his sword and handed it over to one of them. Next, he removed from his cloak a sack of coins and threw it to another man. "See to it that your master gets his reward," he said. "I believe that man would know if a single coin were missing."

Back inside the trader's office, the steward fastened his black cloak and prepared to depart. "I must mention one last matter," he announced. "I expect you will want to know about the safekeeping of the woman."

"She is my guest," said Baern. "I will continue to watch over her."

"Indeed?" replied the steward. "That is most noble of you, good Baern, but my master Circ feels obligated after this unfortunate affair to personally vouchsafe for the woman, at least for the near term. She no longer has a guardian, and my master feels a duty for her safekeeping. Of course, any kinsman may petition to speak to the disposition of such a woman. I suppose some will seek her hand. The woman certainly seems to have her way of enticing men."

"She is a noble woman," Baern answered sternly. "I don't intend to abandon her now. I am prepared to petition on her behalf. If necessary, I will step forward as her redeemer."

"Will you?" the steward replied, arching his eyebrows. "Indeed, you shine with truly noble thoughts today. I will so inform my master. He has told me that he will consider such petitions one week from today."

"A week? Why so long? Let us settle this matter today."

"Ah, Baern, you know that at certain times justice moves slowly. This is such a time. But never fear. You and all the other suitors will have your day before my master. And now I bid you farewell, my kinsman. Farewell."

At Roj's hut, Mirri quickly went looking for the map. With the headman's guard in the room, she retrieved it and handed it over to Arta. The young Pappi regained his sword, climbed atop his horse and set off for the East Point. The lead soldier, meanwhile, told Mirri, "Your mistress's guardian, the MuKierin, has been taken in chains to stand trial in his homeland. Your mistress soon will be delivered to Circ the Headman's fortress. We shall escort you there, too."

Mirri readily agreed. Even as she departed under guard, Baern's servant Tie came running up the road. At the edge of the estate he stopped briefly to catch his breath. As he began to walk down toward the courtyard, he noticed a handful of the headman's guards clustered by the cooking hut. At once, they made for him. For a moment, Tie considered running. But he gritted his teeth and continued down the lane toward Baern's office. He would not forsake Roj now.

The steward's chief guardsman called out to him, "Where are you going, slave?"

"I have news for my master."

"Have you?" he asked. "And I have news for you,

slave." He drew close to Tie and plunged a small dagger into the MuKierin's midsection. Tie toppled. Quickly he realized the wound itself was not deep. For a moment he felt relief, and then the soldier spoke. "The headman's steward put enough poison on this dagger to kill a sea dragon," he announced. "He has decided to pay the slave price for you. Spend your last moments well, horse boy. Very soon, your boat will take you across the waters of death."

Two of the guardsmen dragged Tie over to a nearby shed and flung him on the dirt floor. None of Baern's servants dared help him. They all feared for their lives. And Baern, unaware of his slave's fate, sat at his desk and stared forlornly out his window at the water. So the day passed until Healdin and one of Baern's servants returned from visiting a sick child in the village. Healdin was carrying her bag of medicines. Immediately the chief guardsman approached her.

"Woman, I bring you ill news," he said. "Today, a group of MuKierin brought a warrant and took your guardian away to answer for murder. That makes you a ward of our master, the mighty Circ the Headman. Already your servant has been escorted to his fortress. Gather a few things, and we will escort you there, too."

To the soldiers, it seemed that Healdin took the news with an unnatural calmness. "I will do as you bid," she said. "But first, I will speak with Baern." Immediately she entered her hut and scanned its interior. Still clutching her bag, she grabbed a cloak and made for the trading house. As she crossed the yard she saw Tie rise up from the floor of the shed. He started to stand, but fell over.

"Leave him be," the chief guardsman warned Healdin. "He is a slave."

"He is a man," said Healdin. "Do not stand between me and my duty as a healer or your headman will hear of it." Afraid, the guardsman stepped back as Healdin rushed past him to the shed. She bent over Tie and said, "Rest easy, my friend. You will live."

"Don't worry about me, woman," Tie said. "I've got bad news. Some men kidnapped Roj at the boat builder's shed. They even brought along a MuKierin that Roj knew. I'm not sure who he was. Roj sent me back to warn you, but I'm afraid that I arrived too late. I'm sorry, lady. What a bad day this has become for all of us. What a sorry man, I am. I didn't want to die this way."

Tears began to roll down Healdin's cheeks. Tie saw them fall and began to cry, too. From her bag, she removed a small vial and placed a drop of its elixir on her fingertip. "Behold the Living Fire," she told him. "Taste it, Tie, and live. Rest assured that I will attend to you, and you will survive." She placed her finger on his tongue. Immediately, Tie entered into a deep sleep. Quickly, Healdin examined his wound. She ran to the kitchen and mixed up a gooey concoction, as black as tar and just as sticky. Then she returned to the slave, applied the mixture to his wound and covered him with a blanket.

"Now I will speak to Baern," she told the guardsmen. Their chief soldier followed her into the trading house. Inside, Baern rose anxiously.

"Lady!" he cried. "What a wretched day!"

"Baern," she answered, "your servant Tie has received a poisonous wound." The trader's eyes flashed and he turned in anger to the guardsman. Healdin lifted a hand in order to reassure her host. "Do not fear. I have attended him and he will live, if he's allowed to rest. He now lies in the nearby shed. Please have your servants take him to a hut and keep him warm."

"Of course, I'll see that it is done. I'm sorry, lady. I wanted you to remain here, but the headman has demanded that you go to him for a time and live under his protection. I'm powerless in this matter. I hope you will forgive me. Even so, I will not abandon you. I will seek your release."

"Thank you, Baern. All will be well. I will go willingly to the headman to regain my servant. And I shall send you word as soon as I may." She turned to the guardsman. "I will go with you now."

"I have directed my men to take you to the mighty Circ," he replied. "I will stay behind and return later."

Healdin looked at him soberly. "Do you intend to stay behind so that you can try once more to kill the MuKierin slave?" she asked.

The guardsman gave her a sly grin. "Woman, I tried to keep you from wasting your time on him. Now you must leave."

Healdin, however, did not make for the door. Instead, she reached into her bag and pulled from it a large jewel-like stone. It covered much of the palm of her hand and appeared almost spherical, except at two ends. One rose to a gentle point; the other was flat with a strip of metal fixed to it, and through the metal passed a flat leather thong that was long enough to serve as a necklace. In the daylight the stone gleamed clear, a little like a dull diamond. "Have you ever beheld the White Gem of the Green Lands?" she asked the guardsman. "There is none like it."

The guardsman's eyes fixed on the stone. "Woman," he asked, "do you offer me such a large bribe for such a wretched slave?"

"You misunderstand me," said Healdin, drawing alongside him. "I do not wish to bribe you. I wish to render you senseless." As she spoke those last words she touched the guardsman's hand with the gem. Immediately, he fell over as one dead.

Baern looked on in horror. "What have you done?" he gasped. "What has become of him?"

"Don't be afraid, Baern. I simply stopped him from doing more harm. He still lives, I assure you. But the children of the Dry Lands cannot abide the touch of the White Gem. This stone puts them into a sleep that lasts for days. And in that time, dark nightmares often come upon them. This one likely will dream of being chased by a poisoned knife. When he wakes, he may never touch a dagger again."

"You say that those of the Seven Clans may not touch the gem," said Baern. "But it doesn't have any effect on you, lady. I see once again that you aren't like us. And yet I still can't grasp why you've come among us."

"I have come to prepare the way for a Champion for

238

all the people of the Dry Lands. One day, Baern, that Champion will seek your help. On that day, you must decide whether or not you will follow him."

Healdin stepped outside where the remaining guardsmen were waiting on their horses. She took the reins to a spare horse and mounted. The soldiers looked to Baern. He pointed back inside and tried to speak with composure, "As you know, your chief guardsman has decided to stay behind. You may go. Take this woman and give the mighty Circ my greetings." The soldiers looked strangely at each other. It seemed unusual for the head guardsman to stay inside now. But they had their orders and none dared question Baern, a Pappi of higher rank than themselves. Thus, they surrounded Healdin and rode for home.

What a strange woman she is, Baern thought to himself. *But what will happen next?*

The kidnappers wasted no time reaching the East Point. They pushed their horses to the top of the pass and stopped there, allowing their mounts a few minutes to rest. From atop the point, they could scan the lower hills and valleys all the way back to the lake's shore. The ground below lay empty and still.

As the party halted, Roj and Noli sat despondently in chains on their horses. Neither dared speak to the other. Suddenly in Roj's mind came a vision of the Spotted Stallion standing on a hilltop above the desert. Roj closed his eyes and struggled to see all he could. The visions soon faded, but the young man pondered the meaning.

Nearby, the dark-haired foreigner took one of his underlings with him to a suitable lookout. "You will stay here for four hours," he said as he drew a line in the dirt by a boulder. "When the shadow of this rock comes round to meet this line, you will come and find me.

"But what if the Pappi hasn't come?" the other asked.

"All the more, you must come and find me. Who knows who might try to come after us? Now keep alert and don't fail me.

The foreigner left the man at the lookout and returned to the other kidnappers. Immediately they turned their horses and baggage train east for the place the White Beard called Newell. Roj would lead them there.

At that very hour, Pibbibib and Weakling were making for the East Point. The warriors were keeping among the hills south of the promontory so they wouldn't be spotted. Soon they reached a long slope leading toward their destination. Pibbibib climbed steadily, eager to reach the high ground and scan the country along the lake's eastern shore. Weakling kept a constant watch behind him, knowing they now were exposing themselves as they climbed. Nonetheless, they remained hidden from the kidnapper who had stayed behind at the East Point.

"We should wait until dark," Weakling warned. "If the enemy appears, we'll be caught out here with no place to hide."

"Then we will fight," said Pibbibib. "Now isn't the time to hide. You know that. This is the time to take fortune by the hand."

The night before, the two warriors had been watching the road between the Pappi and the MuKierin. Pibbibib had felt restless. For most of the previous day, he had sensed something in the wind, a feeling he had not experienced in months. The day had passed without event, but still the feeling would not go away. Weakling had cursed Pibbibib when the larger warrior spoke of the sensations. But in the night, the two caught the sound of hooves on the road. Soon enough a Spotted Stallion cantered up the way and continued past them. That was enough for Pibbibib. He was sure the horse was the same one that Roj had won at the Challenge of Orres. Moreover, he concluded that Healdin's scent remained upon the animal. He immediately had declared that the presence of the horse signaled something of great import.

Now, as the two crossed the slope below the East Point, Weakling called to him, "But what will we do when we reach the top there? You don't know where to go next. You're just groping about without a clue."

"Curse you!" growled the Backstabber. "Have you a better plan? My plan is to stand on that high place and look out on the lake and consider my next move. That stallion was a sign, I tell you. And we both know our prey lies near. Remember that traveler we caught a few days back on the road? Before you killed him and made a meal of him, that wretched dog revealed that a MuKierin had brought a healer woman to the eastern side of the lake. He called her a great beauty, even though she wears a veil. We both know that he was speaking about our MuKierin and She of the little light of fire. Surely the human spies for the Red Brigade know this, too. In time, even that stupid miscreant Zhaggee will join the hunt for our horse dog. We can't stand back and act timid now. I feel it in my bones."

On they climbed as the afternoon waned. When they drew near the top, Pibbibib spotted movement in the rocks. He caught Weakling's eye and placed three fingers to his lips. Weakling knew that signal: Dinner! Pibbibib pointed to the high place. The two proceeded with a stealth perfected over hundreds of years and thousands of hunts. The kidnapper above had his back to them and his attention fixed on the deserted trail leading back to the lake. He heard not a pebble slip on the ridge behind him, nor did he sense the danger drawing closer and closer to him. After a time, he turned to examine the sun's shadow in relation to the line in the dirt that would mark his departure time. He looked up to the sky and, behold, Pibbibib rose up on a boulder above him, so close that the warrior could take one jump and pounce upon his prey.

The Backstabber looked on the kidnapper with a merciless satisfaction. "Hello, little one," he said in the Common Tongue. "What brings you here, today?"

The kidnapper turned and ran for his horse, but Weakling stepped out of the rocks to block the path. "Let the feasting begin," the giant gloated.

"Not yet," Pibbibib replied. He leapt down and sprang upright with the balance of a cat. "First, we must talk. Tell us, little one, have you seen our MuKierin? He lives below with a healer woman. Where is he?"

The kidnapper's mind raced as he weighed his choices. "Please let me go," he pleaded. "I do not know the man."

"He lies," said Weakling.

"My chum thinks you lie," said Pibbibib. "You wear a sword and fancy yourself a master of fortune, as do we. We all know how this is going to end for you. Your death will come much swifter if you tell us the truth now, before we have to grip you by the throat. But either way, you're going to tell us all we want to know."

The color drained from the kidnapper's cheeks, but he bit his lip and kept silent. Pibbibib nodded twice toward Weakling. "No blades yet," he ordered. "Just crack bones." He walked away to look over the trail back to the lake. Turning toward Weakling, the kidnapper drew his sword. But that great warrior caught the hand as the blade exited its scabbard. Weakling clamped down on the wrist until sheer pain dropped the kidnapper to his knees. The sword fell useless to the ground.

Weakling chided, "Little one, my chum said, 'no blades yet'." Once more he squeezed, and the main writhed as the cartilage and small bones of the wrist gave way beneath a viselike grip. "Now little one, will you speak? Or must I bite off these little fingers, one at a time?"

Pibbibib, meanwhile, scanned the land beneath him. To his delight, he spotted a rider trotting up the trail. He turned and hustled back to Weakling. "Muffle him," he ordered. "Another dog comes our way. Let's get ready to greet him."

A few minutes later, Arta, the Pappi kidnapper, topped the rise and halted at the East Point. Weakling stepped forth with the other kidnapper clutched in a headlock. Pibbibib slipped from behind a boulder, blocking the horseman's escape. Arta's eyes opened wide. But he made no attempt to flee. Instead, what he said next surprised everyone.

"You're here early," Arta declared in the Common Tongue as calmly as he could muster.

Pibbibib stared cruelly at him, unsure whether the words contained some trickery. "Are we?" he replied inquisitively.

"Indeed, I didn't expect you or the others from your order until after sunset," Arta said. Gaining his confidence, he pointed at the other kidnapper and continued, "I thought I'd have to kill this one on my own. But happily, it appears that you will dispose of him for me."

The other kidnapper could not contain his indignation. "What do you mean by this backstabbing?" he demanded.

Pibbibib was asking himself the same question. He said to Arta, "Go ahead. Tell him."

"It means that you have chosen the wrong side," Arta said. "The Golden Box will be found, but neither you nor your associates will ever hold it or touch the power that lies within."

"You have betrayed us to Equis!" the other kidnapper cursed. "Scum and traitor, you will pay for this! You have turned on your own kind."

"I merely did what you would have done if given the same opportunity. But now the time has come for you to spend a moment contemplating your life because it's about to come to a violent end." Arta turned to Pibbibib and declared, "He's of no further use to us. I suggest you annihilate him."

Pibbibib had to admire such treachery, even as he played his own game of deception with this Pappi. "Let us not be too hasty," he replied. "First, tell us where we can find our MuKierin."

"He's out there east of here. He's chained up and watched by a half-dozen men. We can easily follow their trail. And best of all, I know their destination. I have a map from the MuKierin that shows where the Golden Box lies hidden."

"The Box!" Weakling gasped. Pibbibib could see that even his dull-witted comrade was beginning to grasp that they had stumbled upon a most incredible opportunity.

"Shut up, fool," Pibbibib barked in their rebel tongue. "Take your dog behind the rocks and have your way with him. We'll leave here in five minutes."

Weakling dragged the kidnapper away. The struggling man begged, "No, please wait! Please let me go! I can pay. I can tell you what you want to know. Please!"

Pibbibib strode up to Arta and said, "Get down and show me the map."

"Certainly. At first, I feared you were not with the Red Brigade," the traitor said as he opened a saddlebag and withdrew the map. "My heart went into my throat. Imagine my relief to see the skulls and lightning bolts upon your cheeks."

Pibbibib nodded as he glanced at the map. However, he quickly frowned. "This chart shows the location of a well and a hilltop, not the Golden Box," he observed, not hiding his displeasure.

Arta anxiously noted the other's sour demeanor. "No doubt the mapmaker wanted it so, in order to better protect the hiding place of the great treasure. But the MuKierin said he knows how to find it, and your people will have no trouble overtaking him."

"As you say. Now, we must get your former associate's horse and leave this place."

"Do you not have horses?" the Pappi asked. "The message said you would be bringing them." His eyelids began to blink sharply every few seconds

Pibbibib watched Arta's eyes and grinned mercilessly. "We now have two mounts," he replied. "Let us go."

"But the message said I should wait here for your captain. Your associates and you can overtake the MuKierin in the night. I do not wish to disobey your masters. It would go badly for both of us to anger them."

"I grow tired of your words," Pibbibib warned. "You will do as I say. We will leave this place at once and go after the MuKierin."

Dread fell on Arta, and at last he began to understand that these evil ones might be some sort of renegades, probably out to get the Golden Box for themselves. Even so, he knew he dared speak no more. Slowly, he mounted his horse.

Pibbibib got aboard the other, which was really too small for so large a warrior. Weakling soon emerged and trotted beside them as they set out into the empty lands east of the lake.

With their departure, the East Point remained empty until almost sunset. A group of eight immense warriors approached from the south on horseback—not far from the same path that Pibbibib and Weakling had taken earlier in the day. These new warriors wore the brands of skulls and lightning bolts upon their faces. Among them rode Zhaggee, whom Weakling had greeted recently in the hill country. They climbed to the high place and looked out on the lake as the sun was sinking, its pink and red hues highlighting the mountains in the west. Finding the pass empty, the warriors spread out and searched the ground. Soon, one came back and reported to their captain, "Yonder lies a dead dog, a stranger, killed within the day. One of our own kind did the deed and made a hasty meal of him afterward."

"But where is our own lapdog, the one they call Arta?" the captain replied.

"We have found no sign of him."

"Blast, who has gone sticking their beaks into our business? Some misfits must have snatched our spy and made off with him. Check the tracks and look around for any signs of who did this brash deed. Some scum is going to pay dearly for this."

Zhaggee joined a few warriors in making for the corpse. "Let us enjoy a light repast before the journey," he joked as he approached the dead man. "I trust a morsel or two remains on the bones." But he pulled up short when he beheld the body. For when he looked at the dead kidnapper's head, Zhaggee at once noted that the right earlobe was missing. His eyes grew wide and his jaw dropped.

"Weakwi!" he hissed.

Roj's kidnappers rode until near sunset. The dark-haired foreigner halted them on high ground with a sweeping view back west toward the land of the Pappi. Roj scanned the landscape, with its sage and rocks and a series of small mounts to the north. He calculated in his mind how much farther the party had to travel to reach Newell. He knew it would take more than a day.

The kidnappers at once tied up their horses and started a cooking fire. But they didn't unload the pack horses, and they didn't set out any bedrolls. Roj noted this and surmised that they were waiting to see whether their two comrades would catch up to the main party before nightfall. In the meantime, Roj and Noli were placed on the ground with their backs against a small boulder. Noli looked exhausted. Roj lifted his chained hands and whispered. "Rest on me, brother."

"I can't last much longer, Roj. The last few days have been too much for me. I just want to lie down and never get up again."

"Hold on, Noli. You've got a wife and soon you'll have a child, too. For their sake, please hold on."

Noli shrugged. "Now do you regret getting caught up with that foreign woman? I told you trouble would come of it."

Roj ached at the words, but he couldn't get angry at his brother-in-law after all he had suffered. "Noli, I'm so sorry for what these bad ones have done to you. But I can't turn my back on Healdin. When I first came here to the Lake Country, I made a mess of things. I even got one of our kinsmen killed through my own stupidity. After that, I just wanted to give up. But Healdin stood by me. She wouldn't let me give up. And I don't intend to now. You'll see. Together, we're going to break free of these villains or die trying."

"Do you have a plan?"

"I'm making one. You'll hear it before we get to our destination."

The kidnappers killed and roasted three chickens, which they had brought in a crate on a pack horse. The fresh meat with its roasted juices seemed to briefly lift their spirits. They even ripped off a leg and a wing and threw them to their captives. Roj gave both pieces to Noli. "I've had more meals than you in the last few days," he said. "Please, brother, eat.

We're going to need you to regain your strength." Noli wanted to refuse the extra food but he couldn't. After the meal, he fell asleep on Roj's shoulder.

As dusk was fading, the small one approached Roj. He looked agitated, as if he already had been in one argument and was spoiling for another. "Horse Stalker," he snapped. "Can a man find the Golden Box with only your map?"

The words stirred Roj, but he took his time answering. He lifted the drowsy Noli off his shoulder and rose slowly to his feet. He looked over the camp and concluded that the two other kidnappers had failed to catch up to their comrades. "A smart man might be able to find it," Roj replied. "That man would have some trouble without a guide, but the map is a good one. Haven't your men returned?"

The small one ignored him and retreated to the dark-haired foreigner, who sat on a blanket by the fire. Roj's eyes narrowed. He saw his chance to manipulate these men and push them toward Newell on his timetable. With his hands in chains, he approached the two leaders as they spoke intently to one another in the Common Tongue. Roj called to them, "You're afraid that your two comrades may try to cheat you of the Golden Box. But you may have failed to see another danger."

The small one turned to scrutinize him. "What danger?" he asked skeptically.

"They might have shared the map with the Dark Brood."

"We trust our own. They would not betray us to the Equis."

"Is that so? You're afraid that they might cheat you of the Golden Box but not that they would betray you to the evil ones?"

The foreigner demanded a translation. The two kidnappers spoke to one another and then the small one asked Roj, "Very well, what's your advice?"

"You've got no choice but to push ahead tonight. Perhaps your men are trustworthy, though greedy men will find themselves greatly tempted to take the box for themselves. But the Dark Brood's also chasing me. And if those evils ones capture and torture your men, they'll soon learn everything. They'll find us and attack us all during the night."

The small one carefully studied Roj's face. "So you want us to ride through the night," he said. "Are you more afraid of Equis than me? That would be a mistake."

"Perhaps you'll scare me more after you've battled the Dark Brood and come away victorious. But they've got two fierce warriors hunting for me. They almost killed me once. If they find us here, they'll keep me alive long enough to take them to the Golden Box. But before they do, they'll feast on your corpses."

Roj turned and strode back to Noli. "We're leaving soon," he whispered, squatting down beside his brother-in-law. "It's a bad sign for them that their two friends haven't caught up to us. They're starting to getting scared. Let's try to use that to our advantage."

"Okay," said Noli. "I'll give it all I've got for Remy and our child. All I ask is that you come up with a plan."

Chapter Nineteen

A Flash in the Night

Night had fallen when Circ's guardsmen brought Healdin to the headman's stone fortress on the eastern shore of the lake. Dressed in a tan, hooded robe and still wearing her veil, the healer woman walked beside two guardsmen as they escorted her from an outer courtyard into the great hall of the compound. Candles burned dimly along the granite walls of the passageways, and a fireplace glowed brightly at one end of the hall. There, four women turned and arose to stare at the newcomer. They came forward a few steps, their long gowns skimming over the floor's black stones. Their dresses of reds and greens suggested they were the headman's relatives, quite possibly his wives. Their stern faces showed resentment at the intrusion of another woman. But they kept their distance and said nothing.

The guardsmen led Healdin through a wide passage and up a great stair to the master's chambers. Precious wood, not sticks, but real planks fashioned and varnished, had been used to build the door. To the guardsmen, it was a great honor simply to knock upon that door, to actually rap it and rub across it afterward. An attendant drew the door open and motioned for Healdin to enter. She obeyed and the door swung closed behind her. The attendant led her to a fire in a hearth with two candelabras glowing on either side.

The attendant left her and she stood alone for several minutes, calmly staring into the leaping flames. The headman entered quietly from a side room. He appeared a large man with a round, flat face and a small, gray beard. His blue eyes gleamed as he beheld the woman's profile, still shrouded by the hood and the veil. She seemed unaware of his presence. At last he spoke, "You show patience, woman. That pleases me. I am most pleased to bring you into my home."

Healdin removed her hood and turned to fix her eyes on her host. "Why have I been brought here against my will?" she asked.

"You're a woman without a guardian, without a man. As the headman of this region, the duty falls upon me to see that no one takes advantage of you."

"My guardian has been falsely accused, and you have allowed his abduction."

"Do not insult me, woman. All that has happened has been according to our law. A MuKierin elder signed a warrant for the man and placed his signet ring upon the parchment. My own guard witnessed the arrest and recorded it in my archives. The accused will go back to stand trial among his own people. They will judge him, not I. I merely followed the law of my people."

"And now what is to be my fate?"

"I like your bluntness, woman, so allow me to be blunt, too. You will become my wife, my fifth, if it matters to you. Of course, some of my kinsmen probably will seek your hand, perhaps even that fool of a trader who has been your host in recent months. I foresee a bidding war for who will become your redeemer, and quite a contest, too, given your appeal. But I am the wealthiest man on this side of the lake, and I will have you. I will pay dearly for you, with the money going into the treasury of the common good, which I alone control."

"And what say will I have in this?"

The headman gave her an impish smile. "You get to decide whether or not you will love me. My other wives do not love me, so I can hardly expect such passion from you. Instead, I'll be content to have you, and I'll give you the freedom to be content or miserable, as you wish."

"May I leave you now?"

"Not until I say so. First, I want to unveil you. I have gone to great trouble to oversee your safety, and now I shall reward myself by gazing upon your face. I have no doubt that your veil hides a wondrous radiance, which explains why so many men desire to look upon you."

"You misjudge the world," Healdin said.

The headman stepped forward and reached for the veil. "Do you mean that I have misjudged your beauty?"

From a pocket in her robe Healdin removed the White Gem. She brought it up to collide with the headman's hand. At its touch, he gasped and fell over as if his heart had stopped. Healdin looked down at him and said, "I mean that you misjudge your stature in this world. Now you must face dark and fearful dreams, and you will fear to ever look upon me again."

She opened the chamber door and exited. The waiting attendant jumped off his stool and ran in to wait upon his master. His eyes widened when he found the headman sprawled on the floor by the fire—still as a stone. The servant rushed to his master and found him still breathing. He hurried to a brass gong nearby and beat it several times. In response, guardsmen charged upstairs to the headman's chambers. But on their way, none passed the woman. Quickly the soldiers fanned out throughout the fortress in search of Healdin.

In a darkened turret on the fortress's outer wall, Mirri sat alone. Her eyes brightened at the crash of the gong and the sound of guardsmen shouting and scampering across the courtyard. Next, she heard feet on the steps outside. Slowly the door opened. In strode two young soldiers. One held a torch. "What news, men of the lake?" Mirri asked as she rose.

"The healer woman has worked some devilry on our master," replied the man without the torch. "She has escaped, and we have been ordered to put shackles on you." As the man stepped toward her, Mirri grabbed his left hand with both of hers and yanked apart two of his fingers. The pain dropped the soldier to his knees. As he fell, the old woman pulled his short sword from its scabbard.

"Back!" she threatened, raising the blade. The fallen soldier slid and spun away from her.

The guardsman with the torch drew his sword and advanced. "Drop the weapon old woman, or you will pay dearly," he growled. To his surprise, Mirri attacked him with the fierceness of a panther. Deftly she swung, countered and

251

parried with the short sword. Her blade caught her opponent's forearm. His sword fell and he looked at her in wonder. The old woman advanced, and the two unarmed men scurried out the door and down the steps.

"Flee, you cowards," Mirri called after them. "And do not return." She picked up the second sword and stepped outside to survey the compound. Dark figures scampered across the yard and along the walls. Men with torches hunted near the great hall. And guards with spears stood menacingly by the main gate. At that moment, Healdin appeared from the shadows and made her way up the steps to the turret. Mirri bowed low and said, "Fidden Gadaeyo, my lady. Is all well?"

"Fidden Gadaeyo, Mirri. All is well. Let us make ready to leave."

From across the courtyard a band of guardsmen advanced in formation toward the turret. Mirri turned to Healdin and announced, "The villains approach, my lady. Allow me to send them away."

The soldiers stopped at the foot of the steps leading to the turret. Mirri called down to them, "What do you seek, little men?"

"Drop those swords and come down, old woman," their leader answered. "If you refuse, we will show you no mercy."

"I seek no mercy from such shriveled-up souls. Come up these stairs, little men, and I will teach you of fierceness. Alas, you will not like the lesson."

At her words, the soldiers' faces turned grim. Two by two they trudged up the steps. Other men watched from across the yard. Above them, Mirri stood immovable before the turret door. When the first two men reached the top of the stairs, a light burst forth from inside the turret. The soldiers couldn't see its source, but still the light was so bright they had to turn their heads away.

As they did, Mirri charged them, crying out, "Dare you oppose a servant of the King?" She swung the two swords and drew blood. The wounded soldiers stepped backward, lost their balance and toppled onto the men below. The old woman advanced, swinging with a deft precision. As she did, the light from above seemed to grow stronger. It proved a fearful combination: slicing swords and piercing brightness. The soldiers kept falling over one another and screaming from the cuts and slashes dispatched by their double-bladed foe. Soon the men fled across the yard and disappeared into the great hall. The two guards at the front gate had witnessed the entire scene unfold. Mirri descended the stairs and proceeded toward them. They gave way and ran for the hall.

From the turret, Healdin emerged. Her light, the Vine, blazed brightly in her hand. She returned it to the sheath on her leg, and immediately the light gave way to darkness. Descending the stairs, she hurried across the yard to Mirri. The old woman shook her head. "Child, now you will take ill. Should you not have kept your light sheathed and allowed me to deal with them?"

"No, I wished the light to scare them, and so to spare their lives," Healdin replied. "I did my best to control the power and to keep the Vine out of their direct sight. You will be able to care for me when the illness comes. Now we must wait. I have done what I can for Roj, but still the fear comes upon me. How I long for this night and the next one to pass quickly. Come, let us open the gate. The time of our departure is at hand."

The kidnappers traveled through the night. On horseback, Noli and Roj slept fitfully, but by dawn they had received the benefit of at least a few hours' rest. Their kidnappers, however, appeared worn and sluggish, and in their weariness they gave their prisoners dark, menacing stares. The party stopped in the early morning and rested on a knoll that looked back far over the plains they had traveled. Once more the captives dismounted, and Noli collapsed against Roj. He looked so weary, and he ate little before closing his eyes.

The respite lasted but a few minutes. The small one came to Roj, and the dark-haired foreigner followed behind him. "When will we reach the Golden Box?" the small one demanded.

"At this pace, we should arrive there around nightfall," Roj answered, his eyes almost beaming at the question. "But what are you going to do with the Golden Box?"

The small one laughed scornfully. "Hah!" he scowled. "You think I would tell you."

"That's fine, but which one of you will hold it first?"

"What does that matter to you?"

Roj pointed to the foreigner. "I think he'll take it first," he said. "And then I think he'll remove the power inside the box and use it to kill the rest of you."

The small one sneered and took a step forward. "Guard your mouth, boy, or I'll kick in your teeth." The foreigner demanded an interpretation. The small one snapped at him. The two quarreled a few moments and then the small one turned back to Roj. "He wants you to speak your mind. But I warn you. I won't let you pit us against each other. I will not have you play us for fools."

Roj looked down at his exhausted brother-in-law and began a speech he had been preparing for much of the night. "Tell him he has much to learn of this power. You won't have your way with the contents of the Golden Box. It will have its way with you. One of our ancestors, a man called Troppa, was first among the desert people to steal this power. He took it and beheld its light and then he killed with it. And when he had shed innocent blood, other kinsmen looked upon the fiery light, and they also felt its pull upon their hearts. And that same night they attacked Troppa as he slept. A new man took the power and killed Troppa and many others with him. And that's how the power changed hands from one murderer to the next. Each man felt invincible when he held the great light within his grip, and yet none of them could live without sleep. And when they slept, they died. It seemed that no one could resist stealing it and killing with it. If the power hadn't disappeared, all of us might have died. But somehow it vanished, and we beheld it no more. However, the wise say that every one of us still longs for the light of that power. You'll see tonight the effect that it still has on us. It will reawaken a desire inside you. And only one of us can hold it."

It took a moment for the small one to avert his eyes from Roj, so great was the effect of the horse hunter's words. Slowly, the kidnapper translated the story to the foreigner. The conspirators talked back and forth in clipped bursts. Their words betrayed a touch of wonder. Noli, as tired as he was, lifted an eyelid to observe their sober faces. The small one turned back to Roj and said, "How do you know this story? How do you know what happened so long ago?"

"The healer woman told me. She's not from the Dry Lands, and she knows much of the Golden Box and the power. But your own heart is confirming my story. You can feel the desire for this power, as well as the fear of letting another man get his hands on it before you. That desire has been passed down from generation to generation. And when we draw close to the Golden Box, these other men here will feel the longing for the power, too. And each man is going to want it all to himself."

With somber faces, the two leaders walked away. Noli whispered to Roj, "Brother, you've done it. You've got them riled up inside now."

"Good," said Roj. "We need to make use of that fear tonight. Listen, Noli, I'm ready now to tell you my plan. Let me whisper it to you."

"Are you going to take them to this Golden Box?"

"No."

Noli gave a sly grin. "Well, then I can die in peace. I just want to see their faces when they realized that you've tricked them."

Pibbibib and Weakling lost the kidnappers' tracks during the night. When dawn came, they split up. Weakling took Arta, their Pappi captive, and led him walking on a rope, while each warrior rode upon a stolen horse. They spread far apart from each other and carefully scanned the ground, though they both kept moving in an easterly direction. Pibbibib soon found the tracks. He swung his horse around and cantered back to find Weakling. When they reconnected, they dismounted and set off on foot to follow after Roj.

By early afternoon, Arta was struggling to keep up. Weakling and he fell behind as Pibbibib led his horse up a great rolling hill. Weakling kept his captive behind him on the rope. "Do not exert so much strength, little one," the giant called back to Arta. "Would you not find it more peaceful to simply lay down here and die? If you did, I could help take away all your pain."

Arta gritted his teeth and lifted up his tied hands. "I am an agent of Equis," he declared weakly. "I hold the dark stone in my pocket. Your masters have use of me."

"Those masters cannot hear you now, little one. No, you have only two masters now. One wants to eat you. The other has dreams of grandeur, and he will let your heart beat a little longer in the hope that you may yet prove useful. But when you no longer prove useful to him, you indeed will prove most useful to me."

Pibbibib led his weary horse back down the hill. "I have seen the dogs in the east, perhaps an hour ahead of us. They have crossed the plain on the other side of the rise. Indeed, they do seem bound for the hilltop shown on the map. We still have time to catch them. But we must not be seen. We will move with care until the sun goes down. Then we will run after them and overtake them."

"Our little rabbit here cannot keep up," Weakling said. "Let us spare him the journey."

"No, please," Arta pleaded. "I will help you."

"Silence," Pibbibib warned the captive, and then he turned to his comrade. "This one stays alive for now. He knows those who hold captive our MuKierin. Perhaps that knowledge will benefit us when we reach our destination. If not, your hand will still have a grip on him. Rare is the rabbit that escapes your grasp."

Roj kept a lookout for the signal mount all afternoon.

By his calculation, they would reach it about three hours after sunset. In the meantime, Noli was slumping on his horse's neck, trying to save what little strength remained in him. Roj even nodded off for a brief nap.

Near sunset, the small one rode alongside him. "How much longer must we travel?" he demanded.

"The sun will go down and then we will reach the hilltop," Roj answered.

"And the foul creatures of Equis have not overtaken us. I think you meant to fool us with your stories of a great warrior chasing us."

"Believe me or don't believe me," Roj said. "But I have seen what happens to those who misjudge the Dark Brood.

The small one scoffed, "Indeed, how your heart overflows with kindness. Tell me, merciful one, if the desire for the power of the Golden Box is so great among us, why haven't you reached out and taken it? You say you know its location, and yet you haven't gone after it. How can that be?"

Roj had not anticipated this question. For a moment he felt threatened, as if he might get caught in a lie that could undo his plan. But he remained determined not to let his face show his fear. Slowly he looked down at his shackled hands, even as his mind raced to concoct an answer. "I yearn for it," he said. "But I've known the location of the Golden Box for only a month. I've had no time to act. And the healer woman has sought to dull its pull upon me. But I feel its attraction. I feel it even now. Don't you?"

"Curse you and your lies," his captor replied. "I feel no pull. But I know that you want to break free of us. I'll be watching you tonight. I'll make sure that you never place your hands on the Golden Box. I swear it."

"You do that. And while you keep your eyes on me, your accomplices will keep their eyes on the Golden Box. And the one who touches it first will have fire in his eyes when he looks over at the rest of us, including you."

The small one galloped to the front of the line of kidnappers. Noli said to Roj, "He means to ruin your plans."

Roj nodded. "Yes, but he will keep his eyes on me, not you. We've got to make the most of that."

At last, the sun sank beneath clouds hovering over the western hills. Dusk lingered and then night deepened around them. The clouds shrouded both stars and moon when the kidnappers and their victims came to the valley that the White Beard had named Newell. Roj led the way, with the small one and the foreigner on either side of him. He raised a hand and declared, "There it is. Let's ride up the hill's southern slope. We'll get there quicker that way."

The kidnappers readily agreed to the suggestion and turned for the slope. Even in the darkness they could make out the hilltop's steep eastern face. Soon Roj could hear chatter break out among the six kidnappers. Excitement was building as they approached the hilltop. Noli, however, rode with his head bent almost to his horse's neck. Roj hoped his brother-in-law was merely acting exhausted.

The line of horses wound up the slope until their riders halted at the top of the signal mount. The kidnappers scanned the hilltop but saw nothing to suggest anything special about the ground around them. "Is this really the place?" the small one asked sharply.

"Yes, the spot is meant to be hidden," said Roj as he dismounted and walked over to Noli's horse. "Come on. I'll show you." He helped his kinsman down from the saddle, allowing their horses to freely wander off. Roj let his brother-in-law lean against him as they walked toward the brow of the hill. "Can you do your part?" he asked in a whisper.

"Yes," said Noli. "I'm ready."

To the east, Pibbibib and Weakling approached the edge of the valley. Behind them Arta followed weakly on the rope. They stopped and their Pappi captive fell to his knees, gasping for breath. Pibbibib whispered to his comrade, "Gag the dog and walk beside him. Don't let him make a sound."

Upon the hilltop, the kidnappers dismounted and hurriedly secured their horses to each other—tying the reins and halter ropes to each other's saddles. When the horses were so bound together, one man took his animal's halter

258

rope and tied it to the woody stalk of brush. All the kidnappers then followed Roj as he stepped toward the signal mount's eastern face.

It took the Horse Stalker a few moments to gain his bearings, but soon enough he located the three head-sized rocks that Jerli had shown him. He lowered Noli to the ground besides the stones. "Rest here, brother," he said for all to hear. Next he turned to the others. "Are you ready to help me uncover the Golden Box?"

"Don't ask stupid questions," the small one replied. "Where is it?"

"You're almost standing on top of it. Step over here. I'll show you."

Roj passed through the kidnappers and knelt beside another group of rocks. Slowly, he scraped back a few inches of sandy dirt and revealed part of the cover to the fire chamber. "Here is the entrance to the secret place," he said. "Help me uncover it."

Eagerly, three kidnappers knelt and dug in the loose earth until each had found an edge to the cover. Grabbing it, they tilted it up on end and flung it backwards out of their way. Immediately all the men except Noli gathered around the rectangular fire chamber. To them, it looked about the size of a grave. However, in the darkness the men had trouble making out the walls and the bottom. "I see a hole that leads nowhere," one kidnapper said in MuKierin. The others swayed their heads slightly back and forth in an effort to catch any sight of an entrance.

"Look closer," Roj told them. "There's a door hidden on one side." Two of the men got down on their stomachs and peered into the chamber. Roj, meanwhile, looked up to Noli, who already had dug beneath the three rocks and pulled out the hidden bag of clay vials. Roj stepped around the men and stopped at the end of the chamber nearest the horses. The small one stood opposite him, closer to the signal mount's eastern face. Noli stood up, pulled back his shackled arms on his right side and tossed a clay vial to Roj. His brother-in-law caught it with his cupped hands and hid the vial in his left palm, out of sight.

The small one didn't see the throw, but it alarmed him to suddenly see both captives on their feet. "Sit down, you!" he barked at Noli. "What do you think you're doing?" Noli gave a defiant look but slowly knelt back on the ground.

Roj wondered whether the small one had seen the vial flying through the air. He had wanted to switch it to his right hand, but he feared the kidnappers might see it if he did. Immediately he thought, *You throw a rope left-handed. You can throw the vial with your left hand, too.* Hurriedly he stepped up to the chamber's edge and howled, "Look! I told you. There's the door!" The kidnappers snapped their heads down toward the darkened hole. As they did, Roj raised both shackled hands as one might lift an axe and then flung the vial down with a flick of his left wrist. Only the small one saw this movement. Alarmed, he took a few steps toward Roj. But he was blocked by the dark-haired foreigner peering down as the vial hit the bottom of the chamber. First came the tinkling of clay pottery shattering on rock. That was followed by a thunder-like roar that bellowed from the bottom of the chamber. But an instant before any ear heard the explosion, a blast of fire roared up the shaft and soared high overhead. The flames struck the two men lying on the ground full in the face. The dark-haired foreigner was hit, too. He toppled over, screaming from burns to his hands, chest and face. As he fell, he knocked down the small one, who was shielded from the worst of the blast. The other men were sent reeling, too. Above them, the pillar of fire lit up the night. The amber and orange flames leaped majestically for a few seconds. Then the light died out.

From the valley, Pibbibib looked up in fear at the great flash. He jumped on his horse and turned toward Weakling. "Kill him!" Pibbibib yelled. "Then hurry up that hill. Our enemies surely will see that signal fire." He set his horse to a gallop and turned for the southern end of the signal mount.

Weakling drew his knife and looked in disgust at the frightened Arta. "Oh, I hate it when I cannot toy with you, little one. It is wrong to squander such pleasure." Smoothly he slit the Pappi's throat and left him to bleed to death. The dying man was still tied by a rope to the waiting horse. Weakling took the animal's reins and untied the rope from the saddle. Then, he climbed aboard and set off after Pibbibib.

On the hilltop, Roj had made sure to hit the ground and roll away from the chamber. As soon as the signal flame vanished, he rose up and scrambled to Noli. He helped his brother-in-law struggle to his feet, and the two men dashed away from the burned kidnappers. As they escaped, the small one pulled himself off the ground and watched them flee. He staggered up and ran to get his horse. But all the animals had galloped away in fear. Furious, he turned and ran after the two escaping MuKierin.

Noli and Roj scampered toward the northern edge of the signal mount. Reaching the slope, they lurched and slipped along the rocky descent. Noli turned back and saw a pursuer gaining on them. Roj, meanwhile, led the way, sliding down a steep slope with jutting rocks on either side. "Run, Roj," Noli yelled. "I'm right behind you." Noli slid down the slope, crossed a small gulley at the bottom and climbed halfway up the other side. There, he turned and waited.

The small one reached the slope and drew his sword. "You will pay for this," he yelled to Noli. "You will pay dearly."

"Come here, little man!" Noli shot back. "You and I have a score to settle now that my kinsman is free."

"Oh, I'll catch up with him, too. You can be sure of that. But first I'm going to take great pleasure in killing you."

The small one started down the gravel slope. Noli waited until the man couldn't turn back. Then he took a clay vial from the bag. Hampered by the shackles, he nonetheless imitated Roj's double-armed windup. The throw was a bit off, landing perhaps six feet to the side of the small one. But the vial struck rock. Another explosion erupted, but this time it wasn't contained in a fire chamber. It burst forth as a great ball that spread out along the slope and just out of sight of the wounded kidnappers back on top of the hill. The flames reached the small one, engulfing his cape and clothes in fire. He fell, screaming into the gulley.

Roj ran back and grabbed Noli by the arm. "Come on!" he yelled. "We've got to get out of here!"

"Let me kill him, Roj!" Noli shouted, refusing to budge. "He deserves to die!"

"Yes, he does. But we've got to get away. Please, Noli, come with me for Remy and your child. The evil ones may be near us. We've got to find a hiding place before Pibbibib shows up." Slowly, Roj dragged his reluctant kinsman backward. Once more, they stumbled toward the bottom of the northern slope.

Pibbibib had ridden so close to the signal mount that he had failed to see the second explosion, though he did hear its distant rumble. He continued up to the hilltop. Weakling, however, was in the valley, and he caught sight of the second flash. Immediately, he turned his horse to the right and slapped his animal into a gallop for the northern slope.

Noli and Roj slowed to a walk when they reached the bottom of the hill. They veered east and started to cross the valley. "There's a well on the other side," Roj said. "We can swing wide and come back to it. Let's hope Healdin's people saw that signal flash and will come soon to rescue us." Arm in arm, the two men staggered across a rocky patch of ground. Roj stopped in order to let his kinsman catch his breath. A few moments later, they caught the sound of a horse running hard across the valley. The two men dropped on their stomachs. But the rider was already turning toward them.

Noli sprang back up. "Let's retreat back to that rocky ground," he said, as he began to retrace his steps. "That's where I want to be if we have to fight."

To Roj, the approaching rider looked immense. "That one belongs either to the King or the Dark Brood," he called to Noli. "Let's split apart. If this warrior is an enemy, I've got the weapon for him. But just to be safe, get one of the vials ready. Curse these shackles! How they get in the way!"

Weakling rode ahead of the two MuKierin until he had cut off any retreat toward the signal mount. Slowly he swung back, giving his victims time to become truly afraid. He recognized Noli and called to him, "Little one, remember me? The last time we met, you were the one riding a horse. That day I tripped your mount and dropped you out of the saddle. I am so pleased to find you again and at last to get my hands around your neck."

Noli showed his teeth and growled, "We'll see about that. I didn't escape those villains on the hilltop just so that you could torment me."

"Ah, those little dogs are mere babes in evil compared to me. I'm ready to teach you real fear. Believe me, I can make your heart burst inside you." Weakling climbed off his horse. Immediately he noticed that Roj was circling around to his right. The huge warrior swung a round metal shield off his back and fastened it to his left arm. He walked toward Noli and warned, "Tell your kinsman that he will burn both you and me if he throws fire at us."

Noli's eyes widened at the words. "What makes you think that I can't burn you with fire?" he demanded.

Weakling stopped and considered his adversary. "No, little one, you remain but a mere speck in this great world. I know because I also am a speck. We have others greater than us. But I will remain content, because tonight I will eat you and enjoy every morsel. That is enough for me."

For a moment the three adversaries stood frozen. Then, Roj howled and charged through the sage on Weakling's right. Noli leapt forth from the left. In response, the huge warrior advanced slowly toward Noli, keeping his horse as a barrier on his right, for he still deemed Roj to be the greater danger. But his strategy meant that he had only his shield to protect him on his left. Noli slid to a halt and from the bag grabbed a vial. Winding up, he yelled, "Now!" and heaved the vial at a rock in front of Weakling. The fireball burned both combatants. Weakling's horse reared on its hind legs and toppled over backwards. The warrior couldn't free his grip fast enough from the reins and was yanked onto his back. His metal shield had caught the brunt of the exploding flames, making it shine red on the edges as if fired by a blacksmith. The burned horse struggled to its feet and bolted off in fear. Weakling rolled onto his stomach and struggled to pull his burning arm from the overheated shield. Roj, meanwhile, rushed to his enemy's feet. In his hand he held the black stone knife that the old seeker had given him—the very blade that Healdin had treated. Roj raised it and plunged it deep into the back of Weakling's calf. "For the seeker!" Roj yelled.

The wounded warrior howled mightily and twitched for all he was worth. He rose up on his hands, but then collapsed and rolled into a ball. His body began to rock and convulse. Each movement made him scream anew. Roj waited for a chance to attack again, but it seemed too dangerous to draw near his enemy's whirling arms and legs. Noli, however, stumbled closer to the fallen warrior. The blast had scorched the MuKierin's right arm and side, but still he advanced with a vial in his left hand. "Let me kill him, Roj," Noli said. "We've got to make sure this evil one dies here."

Roj gently grabbed his brother-in-law. "No, Noli, please save the vials," he pleaded. "We'll need them if we have to fight Pibbibib, too. He'll be on his guard now. Our best hope is to get out of here while we can." Reluctantly Noli turned and the two men stumbled away, leaving Weakling howling in agony.

Back on the signal mount, Pibbibib dismounted and made his way stealthily over the top of the rise. He reached the fire chamber unnoticed and found two of the kidnappers already dead. Two others were kneeling beside the dark-haired foreigner, who had collapsed blinded and burned beside the deep hole. The great warrior called to them, "Where is the Horse Stalker?"

The kidnappers looked up in amazement at this new danger. One bolted, but Pibbibib threw a knife and struck him in the back, bringing him down. Quickly he strode to the two remaining men on the ground. Overcome with terror, the one tending the dark-haired foreigner pointed north and stuttered, "The Horse Stalker ran off that way." Pibbibib drew his sword and pierced the man in the chest. Next, he rammed his blade through the dark-haired foreigner. He left the dead men there and went back for his horse. While he was leading the animal back toward the fire chamber, he heard the third explosion, followed by blood-curdling screams. Immediately he realized that Weakling had taken some terrible wound. Pibbibib told himself he now must move forward with caution. The screams went on without ceasing as the warrior led his horse down the northern slope. There, he found the last remaining kidnapper, the small one. He lay smoldering but still alive.

"Where is the Horse Stalker?"

The small one gurgled and moaned, but no words proceeded from his mouth. Pibbibib considered letting this one linger a little longer in torment. But he wanted to make sure that no one knew that Weakling and he had been here. Again, he pulled his sword and thrust it into the dying man. With the last kidnapper vanquished, Pibbibib mounted his horse and proceeded toward the screams on the valley floor. As he did, a strange sensation came upon him. He thought: *Has the enemy drawn near? Is she here?* The valley looked empty but the sensation kept growing stronger. He felt sure he was coming once more into the presence of the lady's power.

He found Weakling still screaming and thrashing in the dirt. "What ails you, fool?" Pibbibib yelled. He received only squeals and bawling in reply. Never had Pibbibib seen his ally in such misery. The larger one dismounted and picked up a rock off the ground. It fit well in his enormous hand. "Here, I shall relieve you of your pain," he said. He raised the rock and pounded Weakling twice on the back of the helm. The screams ended, and the wounded warrior slumped unconscious, his face on the ground. "Now you may rest, idiot. What a relief. Your howls would bring the accursed Tor to us tonight."

Pibbibib quickly surveyed the empty valley. Nothing stirred, but still it felt to him as if the lady were so close that she might rise out of the dust behind him and strike him down. He thought: *The Horse Stalker must still be near. But I cannot risk a search for him. The enemy may arrive at any moment.*

He looked down at Weakling. *And I cannot take you with me. We now have but one worn-out horse between us. And you are no use to me in this state.*

Despite his decision to abandon his old comrade, Pibbibib hesitated. He began to sense the enemy's power surrounding Weakling. Pibbibib cast his eyes down and was shocked by what he saw. Light seemed to be pouring forth from a wound on the back of Weakling's leg. Looking closer, Pibbibib saw distinct specks ablaze in clear ooze that passed from the cut. He blinked and looked up to make sure that the light wasn't a trick from some reflection of stars or another source. But darkness covered both the land and the sky. Kneeling down, he touched the wound. The glowing goop burned him so badly that he screamed, "Great flames!" He arose, shaking his burned hand. "This fool has been touched by The Powers, pure and fierce! Slowly the pain decreased in his singed fingers, and he tried to think. *How can this be? He was not cut by the Great Valuable or even the little light of fire. Surely I would have seen such lights burning in the night. What has afflicted him?*

Pibbibib concluded that here might be some new opportunity, if only he could understand it. But first he must find a way to keep Weakling alive long enough to grasp this mystery. He loaded the unconscious warrior aboard their one remaining horse and set off northwest—the direction that he hoped would best allow the two warriors to escape their enemies.

Once Pibbibib left the field of battle, the night passed quietly. Roj and Noli lay in a small depression about three hundred yards from the site of their skirmish with Weakling. Noli could go no farther and Roj thought that at least they could hide there while the darkness lasted. They huddled close together before exhaustion overtook them. However, Roj didn't sleep for long. Within a few hours, he began to moan from a pain deep inside him. It felt as if his stomach had taken a knife wound and a battle was raging within him. Noli awoke and declared, "Roj, you're bleeding from your mouth! What's wrong with you?"

"Hold me, Noli. Keep me warm. It'll pass soon enough."

"Are you ill because you used that blade on Weakling? Do you have the same illness as the foreign woman?"

"I think I do," said Roj. "It's alright, Noli. I'll live. In a way, this is what I needed. Before tonight I didn't know how much Healdin had suffered for me. Now I know what she endured again and again." After a long pause, he added, "Now I know how much she loves me."

The two men eventually drifted off to sleep. In slumber, Roj caught the sound of a trumpet. Even in his sleep, he recognized it from that first night in the high reaches of the Powder Mountains. On that night, Noli and he had just finished their third bowl of stew and were sprawled on their blankets like the kings of the clan. And Healdin's women were making ready with their instruments. And from somewhere below that sand-colored pass, a horn sounded the five notes of a minor scale: Mi, Rae, Doe, La, Sol. Now, he heard the trumpet sound a second time. It seemed to be drawing closer. The music came a third time and Roj opened his eyes, for he was sure that this time Healdin would raise her bow and her fiddle again would sing to him a story both sweet and bitter. But he beheld the sky, and realized that now the hour wasn't sunset but daybreak. And he looked around and realized that he was resting far from those lofty mountains. Wearily, he pushed himself up on his elbows. Far off he beheld a horse running toward him. At once he knew it was his own Spotted Stallion. Quickly he stood up and called, "Noli, we made it! We're saved! Healdin has sent us help, just like she said she would." Roj raised his shackled hands over his head and began stumbling toward the great horse.

He could now see a company of horsemen following far behind the stallion and making their way up the valley. The riders must have seen him, for immediately they spurred their horses into a canter. Clearly, they belonged to the King. Roj ran back to Noli, who remained too weak to raise himself off the ground. Roj's body shuddered and he felt like weeping, but he refused to drop to his knees. He wanted to meet these warriors standing. And so he did. In a few moments the riders surrounded him. Their captain jumped down and knelt before him. "Fidden Gadaeyo, child of Hannah," he said. "Your stallion has summoned us. We have come to take you to safety."

Roj fought for the composure to speak. "Please, help my kinsman," he said. "He was wounded by the fire from a vial on the signal mount. We had a fight with Weakling. We didn't see Pibbibib, but I'm sure he's lurking somewhere around here. And the men who kidnapped us may still be watching us from that hill."

The captain removed his helm, displaying his close-cropped brown hair, and he motioned for another warrior to dismount. The two knelt and began to examine the two MuKierin. Another warrior brought forth a bag of medicines. "We will treat your kinsman and you, and then you may take a brief rest, as the lady commanded us," the captain said. "But we must not stay here long. We have overcome one company of the enemy, but a stronger force moves toward us. We must ride west today where we can find safety."

Gently, the warriors soothed Noli's burns with salves and oils. They gave Roj a drink that greatly eased the pain in his stomach. Both men also drank water and ate a little jerky and dried fruit from the Green Lands. The simple tastes gave them much comfort. Meanwhile, six warriors rode across the valley and ascended the signal mount. Four soon returned, but two remained on top to keep a lookout for the enemy. A few hours later, the warriors lifted the wounded men onto spare horses and tied each one into his saddle. The captain told Roj, "On the hilltop, we found six corpses and another down here in the valley. All came from the Dry Lands. Most died from a blade, even those who suffered great burns."

"Pibbibib must have killed them," Roj said. "Are you going to go after him?"

"No, my orders are to keep my company together in order to better protect you. Now, let us leave this place."

As the company departed, Pibbibib and Weakling lay

hidden in a deep gully to the northwest of the signal mount. There, the wounded Weakling had collapsed in the dirt. Even the distant trumpet call of the enemy at dawn had failed to rouse him. Pibbibib, however, had cringed at the notes of that horn, for to him it remained a most unsettling melody. It signaled the announcement of the enemy's presence, and that meant a force too great to engage in battle. Still, it was only a single horn, and it likely was sounded in an attempt to find the two MuKierin, not to search for the Dark Brood. As such, Pibbibib continued to hope that he could stay hidden and out of harm's way.

That hope was challenged a few hours later when Weakling began to stir and moan. The wounded warrior lifted himself on his elbows and cried out, "They are coming for us. They are coming this way!"

"What do you mean?" Pibbibib demanded, whipping his head behind him in fear.

"Our enemies, you fool! They draw near. I can sense it."

"What? How can you sense it?"

"In my leg, blast you! Help me escape! They come! They come for me!"

Astounded, Pibbibib turned and scrambled up the steep slope to the flats above them. As he neared the top, he dropped down and found a bush to serve as cover. He saw nothing but dusty sage. Quickly he scanned the small plain and the signal mount in the distance. The high spot appeared empty, but Pibbibib correctly suspected that the enemy would send warriors there to keep watch. Down below, Weakling continued to moan and roll in fear. Pibbibib watched him in confusion. When he looked east again, he was startled to spot a company of warriors circling the base of the hilltop. "By the Great Master," he gasped. "My fool can sense the enemy's approach!"

Immediately he slid and scooted down the slope to his wounded comrade. Weakling had started crawling north in a pitiful attempt to escape his adversaries. His moans began to rise into screeches and his screeches into wails. Pibbibib once

269

more looked for a rock. Quickly he administered two sharp blows to the back of Weakling's helm. Once more the wailing ceased.

Pibbibib took great care when he climbed back to the top of the rise to behold the riders. He judged correctly that the King's company was headed west toward the Lake Country. He felt sure that Roj and Noli were among the party. Crouching there, he watched as two warriors on horseback descended the signal mount and joined the company. He kept hidden until the enemy had passed over the plain.

A few hours later, Weakling began to regain consciousness. Pibbibib came down and uncorked his leather water bag. "I saved the last swig for you," he said.

"Oh, my aching head," Weakling groaned. "Was that you who whacked me?"

"What else could I do? Your screams would have drawn the enemy to us. Those blows I gave you were acts of mercy."

"Such kindness makes my head pound. Why have you become so merciful to me? Why didn't you abandon me?"

"I have gone soft in the heart."

"That will be the day. What game do you play now?"

"I am growing fond of your leg, the wounded one. How is it?"

"Terrible. I think they poisoned me."

"Indeed, it must be a glorious poison."

"Do not mock me."

"Have you looked at it? Take a look."

Weakling swiveled his head and gasped. "My leg is on fire!" He swung an arm and tried to brush away the liquid oozing from the wound. It burned his hand. "Aiee!" he screamed. "Help me! I told you they had poisoned me!"

"Indeed, you have little stars oozing from your leg. You have starlight pouring out of you. And wonder of wonders, you have The Powers living inside you."

"The Powers! Do something! Remove it, lest it kill me."

"Remove it and give back this wondrous gift? Oh, no, my accursed friend, I think not. You were able to sense the enemy warriors as they approached us. None of our ilk have such a gift, except the Great Master himself. Think of it. I can barely detect the leader of the She-ones. But you can sense even her warriors from afar."

Weakling looked aghast. "Then I must rid myself of this gift. It could be the death of me. Why, if the Great Master learns of this, he might butcher me."

"Perhaps, but he need not know of it. First, we must learn more of the power inside you. We must train you to use it and to hide it from all others. I will help you. I will say that it is I who can sense the enemy. No one will suspect that little Weakling possesses such a gift. Oh, we will be masters of fortune. And one day you will help me find the Great Valuable."

"No! I do not want the Great Valuable! I want to go back to the hills. Take me back to the hills. Or take me back to Zhaggee. He cares nothing for The Powers. Let me hide with him."

"Hah! Zhaggee did not save you from the enemy today. I did. You owe me. And I mean to make the most of your new gift. Our old life is over. We will go back to Mackadoo, but we will keep your gift a secret, even from him. And one day we will find the Great Valuable. It is the only thing that will heal your wound. It is the same with me. I touched what is oozing out of you and took a burn that I can never forget. There is only one way to heal such a burn, and that is by the touch of the Great Valuable itself. I am sure of it. We will find that wondrous power, and it will heal the both of us."

Weakling grunted. "I fear it will kill us, not heal us."

Pibbibib made a fire and put his sword in it until it grew as hot as he could make it. He had Weakling bite a rag and then he put his blade against the oozing leg. His patient screamed mightily. Pibbibib bent and examined his effort to cauterize the wound. "This fire lacks the heat I need," he said. "But it will do for now. I have staunched the worst of the

271

ooze. And one day I will hold a greater fire. On that day, I will raise it above me and strike fear into the hearts of all my enemies. And I will be their Master!"

By evening, the King's company had journeyed far from the signal mount and camped in a valley of sage. More warriors had joined their ranks, and many were sent out to scout the surrounding hills. But Roj kept looking to the west. He was waiting for Healdin.

She came at sunset, wrapped in red and riding her gray mare. Roj arose and strode out to meet her. As he did, he thought back over the past months he had known her. He recalled her strange presence that first night on the mountain, her boldness in freeing the two slaves at Sweetwater, her kindness and her care for him. Most of all, he thought about how much she had suffered for him.

He looked at her again and was taken aback. Was she wearing a red courting shawl? He quickly thought back to her special dinner with Arg Wevol. Had she worn such a shawl that night? No, he recalled. She hadn't donned one for the horse trader. He looked at her again to be sure. Yes, it was definitely a courting shawl, tightly woven with a long, red fringe that hung off her shoulders. He also could see that her face was unveiled.

She rode forward and stopped beside him. "I have come for you, Roj," she called.

"Why are you wearing that red shawl?" he asked.

"Is that not the way of your people? I have come for you."

"Usually it's the man who goes to the woman."

"But, unlike you, I have been waiting for this day for generations."

"Generations? What do you mean?"

"The old legends foretold that I would marry the Horse Stalker. Now that you have prevailed over your enemies, I can tell you this. It is a blessed day for me."

For a moment Roj couldn't speak. At last he said, "That night when I first saw Wevol the trader looking at you,

I knew that he wanted you. And I began to realize that I wanted you, too. But for so long, I was too scared to even think such thoughts. I couldn't believe that you could ever want me. I still can't understand why you would have somebody like me—especially after all I've been through. But last night I came to understand that you do love me. I became ill from using the stone blade, and I felt the pain you must have endured for me again and again.

"Perhaps now you can understand how much I also feared for your life. That fear is part of the curse on the Vine. It was why I could not risk staying near you when you faced Pibbibib and those villains from the Seven Clans. The fear of losing you was becoming so great that I could not control the power of my light. In such times, I might have killed everyone, even you. But now, you have prevailed. We can wed tomorrow in the hills above the lake. Baern and Tie can join us, and Noli can stand beside you."

His eyes lit up. "When do I get to kiss you?" he asked. She gave him no answer, but her lips curled into the faintest smile. Roj lifted her from the mare and embraced her.

Epilogue

The next morning was Roj's wedding day. He woke early, threw off his blanket and set out in search of Healdin. The rest of the camp was just beginning to stir, and the cooks were building small fires for the morning tea. But Roj couldn't find the lady anywhere in the camp. The King's warriors told him she had ridden away before dawn. Before breakfast, the captain woke Noli and changed his dressings. His burns were healing well.

The party soon set off on horseback for the high ground near the lake. The clouds had departed and blue sky filled the horizon. Roj kept watching anxiously for Healdin. He was drawing near the first foothills when he spotted her riding in the distance. Immediately he slapped his mount and galloped out to meet her. She smiled to see him coming.

He took a moment to gather his thoughts before he spoke. "Healdin, I need to ask you something. Last night I couldn't sleep. At last, it dawned on me. I'm going to change the future by marrying you. Isn't that so?"

She smiled and said, "I told you that one day you would sense the answer in your heart. Yes, you will change the future when you take my hand. We will have a child and one day that child will become the Champion of the Desert Clans. They will be his people, as they are your people. You and I will help our child. By our love, perhaps we can bring forth a good ending to this bitter tale."

"Are you sure this will happen? How do you know our child will become the Champion?"

"I know this because the King himself told it to me. I am his daughter, and this is what he assured me will come to pass."

"The King's daughter!" Roj jumped off his horse and rushed to her side, gazing up into her eyes. "You're the King's daughter, and he's going to let you marry a horse hunter?"

275

"Yes, he has given his blessing. And you have my love. We still have much that we must endure. Indeed, my child and I must pass through fire. Such will be the burden for the man who walks by my side."

Roj reached up and grasped her hand. "If you and your King are willing, then I'm willing. I couldn't leave you, even if I wanted to. I love you, Healdin. How could I ever live without you?"

She put both her hands on his. "The time has come for you to know more about the stolen Root of Glory. The Vine that I carry one day will connect into the Root. And at the Castle at River's End, a third power awaits the coming Champion. One day our child will take hold of that power."

"And what is its name, Healdin? Is it the Branch or Blossom?"

She looked directly at him. "The Thorn," she said.

Late that afternoon, Baern the trader and Tie his slave journeyed together toward a hilltop overlooking the northeastern edge of the lake. Up the slopes of sage and sparse grasses they rode, trailed by a sorrel packhorse. The autumn sun was sinking behind them. The air was crisp and clear. It reminded Baern of the evening he had spent with Jerli on the same ground. He kept listening for singing, even as his eyes kept watch around him.

On the very ridge where he had spent a wondrous night, Baern found a pavilion standing, and a white flag rose above it with a green horse painted upon it. Healdin and Roj emerged from the pavilion and strode forth to meet the newcomers. The lady was dressed in gold, and her face was uncovered. Both men smiled to look upon her. They turned toward one another, as if to confirm that they weren't dreaming. A moment later, she stood between their horses and touched the hands of both riders. "Welcome, friends," she said. "Welcome to my wedding feast."

"What a blessed day, lady," said Baern, nearly leaping from his horse. "Let me speak now, before the music overpowers me." He motioned to Tie, who dismounted and went back to the packhorse. From it, he untied a bundled load and set it upon the ground. Baern removed the canvas tarp and uncovered a small, carved sea dragon, as gray and fierce as any object of stone ever was. "Behold my gift to you," Baern said. "And I must say more. I want you both to return to my home. I want your man to become my partner."

Healdin smiled and touched the gift. "Thank you," she said. "But we shall have our own home. We will not live far from you. Friends will build us a home in the wild lands along the north shore."

"But will you find safety there?" Baern asked. "Will Circ the Headman leave you alone?"

"We need no longer fear him, I assure you. He will never bother us again. But both Tie and you may visit us whenever you wish. You will always be welcome in our home. And one day we will have a child, and you must help him learn his way upon the lake."

Baern smiled and shrugged. "Then it must be as you say. And I promise I will visit you. I will help both your man and your child learn of the blessed waters. In fact, allow me to do you this favor. Send word when you are settled in your new home, and I will dispatch Tie with a boat. I would be honored to give your family such a gift."

From near the pavilion, the musicians began tuning up. "Ah, my friends," Baern called, his eyes fixed on the pavilion. "Excuse me, I must make my way to the music."

As the trader departed, Tie stepped forward. "Lady," he began, "at last I see you face to face, the woman who saved me. I know I owe you my life. Thank you. But even now, with your face unveiled, I still can't understand you. Forgive me for my bluntness, but I still don't know if it's your beauty or your kindness that draws men to you."

"In time, you shall know," she replied. "On this evening, let it be enough that you have survived a great wound and are restored to life." From around her neck she removed a necklace with a black volcanic stone. Lightly she placed the stone in the slave's palm. She said, "Keep this in remembrance of me, child of Hannah."

277

Tie choked up. "Lady, I can almost believe that with you anything is possible. Thank you. I hope you'll understand that I'm not ready yet to wear this stone. I'm still a slave. But, if I ever become a free man, I'll wear it for the rest of my life. And whatever happens, I'll always keep it in remembrance of you."

Healdin gave him a gentle smile. "Let it be as you say, Tie. If I know your master, the day of your freedom is almost at hand."

CPSIA information can be obtained at www.ICGtesting.com
Printed in the USA
267712BV00002B/2/P